Sunshine With You

A FORT BENDER NOVEL

Sunshine With You

LAYNA JAMES

*You **deserve** to be loved, just as you are.*

CONTENT NOTES

The FMC in this story is living with a few anxiety disorders. Throughout the book, you will see this reflected in the way her internal thoughts are presented. The use of both "I" and "You" statements while in her POV are purposeful and not a mistake. It is used to show how quickly thoughts and fears can assault the mind of those with anxiety. Please look at the list below, and take care of your mental health while reading.

SUNSHINE WITH YOU is intended for adult readers 18+. It depicts explicit language and open door scenes. Other themes to be aware of:

- Anaphylaxis
- Generalized Anxiety Disorder
- Panic Attacks
- Parental Estrangement
- Racial Undertones/Microaggressions from Estranged Parent
- Parental Divorce (result of off-page parental cheating, but discussed in detail)
- Alcohol Use
- Love Triangle (non-cheating)

Fort Bender
N
W   E
S
THE BLUFFS EST
FORT BENDER
VISITOR'S CENTER
AND MUSEUM
LIBRARY
CRYSTAL BEACH

BOTANICAL
RDENS
SHOWER TREE
LODGE
YOUTH CENTER
FORGET
ME NOTS
FORGET ME NOTS
WILLIS
NEIGHBORHOOD
CAMP BENDER
WALLER TREE FARM
RIS
RHOOD
BENDER
ELEMENTARY
BENDER
SECONDARY
HERBERT'S HOLE

CHAPTER ONE
ASHLIE

Don't let your worry keep you from your joy. The refrain whirls through my head, taunting me like the unrealistic expectation it is. When I originally heard the words, they gave five-year-old me the courage to jump in the pool for the first time. Now, the phrase reminds me of my inadequacy. Worry and I are like California and sunshine—you rarely have one without the other. And joy? That's a hard thing to come by these days too.

"Hold still, Ash!" My best friend's voice jerks me out of my mental spiral. "You're going to have pink all over your toes." Kayla swipes her finger around my cuticle. She sits crisscross on my cream faux-fur area rug as I take my turn for a pedicure. The TV casts a reddened glow over her deep bronze skin. I wiggle my toes with a smile, and she glares at me, setting the polish on my mahogany coffee table. "I'll stop right now…"

"And leave me with half-painted toes? Doubtful." There's no way she'd half-ass anything, pedicure or otherwise.

She rolls her eyes and picks up the polish with a sigh, losing to the perfectionist inside her. Settling back into the tan leather sofa with a satisfied smirk, I flick my eyes to the TV mounted on the wall. A *Scandalized Phenomena* marathon, and a night with my best friend is exactly what I need right now. I've missed this—spending time together until we're sick of each other.

Kayla Harris and I have been best friends since we met in high school. We're from a small town up the coast called Fort Bender, but with her living in San Francisco and me here in LA, we haven't been able to have girls' nights like this in a while. After picking her up from the airport this afternoon, we've jam-packed our evening with sushi, ice cream, mani-pedis, and our favorite show on Netvids.

She caps the nail polish and sits next to me, sweeping her black locs over her shoulder. My phone rumbles on the table, and I snatch it up before she can see it. Her eyes narrow immediately. "Who was that?"

"Uh, just Hunter." Strategically turning my phone away from her, I check the message and stifle a laugh.

HUNTER

Next time, you're doing this shit.

Kayla doesn't know this yet, but she's getting engaged tomorrow. And apparently, there's a complication at the cake shop.

"If it's just my brother, why'd you grab it like that?" Her eyes pop wide. "Ew! Did you two—"

"Uh-uh! Nope. That's not *ever* happening." I shake my head emphatically to convince her that her brother—my other best friend—is not someone I have any interest in. Hunter's been a friend for years. *Only* a friend...except for that one time. But we don't talk about that. I refuse. He's the poster child for players et al. Having a casual relationship has never been something I've wanted.

"Hey, it's your life." Her hands tap her knees with nonchalance. Knowing her, she's about to dig for details on my boyfr—scratch that—ex-boyfriend. It'll be the third time she's mentioned him today. "Speaking of... Where's Marcus tonight?"

I sigh, rolling my eyes. "I thought we were having a girls' night. We don't need to talk about Marcus..."

"So, there's something to talk about, then?" Her eyebrow lifts as she pins me with a stare.

"*Ugh*, fine." I swipe to my email and pull up the hurried message my boyfri—*ex-boyfriend*—sent a week ago. Scanning it over again like it'll give me any more clarity on the abrupt end to our relationship probably isn't the best idea. But I do it anyway.

From: Marcus Taylor

To: Ashley Willis

Ashley,

I regret to inform you that I can no longer pursue this relationship.

Best,

Marcus Taylor, MD

Resident Physician in Radiology

University of Los Angeles Medical Hospital

I may not seek out casual flings, but I clearly gravitate toward the emotionally detached, holier-than-thou types who pretend to want a relationship. Releasing a puff of air, I hand my phone to Kayla and bite my thumbnail.

Marcus and I were together long enough that this shitty means of communication shouldn't have happened. Almost nine months, and he went out of his way to send a breakup via form letter, spelling my damn name wrong in the process. Who *does* that? I'll log this into the growing evidence for why I'm such a failure another day. But he could have texted, at the least.

Kayla reads the email and scoffs. "Somehow, this doesn't surprise me."

"What the hell is *that* supposed to mean?" My arms settle over my chest, fists balled tightly.

"It's on brand for you. He was a horrible boyfriend, and I told you he would be after he showed up an hour late for your first three dates."

"He's a doctor. Things come up!" I dig my fingernails into my palms, frustrated that I'm still defending him, and pissed that she's calling me out. *Yes,* I date shitty men. I don't need her making me feel bad about it. "He was everything I was looking for —smart, successful, attractive. So what if he was late a few times? I'm late to things all the time."

The finger aimed in my direction calls me out before her words do. "And that, right there, is why this keeps happening. You get defensive and double down instead of hearing what I'm saying. The guys you date don't treat you well, Ash. You latch on to how they look on paper and won't hear anyone's concerns until they break your heart."

"Oh, I hear you..." My eye roll is unstoppable. "All in my business with no permit." She's been on me about my taste in guys for years, along with Hunter and my sister, Willa. Everyone telling me what to do is really starting to get old. "Since you know everything, why don't you set me up with all the *great guys* you're surrounded by?" She doesn't know any guys besides her boyfriend, so I gasp sarcastically. "Oh, wait..."

Her eyebrow quirks. "Maybe I will."

Wait... Does she actually know a guy? "Whatever. It's not like he came with a warning label."

Kayla's eyes bug out of her head. "He was a walking red flag, Ash! You just saw what you *wanted* to see. At the end of the day, he treated you like an option instead of a priority. No different than Tyson. Or Logan. Or Brett—"

"*Okaaay,* you can stop now. Damn!" Defensive is my middle name, but who the hell wouldn't be when someone's calling out all your flaws?

"I'm just saying, this is your pattern. You're so scared of trying something different and failing that you keep striking out with these douchebags. Ever since Bryan—"

"So, you're calling me a failure now?" That name sends a wall of deflection around me. She knows I don't talk about him. He was the controlling wolf in sheep's clothing who kicked off my string of bad dating habits. The longer we have this conversation, the worse I feel about everything. Bringing him up right now is a low blow.

My doomed relationships aside, I'm fully aware I'm a walking disappointment. I used to be so good at everything. From childhood, all the way until I graduated from the University of Los Angeles, I didn't have to work too hard to be successful. My grades were always A's and B's, and I was the popular girl, no matter where I went. Hell, I was the damn swim team captain my senior year in college. Failure wasn't ever something I experienced. Once I started teaching though, everything changed. I wasn't inherently good at managing my time, or anything else anymore. I struck out *hard*.

Why won't this emptiness go away?

As if she can hear the berating thoughts in my head, Kayla bumps me with her elbow. "Being dumped in a shitty way doesn't make you a failure, girl. You taught me that. But choosing to ignore habits that harm your self-esteem...that's a surefire way to fail." She places a hand on mine and squeezes, sitting with me while I spiral internally. Her words hit deep, but maybe she's right. Maybe it's time for me to do something about my fear of striking out—with dating and everything else in my life.

A tear slips down my cheek, and I close my eyes, blowing a dejected puff of air from my lips. I'm cutting my losses and leaving our conversation where it is. Talk about a melancholic way to end girls' night.

My phone buzzes again.

HUNTER

☹ 🎂 👍 Cake crisis averted.

I have more important things to worry about right now, like my best friend's engagement.

CHAPTER TWO
ASHLIE

"I think you actually pulled it off," I say, fluffing my curls before turning from the window.

"Are you nervous?" Trevor asks, clapping Chase on the shoulder.

Chase adjusts his tie before patting his pocket. "Nope. Not at all." It's early October, but his smile rivals the Los Angeles sunshine gleaming over his sandy blond hair. His ivory skin almost matches the lightly toasted color of his suit as he smooths a hand over it, minutes away from proposing to Kayla. Chase Wilmington might possibly be the most patient man on the planet. It's been five damn years; this step is long overdue.

So far, everything has gone off without a hitch. The event hall is decorated with blush pinks and champagne hues. Fuchsia lilies surround white peonies in the center of each round table. It's absolutely gorgeous. I'm happy for my best friend, but a twinge of longing weaves through me. *When will I find my forever?*

Twenty-six is still young, but the older I get, the more I worry I'll never have the chance to settle down. I *love* love. The butter-flies, public displays of affection—all the cute little clichés that make romance what it is. There's just one problem: love hates me.

Why are you making this day about yourself? So selfish—

The double doors in the back of the room swing open, snapping my attention to where it's supposed to be. Kayla walks from the venue's kitchen completely awestruck, locs swept over the shoulder of her pink floral dress. Chase meets her in the middle of the room with a smile full of so much adoration, it's hard not to smile too. Witnessing their promise to permanently join their lives together brings a few tears to my eyes. I truly love this for them.

"They're pretty great together..." Trevor's deep baritone makes me jump as he sets his drink on the refreshment table beside us. He straightens his navy-blue suit jacket, glancing at the pair, then gives me a dimpled smile. Trevor works with Chase. We briefly met a few years ago when Kayla and Chase moved to their new apartment in San Francisco. He came to help, bulging muscles in all their glory, right as I was leaving.

My shame goes out the window as I glance at the biceps straining Trevor's sleeves. He's tall, which isn't a hard thing to be next to me, and his hazel eyes have lingered on me several times in the last ten minutes. A small scar cuts across his right eyebrow, adding a rugged touch to his otherwise polished persona. Combined with his warm sepia skin tone and auburn buzz cut, it makes for one fine-ass man. I'll admit, it's been tough looking away from him myself.

Not the time.

"They really are. I can't believe they're finally locking each other down," I say.

"So, do you get up to San Francisco very often?"

I tilt my head, completely amused by the smirk playing at the corner of his mouth. "Are you hitting on me at an engagement party?"

"I guess that depends on whether it's working or not," he responds with a smile.

He's cute and looks like he could sling me over his shoulder with ease, but I just got dumped last week. Considering my track record, I don't know that jumping into something else this soon would be in my best interest. Smiling back, I shake my head.

"I don't make it up there often, no." Hopefully, he takes the hint for what it is. He seems nice, and making a scene at this party wouldn't be a good look for me.

Giving a little chuckle, he nods. "Welp, at least you turned me down gently. It was nice talking to you, Ashlie." With one last smile, he walks to a seat next to some of the other EdTechU employees.

The happy couple joins their parents at a table across the room. They look so blissful. Wanting to give them space to celebrate with their families, I stroll toward Hunter to collect my winnings instead. The sleeves of his slate button-down are rolled up a few inches, displaying the rich sienna forearm he has slung around some scrunch-faced woman who clearly wants to be somewhere else. I've never seen her before, which isn't unusual. You could look up the word *player* in the dictionary and find a picture of Hunter just how he is now, with a random brunette under his arm.

I slide into the chair across from him. "Pay up, Hunt."

Annoyance flashes in his light green eyes as he leans to the side and digs out his wallet. Short, dark curls sway slightly when he shakes his head, clearly annoyed at losing his own bet. "I thought she'd figure it out, for sure."

He hands me a twenty, and I tuck it into the cream-colored clutch I matched with my strapless dress. "Your sister's smart, but this plan was foolproof."

"Sister?" the brunette asks, looking between us. "I thought this was your best friend's engagement."

"It is. Chase is my best friend, and Kayla's my sister."

She squints. "I thought your sister was in high school..."

"It's a little complicated." I smile to ease the confusion on her face.

"And who are *you*?" She turns a steely gaze to me, a one-sided challenge I have no interest in accepting. I'm the furthest thing from competition for her. She can miss me with the attitude, though.

"I'm his best friend." I throw my sass behind a smile, knowing it will only add to the confusion. Since she can be rude for no reason, I can add a little snark of my own. Hunter laughs while I keep the sweet-looking grin on my face, staring her down until she looks away.

"This is my other best friend, Ashlie. Ash, this is Ava." Hunter's introduction does nothing to ease the intensity of Ava's glare as she flicks her eyes back to me. It's sad, really. She doesn't seem to know she won't be around next week. "Chase is my best friend, Kayla's my sister, Ashlie is Kayla's best friend. Everyone is friends here. We good?" He takes a sip of his drink, widening his eyes at the ensuing drama.

Ava slowly turns back to him and gives a curt nod. "It's pronounced Awe-vuh, with an *awe* sound."

"Like avocado?" I ask with a straight face. Hunter chokes on his drink, and I bite my cheek to keep from laughing. If looks could kill, I'd be dead. But they don't, so I flash Ava another grin. "Anyway, I'm gonna go check on my sister. Nice meeting you, Ava!"

"It's *Awe*—"

"We still on for Wednesday?" Hunter asks, becoming the newest target of the daggers shooting from Ava's glare. *Always stirring the damn pot.*

We've met for lunch every Wednesday for almost a year now. He already knows the routine. My eyes widen, sending a quiet message. *Why would you ask me that? Your date's about to lose it.*

But he ignores it *and* the glower on Ava's face, staring at me until I purse my lips and nod. When I walk away, I hear the loud "hmph" she snorts in my wake. All I can do is shake my head. *He's always with dramatic-ass women.*

"Hey, Wills." I knock into Willa's shoulder as I slide into the chair next to her. She gives a quick scowl before her face softens, and I bump her shoulder again just to annoy her. The late afternoon sun filters over her through the skylights, her yellow sundress augmenting her rich amber skin with a radiance I haven't seen from her in a while. She smiles and lifts her DSLR camera around her neck, snapping a candid photo of me before taking another of the partygoers over my shoulder. After a few more shots, she pulls her Senegalese twists from under the camera strap and cradles the lens in her hands.

Willa is three years older than me, and from height to hair, we couldn't be more different. My energetic personality has always disrupted her peace and quiet, but we've started getting along in the last few years. It's nice, if not a little awkward sometimes.

"This is fancy," she says, looking around the room. "Kayla planned all of this?"

"She thinks she did. And I guess she technically picked all the details, but Chase is the one who orchestrated everything."

"She looks so happy." Willa snaps another picture of the couple before turning the camera to the centerpieces.

I nod, looking at the smile on my best friend's face. She really hit the lottery with that one. "Are you coming home for Thanksgiving this year?" I ask.

Willa takes a deep breath, holding it briefly before turning to me. The smile from before has fallen into a cool, flat line. I wouldn't call it a frown, but I wouldn't call it anything else either. "I haven't decided yet. Are you?"

"I'll go if you do." I laugh, and she smiles again. Not going isn't an option for me. I can't stand seeing my parents' disappointment. Doing what they expect of me keeps the peace. Willa, on the other hand, couldn't care less and doesn't visit often. When she moved to LA for college, against our parents' wishes, she never looked back. I can count on one hand how many times she's been home since leaving.

"I'll think about it." She sighs, checking her watch. "I have to get to my next photoshoot, but I want to say hi to the happy couple first."

"I'll come with you." I loop my arm around hers as we walk across the room toward my friends.

CHAPTER THREE

HUNTER

*E**nough with the goddamn giggling.* Chase and Kayla are snuggled up across the table from me like they're in some kind of love cocoon. It's adorable in the same way gouging my eyes out with a fork would fix my vision. I understand a candlelit Italian restaurant *sets the mood*, or whatever the fuck people say in the movies. But if I hear *baby* one more time, like it's not the most clichéd term, I'm walking out. There are so many better things I could do on a Saturday night.

Drumming my fingers, I stare at the flickering shadows the tea lights cast across the wooden table. Elevator music playing just under the din of the evening crowd does nothing but amplify the noise in the room. The Tuscan finish on the walls is too orange, as if they used the house vodka sauce instead of paint. *Everything in here is distracting.* My eyes sweep over the arched windows framed by gaudy burgundy curtains, settling on the restroom hallway next to the kitchen.

Ashlie abandoned me for the bathroom ten minutes ago. I'm tempted to head that way just to take a breather, but the sounds of giggling pull me back to the table with a lip-curling grimace. *Give me a fucking break.* Watching these newly engaged lovebirds turns my stomach. Maybe I should be used to it by now, but their PDA still feels like an intrusion.

"You two should really get a room," I say, trying to disrupt the awkwardness.

Without looking at me, Chase dips his head to kiss Kayla's shoulder. "Oh, we intend to..."

Bleh. Scrubbing my eyes with bleach would be more pleasant than watching them sprinkle their vomit-inducing "love parmesan" all over what's left of my pasta. I'm tempted to knock Chase's Chicken Marsala into their laps, but mushrooms are as offensive as their PDA. I reach for my glass and tip a couple of ice cubes in my mouth instead.

Slinging an arm around Kayla, Chase turns to me. "So, I wanted to ask if you'll be my best man."

He already knows the answer is yes. We've been best friends since birth, basically brothers. "Will I have to watch more of this?" I wave my hand in their direction with a scowl.

"Absolutely. But don't bring whoever you brought last night," he says.

"Yeah, don't bring her." Kayla scrunches her nose. "She scowled the entire time. Where did you even meet her, Hunt?"

"Uh, the coffee shop, I think. Or was it the gym?" I shrug, hardly caring to remember the specifics. Women flock to me, and I go along with it. They don't stick around long enough to mean anything, so there's no point of putting my energy into knowing them. I either get bored or distracted before moving on to the next. Ava's no different. We've only had a couple of dates, but she's all sorts of drama. And she was a little *too* excited when she found out I'm the son of a multimillionaire. I don't do drama *or* gold diggers. "It doesn't really matter. I'm not feelin' it with her anymore."

Kayla snorts and shakes her head. "That figures. Are you ever going to settle down?"

"And be whipped like you two? Naw," I say, fidgeting with my fork. "That's not my thing. I like my space too much. And I damn sure don't want to answer to anyone."

She cocks an eyebrow as her head falls to the side. "Do I *look* like I answer to anyone?"

Chase laughs into her shoulder, unwilling to get in the middle of our sibling squabble. I can't blame him. I swallow my smart-ass response too. There's no way I'll win this battle with my sister. Half sister, technically—same dad, different moms. We've only known about each other for five years, learning of our relation right around the time she got together with Chase. She may be a few months younger, but we both know she's not the one to mess with.

"I'm not touching that." I laugh and look up in time to see Ashlie whip around the corner. Her golden-brown coils spill from her high ponytail like a fully bloomed bouquet of curls. The freckles over her nose are illuminated by the flushing across her amber cheeks as she scurries into the seat next to me. She heaves a breath like she just ran a mile, eyes so wide they have to hurt. "You good?" I ask.

"Bryan's here," Ashlie whispers to the table.

"Who?" I look to Kayla to see if she knows what's going on.

"*Bryan*!" Ashlie whisper-screams.

Kayla twists in her seat to look around the room. "*Bryan, Bryan?*"

"Yes! Don't *look*!" Ashlie hunkers down in her chair like Bryan is some ominous reaper coming to take her soul.

"Oh, Ashy Bryan?" I tease, recalling his nickname from our summer in Fort Bender.

Kayla giggles. "I thought it was his babies who were going to be ashy."

"I think anything having to do with Bryan turned ashy," Chase jokes back.

"You three laugh it up, but he's here with his wife. And I'm pretty sure he saw me." Ashlie lifts off her chair, hovering slightly as she peeks across the room.

No sooner than she sits, tall ass Bryan comes around the corner with a very pregnant replica of Ashlie. She's short, with light brown skin and curly hair dyed a golden brown. You can tell it's dyed by the black roots showing. But aside from that, and the ginormous belly, she looks eerily similar.

"Quick"—Ashlie turns to me—"pretend we're together."

My face pinches as I lean back to look at her. *Is she fucking serious?*

"Just do it!" she whispers through her teeth. Picking up my hand, she drapes my arm around her shoulders and laces our fingers. I glance across the table, wide-eyed, and the two lovebirds are cracking up as they watch the exchange.

"Ashlie? I thought that was you," Bryan says with a smile, white teeth gleaming against his dark brown skin. He and his wife stop next to our table, and she rubs her belly in that motherly way, while Ashlie snuggles in closer to me. Close enough that her curls tickle my jaw, the light scent of her jasmine perfume drifting to my nose.

"*Bryan?*" she asks, forcibly changing her panicked expression into one of surprise. "It's been forever!"

"It really has." He nods, turning to look across the table. "And Kayla too? Talk about a blast from the past!"

"Hey, Bryan." Kayla nods to the seat next to her. "This is my fiancé, Chase."

Chase reaches his hand out toward Bryan for a shake.

"Fiancé? Wow, that's exciting! This is my wife, Shaylee." He looks at Ashlie expectantly. It's almost painful to watch. How he found a near-identical replacement to his ex, even down to the similar names, is purely coincidental, I'm sure. *Asshat.* No one in this interaction wants to be here, except maybe Bryan, and I'm getting bored with the niceties. *Time for some fun.*

"Aren't you going to introduce me, *honey bear*?" I ask loudly, hugging Ashlie tight as I nuzzle my face into her hair. I don't know where "honey bear" came from, but it somehow fits her.

She stiffens, subtly jabbing me with her elbow before lobbing back with, "Yes, my *sugar booger*." I nudge her foot, and she kicks me. "This is my"—she flinches when I tickle her side—"this is Hunter." Smiling back at Bryan, she wiggles away from me slightly. Kayla and Chase watch the madness behind covered snickers.

"What's good?" I reach over Ashlie to shake his hand. We've met once, five years ago, but he clearly doesn't recognize me.

"And you're her...?" He's a little too interested, if you ask me. Especially with a wife who looks ready to pop any second.

"I'm the love of her life." I wink at him and drape my arm back over Ashlie's shoulders, wrapping the other around her middle. Discreet snorts float across the table as I turn up the act and nuzzle into Ashlie's cheek. "Right, sunshine?"

"Yep," she says through a gritted smile. I trail my finger over the strap of her dress, and she slaps my hand, playing it off as a tender hand grab. She turns to me with a sassy glint in her eyes. "We met at the car wash. He was shampooing his seats after a case of explosive diarrh—"

With wide eyes, I press two fingers over her lips to silence the rest of her sentence. Kayla has a coughing fit, and Chase's head is in his hands, shoulders shaking violently. "Oh, *sweet cheeks*"—I tut —"some things need to stay between us..."

"Well, that's great. Really, Ashlie. We'd better go, but it was good seeing you. Both of you." Bryan nods toward Kayla and turns to his wife, glancing back at Ashlie one last time before guiding Shaylee to the door. *What a fuckstick.*

"Looks like he has a type," I whisper once they're out of earshot. Ashlie sits still in my arms, holding her breath until they exit the restaurant.

"Boy, if you don't get your hands off me..." She throws my arms from around her and scoots her chair away, causing my suppressed laughter to erupt from my throat. "What was *that*?" she asks, glaring at me. "I said act like we're together, not maul me."

"Hey, you asked for it," I say, breath hitching from residual snickers. Kayla and Chase finally lose it, and Ashlie bites her cheeks, trying to keep herself from falling out too.

"*Honey bear*? What kind of pet name is that?" She covers a giggle with the back of her hand.

"You called me *sugar booger*. I'm pretty sure that's drugs."

"That's booger sugar, you dumbass," Ashlie tries to say with condescension, but she ultimately gives in to the collective snorts and giggles.

"Dumbass? Is that another pet name?" I mimic back.

"*Ugh*! You're so annoying!" She rolls her eyes, arms crossing tightly.

I smile widely. "I know."

"Okay"—Kayla interjects—"let's pivot to the wedding. Since you two are the best man and maid of honor, we wanted to run a few things past you." She glances at Chase, who presses a kiss to her temple. The disgustingly sweet display is enough to make me lose my appetite for dessert. "We're thinking Memorial Day, back in Fort Bender."

"That's only seven months away!" Ashlie gasps, counting on her phone's calendar. "We have to pull all of this together in seven months?"

"Yeah," Chase says. "We'll need to hit the ground running. We just felt like that was *the day* and didn't want to wait another year."

Like waiting one more year when you've been together for five is a big deal. But what do I know? I don't do relationships. These two, on the other hand? They're inseparable. A wedding is just a formality at this point.

Kayla and Chase first met in Fort Bender, where Ashlie and I had a front-row seat to their summer love story. They're different in almost every way—Black and white, reserved and sociable, pessimist and optimist, no-nonsense and goofy as hell—but it works for them.

"I'm ready for whatever you need." Ashlie reaches across the table for Kayla's hand. "I can fly up to San Francisco on the weekends or find vendors in Bender... Ooh, I bet Samson would do your flowers in a heartbeat! Just tell me what else you need, and I'm on it."

"Same. My mandatory day in the office moved to Wednesdays, so I can take off for the weekends whenever," I offer.

The waiter clears our plates and brings the check while we hammer out a few more details. We say our goodbyes in the parking lot, the cool October wind breezing around us as we dole out hugs and handshakes. After another round of congratulations, Kayla and Chase walk off to their rental car. They fly back to San Francisco in the morning.

"Alright, *honey bear*. I'll see you for lunch on Wednesday!" I tease, dodging her incoming swat at me.

"Boy, if you don't leave me alone..." She shakes her head, laughing.

"Are you gonna make me do that anytime we bump into one of your exes? Because I will. We just need to get our backstory straight."

"I think the one I used will work just fine, thank you very much!" Her shoulder swat connects this time before we're both doubled over, laughing at the ridiculous end to the night. Still smiling, she holds up her fist. "Really, though. Thanks for having my back, Hunt."

I meet her fist with mine. "I got you. Always... You good, though?"

"Yeah. I'm okay." She smiles again and climbs behind the wheel of her little red hatchback, but I see in her eyes how shaken she is from running into that manipulative motherfucker again.

Ashlie and I met that same summer in Fort Bender, back when she was still with Bryan. She was safe—off-limits—and she could see straight through my bullshit. Over the years, she's become one of my best friends. I'd do anything for her, including fending off overeager exes.

I wait for her to drive away before crossing the parking lot. When I get in my car, the scent of jasmine on my shirt collar conjures too many memories. The fragrance is faint, but it's there, transporting my mind back to the first time I was close enough to smell her perfume. A time we both promised we'd never talk about again. I won't say a word to anyone about that night, but I'll damn sure think about it the entire drive home. After all, I've been in love with my best friend for the last five years.

CHAPTER FOUR
ASHLIE

S tomach growling, I take another look at the digital clock on the wall. The orange glow from the Fit4U logo highlights all the disheveled tanks hanging up there, and I make a mental note to fix them after lunch. I would have eaten by now, but Wednesdays are lunch days with Hunter. *And he needs to hurry the hell up.* Breathing out a long sigh, I glance out the tinted window, my hands moving on autopilot to fold the legging display. This job gets more tedious when I'm hangry.

The cash register across the room beeps as my coworker, Hannah, rings up the heavily muscled man at the counter. She's giggled so many times, I'll be surprised if she doesn't have a tickle in her throat by the time he takes his bag of supplements out the door. These two flirt multiple days a week. It's so damn cute to watch.

Being a manager at Fit4U for the past year has left me more relaxed than I ever was in the classroom. This athleisure company isn't anything fancy, and gets a little boring sometimes, but I don't leave in tears every day like I did when I was teaching first grade. Talk about feeling like a failure.

The kids were adorably hilarious, but the constant pressure from everyone else was insurmountable. As hard as it was to accept, leaving that environment was worth the risk of disappointing my parents. I stayed four years, just long enough to have my student loans forgiven.

"Have a nice day." I wave at the man. He smiles as he passes by, moving his headphones over his ears before walking out into the sunshine.

Hannah comes straight over to me with wide eyes, her usually pale cheeks as red as the neon Open sign above the door. "That was his second time in here this week!" She bounces on her toes, her blond bob swinging as she clutches her hands.

"And did you talk to him this time?" I ask. "You know he only comes in here to see you."

"I asked him how his day was, and then my brain turned to mush."

"Ooh, girl! You got it bad!" I tease, straightening the case of supplements as I pass by. Might as well fix those tanks on the wall while I wait.

Olivia's sneakers squeak on the orange vinyl flooring as she comes out of the stockroom, carrying a box of our newest zip-ups. One sleek, black braid lays over her shoulder, and she flicks it behind her when she reaches the counter. "Was that Hottie McMuscles I heard?" she asks Hannah, whose cheeks are still flushed. The two of them squeal and giggle about Hannah's failed attempt to talk to the musclehead while they tackle the box.

Chiming snaps my attention to the door, and in walks Hunter, wearing a dark blue EdTechU polo and khakis. His short dark curls dance briefly as the gust of air pressure breezes over him, like he's the star of his own rom-com. If it wasn't Hunter, I'd say he was attractive. But it *is* him, and he doesn't need any kind of ego boosts. Even if they're silent ones in my head.

"Hey, Hunter," Olivia croons dreamily, flipping her braid back over her shoulder. She pets it like a precious mink as he struts closer. Hannah waves, her cheeks flaming the same deep red as before. I roll my eyes. These young college students fawn over him every week as if he wouldn't completely devastate them.

"Ladies, how's it going?" He smiles, and Olivia grips the edge of the table when her knees wobble. Hunter turns to me with the same goofy grin on his face. *Oh, please.* How so many women fall for that look is beyond me. He's cute but *come on.*

"Let me grab my bag." Shaking my head, I step into the break room, walking back into the store right when Hunter leans in and winks at Hannah. The gasp that stutters out of her prompts another eye roll from me as I march past the three of them, right out the door. Waiting outside while the breeze tangles my curls is a small price to pay. *I'm not watching this foolishness.*

Hunter finally joins me on the sidewalk, stuffing his hands in his pockets as he sidles up. "Why are you looking at me like that?" he asks, referencing the scowl on my face.

"You need to leave those poor girls alone..." I turn away and walk down the street.

He follows in step, chuckling at my side. "I'm not doing anything." Shrugging with that smart-ass smirk on his face, he glances at me. "All I did was ask them how school was going. It's not my fault they were fawning all over me."

"Oh, *please.* You knew exactly what you were doing. Those two are off-limits." I huff, jamming my thumb into the crosswalk button. "They're nice girls who don't need your ass contributing to their villain origin stories." He laughs again, but says nothing else about it. Probably because he knows I'm right.

We make it to Lunch-a-Bunch after a few blocks. The redbrick eatery is my favorite, and since it's close to my job, I come here way too often. After a quick greeting, the host scurries off to prepare a table on the patio. Large picture windows bathe the café in crisp, natural light, the calming blue and green walls instantly setting me at ease. Hanging plants scattered among macramé tapestries give this place a free-spirited vibe I've always loved.

"How's Avocado?"

Hunter snorts, shrugging a shoulder like they weren't all over each other a few days ago. "Fine, I guess. Haven't talked to her since the party."

"So, she ghosted you?" I tease, trying to get a rise out of him. With a scrunch of my lips, I wait for his rebuttal, noticing the chiseled angles of his jawline. I'm not saying his face makes me swoon like it does the rookies at work, but I notice it.

"Do I look like I get ghosted?" He cocks his head to the side, green eyes narrowing at my jab. "Naw. She's been blowin' up my phone. I'm just busy." Hunter *is* the ghost. He's probably left the scowl-faced lovely on read, forgetting she even exists, while leading the next girl through the door. We're opposites in that way. I crave connection from the people I date, and he shies away from it. That's why nothing could ever work between us. He's an excellent friend—and we have fun together—but that's where it stops...no matter how much I notice his face.

We follow the waiter out to the elongated patio, enclosed in a black steel lattice fence, with round bistro tables scattered from end to end. Green tablecloths flutter in the breeze as we're led toward the back. Hunter pulls out my chair and waits for me to sit before going around to his seat. "And what about you?" he asks. "I noticed you didn't bring Dr. Doofus to the party..."

"That's because we broke up." I bury my head in the vinyl menu to avoid looking at him.

Even after dating him for almost a year, Marcus never seemed to fully commit. I know doctors have busy schedules, but something else kept our relationship more casual than I would have liked. I couldn't figure out what it was. The romantic in me tried to hold on to the hope that things would work out, but based on that damn email, I should have ended it first.

"I'm sorry, Ash," he says. Looking up, I fully expect Hunter's smug I-told-you-so face. Instead, my eyes are met with sympathy. He may be the biggest goofball around, but one thing Hunter gets right is being supportive. "He's an idiot for breaking up with you."

Crossing my arms, I squint at him. "And what makes you think *he* dumped *me*? Maybe I'm the one who broke it off."

"Well, did you?"

"*Ugh*! No...but I should have. Almost a year together, and I get a 'We regret to inform you' email." I pull out my phone and scroll to the message before handing it over the table.

Hunter crushes his lips between his teeth as he reads, hardly containing his laughter. "I mean, he treated you like a colleague when you were together. Why would it be any different when he broke up with you?"

That's exactly how I'd describe it. Marcus insisted I go to events when he needed an arm-candy ego boost. But whenever we were alone, he seemed uninterested in anything I had going on. Stifling control and stark indifference. I don't know why I put up with it for so long. *Maybe I'm the one who needed the ego boost.*

Hunter levels me with his stare. Even though I know he's speaking truth, I hate it. He saw this happening before I did. *Again*. He's seen right through all the men I've dated, without fail, for years now. Shaking his head, he howls with laughter as he reads the email again. "Ballsy," he says. "I'll give him that."

I snatch my phone back and shove it in my purse, my scalp prickling with sweat as I straighten in my chair. The anger bubbling under the surface when I look at him doesn't surprise me. I wear defensiveness like a battle shield. Yeah, I'm frustrated with myself. But directing my irritation at him feels like it might help right now too. Him and his smug little laugh.

"You want me to say you were right, don't you? That you called it, and he was an ass all along?"

"Naw, chill. I'm not tryna be right or make you feel bad. I just think you keep forgetting who holds the cards here. Guys get away with whatever they can. You keep picking the dusty ones who don't know how to treat you well."

That familiar pang of incompetency twists in my stomach. *He sounds like Kayla.* A glower pinches my face as my protective wall falls into place. "You think I'm doing this on purpose?"

Sitting forward, he looks right into my eyes until I soften my glare. "You deserve someone who wants your happiness as much as their own, Ash." He holds my gaze until I surrender, shifting my focus to the condensation dripping down my peach lemonade. "And delete that email so you stop going back to it."

Grumbling, I reach for my menu, the frustrated heat in my face fizzling away as his words echo in my mind. The way he can say exactly what I need to hear is infuriating sometimes—especially when I don't *want* to hear it. But I have to admit, he's never been wrong.

"How are you so good at spotting the *douchebaggery* in the guys I date?"

"Because I'm an asshole." He smirks, and I snort at the truth in his statement. "Game recognizes game. We can spot each other a mile away."

I try to distract myself with the lunch options in front of me, but my mind wanders to the first time he told me I deserved so much more. Sure, he was talking about a different guy, and it was years ago. But he used that same intense stare that managed to reach through my panic and settle into my psyche. He looked at me like he really saw me, past the bubbly, people-pleasing facade. We don't talk about that night, but I'll always remember how it felt to be seen by him.

MOM
How's the application coming?

ME
Working on it now!

DAD
Wow, look at you getting ahead of the game.

MOM
Don't forget to sign up for the entrance exam.

ME

What entrance exam?

MOM

ASHLIE JANIECE

ME

Kidding! Don't call me. I already signed up.

SETTING MY PHONE DOWN, I ROLL MY EYES AT THE intrusive group text from my parents. Their insistence that I start graduate school gets more intense the closer it gets to the spring deadline. I tell them I'm working on the application when, really, I'm sitting here in my living room, staring at the blank form on my laptop as I try to even out my shaky breathing. I'm sweating buckets while I avoid it, increasingly aware that the looming date is still on my don't-want-to-do list. Basically, I'm lying to get them off my case.

Recalling some tools from my handful of therapy sessions, I take deep breaths and try to name five details I can see around the room: *My comfort NetVids series on the TV, the sunflower painting against the millennial gray wall above it, a burned-out bulb in the kitchen, the contents of my purse spilled across the small wooden table in my entryway, the grad school application taunting me on my laptop.*

Oh God.

I squeeze my eyes shut, breathing deeply through my nose, which does nothing but sound the siren for the beginning stages of this panic attack. I know I haven't called my therapist in a while, but *damn.* Maybe I need to, since that didn't work at all. Another text from Mom pops up on my phone, and I flip it over on the coffee table. I can't deal with her right now.

Being the child of two strict educators, I always did what they expected of me. I couldn't disappoint them and wouldn't ever entertain doing so. Enter my teaching career, where carefree living quickly fell into overstimulation and daily panic attacks. Being in charge of twenty-five six-year-olds was hard enough. Add the intense scrutiny of their parents and my overbearing administrators, and it was the perfect recipe for disaster. I stopped swimming, stopped eating, stopped *caring*. Why have hobbies when I could burn the candle at both ends every day?

When I burned out last year, the only thing that got my parents off my back was a promise to apply for graduate school. I gave them the guarantee of starting a Master of Education to placate them while I took the year off. But honestly, I don't want to go back to school in any capacity—as a teacher or a student. My parents expect me to desire more for myself, and it's easier to let them think I do than it is to stand up to them. I'll tell them eventually, but only when I absolutely have to.

Reaching for my Fit4U tumbler, I take a long sip, hoping the cool water will slow my racing heart. Working there is good for me right now—low stakes and low pressure. I know I don't want to stay there forever, and I'm getting closer to feeling like my old self, but a year just hasn't been enough time. I need more of this slow pace to work through building up my confidence again, more time to gain some courage and reintroduce myself to things I actually enjoy.

Like swimming.

I shake the thought from my head as soon as it comes. As much as I love it, I haven't been in a pool in years. It started feeling like a selfish endeavor when I was struggling so badly at work. With grad school approaching, it still feels selfish. *I* still feel selfish. *Ugh, don't cry.*

Blinking rapidly, I refocus on my computer, my fingers tingling on the keyboard as my pulse pounds in my ears. *I just need to type my name.* It's the easiest thing on the form, but my mind blanks like the blinking cursor wiped the common sense right out of it. Sweat prickles under my arms as I reread the submission requirements—words I could probably recite in my sleep by now. My breathing surges, eyes darting around the words on the application.

GRE. Deadline. Transcripts. Submission. Submission. Submission.

I rub the center of my chest, trying to loosen the tightness gripping me. The walls of my apartment slowly close in as I desperately strain to pull air into my shrinking lungs. *You can't even type your name.*

Disappointment. Selfish. Failure.

Right when I'm about to tuck my head between my knees, my phone buzzes. The loud skittering makes me jump, jolting me out of my panic.

HUNTER

You make it home from work, honey bear?

ME

Yes. And stop calling me that!

HUNTER

Naw, it suits you.

ME

Quit, or I'll tell the car wash story to the girls at work.

HUNTER

Bruh, why are you coming for me?

ME

You started it. Night!

HUNTER

Goodnight, 🍯🐻.

ME

🖕

Finally minimizing the application screen, I check my inbox for the last time. An email sits at the top from the LA County Recreation Centers with a subject line that reads: *Swim Director Position Still Available.*

I sigh. *My dream job.* One where I think I could finally feel successful. I started an application a while ago, getting a confidence boost from a few glasses of wine. But doubts got the best of me and I never finished. Maybe one day I'll feel brave enough to go for it. Right now, though, keeping this dream locked up inside feels like the safest thing for me to do. *No chance of messing it all up.*

CHAPTER FIVE

HUNTER

T he music blasting through the speaker behind me pauses right when the beat drops, a text notification making me lose my focus completely. "Message from Dad," Kiri's robotic voice echoes across my apartment.

Motherfucker. Forgot to set Do Not Disturb again.

Leaning away from my computer, I grab my phone off the filing cabinet against the wall. I keep it up there to help me focus while working, which is only effective about half of the time. The impulse to scroll is always at the back of my mind. Hitting play, I bob my head to the beat as I lounge back in my office chair and check the notification.

DAD

Hey, still good to grab Artie from practice?
Tied up at work.

Shit. Totally spaced it.

ME

Remind me what time...

DAD

5:30

An hour? Looking back at my L-shaped desk, I contemplate whether I've made enough progress to deem myself productive for a Tuesday. I'll have data reports to present in the office tomorrow. Since I'm a remote employee, I need to keep on top of my game, but especially now. After several years at EdTechU, I'm gunning for the remote data analyst supervisor position. My performance review is in a few months, and even with my accuracy rate in the top 5 percent, I don't want a careless mistake fucking up my chances. I double-check my report, cross-referencing a few more numbers before feeling satisfied enough to call it a day.

My home office spans the entire loft of my revamped industrial apartment. Two bedrooms downstairs, a wide-open first floor, and this nook upstairs. Natural light filters in through the two-story paned windows, making it so I rarely need to turn on the overhead light during the day. Exposed brick walls, painted white, offset the black trim and espresso hardwood throughout. It's perfect. Sometimes a little too perfect, leading to midday naps in the beanbag under the window. But it beats having to deal with daily workplace distractions. I get sidetracked easily, and the idea of being distracted at corporate every day sounds like literal torture. Going in only once a week has panned out nicely. The dip in my productivity on Wednesdays is proof of that.

ME

Yep, on my way.

DAD

Stay for dinner? Need to run something past you.

ME

Stretching as I stand, relief shoots through the stagnant muscles in my back. I've been sitting for so long, pins and needles tingle in my feet as my eyes readjust from staring at the screen. I slip off my scratched-up prescription glasses and toss them in my computer bag for work tomorrow. I probably *should* wear them all day, but I've always hated the way glasses look on me. Can't even remember the last time I went in for new ones. The eye doc stopped sending reminders sometime last year after I unintentionally missed a handful of rescheduled appointments. I just had other things going on, and it's not like my eyes are that bad anyway. They get a little fatigued when I'm on the computer or driving at night. The TV is fuzzier too, but getting a bigger one solved that issue. It beats the alternative. Contacts freak me the fuck out. I panic having an eyelash in my eye; why the hell would I purposely stick something in—

"Goddammit..." I grumble, glaring at the stack of papers my elbow just knocked to the floor. *Always when I'm in a rush.* The thought of reorganizing it pisses me off, so after a halfhearted shuffle, I give up and toss it all on the filing cabinet. *A problem for future me.* I triple check that I saved everything before powering down the computer.

AFTER A QUICK SHOWER, I MAKE THE LONG DRIVE through LA traffic, pulling into the loading lane at Mainway Academy forty-five minutes later. Framed by pillars, the white facade is trimmed in black, matching the bulldog logo on the brand-new marquee. Palm trees line the sidewalk of the over-priced private STEAM high school. I spot my baby sister, Artemis, standing under one. She's too close to some scrawny kid with a football helmet in one hand and her cheek in the other. They haven't seen me yet, so I watch their interaction, scrutinizing everything from his pretty boy haircut to how close his face is to hers. She's fifteen—a sophomore—and I know better than anyone that these little high school jocks mean nothing but trouble. I used to be one.

Football Boy takes a step closer, and I honk twice, making them both jump and look in my direction. I roll down the passenger window as she walks to my car, her volleyball bag slung over her shoulder.

"Jeez, Hunt. You didn't have to honk!" She sticks her head through the window, redness still tinting her sienna cheeks. Her long, curly brown hair is tied back into a fluffy ponytail, frizzy where it's been rubbing against her black practice uniform. Artemis throws her bag in the trunk before popping her head back through the window with hope in her eyes. "Can I drive?"

Squinting, I pretend to look past her, then twist to check the backseat.

"What are you looking for?" she asks.

"Whoever you're talking to, 'cuz I know you're not asking to drive *my* car."

"Please, Hunter," she pleads, hands clasped under her chin.

"Hell no." I glare at her puppy dog eyes until her face falls. She flings the door open in a huff, and my head pounds at the thought of her scraping up my midnight blue Torche. This car was a graduation gift from Dad a few years ago. I didn't go through the hassle of having it imported just for her to leave the paint job on every curb in West LA. No one drives it except for me. When she settles into the cream leather seat, I nod back to the tree. "He ever heard of personal space?"

Her head falls to the side like I'm stupid. "What makes you think I want him to give me personal space?"

"You better find the motivation, Artie, or I'm telling Dad you two were sucking face."

"No! Hunter, don't you dare."

My phone buzzes, with a message from Ashlie flashing across the display on the natural wood dashboard.

"*Ooh*, Ashlie's texting." Artie's eyebrows dance, her light green eyes sparkling with mischief as she snatches my phone out of the cup holder. I watch in horror while she taps in my password. "Is she your *girlfriend* yet?"

"Hey!" I reach for my phone right as she leans back against the door. "How do you know my passcode?"

"Because I'm good at snooping, and it's not like Ashlie's birthday was hard to guess." That sly smile on her face while my phone is in her hands makes my palms itch. "Dear Ashlie"—she teases with a deep voice—"we should make this official. Let's go steady."

"Oh, is that supposed to be me? Who talks like that?" I grab for my phone again, and she giggles while some boy band song fills the car. I'm only a little relieved when she finally puts it back in the cup holder. With Artemis, you never really know if she's messing with you or making moves in stealth mode. One minute, she's quiet, and the next, she's showing everyone at the dinner table the "weird water balloons" she found in your nightstand.

I check Ashlie's message, replying to her meme with a laughing GIF. Before I put it down, a text from Ava flashes across the screen, and I open it just to clear the notification. She's fucking relentless. I have no interest in seeing Ava again, but my casual strategy of ignoring all her messages isn't doing a damn thing. Hopefully she gets the picture soon. I don't keep women as friends; Ashlie is the one exception.

"You *looove* her," she taunts.

"You done? 'Cuz I can still tell Dad about Football Boy..."

Her eyes narrow. "And then I'll tell Ashlie that you still have a little bottle of her perfume from five years ago."

"What are you even talking about?" Feigning ignorance is the easiest way for me to call her bluff. I have that perfume so well hidden, even *I* forgot about it. When I found it, I kept it as a memento of something that happened so long ago, I'm not sure it even matters anymore. Still, there's no way in hell I'm letting Artie spread that rumor.

A condescending scowl falls on her face as her arms cross. "In your old room, under that floorboard you ripped up, right on top of your picture collection of girls who—"

"Okay, I got it! *Goddamn.*" I put the car in drive, continuing to cuss under my breath as I pull out of the school grounds. I shouldn't be surprised. Artie's had this idea of being an international super spy since she was little. The older she gets, the better she is at sneaking around. She's a good kid who doesn't get into trouble, but she stays in everyone's business, whether they know it or not.

When we pull into the circular drive of my childhood home —an expansive, white-brick two-story Tudor—Artemis takes off for the shower. I head to the fridge for a snack, stopping to admire the sun gleaming off the pool in the backyard as I crack the lid on my sparkling water. The Tuscan style kitchen is exactly like it was when my parents bought the house fifteen years ago, down to the distressed beige cabinetry and arched stonework over the stovetop.

I grab an apple from the fruit bowl on the gold-veined marble island and head to the TV lounge. Sinking into the plush sectional, I turn on the sports network and pull out my phone as a distraction. I don't plan to focus on the TV, but the sound has a way of calming the rapid-fire thoughts that constantly buzz through my consciousness. My mind is a vast wasteland of noise: never quiet and always chasing stimulation.

I don't know how long I've been scrolling, but the sun is dipping below the skyline when I hear the garage door open. Draping my arm across the back of the sofa, I wave at Dad when he walks in with a few boxes of Chinese takeout—his bad news meal. He looks exhausted from a long day at the office, with worry lines creasing his deep umber skin.

"Uh-oh." I nod to the boxes he's arranging on the kitchen island. "The company's going under? We're about to lose it all?" I tease.

"Funny," he mumbles, pulling plates and utensils out. Dad is the co-founder of EdTechU, one of the top educational technology companies in the country. They just expanded overseas. There's no way the company is going anywhere anytime soon.

"So, what's with the Doom Dinner?" I walk to the kitchen and sit on one of the barstools.

"Hey, Dad," Artemis says, coming down the stairs. She wraps her arms around him, and he kisses the top of her head.

"How was practice, Artie-girl?"

"Good. Coach was on us for losing the last game though. My legs still feel like jelly."

"So, what's with the Doom Dinner?" I ask again, not interested in listening to them go back and forth about improving her game and being a team player. I'm bored already and itching to get out of here.

Dad rubs his chin, his green eyes staring at me longer than is necessary. That recessive gene of his staked its claim in all of his kids—me, Kayla, and Artemis. I tap my foot on the stool, feeling antsy holding his gaze. Judging by his delayed response, he knows I won't be happy about whatever he has to share. He finally glances at Artemis before looking down at his plate. "Your mother is coming for the holidays this year..."

"*Ugh*," I groan.

"Yay!" Artie shouts at the same time.

I don't deal with my mom any more than I have to, which usually means a phone call from her on my birthday and a short text exchange from me on hers. Even though it's been a decade, I still blame her for the divorce. It's childish as hell, but I can't stand to look at her.

Dad's still staring at his plate, mulling something over.

"Is that it?" I press.

"She'll be staying with Theron in the guest house for the six weeks she's here."

"*Here*?" I ask, not even trying to hide the disgust in my voice. The thought of being in the same vicinity of Mom zaps any excitement I could feel about seeing my younger half brother again. "Did you open up a bed-and-breakfast back there I don't know about?"

"Hunter—"

"Nils agreed to that?" My mother's husband and Theron's dad, Nils Johansson, is a Swedish Olympic skier who has been known to rent out entire hotel floors in the past. *Why do they need to spend six weeks holed up in the backyard?*

"She and Nils have separated…"

I don't miss what he said, but I steamroll past it, letting the festering anger over my mother propel me. Standing, I grip the cool edge of the island until I feel it digging into my palms. "How are you okay with this, Dad? Have you forgotten how bad it was? I can't believe—"

"Lower your voice, and sit back down, son," he says with a level voice. Kendall Jackson doesn't yell. He doesn't need to. His presence can go from friendly to intimidating with just the look in his eye and a whispered bass tone. I sit, swallowing the rest of my rant as I look past him, out the window to the guest house in the backyard. Even at the age of twenty-six, I know not to press him. "Of course I remember, but our marriage was over long before she left. It's been ten years, Hunter. Staying angry about it has no benefit, and she's still your mother."

"Naw, not mine. Artie and Theron can have her." I shake my head, reaching for the carton of orange chicken.

"When are they coming?" Artemis asks, bouncing in her seat.

"In a few weeks. From Thanksgiving to New Year's."

"Way to ruin the holidays, Charlotte," I say to no one but myself.

Dad clears his throat. One glance and I take the hint, drop my head, and eat.

CHAPTER SIX
ASHLIE

"I don't understand how he can let her walk back in like nothing happened." Hunter huffs across the table at Lunch-a-Bunch, slumped in the patio chair. We're one of the only tables out here today.

"Letting her use his guest house isn't the same as letting her back in."

"It's close enough." He stabs a fork into his salad. "Too close for comfort."

"I don't know. Your dad's one of the most welcoming people I've ever known. Maybe he feels bad for her. Doesn't want to treat her the same way she treated him..." I've only met Hunter's mom once, briefly, and she made an unsolicited comment about my natural hair that put me off from having any further conversations with her.

"Bullshit." Hunter shakes his head and reaches for his glass, downing half the ice water inside. I don't ever see him riled up like this unless he's talking about Charlotte St. Clair-Johansson. "There goes Thanksgiving. And Christmas. *And* New Year's." The gruff tinge in his voice as he sets down his glass can fool most people. His lip twitching under flared nostrils really sells the rage he's projecting, but I've known him long enough to recognize the hurt in his eyes. He's never told me the specifics surrounding his parents' divorce, but I know it wasn't a good time for him.

"You could come to Bender for Thanksgiving. Chase and Kayla will already be there. We could probably convince them to get some wedding stuff out of the way." I bite into my turkey wrap while he mulls over my suggestion.

Brows knitted together, his tongue juts into his lower lip. "You"—he finally says with a smile—"are a genius."

This isn't one of his signature smirks he lays on unsuspecting women at the coffee shop. It's his honest to God, walls-have-fallen-down smile that makes his entire face light up. The smallest flitter dances inside my belly when I realize I made him smile that way. I shove the feeling away as soon as I sense it, but it was definitely there. Which is a problem because Hunter and I will never be more than the best of friends.

"Anyway, how's your grad school application coming along? Isn't the deadline soon?"

"Check, please." Pretending to look for the waiter, I crane my neck behind me. Hunter laughs again, and that damn flitter threatens to turn into a full flutter. I clear my throat, a feeble attempt to rid myself of the tingles pooling between my legs. *What the hell is happening right now? This is Hunter.* "The deadline is in December, but I haven't started the application yet."

"Why not?"

I roll the corner of my napkin nervously. *Do I tell him the truth?* "I've been busy with work..." I say, but just as soon as I start, his eyes narrow like he knows I'm full of shit. "Okay, fine. All the requirements are a little overwhelming. Whenever I open up my laptop to get started, I panic."

"Panic? About what?" He watches me intensely. He's probably the only person who wouldn't judge me if I told him the truth about this—about the family pressure.

My parents' legacy is teaching, as was their parents before them, and the ones before them. When my sister took her own path, they doubled down on "helping" me choose a teaching career for myself. By helping, I mean taking it upon themselves to insert their will at every chance they could, making it nearly impossible for me to deviate from their plan without severely disappointing them.

I tried it their way. I really did. But *their* pressure mixed with teaching pressure drove me so close to the edge, it was scary. I overworked myself until I had a nervous breakdown, and my confidence took a hit that extended to all facets of my life. I still haven't fully recovered.

Hunter's the one who helped me come up with an exit plan a year ago. The whole reason we have these lunches is because he discovered I wasn't eating well. I don't know what I would have done without him. My therapist, Fit4U, and Hunter literally saved me.

"Ash?" He leans forward in his chair, eyes boring into mine. "Do you want to go to grad school?"

"That's the plan..." My eyes drop as I fidget in my chair. I tuck my thumbnail between my front teeth and nibble furiously.

"That's not what I asked. Do you want to go?"

I shrug, keeping my eyes trained over his shoulder when I look up. Saying no, out loud, feels dangerous. Voicing it will mean I'm willfully going against the legacy my family has built. Who knows what the butterfly effect will be if I admit I don't want to do what I've spent a lifetime working toward? And the disappointment my parents will feel over me throwing it all away? *No thanks.*

"Ashlie, look at me." His voice is soft, and the stark change makes my eyes go back to his. "Forget about everyone else and what they want you to do. Is this something you want?"

"I...don't think so."

"Then don't. Screw anyone who gets mad about it. You only have one life, and you deserve to enjoy the way you're living it."

A tear slips down my cheek, and then another, until my vision is completely blurred by the salty river. *I need to calm down.* People are dying all over the world, and I'm crying over higher education.

I blindly reach for my napkin, moving my hands around the plate in front of me, when I feel the rough cotton swipe against my cheek. Hunter peers up at me, crouching next to my chair as he dabs my face with the cloth. He turns my seat so I'm facing him and props his hands on my knees.

"*Ugh.*" I blow out the emotion clogging my throat. "I don't want to disappoint anyone. I just feel so lost." I slide a finger under my eye to wipe away the smudged mascara.

"Why do they get a say?"

"Because *they* are my family…"

"You're a twenty-six-year-old woman who supports herself. Why do they get a say?"

I shake my head with a shrug. Hunter's thumbs move back and forth across my thighs as he tries to comfort me, wholly unaware that his touch is sending electric currents through my body. Each tender swipe is more searing than the last. He doesn't move until my breathing slows, and when it does, he smiles and slowly trails a thumb across my cheekbone. That damn flitter betrays me, and my stomach flutters wildly.

"Eyelash," he explains, holding it up for me to see. "Make a wish."

Without thinking, I blow the stray lash from his thumb and fly right into dangerous territory. He shudders as my breath fans over him, his eyes flashing with something I'm too scared to name. *No. You're seeing what you want to see, Ashlie.*

Wetting his bottom lip, Hunter's eyes shift to my mouth, and he gravitates toward me. I feel myself lean into him as if we're attached by an invisible string. The flutters from before are now noticeable flops as I remember a moment when being this close led to something I've forced myself to bury time and again.

"Here's your check!" the blond waitress calls cheerily, sending us both flying backward as we're snapped back to reality on the restaurant patio. My head swirls as I try to make sense of being dropped from that cloud of intimacy. Focusing on the green and white striped bistro umbrella flapping in the breeze, I take a deep breath and try to ground myself. "I'll be your cashier whenever you're ready." She smiles at us, sliding the check on the table before walking back into the building.

I reach for my glass and sip away the lingering sensations traveling through me. This is Hunter. *Hunter.* I know how he operates, and that magnetic pull I was feeling moments ago was one-sided. *It had to be.* He was trying to be a supportive friend, and I went and turned it into something more in my head. *Again.* I do this, getting misguided crushes on him every time I break up with a boyfriend. It always seems to last until the next guy comes along. When my logic recalibrates, he's put back into his proper place. This was that, no matter what's going on with my stomach.

As Hunter stands, he brushes the dirt from his knees and settles back into his seat across from me. Clearing my throat, I angle my chair to the table, pretending like I didn't just have a full-on crisis from his touch. He pulls out his phone and scrolls with the same thumb that just sent a jolt through me as it traveled across my cheek.

I want him.

I mentally trample over the wayward thought to put me back into the right headspace. He's probably over there talking to three different women, unfazed by anything that just happened. *Figures.*

Walking back to Fit4U isn't any different than it usually is, with us arguing about who would win in a fight: squid vs. octopus. When we get outside the door to my job, Hunter pulls me in for a hug. We've hugged before, but after the one-sided charge in the air at lunch, I'd be lying if I said my heart didn't tick a beat faster being wrapped up in his arms. Okay, several beats faster. His spicy ginger musk curls around me like a protective blanket, and I lose all my common sense when he squeezes a little tighter than normal. *Maybe I wasn't imagining.*

"Hey, have you been swimming lately?" he asks abruptly.

I freeze in his arms, the question unleashing an onslaught of anxiety. "Not in forever. I stopped having time when I was teaching."

Hunter lets go and nods thoughtfully. "You're just so down on yourself right now. I was thinking it might help you feel better. We could go together, if you want. You still have your membership at McMahon?"

I shake my head slowly. "Nope. That expired a while ago..." My voice cracks, and I let out a frustrated groan. I can already feel the tears pricking behind my eyes, something I don't want to take in to work.

"Another hobby, maybe? Doing something just for you could be the thing that helps rekindle your spark."

"Yeah...maybe." I give a hopeless chuckle as a tear rolls down my cheek. Feeling the way I do, that's all easier said than done.

Hunter throws an arm across my shoulders and pulls me in for another hug. "Hang in there, Ash," he says with a squeeze. "You'll figure it out."

"Hope so... Thanks for lunch."

"Sure thing, *honey bear.*"

He jumps away as I aim for his shoulder, laughing his ass all the way back to his car.

YOU CAN'T DO IT.

My eyes zoom around my living room, unable to focus on anything long enough to ground me. A steamroller irons out my lungs, each shallow inhale doing nothing to help me breathe. Wiping the cold sweat from my forehead, I lean back against the couch cushion, hoping it will give me a little more room for air. Another failed attempt at the grad school application, accented with an all-encompassing panic attack, and I'm convinced. Going back to school isn't happening.

I need to clear my mind, take away the festering dread creeping through my body at this decision. After shutting down my computer, I grab my purse and head for my car. Without really thinking about where I'm going, I drive to the place that always used to put a smile on my face. I give in to every single worry scrolling through my head on the way—work, school, stupid emails from exes, my inability to latch onto a crumb of confidence—everything. Hot tears drip down my cheeks, but I save the downpour, waiting until I find a spot in the back of the parking lot.

The McMahon Swimming Center used to be my favorite place to swim. The year-round double pools—indoor and outdoor—made it easy to come here multiple times a week in college. Now, I can't even step foot in the parking lot. I know Hunter offered to come here with me, but knowing my luck, I'll have a panic attack in the water and drown in the pool. It's been too long. I'm worlds away from who I was back then. That girl was confident and carefree. The woman I am today pretends well, but every little misstep gets logged in my growing book of inadequacy.

I look to the building again, the lights inside glowing like a beacon of hope as the sky grows dark. My mind screams at me to get out of the car, but the seven types of worry pinning me to my seat are relentless.

This isn't helping.

Another tear drips down my cheek right as my phone buzzes in my purse. I dig it out and smile at the name on the screen. The text from my best friend came right on time, like she knew I needed the distraction.

KAYLA

I'm freaking out. There are too many decisions to make.

ME

...Isn't it literally your job to plan events?

KAYLA

Regular ones, not weddings.

ME

You could hire a wedding planner…

KAYLA

I did, and she fired me. Besides, what do I look like hiring someone else to plan my wedding? I'm an Event Planner.

ME

Ooh, girl, you're gonna be such a fun bride 😳

KAYLA

 Can you fly up next weekend?

ME

Girl, yes. And Willa's all in as your photographer.

KAYLA

🙏 🖤

CHAPTER SEVEN

HUNTER

One lone streetlamp lights up the bird icon on The Flamingo, Ashlie's dingbat-style apartment complex. It's more like a giant shoebox covered in faded pink stucco, but the whimsy fits her to a T. Her red hatchback is nestled in her spot under the building. I double park behind it and pull out my phone.

ASHLIE

You're late!

ME

Naw, I'm not. Just pulled up.

ASHLIE

🧚 gimme 10 minutes...

ME

😳 It's already 9:30. Hurry up.

She finally slides into my car with a star-shaped wand, her sleeveless pink dress hugging every curve before giving way to a glittery tutu. I'm pretty sure she's wearing wings, but I'm too busy trying to keep my mouth from dropping open to investigate.

The soft curls framing her face, the glitter dusting her freckled cheeks—she has me in a trance.

"Are you gonna drive?" She motions toward the road like I'm the one making us late, and I spot a pink bandage wrapped around her thumb.

"What happened?" I nod to her hand.

"I tried taking your advice and got burned."

My eyebrows cinch while I wait for an explanation. I have no idea what she's talking about.

"You told me to pick up some old hobbies. I used to bake all the time, so I made cookies."

I'm impressed she actually listened to me. "Were they good, at least?"

"Wouldn't know. I burned my thumb when I took the pan out of the oven and dropped them all on the floor..."

"I mean..." Grimacing playfully, I back out of the parking spot and ease onto the road. "Maybe try a book next time?"

She sighs. "Are you done?"

I glance as she adjusts her hair in the visor mirror, painstakingly tearing my eyes away when she bites her bottom lip. *You can't go there.* "What are you supposed to be, anyway?"

"Really? I have wings and a wand... What do I look like?"

"The Tooth Fairy?" I laugh as she pushes my shoulder.

"Boy, the Tooth Fairy could *never*." She swipes a finger under her glossy lower lip, and I struggled to focus on the road instead of my dick twitching at her costume. "I'm just a fairy. What are *you* supposed to be?"

I flash a grin. My black button-down and jeans give no indication that I'm wearing a Halloween costume. "A Handsome Devil."

She snorts and slaps the visor closed. "I'll get out now. There's not enough room in your car for the three of us."

"Three of who?"

"You know... Me, you, and that big ass ego of yours..."

"Ooh, I see how it is!" I chuckle, squinting at the starbursts from the taillights ahead of me.

"You know, it's a crazy thought, but I *bet* your glasses would help you see the road better..." she teases.

"Naw, I'm good." Driving at night has always been like this. It's not *that* bad, just makes my eyes tired.

Her phone buzzes, and the brightness from the screen frames her face in a sensual glow that has my breath hitching. *Why the fuck can't I stop looking*?

"Willa's meeting us outside. She's bringing a friend," Ashlie mumbles, clearly distracted.

I tap my thumbs on the steering wheel, still fighting to win the internal battle between keeping my eyes on the road and stealing another glance at her. "Cool. Aiden from work is coming too."

Studio 99 puts on the best holiday-themed nights, and Ashlie drags me along to every single one of them. I pay the attendant and creep through the rows of cars, managing to find a parking spot along a concrete retaining wall.

She places her house keys in the glove box before turning to face me. "Okay, club rules apply: leave the same way you came, and send out a warning for any exes."

We made this deal a couple of years ago when we both had multiple exes come out of the woodwork on the same night to terrorize us at the club. Since then, we've had to utilize it a handful of times. I'm sure the full moon in the sky will make it an interesting night.

"Yep. Got it." Climbing out of the car, I bob my head to the muted dance music drifting from the two-story warehouse across the parking lot. The neon *99* buzzes brightly against the black stucco. Ashlie steps next to me, head lowered as her thumbs move swiftly across her phone. In the brightly lit parking lot, my eyes peruse down her short velvet dress to the golden boots zipped up to her thighs, and back up to the matching wings around her shoulders. *Fuck, she's fine as hell*. I take advantage of her distraction, using the extra seconds to let my eyes wander all over her again. "You good?" I ask, dropping my gaze.

"Yeah. Willa's already here." Head down, she starts the long journey through the parking lot. I swat away the thoughts flying into my head as I follow. Thoughts about leaning her against one of these unsuspecting cars to see if that dress feels as soft as it looks. *She's off-limits.* Even without a boyfriend in the way, I'm not her type. She likes the pretty boy fuck nuggets who pretend they want something serious. They front-end all their empty promises and dip when they realize they can't deliver. At least I'm honest about playing the field.

"Ooh, girl, let me borrow that dress!" Ashlie hugs her sister once we make it to the doors.

"Ash, I've got a good five inches on you. This dress will swallow you up." Willa's draped in a white flowy gown that clings to her full curves, reminiscent of a Greek muse. Her brown and black twists are swirled into an intricate *S* shape, and gold jewelry hugs her upper arms.

"Mmm, true. It looks good on you, though! I'm surprised you actually showed up this time."

Willa slips a hand on her hip and rolls her eyes. "Oh, whatever. I'm not *that* bad. Hades here is my friend, Isaiah." She gestures to the tall Black man next to her, his thick locs falling around the shoulders of his mesh shirt. The ring in his nose and snake bite piercings on his lower lip give a modern spin to the Greek mythology theme Willa has going on.

Isaiah waves just as my phone buzzes in my pocket. A message from Aiden prompts me to look around the crowd. I don't see him until he's almost weaved his way to our group. He's dressed in a white button-up and dark slacks, his usual tinted glasses hanging off his nose. Aiden's another remote analyst at work, and we get along better than most coworkers do. "Hey man," I say, bumping his fist as he joins the group. "What are you supposed to be?"

"A data analyst," he says, like it should be obvious. Then he smiles, nudging me with his elbow. "I'm kidding. I'm a pocket door salesman...'cause I'm so short..."

Snorting, I shake my head. Aiden's clever, if anything. "You remember Ashlie. This is her sister, Willa, and Willa's friend, Isa—"

"*Zay?*" Aiden gasps, stepping across the circle to give him a hug. "When did you get back?"

"Hey, Aid." He smiles at my coworker.

"You two know each other?" Willa asks.

"Yeah! Isaiah is a bartender at my favorite bar downtown. Well, he *was* before he took off for the East Coast. How did the show go?"

I don't hear the rest of their catching up since I'm suddenly distracted by the tall butterfly winged brunette walking toward us. Ava's already seen me, which is bad news considering I haven't responded to a single message she's left in the weeks since the engagement party. "*Shit,*" I whisper, turning sideways like I can hide.

Ashlie sneers when I bump into her. "What's your deal?" she grumbles, regaining her feet and glaring up at me. She scans the crowd when she sees my grimace.

"*Hunter?* Is that you?" Ava asks, putting a hand on my arm. I sigh, turning slowly as I force a grin on my face. Her dark green dress clings to her like a second skin, and platform boots set her high enough to be at eye level.

"Oh, *hey,* Ava." Ashlie's cheery voice is eclipsed by her mischievous smile. Ava's eyes narrow as she scowls at the fairy costumed spitfire next to me. "Great minds..." She points between the two of them, and the glower on Ava's face deepens.

"Oh, *please.* I'm not a fairy." Ava scoffs. Ashlie stiffens next to me. If I know anything, I know the one thing Ashlie can't stand is people being rude to her for no reason.

I glance at my best friend, who's tapping her finger on her lip. "Hmm. A giant then? Or an avocado? The green dress really nails that."

Choking back a laugh, I peep the livid sneer on Ava's face.

I'm surprised when Ashlie wraps her arms around my waist and looks up at me through her lashes. If she were any taller, she'd be able to hear the speeding of my heartbeat. "Huntie-baby, can we go in now?" She nuzzles her face into my side as her fingers rub my back, leaving tingling imprints in their wake. *Off-limits, Hunt.*

"I thought you two were just friends," Ava says through her scowl.

"Things change." Ashlie shrugs, flashing a sassy glare that makes Ava take a step back. She pulls me to the entry line, and right before we get to the door, turns and waggles her fingers at Ava.

The thumping bassline swallows Ashlie's laugh once we step inside the doors. Intermittent flashes of color paint the packed main dance floor as she tips on her toes to yell in my ear. "She's gonna follow you all night. You know that, right?" She drops her arms from my waist, and I dig fingers into my palms to resist pulling them back around me. Luckily, Willa, Isaiah, and Aiden manage to make it in right behind us, serving as the perfect distraction. After a brief gameplan, they head upstairs to the lounge.

Pulling Ashlie onto the main dance floor, we move to the beat under the purple and green strobe lights. Tonight's supposed to be fun, and watching her hips sway as she dances circles around me is my idea of a good time.

I LOST ASHLIE ABOUT AN HOUR AGO, BUT THE SCANTILY clad nurse grinding on me right now is cute enough to keep my interest. She tosses a wink over her shoulder and places my hand on her hip. I'm sure it's supposed to be seductive, but her bony ass is wearing a hole in my jeans. *I should touch base with Ash, just to*

check in. Her costume rides up her thigh as she presses into me, and I surprise myself when I look away. *Naw. Not interested.* The crowd is thinning out, anyway. That's my cue.

A strobe light shines right in my eye, and I spot Ashlie's latest ex across the dance floor with some blond in a bikini. I wouldn't even call it a bunny costume, seeing as the only identifiable parts are ears on her head and a puffy tail over her ass. *I really need to find Ashlie.* Whispering a goodbye to the nurse, I dig my phone out of my pocket and head to the stairs. Hopefully, I can get a better view of the dance floor from the balcony.

ME

CODE RED: Marcus spotted downstairs.

I scan the second floor, but she's so damn small, I can't make her out in the blended sea of bodies. Looking over the balcony, I finally spot her at the bar, standing next to Willa. Marcus has crept closer to them with the bunny under his arm. *Shit.*

Springing back toward the stairs, I dodge several wasted dancers who get in my way. I don't know why I have this sudden urge to get down there and save Ashlie from this encounter, but my feet won't stop until I'm next to her. By the time I reach her, Willa's gone, and I'm breathing hard.

"You good?" Ashlie sways backward to look me up and down. I shake my head when she offers me the seat next to her, but she pulls my arm until I'm sitting on the stool. Her eyebrows dip as she takes a sip of her drink.

"You see my text?" I ask.

With a slight tilt of her head, she pulls her phone out of her dress. "*Shit!*" Eyes wide, she looks around the room. "You sent that twenty minutes ago!"

"Yeah, no shit... I looked all over for you."

"Hey, Ashlie. Hunter," a deep voice says from behind us. I turn toward Marcus, who's dressed as a doctor of all things, standing with his spray-tanned arm slung over the bunny's shoulders.

Ashlie stares at her ex with a twisted-up expression, clutching her drink like it's a life preserver. *Is she even breathing?* Feeling like I need to save her from whatever that look is on her face, I pull her between my legs, wrapping my arms around her waist. "Oh, hey, Martin," I say.

"Marcus," the big dumb doctor corrects me. I nod, rubbing Ashlie's upper arm to ease her out of her haze. Her hold on that glass is so tight, I'm surprised it hasn't cracked under her fingers.

"I got you," I whisper in her ear, and it snaps her back down to earth.

"Hi, Marcus." She takes a sip of her drink, and then another, before settling back against my chest.

"I just wanted to make sure we don't have any hard feelings." He slides a hand through his slicked-back hair before extending it toward Ashlie. "I thought we could be friends."

"Naw," I say, pulling her closer. "She's good on friends."

"I'd like to hear that from her..."

"How about she gets back to you by email? Five to seven business days sound good?" My molars grind as I stare at the idiot next to me. This asshat really has no idea how close I am to toppling the stool and ramming his face in. The fucking audacity he has to do this with another woman under his arm is astounding.

"Are you two—I thought you were just friends."

"Things change." Ashlie turns away from Marcus and leans into my chest, her hair tickling my chin. She's wedged into me so tightly; the smell of jasmine threatens to override the few logical thoughts I have left. It would be the easiest thing to kiss her right now. Just completely ravage her mouth the way I've been wanting to all night. Blaming it on the ruse of being together would be the perfect fallback. But as much as I want to, it would devastate our friendship, just like the first time.

"Bye, Marcus." Dismissing him with a nod, I move Ashlie with me and swivel toward the bar. I don't check to see if he's left, knowing my fist won't leave his face alone if he's still behind us.

"Thank you," Ashlie whispers, staring into her drink. She's

carried a brave face since the breakup, but I know her better than that. The slump in her shoulders gives her away, her shaky breathing adding a cherry on top.

"Hey." I lower my face to hers until our eyes meet, and damn it if my breath doesn't catch at those honey-brown irises looking so distraught. "I got you. Always," I say softly. She gives me a sad smile before downing the rest of her drink in one large gulp. Signaling the bartender to send another, she sets the empty glass on the bar top. "How many of those have you had?" I ask.

"Not enough to make up for that interaction."

"And how many is that?"

"Not enough, *nosy.*" She shakes her head while looking over my shoulder. "And now Ava's shooting daggers at me."

I start to turn, but Ashlie brackets my head to stop me. My breath stalls as her thumbs stroke my face. *Fuck, her fingers are the softest damn things I've ever felt.*

"Don't look. That's what she wants. Do you trust me?" The mischievous twinkle in her eye knocks me speechless. I nod, swallowing hard at the stroke of her silken fingertips grazing my neck. "You should see her face, Hunt." She leans in close, giggling quietly as her gaze darts over my shoulder and back. Her eyes lock onto mine just as someone slams into the seat next to her, knocking her forward.

With a near silent gasp from her, we're nose to nose. I slip my hands around her waist to steady her, the warm stream of her breath tickling my lips. I can almost taste the fruity hints of her drink. Her touch, something I didn't know I still craved this much, is the only thing that matters. My thoughts scatter as I wet my lips, my body mindlessly drifting closer. I'm teetering on the brink of burning our friendship to the ground, but still, I lean in. Then her eyes flick behind me, shattering the moment completely.

"That was too easy," she whispers with a smile, dropping her hands and pulling away from me. My arms fall limply to my sides, aching as I resist the urge to latch back onto her. These last few weeks have been dangerous; giving in to my impulses is like playing with fire. Touching her is inane when I know damn fucking well that crossing the friendship line would be a death sentence. I can't give her what she needs, and she deserves someone who can.

That's the thing about being in love with your best friend. The glances, touching, it all gets logged by her as innocent interactions. *Shit, she's drowning in her feelings for some other guy right now.* My stupid ass is holding onto moments that mean nothing to her, wrestling with the undeniable reality that I'm no better for her than he is.

CHAPTER EIGHT

HUNTER

"I'm cutting you off." Taking the drink out of Ashlie's hand, I set it on a nearby table.

She puffs out her bottom lip and whines, "You're no fun!"

Holy hell, I want that lip between my teeth. "You're drunk, and it's time to go."

"Just let me finish it." She stumbles, reaching around me for the cup. "I already paid for it."

"Naw. I'll pay you back tomorrow. Let's find you some water."

"Can we get tacos?" she slurs, holding onto my arm for balance. I won't be surprised if she loses the high-heeled boots before we make it to the parking lot.

"So you can puke all over my car again? Naw, I'm good..." I dig out my phone and shoot off a text to Aiden. "Give me your phone so I can text Willa."

"Oh, no. Is she okay?" Willa pops up out of nowhere while Ashlie relearns how pockets work. "What happened? Who did she run into?"

"Marcus." I shift my body to catch Ashlie as she sways to the music unsteadily. She drops her phone, and Willa hands it to me.

"*Ugh*. Asshole." She offers her water to Ashlie, who pushes it away. "Let me help you get her to the car."

"Have you seen Aiden?"

"I'm pretty sure he left with Isaiah to 'catch up.'" She throws up air quotes. Wrapping her arm around Ashlie, she maneuvers through the crowd. I follow closely behind, steadying the drunken fairy when she sways too far, knocking Willa off balance. I'm focused on the doors in front of us when Ashlie pulls out of Willa's grasp suddenly, catching her heel on the top step. Her body lurches forward and slams onto the stairs.

"*Shit!*" Willa and I say collectively.

"*Owww*," Ashlie groans, sprawled out like a marionette. We scramble to sit her up, and I scan her body for injuries. No blood, but the heel broke off her boot in the spill. Willa stops me when I reach for the zipper around Ashlie's thigh.

"She can't walk barefoot with all that broken glass in the parking lot."

"I planned on carrying her." I reach again for the zipper and slip off the boot. My hand pauses on her foot as I home in on the sexy-as-fuck pink polish on her toenails. Willa clears her throat, and I'm met with a stifled smirk when I look at her. "What?" I say, a little too sharply.

"*Nothing...*" She holds up her hands defensively, then gets to work on the other boot.

We help her stand, and I put my hands on Ashlie's cheeks until her glazed eyes focus on me. "Ash, I'm gonna pick you up."

She nods lazily as I lift her, wrapping her arms around my shoulders and snuggling into my chest. "Don't drop me."

Goosebumps scatter across my body when she nuzzles her nose against my neck, her parted lips noticeably close to my skin. "Just...hold on." That damn perfume drives right through my senses like a drug I'll always seek. Gritting my teeth, I fail to avoid taking a breath without another hit of the sweet scent. Willa's watching us with the same annoying smirk, one hand holding the boots while the other sits on her hip. "Ready?" I ask, ignoring the look on her face. She gives a curt nod and walks past me to the exit.

Once I buckle Ashlie in, I take a look at her ankle. It's double the size it was, and turning redder by the second. There's no way she's walking on that in the morning. "Hop in the back," I say to Willa as I close the door. "I'll drive you to your car."

"I'm good. I parked right there." She points to a purple car parked a couple of spots away. "Hey..." That fucking look is back on her face as we walk around to the trunk. "You're in love with my sister."

I scoff, shaking my head. "Naw."

The condescension in her eyes makes it obvious she's called my bluff before I ever said a thing. "Look, it's not my business. I'm just saying, I see it. And whenever you two figure out your shit, I approve. Make sure she gets some ice on her ankle." She doesn't wait for me to respond before turning on her heel and strolling to her car.

"Figure out our shit"? What the hell does that mean? I know *I* have shit, but it's got nothing to do with Ashlie. We're friends, and that's how it needs to be. I shake away the nonsense and slide behind the wheel. *There's nothing to figure out.*

WHEN WE GET TO ASHLIE'S APARTMENT, I SET HER ON the couch and arrange the throw pillows into a plushy throne. "Eat your tacos, honey bear," I say, ripping the paper bag open for her. I don't know why I keep calling her *honey bear*, but she's too wasted to complain tonight. I don't hate the way it sounds coming out of my mouth either. With how hard she went at the club, I'll be surprised if she remembers a thing about it tomorrow.

"My ankle hurts." Ashlie falls sideways against a pillow, wincing as I prop her leg on the coffee table.

"I know, Ash. Let me get you some ice." I kick my shoes off and head to the freezer, snagging a couple of water bottles from the fridge before grabbing an ice pack. When I return, she's halfway through her second taco, eyes closed, shimmying her shoulders in a "happy food" dance. Despite how annoyed I was at myself for giving in to her incessant pouty-lipped request, she's fucking adorable right now. Chuckling, I sit on the cushion next to her, moving her bad leg onto my lap so I can wrap the ice around it. She's staring at me when I look up.

"What's up?" I ask.

"You're a good guy, Hunter." Her bobblehead nod is a clear indication of how far gone she is. "You don't let other people see it, but you are...and you have pretty eyes." She giggles as she leans her head back.

Laughing, I look to the floor. "Yeah, well, you're drunk and not going to remember any of this tomorrow."

"Maybe. But it's still true. You know how to take care of people when it matters." Our eyes lock, and the urge to press my lips to hers is alarming.

Doing the first thing I can think of, I crack open some water. "You need to drink this, and go to sleep," I say, securing her hands around the bottle. After a couple of tries, she finds her mouth. "I'll help you to your bed whenever you're done eating."

She takes a few gulps, giggles again, and snores lightly as she starts to fall asleep. Smiling, I let myself take her in, just for a minute. Her eyelashes cast a shadow over the glittered freckles on her nose, and I stifle that nagging urge to kiss her. *Fuck, man. Off-limits.*

It has to be the full moon. That's maybe the tenth time I've had to ignore the impulse to drown in her tonight. Willa's sidebar from the parking lot echoes in my head. *Figure out your shit.* There's nothing to figure out. Ashlie needs stable relationships, and I can't stand the thought of being tied to anyone longer than a couple of weeks. *We want different things.*

The food wrappers crinkle in my hands as I gather the garbage from Ashlie's lap and move it to the coffee table. "Ash," I whisper. "I'm gonna carry you to bed. You ready?"

She responds with a snore, so I cradle her in my arms and walk her into her dark bedroom. I lay her on the pillow, rolling her to the side to slip the fairy wings off her shoulders. She instantly curls her body, slipping praying hands under her cheek as if she's already lost in dreamland.

Her silk hair bonnet peeks out from under the pillow, and I slide it over her curls. If I've learned anything from watching Ashlie help my sister, it's the necessity to protect the curls at all costs. She'll thank me in the morning.

She groans about her ankle again, and her pinched expression hits me square in the chest. Folding the other bed pillow in half, I reach under the comforter to prop up her foot. I doubt she'll keep it there all night, but it's better than nothing. She already has ibuprofen on her nightstand, so I head back into the living room to grab her water bottle. When I stick it on the small table, she stirs.

"Hunt," she whispers. "Can you stay with me?"

"Yeah, I'll be out on the couch."

"No"—she pats the space next to her—"right here. Just until I fall asleep."

I shouldn't do it. Tonight has been too charged on my end. I need to walk my ass out to the couch, but she looks right at me with those sleepy doe eyes, and I can't say no.

Silently, I climb on top of the blanket, utilizing the bedspread between us as a safety barrier. I slide my hands behind my head and stare up at the ceiling, thinking of every random thing besides how much I want to pull her closer. She's quiet for several minutes, but when I look over, she's watching me. "Ash, go to sleep."

She props on her elbow, leaning in close enough for me to see her freckles in the pale moonlight streaming through her window. "Thank you," she whispers, then brushes her lips against mine. Her featherlight fingertips graze my cheek, and I freeze as she kisses me again, pushing the tip of her tongue past my parted lips.

Give in, dummy. Latch on and drown in her. But the voice of reason in the back of my head is louder than my desire. "Ash, no," I say, pulling away. "You're drunk."

"I just wanted to know if you tasted the same." She leans in one last time. The soft pressure of her mouth on mine opens a trapdoor that drops me straight into devastation. I kiss her back, and everything around me stills. Buzzing warmth washes over me, each molecule in my body rejoicing at the reunion of our lips. Just as I grip her waist, she pulls away with a sigh and lays back on her pillow. "You do," she whispers, her drowsy eyes falling shut as if she didn't just turn my world on its head.

I lie next to her for a while before creeping out to the couch. My mind reels while I savor the tingles still coursing through my lips. *What the fuck just happened?*

CHAPTER NINE

ASHLIE

Groaning, I shield my eyes from the sunbeams assaulting me through the blinds. I swipe my tongue around my teeth to work the stale taste out of my mouth. The bitter film makes me gag, but I stay horizontal while looking for water, hoping to appease the headache gods. I reach for the bottle on my night-stand and chug, which does nothing to ease the pounding haze. Everything after seeing Marcus last night is a little fuzzy. Taking another drink, I walk myself through the timeline of events. *Marcus, skimpy blond bunny, Ava, Hunter's soft lips.*

Shit. I jolt upright, wincing immediately at the pounding in my head as I lean back on the headboard. *I kissed Hunter last night.* I turn slowly, confirming he isn't still next to me. Maybe he went home. I can't blame him. *That* is a boundary neither of us can cross. Except I *did*, and he tasted just as good as before. *Shit.*

I reach up to soothe my temple, and my hand brushes against the edges of my bonnet, which I don't remember putting on. My heart thumps wildly at the thought of noncommittal Hunter caring for sloppy drunk me last night. *And then I kissed him. Ugh.* My hair spills around my face as I slide off the bonnet. When I stretch my legs, a dull ache shoots across my left ankle. A bruise, wrapped around swollen flesh, throbs as I swing my legs off the bed. Despite the pain, the memory of being tucked inside Hunter's arms as he carried me across the parking lot flashes in my mind. I groan at a different kind of throbbing between my legs.

Absolutely not!

Getting turned on by being close to him, biting my lip as my fingers graze the spot where his warm hand gripped my thigh, moaning at the memory of the spicy ginger musk on his shirt collar—it all needs to stop. I squeeze my legs together, which only makes me whimper at the relieving pressure. *Damn it. Get a hold of yourself.*

My head and leg compete in a pain biathlon as I hobble out of bed. I almost fall trying to keep my full weight off my foot while heading to the bathroom in the hallway. But I halt at the sight of Hunter sitting on the couch, drinking coffee from a to-go cup.

"Morning, Tooth Fairy," he teases, nodding at my crumpled dress.

"What are you still doing here?" Ignoring the fluttering in my chest, I continue my journey to the bathroom, pausing at the door for his answer.

"I wanted to make sure you were okay after last night."

"Last night?" Sweat prickles on my scalp. I hope with everything I have that he doesn't bring up the kissing. "I don't even remember last night."

"You drank up the bar after our run-in with Marcus, and then you tripped down the stairs and broke your boot. You should probably get more ice on your ankle."

"That's it?"

"Yeah"—he nods—"that's it. You were blasted though. How's your head?"

I grimace as the dull riot settles at the base of my skull. "Like a tiny jackhammer has taken up residence."

He smiles, eyes falling to the coffee in his hand.

"Gimme a minute." Closing the bathroom door, I breathe out all the anxiety rifling through my body. He didn't bring up the kissing. *He's acting like it didn't happen. This is good.* I can just pretend I remember nothing, and he can chalk it up to all the drinks I had last night. We can forget it.

When I limp back into the living room, Hunter's digging in the freezer. I crash onto the couch, losing my balance while trying to avoid stepping on my foot. He chuckles as he watches me, ice in hand.

"Here." Stacking throw pillows on the coffee table, he motions for me to rest my foot on top. I don't move, a little in awe of how he's taking care of me right now. "Put your foot up." He gestures toward the pillows again.

"It's too early for you to be this nice."

"It's 10 a.m., and I'm always this nice." A smirk slides across his lips as he lays the ice on my ankle. "You said so yourself last night. Called me pretty too."

"Mmm, don't think so. Must have been that other fairy." I crane my neck toward the extra cup of coffee on the table and spot a lemon poppyseed muffin. *My favorite.*

He chuckles, handing me a bottle of water. "Water first, then muffin, then coffee."

"Bossy," I tease before guzzling.

"If you say so."

"I say so."

"You said I was pretty too, so..."

"No, I said your *eyes* were pretty..." I cringe immediately. *Damn it!* I just couldn't resist arguing with his smart-ass goading. He'll never let me live this down.

His eyebrows tick up as he smirks. "So you *do* remember?"

"Bits and pieces," I say, making grabbing motions to signal for the muffin. "Did I do anything else?" Bracing for him to mention the kiss, I force myself to look into his eyes. He gives me a cool green stare, not even blinking.

"No*p*e." He pops the *p* and hands me the muffin. "Nothing."

Thank God he's playing along. Relief floods through me, but I shouldn't be surprised by this. We're good at pretending.

CHAPTER TEN

ASHLIE

Flying always relaxes me. Something about sitting inside the clouds makes me feel like I'm untouchable. No demands. No stress. I can simply *be*, and this sparse Friday morning flight gives me the perfect opportunity.

Disappointment snakes through me when the pilot announces our descent into San Francisco. I'm excited to help Kayla with wedding planning, but I'm not looking forward to the ache I'll feel in my ankle after weaving through the throng in the terminal. The doctor said it's not broken, but the past week at work has been a struggle on my feet. Hurrying through crowds on a still-bruised sprain is not my idea of a good time.

Chase is parked right outside the doors when I make it into the hazy sunshine. His Ivy League crew cut ripples in the breeze as he tucks his phone in his pocket and waves. "Hey, Ash!" He gives me a side hug before placing my carry-on in the trunk. "How was the flight, and why are you limping?"

"I lost a battle with some stairs. My ankle is still fighting for its life."

His eyes widen as he tilts his head with concern. "I'll grab you some ice at the office. I have to wrap a couple things up before taking you back to the apartment."

"It's really okay," I say. "I just need to rest it."

"I can see the bruise from here. Ice and elevation, for sure." He chuckles at my eye roll and opens my door. None of his kind gestures surprise me anymore, so I don't fight him too hard about the ice. He might be one of the most attentive people I've ever met. That charming personality is why I used to call him a Golden Retriever. He's friendly, reliable, and self-aware. No wonder Kayla is sure she can find a better guy for me. She already found a good one for herself.

When we make it to the EdTechU building, Chase sets me up in a chair by the window. He moves a side table for me to rest my leg on and steps out to grab ice from the break room. I pull out my phone, pop in my earbuds, and settle in for a long social media scroll. Just as I get to some juicy celebrity drama, I'm interrupted by a banner across the screen.

HUNTER

Put some ice on that ankle.

ME

Thanks Dad. Chase is already on it.

HUNTER

Don't forget to talk to them about Thanksgiving.

ME

OKAY DAD...

HUNTER

👍 I'll see you Sunday.

I shake my head at the overprotective tone in his messages and toggle back to my feed. Hunter's mom and younger brother fly in today. Based on the conversation we had at lunch on Wednesday, I know he's stressed. In the past, I've been around to distract him, but this weekend he's on his own.

Chase walks back into the office with his coworker, Trevor, in tow. Slipping a bud out of my ear, I thank him as he settles the ice on my pulsing ankle. "Hey, Trevor." I smile at the towering, dimpled man leaning against the doorway. He folds his arms, which only accentuates the curves of his corded biceps as they stretch the short sleeves of his navy EdTechU polo.

"In San Francisco so soon?" Trevor teases with a smirk, referencing the line he tried on me at the engagement party. He's got a great smile, and without the obstruction of a suit coat, my eyes take in the tattoo sleeve snaking its way up his left arm. I *love* men with tattoos.

"What can I say? I like to keep people on their toes."

"Speaking of toes, what happened to your foot?"

"I stopped a purse snatcher with my bare hands." I make a karate chop motion with my arms for effect.

"Really?" His eyes widen as he straightens his back, arms falling to his sides as if my imaginary attacker is in the room with us. Keeping a straight face, I nod to sell the story. Chase laughs and claps him on the shoulder before walking to his desk.

"Yep," I say. "If you replaced all those words with 'fell down the stairs at the club.'"

It takes him a second, but the laughter that booms out of him as he puts together what I said makes me laugh too. "You're pretty *and* funny?" he asks, resuming his lean against the doorway.

Okay now, fine ass, flirty man. My eyes fall to my lap as heat creeps into my cheeks. That "new crush" tingle sparks to life, and I'm not mad about it one bit.

"Are you alright though?" His deep baritone skitters through me as I admire the ink on his sepia skin, fully appreciating his entire aesthetic.

"Pretty sure I'll live. Chase came in clutch with the ice."

"I hate to break up this cute little flirting session, but I've got to get these reports in before three..." Chase says, glancing at his watch.

Trevor nods and taps the door frame twice. "Welp, it was nice seeing you again so soon, Ashlie." That smile is still plastered on his face as he walks away.

I squint at Chase. "You planned that, didn't you?" I wouldn't put it past him. It's not the first time he's tried to play matchmaker.

"Nope," he says distractedly. "That was all Kayla."

"She *would* try to set me up with the only single man she knows..."

"He's a good guy, Ash." He shrugs, glancing at me before turning back to his computer. "Might be worth it."

Sliding my earbuds back in, I continue scrolling on my phone. Kayla *was* right. I gravitate toward shitty men like they're the center of the universe, and it bites me in the ass every time. Swallowing my nerves and dating a different type could be the thing I need to break out of my rut.

Or it could be even worse for you.

That's where the hesitation lies. I don't know what to expect. Shaking the worry from my head before it has the chance to grow, my eyes scan the room and land on a picture of Kayla and Chase from the summer they met. I smile at the memory of him trying to win her over. He's one of the good ones. If he says Trevor is too, I believe him. Being set up by my best friends might not be the worst thing in the world since my radar is *clearly* broken.

CHAPTER ELEVEN
ASHLIE

Why the hell are there so many kinds of lace? I've been surrounded by itchy tulle and shiny taffeta for too many hours. My face hurts from laughing at all the frilly gowns, each comically wrong for Kayla. She decided which looks she absolutely hates, but other than that, our first dress shopping trip was a bust. The only upside has been spending an entire Saturday with my best friend.

The elevator doors clamp shut, jostling us as it climbs to her fourth-floor apartment. "I'm just saying, if we're all in Bender for Thanksgiving, we could knock out a bunch of the planning. Shower Tree Lodge would be perfect." I place a hand on Kayla's arm to pacify the ensuing argument radiating from her. "It's big enough for all of us, with a little room to spare. We could have a joint dinner with our families; make a vacation out of it. Just think, five days back home in the mountains."

Kayla scrunches her face. "Oh, having everyone in the same place makes sense. I just don't know about renting an entire lodge when we can stay at our parents' houses for free."

"Is it a money thing? You know your dad will take care of that."

She slides a hand on her hip. "Yeah, but it doesn't mean I'm any more comfortable asking for money than I have been in the past."

Kayla didn't grow up with her dad—didn't even know who he was until we all met that summer in Bender. She grew up having to scrimp and save for everything, and five years hasn't been long enough to convince her that she has so much more support than she used to. Kayla's dad, Kendall, and Chase's dad, Russell, co-founded EdTechU. My best friends are technology royalty twice over, even though Kayla doesn't see it that way. She still tries to rely on her own hard-earned money at all times. I understand her hesitation, but she's not going to realize she has breathing room until she practices breathing.

"Let's talk to Chase about it and see what he thinks," I say, following her down the hallway. I'm 95 percent sure I'll have to go over her head on this one.

"You already know he'll love the idea, Ash."

"Exactly. Even more reason for us to do it."

When we step inside, we're greeted by a basketball game on the wall-mounted TV. Two grown men in jerseys shout at the screen as the door falls closed behind us. Their hollering bounces off the floor-to-ceiling windows at another bad call. *This has to be another setup.* I glare at Kayla suspiciously, and she shrugs, evading my eyes while she hangs her bag on the hook by the door. Without a word, she walks across the maple hardwood and perches on the gray sofa arm. Chase instantly reaches around her waist, pulling her onto his lap like the doting fiancé he is.

"Are we winning?" I ask once I reach the couch.

Trevor pops his head out from behind the other two with a smile. "Hey! You like basketball?"

"Basketball, football, it all came with the territory." I walk around the couch, arms settling across my chest when I stop next to him.

"Did you play...?"

"Cheerleader."

Trevor stands, motioning for me to take his seat. The jolt that zings up my arm as I brush past him is certainly welcome.

"Hey, Trev." Kayla smirks at her phone, clearly avoiding my scrutiny. "You staying for dinner? I'm ordering Mexican." She knows *I* know what she's up to. I glance at Chase, and he mouths the words *told you* before moving his attention back to the game.

"Sounds good." Trevor tucks his hands in his pockets and turns back toward the TV.

"Well since you're staying, you might as well sit back down." I scoot to the middle, but with the other two next to me, it only leaves a narrow space for him to squeeze into. The heat of his thigh smashed against mine sends my lower lip between my teeth. When he slides his arm across the back of the couch out of necessity, the spiced orange and clove notes on his skin tempt me to curl into him. I don't, but it's like being snuggled up next to a warm holiday TV special.

AFTER DINNER, I TAKE UP RESIDENCE IN THE KITCHEN, tackling the dishes. I have an early morning flight, so the least I can do is handle cleanup tonight. I'm elbow deep in hot soapy water when Trevor comes over, dish towel in hand.

"Need any help?" he asks. "I'm pretty good at drying."

"Is anyone ever bad at that? It's the easiest part."

He grabs a plate from the drying rack, brushing my arm in the process. My cheeks heat, and he gives a knowing smile. "You got me there..."

"So, you're from the Midwest?" I ask, hoping the shake in my voice isn't obvious.

"Yep, Nebraska."

"Nebraska has Black people?"

"A few." He chuckles, and it puts a smile on my face. "Heritage has more than other small towns in the area. Still hated it though."

"Too much corn?" I tease. That earns another laugh as he swipes the towel over the plate in his hand.

"You'd think, but no. I got tired of being around the same people all the time. Everyone acted like we lived in some perfect little bubble where learning about the real world was unnecessary. I tried to go back when I got out of the Coast Guard, but I couldn't stand it. California is good for me."

Attractive and genuine? Yes, please! With my track record, it's refreshing to have a conversation with a guy who actually seems interested. We stare at each other for several seconds before I snap out of it and look back into the greige dish water. "They planned this, you know..." I jut my chin toward our friends snuggled up on the couch.

"I do know. I asked them to."

My eyes snap to his, and the smile on his face has fallen into a cute little crooked grin. "*Oh?*" I raise an amused brow. "Why's that?"

"Because I want to get to know you." His deep voice scatters tingles through me, and I glance away.

"Do you, now?" Plunging my hands back into the water, I fish around for the last few utensils. My heart thumps from his forwardness, but I'm not sure if I'm nervous or excited.

"Very much." He steps closer, giving me a clear view of the green scattered through his hazel eyes. "I'll be in LA for New Year's. I know it's a couple of months away, but can I take you out?"

Pause. Planning a date for two months from now? Who does that? What's his motive? This is the kind of early enthusiasm men hook me with all the time. I consider saying no, but then I catch a glimpse of my friends watching us from the couch. Kayla shoots me an obvious look with her eyebrows, while Chase gives a sly thumbs-up. They think Trevor would be good for me. Something inside me wants to trust that. *What if he's the "something new" I've been looking for?*

"Yeah, I think that would be fun," I say with a smile.

He digs his phone from his pocket, and we exchange numbers. The smile doesn't leave his face as we finish the dishes, and mine is ever present until he heads home.

"So...?" Kayla raises her brow as she sits at the counter.

"Girl, you're not subtle *at all*. You planned that." I laugh, shaking my head.

"Someone had to! It worked, didn't it? He asked you out?"

"Sure, for almost two months from now..."

"Hey, a win is a win." She shrugs. "Rushing is overrated anyway."

"Well, I'm calling it a night. You two don't stay up too late." Chase stands from the couch, stretching and stifling a yawn.

"Wait, Chase"—I ignore Kayla's eyeroll—"we need to run something by you."

"No," Kayla says through gritted teeth, staring right at me. "We don't. It's nothing."

"Kay, it's a good idea."

Chase cocks his head and walks toward us. "Well, now I'm intrigued... What's up?"

I explain the plan for Thanksgiving, including Hunter flying in.

Chase shrugs and wraps his arms around his bride-to-be. "Sounds good to me..."

"Expensive is what it sounds like." Kayla turns to him.

"Baby, *it's fine*." He nuzzles into her neck. "You know Dad and Kendall would give you the world if you'd let them. This is a good idea." He looks at me and nods. "I'll get it all set up on Monday and send out details." After another yawn, he kisses Kayla's cheek, says goodnight, and disappears into their bedroom.

She rolls her eyes again, puffing out an annoyed huff at losing the battle of the lodge. But my mind is filled with the hope that I'll be as lucky as she is one day. She's acquired the ultimate prize and found someone willing to give her the world without any hesitation. *Must be nice.*

CHAPTER TWELVE

HUNTER

Mom has been here all week, and I've managed to avoid seeing her. That streak ends in approximately thirty minutes, all because my baby sister got herself a date to the Winter Formal. My only saving grace right now is Ashlie, who offered to do Artie's hair for the dance. I agreed to a quick dinner at Dad's. That's all I'm willing to give.

"You look so cute!" Ashlie squeals, and Artemis beams back at her. The tiniest smile teases my lips as I watch their interaction from the bathroom doorway. They've been in front of the double basin vanity for hours, makeup and hair supplies strewn across the beige travertine marble. With some products from her magic hair box, Ashlie has morphed Artie's tight curls into large ringlets that flow down her back. Wearing makeup and a sparkly, floor-length lavender gown, my baby sister has transformed into a fifteen-year-old princess. "Now sit still so I can finish your eyes."

"Can I look yet?"

"No, Artie. The sculptor decides when the masterpiece is ready."

"He's gonna be here soon..." Artie whines, kicking her feet in the air as they dangle off one of the kitchen stools. "Are you almost done?"

"If he's the guy for you, he won't mind waiting. You're worth it, girl," Ashlie replies, pushing on her shoulders to stop her from moving.

The sisterly nature of their relationship has always been like this. Ashlie came along at a time when Artemis needed a role model who looked like her. She showed Artemis it was okay to be herself. There are still those teenage moments of insecurity, but Ashlie continues to build up Artie's confidence. It's something I will always adore about Ash.

The doorbell rings, and I snort at the matching panic in their eyes. "That's my cue." I smirk.

"Hunter, if you embarrass me, I swear—"

"Huh?" I tease as I walk down the hallway. "Can't hear you. Gotta go answer that!"

By the time I make it down the curved staircase, Dad is standing by the Tudor panel door next to a trembling football player. The poor kid is shaking all the petals off the corsage in his hand. He straightens his pale purple suit, and the light gleams over what looks like an entire tub of gel in his brown hair. Meanwhile, Dad peppers him with questions about where they're going for dinner and how the football team is playing this year.

"Hunter!" The back door slams, and I hear him before I see him. By the time I catch a glimpse of the strawberry blond hair, my younger half brother, Theron, already has his arms wrapped around my waist.

"Hey, T." I ruffle the unruly strands on his head and smile at the almost eight-year-old. "How you been?"

"This place is so cool! Yesterday, we got to swim in the pool, *and then* Ken let me play in the game room!" He stands straight, beaming up at me. That's probably the most action the game room has seen in years. I have no doubt Theron will be in there every day.

"Yeah? Maybe we can have a game day while you're here."

"*Really*? Like a brothers' day?"

The pang of guilt hits me out of nowhere, and I glance away

from his eager expression. Avoiding our mother the entire week has meant inadvertently avoiding him too. "Yeah, bro, the whole day. We can get pizza and whatever other snacks you want."

"Well, that sounds fun." I look up into the dark brown eyes of my mother as she smiles timidly. "Hi, Hunter."

"Charlotte." Setting my jaw, I glare back, watching the hope in her eyes fizzle into wounded disappointment. *Good.* It's about time she felt some kind of remorse. Her straight black hair is shorter than I remember, hitting just above her shoulders as it frames her olive-toned face. Dad clears his throat, and I recognize the sound and his expression for the warning they are. I suck my teeth before turning back. "Hey, Mom."

Ashlie appears at the top of the stairs, followed by a beaming Artemis. Shuffling across the diamond lattice tiled floor, Ash stands next to me, already snapping pictures on her phone.

"You look beautiful, Artie-girl," Dad says as she reaches the bottom step. We all turn to Football Boy, who's standing in front of her, catching flies with his gaping mouth.

Sidestepping, I bump his shoulder and whisper, "This is the part where you tell her how great she looks…"

Artemis takes a tentative step forward, but her heel catches on the hem of her dress. She lunges toward the floor, and all of us pitch forward to catch her. The football player reaches her first, dropping the corsage in the process.

"Are you okay?" he asks, brows pulling together while he holds on to her elbows. She nods, and he smiles. "You look so amazing." He stoops to pick up the discarded flowers and secures them around her wrist.

If this isn't the cutest little puke-inducing epitome of high school dances, I don't know what is. I feel like I'm watching a preview for the newest coming-of-age movie.

"Home by eleven." Dad smiles as he opens the door for them. The pair giggle as they hurry down the front steps. Dad waits, waving at them once they reach the car.

"That was adorable," Ashlie squeals next to me. "He was so nervous! Were you that nervous for your first dance?"

"Naw. I don't even remember who I took to my first dance."

"*Wooow*." She draws out the word dramatically. "Noncommittal even in your youth. That shouldn't surprise me."

"Isn't that what your youth is supposed to be?"

With a slight head tilt, she scrunches her mouth to the side. "So what's your excuse now?"

"I'm still young." I smirk and toss her a wink before walking into the dining room for dinner.

Ornate mahogany beams arch across the ceiling and trim the cream-colored walls. A matching dining table is set in the middle of the room, with Dad's baked ziti cooling in the center. He's busy dishing up servings while we find our seats. Theron and I sit on one side, facing Ashlie and Mom, while we save the head of the table for Dad.

"Didn't Artie look magical?" Ashlie asks as we dig into the food.

"That dress contrasted nicely against the dark summer tan she's hanging on to. I just wish Artemis would have let me straighten her hair. It gets so wild when it's curly, and I'd love to see how long it's gotten."

The room falls silent after Mom's criticism. She constantly compares Artie and I to her French ancestry like procreating with a dark-skinned Black man wouldn't produce Black-ass kids.

Ashlie purses her lips and glances at me. "I put so much product in there, I'd be surprised if any of her curls frizz by the time she makes it home. You'll have to let me know." She smiles sweetly, but that look in her eyes is anything but.

"Don't get me wrong. You did a great job. I just wish she knew how much prettier she would be with her hair sleek and smooth instead of—"

"Curly like mine?" That faux smile glitches so briefly I doubt anyone else caught it.

Mom has always had this weird complex about Artemis. Constantly commenting on the shade of her skin or her curl pattern. How polished she would look if she changed this or that. Ashlie's defensiveness is in direct correlation to some of those harmful things Mom has said. Things that Ashlie has worked hard to eliminate from Artie's psyche over the years.

"She doesn't like to straighten her hair," I say, scowling at Mom across the table. "You'd know that if you took the time to listen to her."

Mom slowly meets my eyes, face flushing before she returns to her food. After a few minutes of silence, she tries again with a smile on her face. "Hunter, your dad was telling me you work from home now."

"Yep." I take a sip of water so I don't have to say anything else.

"That must be so distracting. How do you get anything done?"

"Oh, I don't." The sarcastic bite in my voice makes her shoulders tense. "I just sit at home and let Daddy Wallet over there promote me through his company."

Her smile falls. "I just meant that you were so unfocused when you were younger. I imagine that would make it hard to be home all the time."

"Yeah, well, I'm not a child anymore." I stare at her until she lowers her eyes, which only amplifies the pulse pounding in my ears.

Dad clears his throat. "Hunter is one of our top data analysts. Being at home without the office distractions has vastly improved his work. He's up for a supervisor position."

"That's fantastic, Hunter. I'm proud of you!" She grins, and the crinkle lines around her eyes are as familiar as I remember... *before she left and everything went to shit.*

"Thanks," I murmur, wishing Dad wouldn't have opened up the door for her to be in my business. I set my eyes on Ashlie, who's been silently watching the whole exchange. "You ready?"

"Oh, you're leaving already?" Mom asks. "You just got here."

"*We* have been here for hours," I say. "*You* just got here."

Ashlie pushes back from the table, placing her napkin next to her plate. "Thanks for dinner, Kendall. It was delicious."

"Come over anytime. And thank you for helping Artie. You did a great job." He smiles and stands from his chair. "I'll walk you to the door."

When we reach the stairs, Ashlie runs up to grab her things. I avoid looking at Dad, knowing he's about to give me one of his abbreviated lectures. My scalp prickles as he watches me. "Just say it!" I snap.

"Cool it, Hunter." That's all he says. I know exactly what he's talking about, and he knows I know. He claps me on the shoulder, his stare softening. "It's nice seeing you, son. Don't let your mom keep you from coming over. This is your home, not hers."

I nod and open the door for Ashlie, who's almost to the bottom of the stairs. "Bye, Dad," I say, before jogging down the front steps.

"WELL, *THAT* WAS THE MOST INTENSE DINNER I'VE EVER sat through," Ashlie jokes once we get in the car.

"Yeah. Charlotte St. Clair tends to have that effect on people." My mind fills with the worst kind of memories as I head toward the freeway. We drive most of the way back to Ashlie's apartment in silence until she breaks it when we reach her neighborhood.

"...Are you okay?"

"Peachy," I mumble. From the corner of my eye, I watch her stick her thumbnail between her teeth. *She's gonna ask for details.*

"I've never heard you talk about it. Can I ask what happened?"

Fucking called it. Laughing to keep the searing rage in my chest from taking over, I remember why I don't talk about what happened after Mom left. I'm still livid as fuck about it. No amount of time or distance can put a damper on the emotion roiling through me.

"O-oh, let me tell you." I huff a humorless chuckle. "When I was sixteen, I came home from school early and found my mom and Nils in bed together."

Ashlie covers her mouth with both hands. "Oh my God."

"Yeah. Imagine hiring a babysitter so you could cheat on your husband in his own bed." My throat tightens, and the longer I talk about this, the harder it is to concentrate on the road. Thankfully, Ashlie doesn't ask another question until I park behind her car and rub my eyes.

"Did she see you?" Ashlie's facing me now, seatbelt dangling behind her, legs crisscrossed on the seat. The concern on her face as she listens makes me want to run and hide *and* reach out toward her for comfort all at the same time.

Nodding, I blow a puff of air from my lips. I hate talking about this, but with Ashlie, I can't seem to keep the words from spilling out. "I went back to my room, and she followed me, wrapped in the blanket from her bed, begging me not to say anything to Dad."

The memories flood through me while I stare out the windshield. I've spent a decade trying to push them all down, but here they are, as vivid as the day they happened. "Of course I told him. He's my dad. I told him, and everything fell apart. Every time I looked at her, I saw red. It was so bad, I stayed with Chase's family for weeks. I couldn't get the image out of my head—her and *him*. The thought of going back to that house made me want to break things."

"Shit, Hunt..."

"That day is the only time I've ever heard my dad yell. They screamed at each other for hours. Mom blamed me, saying I should have minded my business. Dad completely closed himself off. And my girlfriend at the time dumped me because I was pissed at everything."

Ashlie reaches across the center console, putting her hand on mine. The soft pressure serves as a distraction from the torrential hurricane swirling inside of me. Focusing on her, I breathe out the emotion building in my throat.

"This explains so much about you, and I hate that you had to go through that," she says with a squeeze. "But Hunter, it wasn't your fault."

"No? If I would have kept my mouth shut, we could have avoided all the drama. Mom blamed me for it, and I think Dad did too, for a while."

She shakes her head with a frown, scrunching her lips. "It wouldn't have mattered. If she was bold enough to do what she did in her own bed, she would have slipped up some other way. Your dad would have found out eventually." Her thumb strokes mine tenderly, but I can't dwell on it. "She was wrong for asking you to keep it a secret, Hunter. It wasn't your responsibility to—"

"I know it wasn't, but what was I supposed to do? She completely broke him and left me to pick up the pieces."

Ashlie's eyebrows dip in confusion. "What do you mean?"

"He was okay after finding out she cheated on him. Angry, but still functioning. But when Mom took Artemis, Dad stopped eating and sleeping. He hyperfocused on work. Nothing else mattered."

"*Took her*? That sounds scary as hell."

It was terrifying. I was a kid and didn't know how to deal with any of that shit. There were some nights he didn't come home from work, opting to power through at the office. He always made sure I had the Wilmingtons to fall back on, but I was left to my own devices often.

The warmth from Ashlie's fingers seems to travel through me, wrapping me in a cocoon of safety where it's just me and her. For the first time in a long time, it's okay to talk about this —okay to *feel*. I blow out another breath, searching for some sense of calm in the storm of memories. "Chase's parents were the ones who stepped in, got Dad back on track, and helped us get Artie home. It took years. It was a nightmare, and I hate her for it."

Ashlie rubs her hand up my arm, a consolation prize that would, under any other circumstance, leave me with goosebumps. Now, though, it just makes me want to dive into her comfort. "I think that's valid." Ashlie nods. "Your mom—"

"Naw." I suck my teeth, looking straight ahead. "She's not though. Moms don't leave their kids like that. She made it perfectly clear which children she wanted, and she lost that title with me ten years ago."

Ashlie cups my face in her hands, turning my head so I have to look at her. "Listen to me, Hunt. This was not your fault—"

"I know that!"

Hot tears prick my eyes as I stare at Ashlie. I choke them back and try to turn away, but she keeps my head steady. "Hunter, her abandoning you, that was not your fault. She was wrong, and she shouldn't have left. No amount of you doing anything differently would have changed the choices she made. That was all her. It all falls on her."

Ashlie leans in, the compassion in her brown eyes lancing me. She isn't doling out judgment or telling me I'm wrong for feeling this way. And like a flash of lightning, I'm hyperaware of the beating of my heart while her thumbs stroke my face. Her touch engraves possibilities into the desire I've stifled for years, her memory-inducing scent fogging through my head like an ether leading me to delirium. I could kiss her.

And I do.

It happens in slow motion, me leaning forward to press my lips to hers. For the briefest moment, she kisses me back, a soft and slow tug-of-war while we sample this forbidden fruit. I reach toward her for more, but just as fast, she drops her hands from my face and pulls away, leaving me craving her touch as soon as it's gone.

"Hunter." She shakes her head, eyes plastered below my chin. "Y-you're upset," she says in a breathless whisper.

"*Shit.*" I press the heels of my hands to my eyes, fully aware I just messed up. We don't cross this line. I don't even know what I was thinking. I *wasn't* thinking. "Fuck!"

"Hey…" The gentle soothe in her voice makes all of this worse. "It's not a big deal. We can forget it even happened."

"Yeah." I scoff with a sardonic snort.

"Why don't you come in? We can watch a movie or something."

"Naw." Shaking my head, I turn back to the road. "I need to go home."

"Then I'll come with you. I don't like the idea of you being by yourself when you're upset like this."

"I'm not upset, I just want to be alone. I'm fine." I feel her studying me, but I don't risk another glance, fearing I'll latch back on and drown in her vortex. I need to go home and sleep off whatever hex my mother's presence has put on this day.

"Hunter, it's okay to need people…" She puts her hand back over my arm, and I shrug away. As much as I craved her touch moments ago, it's too intense right now. I just need to get out of here. "Will you text me when you get home?" she asks quietly.

I nod, feeling her eyes on me again before she slides out of the car. Without another word, she grabs her supplies from the back and walks up the stairs to her apartment. *What the fuck did I just do?*

ASHLIE

Did you make it back okay?

It's been two hours…

HUNTER, IF YOU DON'T ANSWER, I'M COMING OVER.

ME

My bad. I'm fine…fell asleep.

ASHLIE

Boy! You irk me.

ME

CHAPTER THIRTEEN
ASHLIE

"It looks the same as the other one, which you didn't like…" I remind Kayla. She frowns in the illuminated mirror at the frilly A-line gown pinned to her body. White floral wallpaper lines the showroom at Wedded Bliss, with plush ivory carpet throughout. The warm track lighting in the bridal shop casts a glow over her locs that would make her appear angelic if it weren't for the scowl on her face. This Saturday dress shopping excursion in LA has been much like the last one in San Francisco, except we've found my maid of honor gown.

"I thought the silver accents might look better than the all-white."

"But you didn't like the *shape* of the dress…"

"*Ugh*, I know!" Her shoulders slump as she buries her face in her hands. "I'm never going to find it."

I grip the mauve velvet arms of my chair to stand, my pink taffeta gown making an annoying swish with every step I take toward the pedestal. "That's not true. We have plenty of time to find something. And if we don't, you know that man will marry you even if you're wearing a plastic bag. Hell, he'd probably elope if you told him that's what you wanted."

"I know." She nods, still hiding behind her hands.

I peel them away from her face, making sure she's looking me in the eye when I ask my next question. "What's the mental block? You can't possibly hate every dress here in California. Something else is going on..."

She sighs, her grimace melting into scrunched eyebrows and downturned lips. *She needs a break.* Pulling her by the hand, I lead her to the velvet sofa on the floor. "What if I'm not good at it?" she asks, scraping her thumbnail with her finger.

"You're good at everything," I tease, giggling at her eye roll. "Can you be more specific?"

"The marriage thing. The wife thing. The mom thing."

"*Are you*—?" I gasp, because if this is how I find out she's knocked up, she's dead to me.

"*No*! Not pregnant. I'm just saying, I've never done this before. What if I'm not good at it?"

"Not good at the thing you're already doing?" My eyebrows tick up, waiting for her to recognize her fallacy. "Girl, you two have been attached at the hip since you got together. It's been five years, and he still looks at you like you were crafted straight from the cosmos. None of that is changing when you take his last name."

"But what if it does?" Tears well in her eyes, and she races to catch them before they trail down her cheeks. "Everything has been so great. What if *this* changes it all?"

"Hey." I slide my arm around her shoulders. "Have you talked to Chase about this?"

She shakes her head, a fresh wave of emotion hitching in her throat. "You know him. He's so excited about the whole process. I don't want to ruin the experience for him. I'm excited too, I'm just..."

"Scared." I smile, leaning away to see her face. Kayla and fear of the unknown go together like peanut butter and chocolate. If she can't see what's over the hill, she spirals until the horizon is right in her face. It's no wonder we get along so well. "You need to talk to him. It'll make you feel better. Promise me?"

Nodding, she swipes her face one last time before getting back on the pedestal. She tortures herself with another glance in the mirror.

"How's it going?" The bridal shop attendant peeks in to check on us.

"This is *not* the dress," Kayla says, shaking her head as she walks toward the dressing room.

"I agree. This one doesn't give you that 'glow.' I have a few more for you to try."

They disappear through the curtain, and after a couple of minutes, Kayla walks back out in a flowy cream chiffon dress. Long lace sleeves enhance the champagne blossoms clustered across an empire waist. The flowers cascade down the full skirt with simple elegance. She's beaming from ear to ear, not a tear in sight.

"You're glowing," I say, smiling back at her. "Is this the dress?"

She nods quickly. "This is it!"

KAYLA SEEMS LIGHTER AS WE DRIVE TO MEET THE GUYS for lunch. She's smiling and joking, and any traces of the fear she presented at the dress shop have disappeared. I guess wedding jitters are normal, even when you're five years deep in a relationship.

"I've been meaning to ask, how's the grad school application coming along?"

"Oh, it's not." I tap my thumbs on the steering wheel casually.

"What do you mean 'it's not'?"

"I mean, I haven't started the application and won't be going to grad school."

"*Girl*! Do your parents know?"

"Nope. I'll tell them when I have to, and not a second before."

With a nervous grin, I slide my eyes over to see her reaction. After the conversation with Hunter, a few more panic attacks, and a pep talk from Willa, I decided it's not worth it. My parents' approval isn't worth my mental health. I just need to work up the courage to tell them.

"They're so intense; I don't blame you. But what made you change your mind?"

"Hunter. He told me to stop living for everyone else and do what makes me happy." Pulling in at Lunch-a-Bunch, I manage to find a spot next to the door.

"Huh…" Kayla makes a face. "I actually agree with my brother about something. Never thought *that* would happen. Where are the pigs?" She looks up into the sky through her window, making me laugh. "And if you tell him I agreed with something he said, I'll disown you."

We walk into the bustling restaurant and, suddenly, I'm nervous. I was sick on Wednesday, which eliminated our regular lunch outing. This will be my first time seeing Hunter since he opened up about his family a week ago. *Since we kissed.* Seven confusing days where my mind has replayed the soft pressure of his lips on mine. I liked it more than I care to admit.

One drunken kiss can be chalked up to an accidental misstep. I take full responsibility for my loss of inhibition after the club. Kissing him twice, just weeks apart? That's a choice. And having that brief moment when we locked eyes, and I felt like he wanted it as much as I did—that was the pin being pulled from the grenade. I haven't stopped thinking about him, despite all my warning sirens blaring.

The guys don't notice us until we're right next to the table, the restaurant patio empty enough that their conversation carries in the wind. "So, it'll just be you as the best man and Trevor as the lone groomsman. Kayla will have Ash and Artie," Chase explains.

"Trevor is your groomsman?" The pitch of my voice floats higher than normal. Chase nods as he pulls out Kayla's chair, then pecks a kiss on her cheek. When they embrace, they fall into a torrent of sweet nothings. It's so cute, I can't help but wonder when I'll find that for myself.

Hunter lifts a finger in greeting and reaches over to pull out my chair. When I sit, he leans in and whispers, "I'm sorry about last week. I shouldn't hav—"

"Don't even worry about it," I whisper back with a smile, relief hitting me in the chest that he wants to sweep this under the rug too. *We're good at pretending.*

On his part, I don't chalk up the misstep to anything other than him being upset and me being present during a moment of weakness. I have no doubt in my mind that whatever spark I felt when he pressed his lips to mine is one-sided. Hunter doesn't catch feelings, and I very easily do. This is why, no matter how much I liked it, I can't go there with him. I'd be willingly throwing myself into the center of a bubbling volcano.

"What are you two whispering about over there?" Kayla cocks her head at us.

"Oh, just about how disgustingly cute you two are together." Hunter makes a playful retching sound while I pretend to dry heave at their PDA. Chase laughs, and Kayla rolls her eyes. "What about Avery and Hadley?" Hunter asks about Chase's sisters.

"Av is still studying abroad and can't make it back. Hadley will be the MC slash DJ."

"She's actually pretty good." Kayla nods before taking a sip of water. "She's excited to be doing something other than standing up on display."

"Ooh, hear me out! You two could elope, and then none of us have to stand up there on display. Win-win," Hunter says.

"Nuh-uh, nope. Not after all the time we spent finding that dress. She's gonna stand up there and be seen by *everyone*," I say.

"You found it, baby?" Chase's eyes spark as he whips his head over to Kayla. She bites her smile, nodding quickly, and they're back at it with the kissing and whispering.

"*Great.* Look what you started." Hunter groans. He silently mimics the word *baby* with a grimaced glare.

"You just said it was cute," I reply.

"I also said it was disgusting. That preceded the cuteness."

"You don't have to watch, ya know," Chase says without looking at either of us. He's busy staring at his bride-to-be, who's studying the menu, shaking her head at the nonsense around her.

"Are we all set for the lodge next week?" Hunter asks, interrupting the love-fueled intensity across the table.

Chase slowly drags his eyes away. "Yep. Check-in is on Tuesday after three. We have the entire property until Saturday checkout at eleven. Did you see the email I sent last week?"

"Forgot." Hunter shrugs. "And what's so great about this place? We have to shower in trees or something?"

Kayla and I laugh. Fort Bender is not Hunter's favorite place. He complains every time we suggest going. I suspect the only reason he hasn't started this time is because it easily gets him out of having to deal with his mom.

"There's *one* shower in *one* tree, and no one has to use it if they don't want to. There are regular showers inside. It's just a gimmick to pull the tourists in," Kayla explains.

"I mean, I'll shower outside for all to see if that's what everyone wants. It can't be more awkward than watching you two." The table shakes when Chase kicks Hunter's foot. I push on his shoulder, and Kayla shoots an icy glare at him, all while he cracks up.

"Boy, *no one* wants to see you in the shower," I say.

"Debatable." He smirks at me. If I didn't know better, I'd say his eyes lingered a few seconds longer than usual.

I do know better though, and before I can think more about it, he clears his throat and looks at his phone. *You see what you want to see, Ash.*

CHAPTER FOURTEEN

ASHLIE

After landing in Fort Bender, we pop into Patti's Place for lunch. The dark weathered wood gives the diner a rustic feel, bringing back some nostalgia from my teenage years when the bell tinkles overhead. This place holds a lot of memories.

"Grab a seat wherever," Ms. Patti calls over her shoulder, tending to the few regulars on this slow Tuesday afternoon. "I'll be there in a sec."

Hunter leads the way to a booth at the far side of the diner. As soon as he slides into the vinyl seat, he twists to look around the room. "It looks exactly the same."

"I forget you haven't been back since then." The faded photos of surfers and anglers lining the walls are just as I remember. My eyes drift to the brown and white striped surfboards anchored at the end of the diner. "That summer was iconic."

"It was alright." He shrugs. "I would've sat at the counter, but someone's already in 'your seat.'"

"My seat?"

Hunter points to the stool in the middle. "Yeah. The first time we met, you said, 'Chase, you better tell your friend to get out of my seat.'" He uses a high-pitched voice and splays his fingers, pretending to be me. "Then you pulled out a book and ignored us for the rest of lunch."

"I mean, that *was* my seat. But that's not the first time we met..."

"Yeah, it was."

"The first time I saw you was at the museum with Artie."

"Naw. It was right there. You were wearing that swim captain jacket and had your hair piled on top of your head."

I blink at him, not only realizing he's right, but also taken aback by the details. "You remember what I was wearing?" I ask.

"I..." He pauses, mouth gaping as he drops his eyes.

"Well, talk about a blast from the past!" Patti places menus and glasses of ice water on the table. Her dark hair is graying now at the edges, but her friendly smile and plump frame still give off young Mrs. Claus vibes—glasses and all. The flour-stained apron only adds to it. "I haven't seen you two together in years. How you been?"

"I'm good! Glad to be back home," I say.

"Can't complain," Hunter replies, sliding out of the booth seat. "I'm gonna head to the restroom. Can I get a burger and fries please, Ms. Patti?"

"You got it!" She nods and waits until he's out of earshot before turning to me. "Well, it took you two long enough to figure it out." Patti gives me a knowing smile.

My head juts back, brows pulling together. "Me and Hunter? We're just friends, Ms. Patti."

"You mean to tell me he *still* looks at you like that and you *still* haven't noticed?"

"What are you talking about?"

Her head falls to the side as she shoots a playful glare over her glasses. "Back when you two would come in with Chase and Kayla, that boy looked at you like you hung the moon. You did have that preppy boyfriend, so I get the distraction back then. But what's your excuse now?"

"He doesn't...*look* at me." Heat creeps up my neck despite my fumbled protest.

"If you say so." Patti shrugs with a smile. "What can I get you with that steaming plate of denial?"

"Um, a turkey wrap..."

"You got it." She winks before collecting the menus and shuffling behind the counter.

Staring at the condensation dripping down my glass, I reassure myself that Patti's wrong. *She has to be. Hunter doesn't look at me any differently than he always has.* But it's no help because Patti *just* said he's always looked at me that way. Closing my eyes, I shake the confusing thoughts from my head. *He doesn't see me like that. We're friends. Just friends.* But the heat hasn't left my neck and is steadily rushing toward my face.

"You good?" Hunter asks, sliding back into his seat.

My cheeks flush as I nod. I was so caught up replaying Patti's words, I didn't hear him come back.

"Are you *blushing*?"

Unable to meet his eyes, I reach for my glass. Patti's wrong, and even though I know it, I'm finding it hard to look at him and prove it to myself right now. "No. It's just hot in here."

"Who is it?" The amusement in his voice as he scans the room makes this even more embarrassing. "Is it the baseball cap in the corner?" He leans over the table, whispering, "Ooh, no, it's Bert, isn't it? I knew you liked older guys."

I glance at the dozing older gentleman at the booth. He's been a regular ever since Patti's Place opened. A giggle slips out at Hunter's teasing, releasing some of the anxious energy Patti left me with.

"Naw...it's that monster peen book you were reading on the plane, huh?"

"*Ugh*, why are you in my business?" I ask, my shoulders shaking from laughter. "You told me to pick up a book. Let me live!"

He chuckles too, a deep, heartwarming sound that causes my

eyes to betray me. When they slide up to his, he's staring right at me, and my face ignites. Patti was right. He's *looking*.

HUNTER DRUMS HIS FINGERS ON THE BOTTOM OF THE steering wheel, tapping to the beat of the hip-hop song on the radio as we pull into the grocery store parking lot. Since we were the first to get into town, Hunter and I are tasked with stocking the fridge for the week. The afternoon sun illuminates the brown highlights scattered in his dark curls, and I can't turn away. As much shit as I give him about his cockiness, Hunter's a sight to behold. Right now, I'm definitely the one *looking*.

I managed to tamp down the blushing once we started eating lunch, but I've had the hardest time keeping my eyes off him. I've tried to busy myself with my phone so he doesn't notice *my* noticing, but it's not working. The last few weeks have been more confusing than ever with thoughts about him—his eyes, his lips—and what it would be like to go there with him. *Disaster, that's what*. I shake my head and turn toward the window as a distraction. *Hunter and I would be complete chaos together. Right*?

Once inside the store, Hunter pushes the cart through the aisles while I ride on the end. I hop off periodically to grab items from our list and jump right back on as we weave through the store. He sails around corners, tittering at my high-pitched squeals as I try to hang on. The older couple we speed past in the cracker aisle scowls at us like we're two teens goofing off, which only makes us laugh harder. When we reach the bread aisle, I leap off and drop bagels in the cart with a yawn. That's the last thing on our list. I can't wait to settle in at the lodge.

"Hey, Ash, catch." Hunter hurls a bottle across the cart, and I look just in time.

It slips through my fingers as I juggle it in the air before finally grasping the plastic bear. *What do we need honey for?*

"Just thought you could use a friend, *honey bear*." A smile crawls up his face as he waits for me to make the connection. The way he's hung on to that stupid name from the night we ran into Bryan is ridiculous. As soon as I think he's let it go, he slips it into conversation just to irk me.

"Ha. Ha." Rolling my eyes, I slide around the cart to put the bottle back on the shelf. "You're a riot." A thud in the basket behind me makes me turn. *Another damn honey bear.*

There's a smart-ass glint in his stare when he says, "Maybe I *want* the honey bear."

Actually honey, Ash. Not you...

I resist the urge to bite my lip and grab the bottle from the cart. "You don't even like honey."

"Wanna bet?" he asks, stepping in my path.

"Hunt, you can't turn everything into a bet."

"Wanna bet?" he asks again, waggling his eyebrows.

"Boy, move." Nudging him out of the way with my hip, I'm just about to get the honey back on the shelf when he wraps his hand around mine.

"Naw. I want it." He's *looking* again. His stare, combined with his roughened fingers covering mine makes my breath catch.

"Why? So you can say 'honey bear' all week and act like you're not teasing me? No thanks..."

"Why does it bother you so much?"

"It doesn't bother me," I lie, stepping back. Heat creeps up my neck again as his eyes dip to my lips and back.

"Ooh, so you *like* when I call you 'honey bear' then?"

"Nope. Didn't say that either." I turn away from him as my cheeks warm.

"So why are you blushing again?"

Damn it! "I'm not."

"Then look at me."

Taking a deep breath, I count to three before turning, hopeful the flushing in my face has dissipated enough that he won't have the satisfaction of seeing it. "See. Nothing. Can we go now?" I toss the honey in the basket, sick of this little game he's playing.

"Sure thing, *honey bear...*" His eyes lock on mine, his tongue darting out to wet his bottom lip like he's savoring the redness seeping back into my cheeks.

"*Ugh!*" I whip around on my heel, scurrying quickly as his chuckle chases me down the aisle. The most annoying part of him calling me honey bear isn't the reminder of that night we ran into Bryan. It's the bravado in his voice that sends guppies swimming through me whenever he says it. The awareness of the wetness between my thighs. *How much I enjoy it.*

CHAPTER FIFTEEN

HUNTER

"You're kidding." Ashlie paces outside the office door at Shower Tree Lodge. "Both cars? Do you want me to come get you? ...Okay... Got it. We'll see you tomorrow."

"Tomorrow?" I ask. She was talking to Kayla or Chase, I'm not sure who, but it didn't sound like whatever is going on is a good thing. It's almost three. Between lunch and the store, I'm ready to get inside and relax.

"Someone went on a tire slashing spree in their parking garage and got both of their cars. The tow truck can't pick up for another hour, and the tire shop won't be done with them until the morning. They're going to leave first thing, but it looks like it's just us tonight. Chase is calling the front desk now so we can check in."

I puff out a breath and look toward the trees. The plane ride over here was hard enough, especially when Ashlie fell asleep on my shoulder. I had to spend forty-five minutes smelling her perfume, resisting the urge to wrap my arm around her. Now I have to make it through an entire evening with her in a cozy cabin. Alone? I might need to call it an early night just to survive this.

Ever since I kissed Ashlie in my car, I haven't been able to get her out of my head. It's not that she's ever really left, but thoughts of her are usually a dull roar that I can ignore in the background. The last two weeks, they have been a constant clanging in my ears. *What is she doing? Who is she with? Is it Wednesday yet?* I can't shut it off like I could in the past. I'm not even sure how much I want to anymore.

Ashlie starts toward the office while I open the back for our bags. The secluded two-story lodge is set high on a hill, surrounded by redwood and oak trees. Wrapped with tawny-brown log siding and a forest green metal roof, it would be the perfect fall hideaway for someone who doesn't hate this town. Inside, large windows lining the walls give an airy ambiance to the otherwise cozy main room and kitchen. Light hardwood floors span both rooms, with the same logs from outside trimming the walls and staircase. I lean against the leather couch as I take in the space, my eyes landing on the stonework fireplace that's already burning.

"Perfect, right?" Ashlie asks from behind me. "I'm taking a room upstairs." She breezes up the staircase with her suitcase and disappears down a long hallway.

I continue through the living room and down the hall to a glass door at the back of the cabin, revealing a large patio that overlooks the redwoods. A hot tub sits to the left, with the lodge's namesake tree just beyond it. The craggy bluffs lining the Pacific Ocean in the distance make this view look like one of those old-timey postcards.

Ducking back inside, I drop my bag in the room closest to the back patio, far away from the others. I'm the last person who wants to hear any late-night couple noises on this trip. And being upstairs where I might bump into Ashlie in the middle of the night isn't the greatest idea either.

I head back out to the car, the cool autumn breeze sending a chill through me as I unload the groceries. Even with the sun peeking out from behind the clouds, this place is always gloomy, rainy, or both. It's horrible. I need sun and warmth. Noise. The weather here just makes me want to stay inside and sleep. But it beats the hell out of being stuck at a dinner table with Charlotte.

Once I've put everything away in the kitchen, I realize I haven't heard any movement upstairs since Ashlie disappeared an hour ago. Curious to see what's got her attention, I climb the stairs and find her curled up on a bed, breathing softly through her parted lips. The muted rays of the sunset streak across her face, her long lashes casting soft shadows across the freckles on her nose. My heart skips a beat, and my jaw goes slack. *She's so fucking beautiful.* No. Beautiful doesn't even begin to describe her. *Exquisite. Inimitable. Radiant—without even trying.*

What am I doing?

The force it takes to tear my eyes away is borderline pathetic. Watching her sleep, pining like I'm some jackass doped up on love, is fucking pointless. She needs more than I can give— *deserves* more. Someone who can offer commitment. Stability. Communication. I can't give her any of that.

With a sigh, I walk straight down to the kitchen and pull out ingredients to cook her dinner. *Like that's any less dopey. Fucking dummy.*

CHAPTER SIXTEEN

HUNTER

"It smells good," Ashlie says from the stairs behind me. She's changed out of her travel clothes into a gray slouchy University of Los Angeles (ULA) sweater with light pink leggings underneath. If I was struggling before, tearing my eyes away from her now is a full-on battle.

"I was wondering if you were out for the night. You've been asleep for hours." I turn back to the gas stove as soon as I feel my eyes threaten to wander to the dip in her waist. It's hard enough without the added temptation of her loungewear. Seeing her dressed down with a relaxed smile like this is a long-held favorite of mine. She looks like she did when we—*no*.

That's what this is. We're back in Fort Bender, and I'm reminiscing over a moment we shared years ago. A moment we agreed meant nothing. One I think about every time her jasmine perfume lingers and I'm alone.

"I guess my nap on the plane wasn't enough." Her shrug is paired with a sexy giggle that would make even the strongest man crumble. "Wine?" she asks, moving to the small bottle cooler sitting next to the fridge.

From the corner of my eye, I watch as her tip-toed stretch for wine glasses lifts the side of her sweater, exposing a thin gold strand of waist beads. My hand twitches, threatening to drop the mixing spoon I'm holding for the sole purpose of brushing my fingers against—*Shit*. I clear my throat and shake the thought from my head.

"It was long enough for you to drool down my arm." I smirk, dodging the playful swat coming my way. Teasing her is my go-to strategy for distraction. Makes it easier to focus on something other than her bare shoulder and the curve of her ass—*Stop. What the fuck is wrong with me right now?*

"I do *not* drool!" She laughs, balancing the wine bottle and glasses as she sets them on the speckled granite island.

"Oh? Then what's this on my sleeve?"

Her mouth drops as she comes to inspect my shirt, eyebrows scrunching when she can't find anything. "Where?"

I flick her nose when she leans closer. "Right there."

"*Ugh!*" She rolls her eyes but laughs as she pushes on my shoulder again. "Annoying!"

"I know." I grin. My eyes linger on that smile, and God, I just want to—*Fucking hell, bruh*. I clear my throat again, like doing so repeatedly has helped dissipate my wayward thoughts.

Her face falls, and she slides delicate fingers over my forearm. Goosebumps instantly scatter under her touch. "You getting sick?"

"Huh?" My voice cracks like I'm pubescent, and I cringe, trying to hide it by focusing on the bubbling sea of red sauce.

"You keep clearing your throat...and you sound weird." Her slight caress makes me jolt, and her eyes narrow. "Kinda jumpy too."

"Na—" *Goddammit*. I catch the heightened pitch and "ahem" one last time. "Naw, I'm good." One more swipe of her thumb, and my heart will careen across the floor. "Can you grab those bowls on the counter? Dinner's ready."

"Sure. Thanks for cooking...and for letting me sleep."

I nod, my eyes fixed on the stove. I don't cook for anyone. Don't keep women around long enough to *want* to cook for them. But these past few weeks, I'm realizing just how much I would do for Ashlie, without her even having to ask.

"You were such an asshole back then!" Ashlie laughs and takes another sip of wine as we reminisce about the summer we met. Dinner has long since been put away, and we're on the sofa by the nearly exhausted fireplace. With her legs stretched toward me, I've been spending our time stealing glances in the sultry glow. She's damn near irresistible tonight. Her light-hearted giggles and sass are just like they used to be, and I can't help but laugh along. This is the most confident I've seen her in a while. Maybe Fort Bender isn't all bad, if it gives Ashlie the little boost she's needed.

"I'm still an asshole." I smirk. Her carefree smile has me thinking all the thoughts I shut down earlier. In this intimate darkness, I keep my eyes on her for longer than I've allowed myself all night. "You're just used to it now."

"You're not an ass to me, though…"

"Naw, 'cuz you're always calling me out." I'm trying so damn hard to resist brushing a thumb over her pink toenail polish. I'm a fucking sucker for painted toes. "You don't let me get away with it."

"Damn right! *Can't* let you get away with it." Her self-assured nod is accented by another giggle that has me biting my lip before I can stop myself. She could always see through my bullshit, and I didn't have to worry about her pretending with me. I think her ability to call me out is part of what made it easy to let her get so close. She'd keep it real no matter who was around. "But really, why were you such an ass to everyone but me?"

"Because everyone else sucked." I shrug, turning to the

lowering embers. Vulnerability, even in the dark, isn't my strong suit.

"Everyone, except me?"

"You were alright," I tease, giving in and nudging her foot. I take the opportunity to swipe over the pink polish before letting go. Her silky skin gets impossibly softer each time we touch, which does nothing to discourage my desire to *keep* touching her.

She's quiet for a couple of minutes, long enough that I wonder if she's fallen asleep again. When I slide my eyes over to her, she's watching me while nibbling on her thumbnail. Holding my gaze, she places her wine glass next to the empty bottle on the coffee table and sits back again.

"What's up?" I ask.

"You know why I was blushing earlier? At the diner?"

"Yeah. Ole Bert in the corner," I tease. She doesn't laugh, though, shaking her head instead. The undeniable shift of energy in the air prickles my skin as we stare at each other.

"Patti told me you used to look at me like I hung the moon."

"Eh, Patti says a lot of things." My pulse pounds in my ears as I realize we're stepping into some uncharted territory. This doesn't feel like friendly reminiscing anymore. This feels dangerous.

"She told me you still look at me that way..."

"Patti's got a thick prescription on those glasses..." I try to joke, but my voice cracks halfway through the delivery.

"You remember what I was wearing the first time we met."

"Yeah. So what? I have a good memory."

She looks at her toes and chews on her thumbnail as she asks quietly, "Do you ever think about that night?"

"Which night?" I know exactly which night she's talking about, but I'm not letting on until she calls my bluff. Of course I think of it. I've thought about it for years. I thought about it a few hours ago. I'm always remembering that night, and what could have been if we weren't who we are.

"The one we said we'd never talk about..." Her eyes slowly

drift back to mine, her hands dropping to her lap. "I sometimes wonder what would have happened...if we were—"

"Different people," I finish for her.

She nods, biting her bottom lip. "Yeah. If we were just two people, open to the possibilities of each other instead of—"

"A noncommittal player and a codependent romantic?"

"Harsh...but yeah."

"I'm pretty sure those were your exact words when you turned me down back then..."

"Wha—I never turned you down! I was just being realistic. Besides, you didn't object..."

"Would it have mattered if I did?"

"What?" Her mouth hangs open like she really has no idea the effect she had on me back then.

"You were fresh out of a two-year relationship, and I was just some tourist visiting for the summer. If I told you then that I was into you, would it have even mattered?"

"You were into me?"

"Don't act like you didn't know, Ash... I was ready to give it a shot after that night, but you wanted to forget it."

"So you *do* think about that night?"

With an exasperated exhale, I grip the arm of the couch to stand. The way my heart is pounding, it's becoming more evident that being this close to her is a bad idea right now. I grab the glasses and wine bottle, then walk into the kitchen, flipping on the light as I go.

"What I *think*"—I say over my shoulder—"is that we've both been drinking tonight, and we shouldn't be talking about the night we said we'd never talk about." The glasses clink as I set them in the sink.

When I turn back around, Ashlie's standing behind me, leaning a hip against the kitchen island. Her sweater has slipped past her shoulder, exposing the sharp angles of her collarbone. *That* is one visual I don't need clouding my judgment right now.

"We've shared one bottle over two hours, with food. I'm not

drunk, and neither are you... You didn't answer the question, Hunt." She bites her nail again, looking up at me through her lashes. The vulnerability in her eyes makes me want to come undone and tell her so many things—*you're beautiful, I want you, I love you*. But I know the words wouldn't come out right, and even if they did, it would be a death sentence for our friendship. For the sake of my sanity, I push it down and give what I can.

"Of course I think about it, Ash. I've thought about it almost every day for five years. I've never been able to get you out of my head. Not once."

My words set her in motion, and even though her steps are slow and tentative, they pin me in place. She doesn't stop until we're wedged together, my hand falling to her waist. *This is a bad fucking idea*. The refrain echoes in my mind as her soft fingers slide behind my neck. Pulling me toward her, she pauses just short of my mouth. "You're in my head too," she whispers, then laces our lips together.

For just a moment, my thoughts stutter, battling my better judgment with the need growing in my pants. Logic wins, despite the screaming elation in my head, and I pull back slightly. "Ash," I warn, looking into her eyes. The warmth I'm accustomed to seeing blazes with a fire brighter than the smoldering embers across the room.

"We could be those people, just for tonight."

I shake my head, closing my eyes as the fight between rationality and desire rages in my head and heart...and jeans.

"We can pretend this didn't happen in the morning. We're good at pretending..." Her nails scrape over my shoulders, sending shivers through me that loosen the last strands of my resolve.

"Ash—"

"Just for tonight," she whispers, and it's like life itself has decided to spring inside me. "I want this. I want *you*."

I *should* say no. Find the strength for both of us to stop this before we ruin so many years of friendship and trust and pretending. I should walk away, but I don't. I *can't*. Something inside me

—deeper than the restraint that's been holding me back all these years—wants this more than anything I've ever wanted before. I have no more desire to keep it buried.

"*Fuck it*," I murmur, pulling her into me. Lips meet lips, tongues swirling wildly as the curve of her body melts into the crook of mine. She tastes like sweet red wine and all my wildest dreams. She whimpers, and I can't stop the groan that escapes my mouth as my fingers brush her smooth glass waist beads. *I need her.* Need to bite and lick and soothe every inch of her. I trail fingers up her curves, under her loose sweater, and damn near lose my mind when my thumbs graze the silky skin above her ribcage. *Shiiit. No. Fucking. Bra.*

Ashlie pulls me with her until I'm leaning her against the island. I lift and set her on the cool granite, kissing down the jasmine scented skin on her neck. Wrapping her legs around my waist, her whimpers plead for me. "Please. Just for tonight."

Her warm breath sends an intense need through me, tempting me to get lost in her frantic pacing. But I don't want to do this frenzied, on the countertop. I want to take my time, want her to enjoy it as much as I will. I want her to remember past tonight.

My lips melt back into hers as I carry her through the lodge. The thoughts racing through my head merge into a single question—*What will it be like to feel Ashlie's body on mine again?* Her hands rove through my hair, sending goosebumps across my skin as her nails scratch against my scalp. I put her down in my darkened bedroom, walking her back toward the bed, our lips never separating.

She fumbles with the button on my jeans, before grabbing my face in her hands, kissing me deeply like she can't get enough. Her sucking on my bottom lip takes my brain offline, waking every primal urge I have to toss her on the bed. It's as if she's feasting after a long famine, and I'm the lifesaving sustenance. I grip her hips tightly as I grind into her.

"Do you have...?" she whispers into my mouth.

"Yeah." Pulling away is a feat, but I step over to my bag, using the light from the hallway to dig out the few condoms I left inside from my last trip. I smirk at her when I toss them on the bed.

"Of course you do." She huffs, shaking her head. "You're always prepared, aren't you?"

"Always." I pull her into me. Brushing my lips along her jaw, I stop to nibble her ear and let the jasmine fog through my senses. I could get lost in this scent, traipsing around in her orbit for eternity if we had the time.

"Good," she says breathlessly. "Who knows how many girls you've been with...?"

That stops me dead, and I pull away to look in her eyes. "You think I sleep with all of them?"

"Don't you?" She cocks her head to the side like she's already convinced.

I bite my tongue at the distinct urge to prove her wrong. Pulling out my phone, I scroll through my email to locate my latest MedTest results. "All clear," I say, holding the screen up to her face, smirking as I watch her self-satisfied look turn into genuine shock. "And no, I don't sleep with all of them. I don't even sleep with most of them. It's been months."

She scoffs. "What? Like two?"

"More like six." I toss my phone on the nightstand. I'd be offended at the surprise on her face, but my mind is racing ahead to the faces I imagine she'll be making in a few minutes. "You've gotten laid more than I have this year with that dumbass doctor."

"I—oh. No. Marcus and I didn't... He was always too tired from work, so we didn't do much..."

"Even better," I say, kicking off my jeans and sitting on the edge of the bed. "He didn't deserve you. Now, come here..."

"Make me."

The bratty response shouldn't surprise me, but I pause and stare at her sassy head tilt. Raising an eyebrow, I grab her wrist and pull her between my legs. My dick twitches at the shiver that runs through her when I palm her waist. I reach up and trace the line of her cheekbone, taking in her soft curls, the freckles over that perfectly peaked nose, those full lips—still puffy from wrestling with mine. *Her.* My thumb tugging lightly on her chin, I part her lips, chuckling as her breath hitches. Goosebumps race across her skin, and I lean in close to her mouth. "We don't have to do this, Ash... It's not too late to—"

"What part of *make me* don't you understand?" Her lips ghost mine until I grip the back of her neck, pulling her into my mouth with the same eagerness as before. But as much fun as the fast pace is, I want to savor this. Enjoy tonight. Worship her. I only get this one moment, and I want to finish what we started five years ago while committing her body to memory.

She inhales sharply when I whip my shirt over my head, her eyes wide as she runs her hand up the tattoo on my side. The sinful way she bites her lip as she touches me makes the strain in my boxer briefs unbearable. I wrap my fingers around hers when they breach my chest, and dip to kiss her thumb. The burn of her gaze glitches, her forehead creasing at my sudden change of pace.

"If I only get you for tonight, I'm about to have the time of my life with every single inch of you." I lift her sweater over her head and toss it on the floor. She gasps when I tug her forward by her waist beads, something I've imagined doing since I first saw them. By the hooded look in her eyes alone, the experience lived up to my fantasy.

"You're beautiful, honey bear," I murmur, placing kisses over the swells of her breasts, taking my time to savor the way she moans when I suck her nipple into my mouth. She rakes her fingernails over my back as she arches into my touch, her sweet whimpers swirling around me while my tongue flicks her stiffened peak. I slip my hands over her ass and squeeze. "You, in these fucking leggings, have been driving me crazy all night. Take them off for me." Licking her lips, she stares right into my eyes and shimmies them down to her ankles. The pink thong goes next. "Good fucking girl. Now do me a favor?"

She tilts her head but doesn't say a thing.

"Sit your pretty ass on my lap."

Her eyes spark briefly before she lowers onto my lap, knees around my waist, pinning me in place. "Don't tell me what to do, Hunt."

I moan when she rolls her hips. Her teeth sink into her bottom lip as she pushes me back on the bed, sending my sanity into oblivion. *So, my girl likes to play?* She's been quiet, taking my directions so well, but from the way she has me pinned down, it's clear she's been the one in charge all along. I press my lips to her neck, sighing as her silky fingertips dip into my waistband and graze my dick, pulling it free. The sensual sway of her body as she teases her clit up and down my shaft sends me floating through the cosmos, her whimpers illuminating every single star I pass by.

Ashlie reaches for a condom and rips the foil with her teeth. The soft pressure of her fingers as she rolls it on almost undoes me, my hands tightening on her waist with a groan. She grips the base just long enough to seat herself around me. The warmth that scrolls through my body as I fill her is like being bathed in sunlight. "Fuck, Ash, you're so wet. You've been aching for me, haven't you?"

"All day." She presses a gentle kiss to my lips and tosses her head back. "Now shut up and let me enjoy myself."

With one roll of her hips, she's found a way to devastate me for anyone else. I wholly accept the ruination, pulling her mouth to mine to plunder. Ravage. *Claim.* My hips buck, the powerful thrust stealing her breath in a piercing gasp. The pinched bliss on her face threatens to make me come, but I grit my teeth to stave off my excitement. I want this moment seared into my memory. Her cries of passion are mine tonight, every single one.

"You like how my dick fills you up, don't you? Being stuffed so full you can't breathe?"

"*Shit*, Hunt. *Yes.*" She moans against my lips, grinding methodically like we'll be doing this for eternity.

Her pussy strangles my dick when my teeth graze her nipple, and stars dance across my vision. "That's it, filthy girl." I grunt, her quaking walls luring me into delicious agony with each glide. "Ride me until you're dripping." Her sweet whimpers send searing waves through my body, nails digging into my chest as her hips jerk wildly. I could watch her like this forever. "God, look how pretty you are, fucking the life out of me."

"You feel so good." She pants, her clit painting my skin with her arousal as she chases her orgasm.

"Use me, honey bear. Make a fucking mess all over me, because once I have you pinned to this bed, I won't stop until you're a trembling wreck."

A few curls stick to the sweat on her forehead, her eyes glassy, pupils blown wide. She's as stunning as she was all those years ago, and I anchor my hands to her waist, lost to this moment and the memories of that one night.

CHAPTER SEVENTEEN

HUNTER

Five Years Ago
That One Night

"Bryan, you're not listening to me!" Ashlie's yell penetrates through the closed dining room window. I turn sideways on the couch to look, and she's holding her phone to her ear, waving her other hand wildly. Her white tee and sweats stand out against the navy patio as she paces outside The Bluffs Estates.

"Wow, she's really mad at him," Artie says from the stool in the middle of the coastal white kitchen. Ashlie was about to show her how to set her curls when her phone rang.

"Mind your business, Art," I warn. "Don't ask her about it when she comes inside either." My sister rolls her eyes, and we both turn our attention back to the picture window.

"No... No! I don't care anymore!" Ashlie shakes her head, scowling as she leans against the railing. One look, and I can tell this conversation is a bad one. Bryan has been blowing up her phone since she got here an hour ago. Her scoffs of irritation have morphed into huffed cursing with each notification. He's interrupted her progress so many times, the sun is setting on the horizon behind her. "I don't want your ashy babies, Bryan! *I'm done!*" She turns her phone at that last part, hollering into the speaker end, then taps furiously on the screen with a guttural, "*Gah!*"

When Ashlie opens the door, Artie and I whip around like we're fixated with the detective rerun on the TV.

"I know you two heard all of that. It's fine." Ashlie blows out a breath, shuffles across the tile floor to Artie, and turns on the blow dryer. It takes about twenty minutes, but when they're done, Artemis is all smiles. With a squeal, she runs next door to show Dad. I smile to myself at her excitement. *She needs this.*

"Hey," I say, walking into the kitchen. "Thanks for helping her. Dad takes her to salons, but she doesn't really have anyone to show her how to do it on her own."

"Yeah, no problem." She doesn't smile, which is unusual. I've only known her for a few weeks, but she's always laughing. Looking at her now, you'd never guess she's got a cute smile and bubbly personality. I'm kinda drawn to it, which says a lot. "Hey, can I stay here for a little bit? I don't really want to go home, but Kayla's at work."

"Uh, sure. You good?"

"I'm great!" she says with a straight face. "Got anything to drink?"

"Yeah...water, juice, soda—"

"Anything *stronger*?"

"Yeah." I laugh, finally realizing what she's asking for. "You're in the summertime equivalent of a bachelor pad. We've got it all. What do you want?"

"Surprise me." Shrugging, she plops on the beige sectional, kicking off her shoes on the jute rug. I bring over a safe bottle of blackberry wine and a glass, fill it halfway, and hand it to her. She drains it in three gulps and slams it down next to the bottle. "More," she says, breathing deeply to compensate for the amount of liquid she just inhaled.

Despite being tiny, this girl is a force to be reckoned with. Friendly. Sassy. Hot as hell but knows how to pack a punch when needed. She's safe—unobtainable—because she has a long-term boyfriend... *Had a long-term boyfriend*. I don't even know what's going on there. But she's a friend, which feels weird considering I don't have girls who are friends. Girlfriends, yes. Girl friends, naw.

"Do you just want the whole bottle or..." I joke as she slumps against the couch.

"What if I do?" Her glare sparks with the residual heat from her conversation outside, clearly shouting *proceed with caution*. Without taking my eyes off her, I reach for the bottle and hand it over with a smirk. In a power move, she tips it to her lips, maintaining eye contact until I look away. I stifle a laugh at her obstinance as I sit next to her.

"Here." She shoves the wine at me, waving it side to side until I take it from her. "I'm not drinking alone, so here. Drink."

Tilting it to my lips, I shake my head as I sip the fruity blend. *Damn, she's feisty.*

"*Why* are men?" she asks abruptly, making me choke on the wine in my mouth as I laugh.

"Why are men what?"

"Aggravating? Demanding? Stupid? Take your pick."

I shrug, setting the bottle on my leg. "Men get away with whatever they're allowed to."

She grabs the bottle from my hands and takes a long draw, then sticks it between her knees. "That's shitty."

"Yeah, maybe... Still true though. Do you want to talk about it?"

"He called me selfish and aimless, just because I don't want to get married and have his—"

"Ashy babies," I finish for her with a chuckle. "I heard that part."

"*Ugh!*" she groans into her hands before taking another swig.

"Why they gotta be ashy though?" I ask, trying to tease a smile out of her.

Her shoulders shake as she lets out a laugh. "It was the only thing I could think of to get him to shut up. He kept talking over me, telling me all the things I'm supposed to be doing with my life, and I lost it." She focuses on the TV, and the next thing I know, her giggles have turned to sobs. Big ones.

Fuck.

I don't do tears. People crying gives me a headache. This is usually when I make my exit. Let someone else handle it. But I'm the only one here, and her weeping does things to my stone-cold heart that I'm not accustomed to. I can't leave her like this, even if it's uncomfortable.

"Hey...don't... It's okay." I slide over, rubbing her back with one hand while moving the bottle of wine to the table with the other. "I bet you twenty bucks he calls you tomorrow to work it out."

"Yeah, and I'll probably answer, *like an idiot*, because I can't stand disappointing people." Her sniffles slow, and she looks down at her hands.

"You don't want to work it out?"

She shrugs with a sigh. "He doesn't leave enough space for me to figure anything out for myself. I don't know if we want the same things anymore." Her tears were short-lived, but she still looks sad as hell. It punches me in the gut—like someone snuffed all the light out of the room. I fucking hate it.

"Want to watch funny videos?" I ask, trying to think of anything that might help. Standing, I nod toward the stairs. "There's a projector set up in the loft we could stream to. It might help get your mind off of it."

Sniffling, she takes my outstretched hand and grabs the wine before following me up the stairs. A couple of hours and another half bottle of wine later, Ashlie looks sufficiently humored and thoroughly relaxed. She turns to me with a smile. "You're good at this, Hunter."

"Good at what?"

"Being there for people."

"Am I?" I didn't think I was doing anything other than trying to make her laugh. It's what I would want in her situation. I know better than anyone that telling someone how to feel is a waste of time.

"Yeah. You didn't try to change my mind. It's a different approach than most people have. It's a gift."

"I'm just tryna be a good friend." I shrug.

"Well, you are." She stands and grabs the phone that tumbled out of her lap. "I should go."

"Whoa, wait. Naw. You can't drive right now."

"I'm so tired, I can barely keep my eyes open. I just want sleep."

"You can sleep it off here. All these rooms are empty except that one." I point to my bedroom door.

Leaving her to pick a room, I jog down the stairs to grab her bag and jacket. When I return, she's sitting on the spare queen-sized bed at the end of the hall, staring out the French windows—barefoot, cross-legged, and crying. "Hey…" I sit next to her on the tufted ivory bedspread and pull her in for a side hug. My shirt sops up the tears soaking her face as her arms wrap around my torso. My eyes sweep the canvas paintings of seashells on the walls while I stiffly comfort her. Another wave passes, and I rub her back. I've already done this once tonight. After bonding over ridiculous videos, it's not so hard comforting her again.

"I—" She shakes her head, choking back a sob. Her shoulders tremble as she draws in a shaky breath.

"Do you need anything? Water? Phone charger?" I feel like I should do something other than cuddle this newly single, hot, sassy *friend* in her bed.

Shaking her head again, she sits up straight, a timid look in her eyes. "Am I being selfish?"

"Naw, I don't think so."

"But he said—"

"Look, Bryan's an idiot," I say. "He doesn't know how to treat someone like you, so he's trying to knock you down to his level." Her mouth gapes, shock flashing in her warm brown eyes.

"You deserve someone who wants your happiness as much as their own, Ashlie."

Her mouth is on mine before I register what's happening. Slowly, she paints my lips with a kiss, teasing them open as she shifts her body closer. I slide my tongue against hers and fucking fall through the abyss.

She tastes so damn sweet, with a hint of the blackberry wine still on her tongue, and her lips might possibly be the softest things I've ever felt. Her fingertips stroke my face, her touch marking my soul as it sends jolts through me. *I need more of her.*

Pulling her close, I deepen the waltz of our kiss as she moves her knees around my hips. When she grinds into the bulge in my sweatpants, I'm ready to toss my "no commitment" rule right out the window.

I slip my hands under her shirt, grazing the smooth waist beads underneath. A shiver travels through her body when I give a little tug on the jewelry, and I lose my mind. *More.* She bucks her hips forward, and a moan escapes my lips, causing her to smile against my mouth. *Goddamn.* Being this close to that smile is mind-blowing.

This feels different from anything I'm used to, and the intrigue has my guard melting away. I strictly seek out casual, heated frenzy, but *this*—slow, methodical, sensual—it's like our souls are colliding. I can't get enough.

Ashlie leans back, gasping for air. That brief loss of connection has me chasing, pulling her closer to taste her skin. She rolls her hips again, rubbing herself back and forth against my dick in a steady pace that grows more frantic with each pass. By the sounds she's making, I don't think she'll last long.

With my hands stuck to those waist beads, I bury my face into her neck and suck the delicate skin above her collarbone. The sweet jasmine overtakes me. *This?* With her, every day? I can see myself craving her touch.

The sharp hiss of her moaning in my ear as she pushes me down flat on the mattress almost sends me over the edge. Her panted breath hitches, and she tips her head back, her hips jerking wildly while she slides against me. "*Sh-shit, Hunter,*" she stutters.

"That's it," I urge, gripping her ass to grind into her. She's so fucking sexy like this, taking what she wants from me. Biting my lip, my eyes plastered on her blissed-out face, I watch for that rewarding moment when she spirals into ecstasy.

And then her phone rings.

We go still, and it rings again before she sits up straight, looking into my eyes. "I don't want to answer it…" she whispers.

"Then don't." I keep my gaze locked with hers. My hands move to her waist, my thumbs tracing circles on her skin, just trying to keep this undeniable connection alive. We watch each other until the phone goes silent, my chest rising and falling in time with hers. Slowly, she climbs off my lap and sits next to me on the bed.

Well shit. I don't know where we're supposed to go from here. *Is lying here quietly helping? Am I making the tension worse?*

"Can you stay with me?" She bites the tip of her thumbnail. "I don't want to be alone…"

"Uh, yeah…sure," I say, thrown off by the rapid change of pace. She slides back to lie on one side of the bed. "I have to warn you, though…" I move to the other pillow. "I can't sleep unless I'm holding onto something."

"Can't you use an extra pillow or something?"

"You mean the one you're on?"

"I mean the plethora of pillows all over this house…"

"I'm tired and already lying down. If I have to get a pillow from my room, I'm staying in there."

"So, you're saying if I want you to stay with me, we have to cuddle?"

"Yep."

"Are you—you're joking."

"Naw. It's been a thing since I was little. If I don't start the night with something in my arms, whatever's closest ends up there by morning. I usually *do* use an extra pillow, but unless you're giving yours up, it'll have to be you."

"I can't sleep without a pillow."

"Me neither. So I guess we're cuddling then." I smirk, waiting for her move. Holding her all night sounds fantastic, as long as she agrees to it. Dry humping aside, I'm not enough of an ass to touch her uninvited.

"Fine. But if I feel any poking, you're gonna get it, Hunter."

"I think I'd be fine with 'getting it' after what just happened..." I tease, and she pushes on my shoulder.

"You're so annoying!" She laughs, turning her back to me. Lifting her elbow in the air, she waits for me to settle around her. When I do, her hand slides down the length of my forearm in a soft caress, lacing her fingers with mine. I'd be surprised if she can't feel the goosebumps rising in her wake. "Is this good, *Mr. Snuggles*?"

"It's perfect." I nuzzle into her shoulder, immersing myself in her jasmine perfume as I breathe her in. The tension in her back melts into me, and her breathing slows. The last thing I think before falling asleep is how nicely our bodies fit together. *Yeah, I could get used to this.*

CHAPTER EIGHTEEN
ASHLIE

Five Years Ago
The Morning After

It's early when I wake at The Bluffs to the sound of phones buzzing—Hunter's in his pocket and mine on the nightstand. His arm is still draped over me. I don't think he's moved all night. I reach for my phone, and even in his sleep, Hunter pulls me back against him. It would be the cutest thing if it weren't for the all-encompassing dread falling over me.

I crossed a line with him last night that I shouldn't have. It wasn't fair to him...or me...or Bryan, for that matter, seeing as we just broke up. Regardless of how electric it felt having Hunter's lips on mine, and how my body hummed under his touch, last night can't—*won't*—happen again. I wasn't thinking straight, but being upset is no excuse. Thank God my phone rang when it did, or there would be so much more for me to apologize for.

My phone shows an 11 p.m. call from Bryan, along with a recently missed call and group text from Chase. *Why would Chase be calling at five-twenty in the morning?*

CHASE

Hey, Kayla needs reinforcements at the diner.

ME

What happened? Is she okay?

CHASE

Woke up late for work and she's panicking.
HELP.

I fluff my flattened curls as I scramble out of bed, ignoring the thought of the dry tangles that cotton pillowcase gave me last night. Slipping my jacket over my shoulders, I zip it halfway before moving on to my shoes.

"Ugh, it's too early." Hunter groans. "Who's blowing up my phone?"

"It's Chase. Kayla needs help. I gotta go."

Hunter sits with a yawn, squinting at my racing around the room. He taps on his phone before heading down the hall. Mine buzzes again as I wiggle my shoe on my foot.

HUNTER

Bruh, really? It's 5 a.m.

CHASE

Just get down here.

HUNTER

We're on our way.

CHASE

We? You're together?

Damn it, Hunter. Scrunching my face, I grab at the pounding in my head. It's partly from the wine last night, but mostly from the realization that this private complication is about to get a whole lot more public.

What was I thinking? I don't jump on top of someone new hours after breaking up with my boyfriend. *What kind of person does this make me? Maybe I am selfish.*

I sling my purse over my shoulder and fluff my hair again as I walk from the bedroom. Hunter meets me at the bottom of the stairs—holding out a bottle of water—and we silently hurry to my little red car.

Neither of us speak during the short drive from The Bluffs Estates to Patti's Place. The music on the radio swirls around the awkward quiet between us, leaving the loose ends flapping wildly in the uncomfortable breeze.

I can't reach for the door handle fast enough once I park, but Hunter stops me with a hand on my wrist. "Hey, about last night..." He hesitates as I turn to look at him.

"I'm sorry about last night. It shouldn't have happened." Shaking my head, I stare at the console.

"But it *did* happen, so we should probably talk—"

"Look, Hunter, we don't need to talk about anything. I was buzzed and upset, and you were just trying to help me feel better. I shouldn't have taken advantage of that by kissing you...or humping you..."

My words hang in the air as he scratches his jaw, nodding slowly. "Alright, then."

"Besides, we both know there could never be anything between us. You're a noncommittal player, and I'm a codependent romantic. We're polar opposites. Can we just pretend it never happened?"

Blinking a few times, he nods again. "Yeah, consider it forgotten. I won't mention it again..." He turns to the window. "You might want to cover that spot on your neck, though."

My eyes widen, and I slam down the visor to see what he's talking about. In the warm light surrounding the mirror, my mouth drops as I spot the lovely bruising on my collarbone. "*Damn it!*" I whine, rubbing vigorously at the spot on my neck like it will erase the last twenty-four hours. "*A fucking hickey!* Why did you do that, Hunter?" I turn to him, and he's laughing, like this isn't the most embarrassing thing. Like I'm not walking around with his mark prominently displayed right before we're supposed to see our *very* nosy best friends. How is this going to look to them? To my parents? *Oh God.*

"I don't know what you're talking about... Nothing happened last night, remember?" He sets his jaw and stares at me, but I'm too stressed to do anything other than glare back and seethe. *Always stirring shit up. He put the hickey right in a spot I can't cover, just to mess with me.* If I never talk to him again, it'll be too soon.

Chase knocking on my window makes me jump. Hunter gets out of the car, and I try to zip my jacket high enough to hide my neck before following. We stand at the locked entrance of Patti's Place, waiting for Kayla to open the door. Chase fills us in on what's happening—a lost phone, no alarm, and a rushed panic—as I peer into the diner windows.

When Kayla makes it outside and explains she has an unscheduled day off, I'm a little relieved I can go straight home. I just want to climb into bed and forget the last twenty-four hours. The three of them are going back and forth about something, but my mind is elsewhere, rehashing everything that happened yesterday.

"I think the better question is why they were *together* at the ass-crack of dawn," Chase says.

My stomach drops into my ass.

"We were hanging out and fell asleep." Hunter kicks at the ground. I stare at the sidewalk, trying to avoid Kayla reading me like a book. If I look at her, she'll know something happened.

"And that hickey there is a what?" Chase says, pointing at my neck. "Mosquito bite?"

Damn it. I pull my jacket over the spot, wide eyes sliding up to Kayla's.

"*Spill!*" Kayla gasps, looking from me to Hunter and back. The tears burning behind my eyes threaten to roll down my face if I stay here for much longer. Sobbing on the sidewalk would be the cherry on top of a shitty situational sundae.

I jam my fists into my jacket pockets, bouncing on my feet while the anxiety courses through me. "Can we *not* do this here?"

I whine, looking down at my shoes. A tear slips past my defenses and lands on the gravel below.

"Yeah, okay," she says with a gentle voice. "Give me a ride home?"

Nodding silently, I trudge back to my car and slide into the driver's seat. As soon as the door latches, I'm lost to the blurry river raging down my cheeks. Almost giving it up to Hunter on the same night I broke up with my boyfriend over the phone? I don't do things like that. *Shit*. I really messed everything up last night, and I have no idea how to fix it. *Shit. Shit. Shit.*

CHAPTER NINETEEN
ASHLIE

Present Day

"Shit..." Hunter tightens his grip on my hips. "Look how well you take me, Ash." My hands and knees dig into the mattress as I cry out in ecstasy, his hips slapping my ass with each thrust. "Fuck, baby," he murmurs.

Baby?

There's no way he meant to say that out loud, but the word falling from his lips as he pounds me into oblivion undoes me. I dart a desperate hand between my legs to soothe my throbbing clit, but he catches my wrist. "Please..." I whine. "I need..."

"I said *no touching*..." Chest pressed to my back, he kisses my shoulder and sits me upright in his lap, hard length still inside me. I bite my lip, moaning as pleasure courses through my body from his restrictive grasp. He's fucked the rebellion right out of me, and I've never been this turned on. "Every moan"—thrust—"every shudder"—thrust—"is mine tonight..." My breath hitches when he rolls my nipple with his fingers, teeth grazing my ear as he whispers, "Who makes you come, honey bear?"

My eyes flutter closed as I settle against him. I wasn't prepared for his mouth, in more ways than one. "You do."

"You're my needy little brat tonight, aren't you?" he rasps. "Gonna leave a mess all over my sheets?" His lips suction to my neck, and I don't even care if he leaves a mark. "Scream my name while I fuck you senseless?" *God, yes.* I nod lazily. "Open your eyes." He loosens his grip on my wrist, his fingers pausing over my slick bud, waiting for me to comply. I flush at the sight of him stroking me slowly, just inches away from where he's buried inside me. "Watch how I make you come."

His fingers strum my clit, the sensation pulling his name from my throat in a desperate plea. My cries turn hoarse as he bounces me on his dick, plunging quick and deep, prolonging my orgasm for an eternity. Convulsing, I clutch his forearm, hardly recognizing my name hissing from his lips when he falls apart. One last shiver runs through me while we ride out the lingering waves of euphoria together.

When we collapse on the bed, he tosses the condom and rolls me onto his heaving chest, both of us a sweaty mess. He presses a quick kiss to the same wrist he restrained moments ago. "You okay?"

I'm too blissed out to respond with words, so I nod quickly, dazedly listening to the pounding of his heart.

His fingers trace my spine like he's inputting a lock code on our newest memory. "Again?" he asks, hands smoothing over my thighs.

"I can't..." I laugh breathlessly, my smile growing when he chuckles in my ear. He's turned me seven ways to Sunday, and I'm still quaking from the razing his tongue performed on my clit earlier. I'm boneless. "I can't do another one."

We lie in his darkened bedroom for a while, just existing together while light streams in from the hallway. This close, I study the details of his ink. Keeping my head on his chest, I shift my legs from around his hips. "Tell me about this." I trace over the expansive tattoo that snakes up Hunter's left side and around his pec. I've seen it before, but it always felt too intimate to ask about. Since tonight is our chance to be vulnerable, I don't hold back.

"It's Atlas." His fingers draw small circles over my shoulder.

"Like maps?"

"Yeah, kind of. Same guy." He chuckles softly. "Atlas was a Greek Titan who waged war on Zeus but failed in the end. All the other Titans were sent to suffer in the underworld, but Zeus saved a special punishment for Atlas."

"He's the one that had to carry the world on his back, right?"

"Not the world. He had to uphold the entire celestial sphere, for eternity, to keep it from crushing everything below."

I pop up on my elbow to see him straight on, and unease hits his eyes before they shift away from mine. "That sounds like a lot to carry," I say, running my fingers over his chest.

"It was," he whispers, and I know we're no longer talking about Greek mythology.

"When did you get it?"

"At seventeen, in the middle of the custody battle for Artie. Everyone was busy with that, so I used my fake ID and dragged Chase to the tattoo shop with me." He smiles at the memory, and I reach up to stroke his face.

"Did it hurt?"

"Chase puked just watching me get it done, so it probably wasn't too pleasant." He snorts, his fingers dancing lazy trails over my skin. I snuggle in closer and peck a kiss on his chest. "Naw, I don't really remember. Everything was kind of numb back then."

"We don't have to talk about this," I whisper, remembering how hard it was for him to relive it all a few weeks ago.

"It's okay. I don't mind telling you." He shifts underneath me and rubs a hand over his curls. "You know, the worst part about that time wasn't even the cheating. It was bad, but coming home from school to a note on the fridge was worse. She couldn't even be bothered to use the grocery list notepad. Just a crumpled receipt on the fucking fridge saying she was taking Artie and moving to be with Nils in Europe. Then they were gone. No warning. No goodbyes or apologies. She took my five-year-old baby sister and left us."

"That sounds like a nightmare," I say, brushing my fingers over his jaw.

He nods as he stares up at the ceiling, lost to whichever memories are filtering through his mind. I hate that he's had to deal with this all alone. Seeing him like this, knowing I can't do anything to make it better, hits a spot right in my chest that makes me ache for him. I press a kiss to his chin, and he grips me around my waist, keeping me in place while he leans down to reach my lips.

We kiss without reservation, like we've been doing it for a lifetime. Touch as if the caresses will last forever. I allow myself to get lost in the fleeting feeling of being his, just for a moment. When we break apart, I'm left wondering if this thing between us could survive daylight. Lying in this temporary bubble of intimacy gives my mind permission to run wild, and I have to remind myself this is temporary.

This was reckless. I take one last draw on his lips, before rolling away. *What were you thinking?*

"Where do you think you're going?" Hunter whispers in my ear as I try to slide out of bed. I squeal as he flips me around and pulls me against him, throwing the comforter over us. "The night isn't over, and I'm not letting go of you until morning. That was the deal."

"Is this about your cuddling thing?"

"That's part of it."

"And what's the other part?"

He smirks. "I don't want you to leave yet..."

"Aww, Hunter, I'm touched," I say sarcastically, slipping my palm over my chest.

"I mean, yeah. I'd say you've been *sufficiently* touched tonight." He chuckles as I swat his shoulder.

"You're so irritating." I laugh, tipping my head to his chest. He lifts my chin, looking into my eyes with an intensity that makes my insides flutter. The light humor we just shared has burnt to a crisp in the heat of his gaze. I clear my throat, breaking the hold. "I'm just going to the bathroom."

"And then back here." He isn't asking, which puts a little hitch in my attitude at him telling me what to do.

"If you're lucky." I slide out of bed and pad across the darkened hallway. When I get to the bathroom, I flip on the light and wrap a towel around myself. Doing all the things we just did in the dark is one thing, but I'm not ready to face my naked self in the mirror tonight. I'll save all of that, plus a quick panic session, for the morning.

I hesitate before leaving the bathroom. It would be the easiest thing to spring past Hunter's door, up the stairs, and back to the reality waiting for me in my room. That would be a surefire way to draw a line in the sand with him about tonight. Make it crystal clear that this is one and done. I enjoyed every bit of our time together, but it can't ever happen again. We want different things; *we're* too different. Hopefully, he'll be out of my system for good after tonight.

Fluffing my curls, I take one last look in the mirror and smile at the hickey he left on me. I brush my fingers across the sensitive spot under my collarbone—placed just low enough that I'll easily be able to cover it with a shirt in the morning. *He's learned a thing or two.* There's no doubt in my mind he remembered from last time and purposefully left his mark where I could hide it.

I smile at the thought, unable to ignore the curiosity inside that wants to see tonight through. *Tonight, and then no more.* The towel stays, though. I may not have the sense to draw the line right now, but I'm putting some caution cones around the perimeter of my body, for sure.

When I walk back into Hunter's room, towel tied tightly under my arms, he's sitting against the headboard, boxer briefs on, with my bonnet in his hands. All I can do is gape, frozen mid-step. *He went upstairs for that?*

"I, uh"—he clears his throat—"didn't want you to leave

again...so I grabbed it for you." He fidgets with the ruffled edge, but his eyes don't leave mine.

It takes a second before I snap out of my surprise, eventually grabbing my phone off the floor. "...Thanks...." I saunter around the bed like this is completely normal and reach over him to put it on his charger. He fingers the edge of the towel as I drop next to him, shaking his head and letting out a soft laugh. But he says nothing as his eyes meet mine. Instead, his thumb brushes my cheek, and he presses the sweetest kiss to my lips. Tingles scatter through me, and I melt. *Only tonight?*

He lingers on my lips for a lifetime before whispering, "Patti was wrong..."

My brows knit while I wait for him to explain.

"Back then, I didn't look at you like you hung the moon... I looked at you like you were the sun. You lit up my world in a way I didn't know was possible."

My jaw drops, and a timid smile slides across his lips. He pushes a finger under my chin to close my mouth, then slips my bonnet over my hair, taking care to tuck in the stray curls.

"There's another thing we can forget in the morning, honey bear." He turns me away from him and nuzzles into my neck. Molding his body to mine, his breath grows deep, leaving me to deal with that bombshell confession on my own.

MORNING COMES TOO FAST, THE SUN WAKING ME slowly as it streams through the window. Blinking a few times, the room comes into focus while soft, slow kisses land on my bare shoulder. A quiet moan eases from my lips, a surprising calm washing over me with each tender brush of his. All through the night, I seemed to be aware of his roughened fingers caressing my stomach in his sleep, his musky cologne easing me into a hazy comfort. I could get used to feeling his skin on mine, and I sleepily wonder if we could work in the light of day. *Maybe we could.*

"Good morning, honey bear," Hunter's gruff voice whispers in my ear from behind. His arm is draped lazily over my hip, the same as it was when he fell asleep last night. He kisses my shoulder one last time and tugs me closer with a sigh. The mattress shifts, and then he's gone, feet padding against the hardwood as he walks out into the hallway.

My phone buzzes on the nightstand. When I tap the screen, I get an eyeful of a scantily clad Ava before I realize it isn't my phone in my hand. A lump forms in my throat as reality slaps me in the face, waking me up completely. Slipping Hunter's phone back on the small wooden table, I use the sobering realization crashing down around me to find my resolve. *He's still talking to Ava.*

Last night was earthshaking and devastating, all at once. He was true to his word and took his time, thoroughly enjoying every inch of me. By the end of the night, I felt like an untouchable goddess. But seeing that message on his phone is a stark reminder that we're no different from who we were before. Nothing will come of this—nothing can. We're still, after the most amazing night together, complete opposites who want different things.

All of that aside; this was the arrangement. We pretend to be who we're not for one night, and then we forget it. We go back to life as normal. Random women throwing themselves at his feet *is* a normal occurrence for him. And I don't want to look like the unhinged codependent who went through his phone after sex. It's none of my business who he's talking to, anyway. That text was the splash of cold water I needed to snap out of the passionate haze I succumbed to last night. *It ends here.*

I jump up, snatch *my* phone off the nightstand, and retighten the gaping towel I fell asleep in as I search the room for my scattered clothes. Gathering them in one arm, I slide off my bonnet and clutch the towel to my body with the other, scanning the floor for my panties.

"Looking for this?" Hunter asks, dangling my thong from the tip of his finger. He leans against the door frame, all brown taught muscles in their glory, wearing nothing more than his boxer briefs and a smart-ass smirk.

"Give. Them. Back." I glare at him, punctuating each word. He's playing games with me—games that I don't have the patience for this morning.

"Come get them..."

"No. Bring them here. And stop looking at me like that!" I snap back at him.

"Like what?"

"Like you can"—tortured squeaks bubble from my throat as my mouth tries to find the right words, landing on—"see me naked."

"Forgive me if I'm wrong, but aren't you butt-ass naked under that towel? It wasn't exactly secure when we woke up..." He bites his lip, taking his sweet time looking me up and down. I could punch him.

"Knock. It. Off. This was a onetime, late-night lapse in judgme—"

"Three."

"Three what?" Exasperation wheezes out of me as I scan the room for anything else that may have gotten removed. The irritation in my voice only deepens the amusement on his face.

"Three times... It was a *three-time* lapse in judgment for you, but who's counting?"

"*Ugh*!" I groan into the clothes in my hand. "You're so damn—"

"Irresistible?" Smiling widely, he twirls my thong around his finger.

I stomp over to him, the terry cloth chafing my skin with each determined step. "You agreed never to talk about last night," I say, poking his chest.

"Naw." He shakes his head. "I didn't agree to anything. *You* said we could pretend it didn't happen, and then you kissed me. So *I'm* going to pretend I didn't hear you and kiss you."

He pulls me toward him so quickly, I let out a gasp before his lips smother mine. *Why is he so damn good at this?* Kissing is basic —elementary. And yet, when he kisses me, it feels multifaceted. Like the threads of his heart weave intricately with mine, through space and time, organizing in the most perfect way that leaves me lightheaded and flustered. As if past, present, and future are one and the same, and kissing me is the only thing holding the universe together. He kisses me like he wants to *keep* kissing me, and it's easy to get lost in it.

"Hello?" a voice calls down the hall.

I pull away, wide-eyed. He tosses my panties in his open bag, then ushers me behind the door.

"Hey." Hunter holds up a couple of fingers in greeting. I try to slow my panicked breathing as footsteps stop near the door.

"You just wake up?" Chase asks, leaning on the opposite side of the door frame. "It's almost nine-thirty."

"Naw, I've been up for a while. Just taking my time."

"Ew, Hunter, put some damn clothes on!" Kayla's voice sounds from the hallway. I'm no longer breathing. If I die, I die. The only thing keeping them from seeing me wrapped up in a towel in Hunter's bedroom is the gap where the door meets the frame. I peek around to shoot Hunter a look.

"Yeah, yeah." Hunter shifts his weight to his other foot, glancing at me quickly before continuing the conversation. "You two make sure to choose a room far away from mine."

"Hey," a third voice echoes from the hallway.

Hunter nods, scrunching his forehead with a confused look. "How's it going, Trevor?"

Trevor? Great. It's a goddamn party out there, and Hunter's entertaining it, while I'm just here, naked, in his room.

"Where's Ash?" Kayla asks.

"Mmm, I think she said she was taking a walk. Should be back soon."

"You let her walk out there alone? There are bears out there, Hunter! What's wrong with you?" Kayla chides.

"Maybe you should go out there and look for her, then." He tips his head toward the back door. "Give the bears a two-for-one deal."

"Chase, handle your friend," she says in a huff, turning back down the hallway. I hear a door shut in the distance.

"Not even five minutes and you've already pissed her off. Cool. Thanks, man." Chase blows out a breath, his steps retreating until another door closes.

As soon as Hunter shuts his door, I throw my sweater over my head, sliding the towel off only after I'm sufficiently covered in my oversized top. Hopping on one leg, I hike up my leggings and catch Hunter watching me with that stupid smirk. I jam my phone in my pocket with a scowl.

Rolling my eyes, I tuck my bonnet under my arm and reach up to twirl my hair into a messy top knot. I stomp over to him and put my finger in his face. "If you say anything—"

"I won't." He wraps his hand around mine, lifts it to his lips, and dusts it with a kiss. "But you need to be quiet before they hear you."

"Hunter," I growl, shaking my head at him.

"*Shh*! I won't. Just...go, before they get suspicious." He moves me behind him as he opens the door and peeks into the hallway. With the coast clear, he shoves me out and swats me on the ass, making me yelp in surprise. I turn around, my mouth gaping at his audacity. Shrugging, he winks and closes the door. *Like hell he's letting last night go.*

CHAPTER TWENTY

ASHLIE

You were the sun...

Hunter's words echo in my head, distracting me as I creep through the kitchen. I turn toward the stairs and bump right into Trevor. "Oh!" I say, putting a hand on his arm to steady myself.

"Ope! You okay?"

That simple question shoots memories of last night through my mind, of Hunter kissing my wrist before asking the same thing. The cuddling. His confession. But the image of a brunette in lingerie chases it all away. *One night. No more.* I shake my head to clear the haze. "Hi! Yeah, sorry... Just distracted. What are you doing here?"

"Chayla's cars weren't ready, so I gave them a ride. They invited me for Thanksgiving a few weeks ago; we probably should have carpooled in the first place.

"Chayla?" *Did he really just make a portmanteau of my best friends' names?*

"Yeah." He smiles. "It's easier than saying 'Chase and Kayla' all the time."

"Kayla's going to hate that... I love it!"

He nods and shifts on his feet, but doesn't move out of the

way. "So, I was looking into things to do up here, and I guess there's a ton of hiking trails…"

You lit up my worl—

Ugh, quit it! "Yep." I grin like my thoughts aren't beating the hell out of me. "Everything from beginner to advanced."

"It's supposed to be warmer today. Would you like to go on a hike later? With me? Maybe after lunch?" The eager look in his eyes sends flutters through my belly. Subtle assertiveness. *I like.*

"Uh…" My phone buzzes, reminding me again of that picture of Ava as I dig it from my pocket. It's the last bit of resolve I need to let it all go. "Sorry, hang on. This is my sister." I don't bother stepping away before answering.

"Wills?"

"*Get me out of this fucking house!*" she whisper-screams into the phone.

"Wha—you came home?"

"Clearly, I've lost my mind. And I'll be on the first flight back to LA if you don't come get me *right now!*"

"Okay, let me shower, and I'll be right there."

"It better be the fastest damn shower of your life, Ash. I swear."

I laugh, fully entertained by her intense tone. She says *I'm* the dramatic one. "I'll be there in thirty minutes."

"Sorry," I say again, turning back to Trevor.

"Everything okay?"

"My sister decided to come home for the holiday, and my parents are already driving her crazy. I have to go get her, but a hike after lunch sounds fun." I smile, and he returns it.

"Yeah? Okay, cool. It's a date…"

"Cool… Well, I have to…" I point up the stairs.

"Right. Yeah. Go get your sister." He chuckles nervously as he steps to the side, and I slide past him.

Sitting under the shower stream magnifies everything I've just done. I groan, trying—and failing—to rationalize sleeping with Hunter last night and accepting a date with Trevor this morning. *What the hell is wrong with me?* "*Ugh!*" Scrubbing hard with my washcloth does nothing to dull the sting of my impulsiveness.

Hunter knows last night has to stay in the past, and he told me he wouldn't mention it again. But I can't get him touching, holding, kissing me out of *my* head. And the "honey bear" that started as a joke? The way he said it as he pleasured me to bliss felt intimate and intrinsic rolling off his tongue. Don't get me started on "baby."

In the heat of it, our connection felt momentous. But now, in the reality of daylight, I see last night was cataclysmic. I have to face the fact that he's still Hunter. He's never been any other way, always been up front about relationships. I have to see things how they are, not the way I want them to be.

Hunter's just like the guys I've dated in the past. He's the pattern. It's time for me to break free from that. I need to move on before I get in too deep and end up hurt again. *I'm so damn tired of being hurt.* Starting today, I'm taking Kayla's advice, and my first step is a date with Trevor after lunch.

When I walk down to the kitchen with my purse, Chase and Kayla are sitting at the island, browsing through table linens on her phone. "Hey, *Chayla*," I tease, reaching into the fruit bowl for an apple.

"Oh, great. It's a thing now." Kayla rolls her eyes and turns to Chase. "I told you it was going to be a thing."

"It's cute, and I like it." He kisses her cheek before walking around the island to get a glass from the cabinet. "Hey, Hunt." He nods behind me.

I don't turn around, suddenly unprepared to face Hunter despite my pep talk in the shower. I'm about to bite into my apple when Hunter's breath fans over my ear. "You left something in my room," he whispers, tapping my hip with his hand. I look underneath the counter, gasping quietly as I snatch my thong out of his hand and stuff it in my bag.

"You said you were going to play nice," I whisper through gritted teeth, placing my apple on the counter.

"Naw, I never said I'd play nice. I said I wouldn't tell anyone," he whispers back.

Pursing my lips, I roll my eyes, and they land right on Chase. He's standing with a glass of milk halfway to his mouth, looking between Hunter and me with confusion all over his face. *Damn it.* I glance at Kayla, who's fully immersed in her phone and hasn't seen a thing.

Dropping my eyes to the countertop, I clear my throat and turn toward Hunter. "I need the car keys"—I hold out an upturned palm—"to get Willa from my parent's house."

"I can take you," Hunter says.

Tracing the pattern of the granite with my eyes, I avoid his stare. My pulse pounds in my ears at the thought of being trapped in a car with him after everything. I just know he wants to get me alone to talk about last night, but there's no way in hell I'm digging up the freshly buried memories. The deal was to forget. That's what I intend to do.

"Oh, I need to check in on my mom. I'll come with you," Kayla says, still buried deep in her phone. She has no idea she just saved the damn day.

"How about you two head into town, and I can fill Hunter in on some of the wedding details?" Chase offers. *He knows.* He may not have specifics, but he knows something happened. *How could he not?* He just watched the awkward panty exchange. Chase is throwing me a lifeline, and I'm holding on for dear life.

"Great!" I smile at Chase before turning to Hunter, finally looking at him as I wiggle my fingers. "Keys?"

His eyes never leave mine as he reaches into his pocket and dangles the keys in the air. I grab for them, but he pulls his arm back with a smirk, causing me to press my body into his. Rage simmers in my chest as I glower. He's lucky we have an audience, or I'd be going off.

Hunter's brow ticks up like we're embroiled in a sudden death match. Tipping on my toes, I snatch the keys out of his grasp, trying to ignore the way our bodies meld together. When I steady myself with a hand on his rippled stomach, I scramble back a few steps, the heat in his stare undeniable.

"Let me get my bag," Kayla mumbles, keeping the phone up to her face as she walks down the hallway.

"I'm going for a run." Hunter turns and walks down the same hallway, and once he's gone, I let out a frustration-filled breath. Chase, still in front of the fridge, shakes his head and takes another drink.

With keys and apple in hand, I walk around the island toward the front door. "Thanks..." I say, pausing next to Chase.

He nods quietly, taking another drink from his glass.

"Tell Kayla I'm in the car?"

"Yep, sure. Hey." He stops me with a hand on my shoulder. "Whatever's going on between you two, don't tell her. She's stressed enough." He cocks his head slightly, waiting for my nod before he lets go. He's got nothing to worry about. I'm not telling anyone a damn thing.

HUNTER

Standing out on the deck, I grip the banister and stretch my legs, staring into the yellowing trees. *What the fuck is this feeling? Regret? No.* I don't regret anything about last night, except for wishing it would have happened sooner. She—we—*us*. Being together in that way was beyond words. Electric. Kismet. It felt right, no matter the ambiguous feeling in my gut right now. I can't ever go back to what life was like before knowing how it feels to be with Ashlie, and I wouldn't want to go back, even if I could.

"What did you do?" The door slams behind Chase, and I turn as he stalks toward me, dressed in gym clothes. *So much for my solo run.*

"What the hell are you talking about?" I ask, my eyes falling to the ground. I'm not offering any information if I don't have to.

"You know what the hell I'm talking about, man. Did you kiss her? Sleep with her? What?"

"Can you talk any louder? I don't think the bears heard you."

"Hunter." He scrubs a hand over his face. "What are you *thinking*? You know your sister's going to lose it on you. That's her best friend."

"Naw, Kayla's not gonna lose it because *you're* not telling her. Now are we running or what?"

"Or what." He nudges my shoulder and jogs down the dirt covered path, not bothering to wait for me to join him. "You're telling me what happened on the trail," he calls.

I set up the music in my earbuds, heavy bass blasting so loud it liquifies my thoughts as I catch up to Chase. We both grew up running on track teams, but he stopped after high school while I ran throughout college. He's good at distance, but I'm faster and able to catch up to him in a couple of minutes. The spongy trail is only a few miles long, so we jog side-by-side until we spot a glade covered in copper and rust-colored leaves. Trees surround the clearing, branches clinging to their last signs of warmer weather. Like we've got some kind of internal competition meter, Chase and I glance at each other and take off for the clearing. I let him gain the lead for a few seconds, playing mind games to make him think he's bested me. But right before we get to the end of the trail, I push with everything I have to edge forward. I slip out an earbud, grinning ear to ear as the annoyance on Chase's face melts into amusement.

"You tricked me," he says, breathing hard as he crosses his arms over his head.

"Naw, you got rusty. Don't blame me." I grab my hips, gulping the mountain air. We slowly pace around the clearing, letting our breathing slow.

"So, what is this?" Chase asks after a while. "Ash is strictly into relationships."

"I know that!" I snap. He whistles, recognition falling across his face, and my eyes dart to the ground.

"Oh, you *like*-like her." He chuckles as he pieces it all together. "Wait, look at me again. Let me see it in your face."

"Bruh, fuck off." I try to knock his arm with my elbow, but he dodges out of the way, laughing.

"Ooh, you've got it bad. I don't even know the last time you were into someone. So spill it. What happened last night?"

"A lot... Everything."

His eyes widen. "Like, *everything*-everything?"

"What are you, a parrot? Yes, *everything*. She initiated it, but I didn't put a stop to it. And she wanted to sweep it all under the rug this morning, but I'm—I can't stop thinking—I..."

"You're—wait... Are you *in love* with Ashlie?" All the teasing humor has left his face as he watches me. I don't admit it right away. The thought of saying it out loud makes me want to crawl out of my skin and find a bear cave to hide in. "Are you, man?"

Leaning against a tree trunk, I look up through the barren branches and nod.

"*Oh, shit*!" Chase whistles. "Dude, that's... I mean, it's big. Uh... Does she know?"

"Hell no. No one knows...except Willa."

"Hold on. You told her estranged sister before you told me? Should I be offended?" He whacks my shoulder, trying to lighten the serious tone our conversation has taken.

"Naw, I didn't tell Willa. She figured it out on her own."

"So, what are you going to do about it?"

"Nothing." I shrug, rubbing the back of my neck. "Ash wants to pretend like last night never happened, so that's what we're doing."

"I'm confused. You love her, but you don't want to be with her?"

"I...can't. You said it yourself; she doesn't do casual flings, and we all know I can't do serious relationships."

"Eh... You *can*. You just won't."

"What the hell is that supposed to mean?"

"Just that you'd much rather cut and run before anyone gets too close to you. You call it 'avoiding unnecessary drama,' but it's really your fear of being abandoned holding you back. You've been this way since your parents' divorce." He shrugs, waiting for my reaction. When I don't say anything, he continues, "Look, take my advice or don't, but if you're really doing nothing about this Ashlie thing, you've got to leave her alone. *All the way* alone. If you can't offer a stable commitment to her, you need to shut this down and let her find someone who can. If you really love her, you need to guard her happiness, even if it means protecting her from yourself."

I puff out a breath. How do I reconcile my best friend's wisdom with the way I feel after last night? He's not wrong about any of it—me, my fear, Ashlie. It's all true, which makes my feelings surrounding our time together even harder to deal with. I love her. I've loved her for years, but I have to bury this and let her move on. We can be friends, and I can keep loving her quietly while I hide in my little corner of commitment issues. "You're right," I say. "She deserves more. I can't give her what she needs."

"Great. Yeah... So this is probably a good time to tell you that she and Trev are going on a date later today."

"The hell? Trevor? Why?"

Chase laughs, shaking his head. "What do you mean 'why'? He likes her, and Kayla's been trying to set them up for months."

"Naw, fuck that!" Heat courses through my body, my head pounding at the thought of Ashlie and Trevor together. *I have to sit and watch her go off with that asswipe?* I curl my fingers into fists, cracking my knuckles as I try to contain the jealous rage bubbling under the surface. It's an unusual feeling for me. The women I've been with have never elicited jealousy; they don't last long enough to matter. Ashlie is a different story. My eyebrows knit, and just as quickly fall as my face morphs into a display of the emotions filtering through me. Chase laughs again and claps my shoulder. "Are you screwing with me?" The brash question erupts out of me, but he takes it in stride.

"Nope. But based on your reaction, you might want to reconsider the whole 'letting her go' thing."

"Is that why he's here? They have a thing? Why wouldn't you tell me they have a thing?"

"Hey, don't blame me"—he holds up his palms, backing up toward the trail—"I just found out about *your* thing. Maybe don't keep me in the dark next time."

I curse under my breath when he takes off and slip the buds in my ears, hoping the beat will drown out the noise in my head.

When I make it back to the deck, Chase is stretching against the railing.

"Hey, Hunt..."

"*What*?" I breathe out, exasperated by him and this entire conversation. I'm pretty sure I've gone through every conflicting emotion in the last forty-five minutes.

"People aren't always going to leave you, man. Don't miss out on life because you're scared of the what-ifs. Happiness is worth the risk." He claps me on the shoulder and walks inside the lodge, leaving me to sort out the tangled thatch of thoughts in my head.

CHAPTER TWENTY-TWO
ASHLIE

"Let me get this straight," I say to Trevor. "You're a tech nerd, you served in the Coast Guard, *and* you play piano? You got a cape hidden under that T-shirt too?"

"Eh, I'm well-rounded, but I'm still working on the superhero alter ego." He winks, and the school-girl giggle that erupts out of me is only a bit of a surprise. He's been making me laugh like this the entire hike, completely taking my mind off the mess waiting at the cabin. We reach a clearing, crunching through red and yellow maple leaves until we settle onto a fallen log. The sun hangs high in the sky, highlighting the rusted color of his hair in an easy comparison to the leaves dropping from the trees.

"I can grab you some leggings from work whenever you're ready for that part. You're on your own with the cape, though..." I tease. "Is there anything else I should know?"

"Hmm"—he stretches his long legs out in front of him—"I was a theater kid, played football, and joined the swim team."

"You're kidding!" I grip his arm from excitement, only to drop my hand quickly when I realize the intimacy. "I was on the swim team too."

"Oh, yeah?" His brows rise with interest. "Swim is what got the Coast Guard on my radar. So, you did cheer and swim?"

Nodding, I pull some bark off the log, breaking little bits with my fingers and sprinkling them on the ground to occupy my hands. "Cheerleading was for my parents, but swimming was all mine. It kept me sane, and, despite being short, I broke some records at ULA. Earned the team captain spot my senior year too."

"That's impressive." He nudges my shoulder with a flirty grin. "I was too involved with everything else to be good at swimming competitively, but it was fun."

I nod as the smile grows on my face. The more Trevor shares with me on this trail, the more I want to know. He's genuinely interested in learning about me too. I haven't seen a red flag yet, and the green ones are steadily glowing more vibrant. "Why *were* you so involved? It sounds like you did everything." I tap his foot with mine and smile.

"I did." He chuckles. "Where I'm from, there's not much to do besides get drunk in cornfields and get arrested. Staying busy kept me out of trouble long enough to get out of there. I finished high school early just to leave that place."

"Okay, smarty-pants," I tease. "You mentioned before that you hated growing up there. Do you go back very often?"

"Christmas is all I can handle back home. I give my family that week every year. If they want to see me more than that, I convince them to go on vacation."

"Come on, Trev." I place a hand on his knee, giving it a little shake. His eyes drop to our connection, and a migration of butterflies surges through me when the smallest smirk quirks the corner of his mouth. "Small towns aren't all bad. I love this place. The city has its perks, but being able to slow down when I come home is the best."

I pat his knee, and as I pull away, he covers my hand with his. Biting my lip, I take a breath before looking into his eyes. They're so warm and inviting. *Safe*. Sitting with him is surprisingly comfortable.

"You grew up here, right?" His thumb slides across my hand, leaving a trail of tingles in its wake.

"Uh, kind of. We moved from Vegas when I started middle school, which sucked at first. Going from a diverse city to a quiet place where no one looked like me was tough. I didn't feel like I really fit in until I met Kayla in high school. But it's grown on me, and now it's home."

"I get that. What about your sister? You two had each other, yeah?"

"Mmm, not really." I slip my hand from his, shifting uncomfortably on the log. My butt is going numb from sitting here, but I like Trevor's company. "Willa and I didn't get along as kids. I don't know if it was the age difference or our personalities or what, but we weren't close back then. We're just now starting to understand each other." Suddenly feeling like I've shared too much with the enchanting hazel eyes across from me, I drop my gaze and change the subject. "So, do you have siblings?"

"Yep. Three: Maya, Lainey, and Eli. They all love it back home in Heritage. I don't get it, but they're happy, so I'm happy." Trevor stands from the log with a smile, dusting off the back of his jeans. "Welp, you ready to head back? I can't feel my legs."

"Yeah." I laugh, moving back toward the trail. "I'm sure they'll be sending out a search party soon."

Trevor falls in step with me and bumps into my shoulder playfully. "Successful first date?" he asks.

"Mm-hmm, I'd say so. You're full of surprises, Jack."

"*Jack*?" He clutches his heart, and another giggle bursts out of me. "I made such a good impression, you forgot my name?"

"Jack-of-all-trades, since you do any- and everything."

"Whatever you say, pretty lady."

Heat creeps up my neck with his flirtatious nickname. This crush on Trevor didn't take long at all. He's silly, easy to talk to, and his straightforward flirting eliminates the guessing games I'm used to. I feel so giddy, and I admit, Kayla was right. It's refreshing, being pursued for the right reasons. He's crystal clear about his intentions, an element I think I've been missing up till now.

When we get back to the lodge, I've mostly forgotten about the awkwardness that awaits. One minute, Trevor and I are bumping into each other, laughing about his childhood obsession with chicken nuggets dipped in applesauce. And the next, we're face-to-face with our friends around the kitchen island.

"Looks like you two had a good time." Kayla's eyebrows dance suggestively. Chase darts a glance at Hunter before looking back at me.

Trevor brushes his arm against mine with a sly smile before walking toward the fridge. "Yeah, you could say that."

"Which trail did you do?" Willa asks from across the counter.

"The Horizon Trail. It was beautiful up there," I reply.

"It sure was..." Trevor says, shooting a wink my way.

I bite my cheek to temper the timid grin sliding across my face, but it's no use. Mashing my lips together doesn't help either —not with the way my belly is flopping around inside. But then my gaze drifts across the island, meeting Hunter's. We stare for a couple seconds before he drops his eyes to his phone. His face is unreadable, but all those flutters are now dead weight in my gut.

I asked for this, told him to act like nothing happened. So why do I have this creeping doubt spreading through me? Why do I feel a pang of remorse? Last night was right up Hunter's alley. He's good at detached intimacy—he *prefers* it. Plus, he's still talking to Ava. I'm the one who doesn't do casual flings. But when I look at whatever mask he's slipped on his face, it's definitely not the unbothered one I'm used to seeing.

CHAPTER TWENTY-THREE

HUNTER

"Not a football person?"

I glance over my shoulder as Willa strides across the deck. Dejection slumps my shoulders, and I resume watching the autumn foliage lose hope. *Not her.* "Just needed some air." I've been checking the score on my phone, but watching Ashlie and Trevor bond over football—and everything else—sounds worse than throwing myself into a woodchipper. Yesterday was brutal enough. I made up my mind about Ashlie on my run, and swiftly unmade it when I found out about her date with Trevor. Watching them leave for their date excitedly, and return standing much closer than they had been before, tore me apart inside. For the last twenty-four hours, I've taken silent shots to the chest each time she's giggled at his jokes or made eyes at him. And the visceral reaction I fight every time he flirts with her—touches her. *I'm fucking pathetic.*

I finally went to bed early last night, only to hear them talking in the hot tub outside my window until one in the morning. When I rolled over to sleep, my damn pillow smelled like jasmine, memories, and misery. I hardly slept.

"I don't think it will last." Willa zips her purple jacket, then sits in the weathered Adirondack chair next to mine, looking out at the scenery.

"The game? It's almost over ..."

"Don't play dumb. I'm talking about Ashlie and Trevor." She shakes her head like I should already know.

"And what makes you say that?"

"Because he's just like Bryan." She shrugs, watching me.

"Care to expound on that?"

"Bryan was nice enough at first. He was the type of guy Ashlie thought she was supposed to be with, so she tried to make it fit when it clearly wasn't what she wanted. She may not know it yet, but this Trevor thing is the same. He's the friendly, All-American type who always does the right thing. Ashlie walks around like she gets paid to keep people from being disappointed. She thinks he's the kind of guy she's supposed to go for."

"Why are you telling me this? She can date who she wants. It's none of my business."

Willa rolls her eyes before scowling at me. "She chases the wrong type, and *you* chase the wrong type when, really, you two should be running toward each other. I'm telling you so you can get your shit together and finally be with her."

"What shit, Willa?" My scalp prickles at her insistence that she knows me. She barely knows her own sister. What makes her think she has me pegged? I run my tongue along my bottom lip, breathing out my irritation. "Why don't you go ahead and tell me about myself...?"

She bellows a loud, hearty laugh, wiping tears from her eyes. "Oh please, Hunter. You very clearly have the deepest type of 'mommy issues.' Every girl I've ever seen you with looks the same as the one before—*skin tones may vary*," she lilts like an infomercial. "I bet you twenty bucks I know what your mom looks like based off of them. And the way you leave them, quickly and quietly, I know there's a reason for that too."

"Willa...why the fuck do you care?"

"Because she's my sister, and you're the only one able to

convince her to choose the things she really wants in life. If you could get past your commitment issues, you two would be unstoppable."

All I can do is stare. She and Chase are the annoying angel and devil combo on my shoulder. Chase sits on one side, telling me to be the bigger person and let Ashlie go, while Willa sits on the other, encouraging me to keep her for myself. There's a whole lot of noise in my head right now, and all of it is stressing me out. This kind of drama is my sign to cut and run. Shut it all out and push down whatever these conflicted feelings are. But there's a nagging part inside of me that keeps asking: *What if, this time, you didn't?*

EVERYONE'S SCATTERED AROUND THE PROPERTY AFTER Thanksgiving dinner. Kayla and Chase are outside at the fire pit, Trevor is getting smoked by Willa in a chess game at the dining table, and Kayla's mom is chatting it up with Ashlie's parents by the fireplace. I don't know where Ash is, but honestly, that's kind of a relief right now. Trying to clear my mind, I busy myself with the cleanup process, filling the single basin copper sink with soap and water. As I'm about to dump in the dirty dishes, a bump on my hip snaps me out of my daze.

"Need any help?" Ashlie asks, grinning up at me. She's pulled her hair back, a few curly tendrils framing her face. My eyes dip to the mustard sweater dress clinging to her body before I catch myself.

I haven't said two words to her today, and I'm at a loss for any sort of meaningful conversation right now. Shaking my head, I turn back to the sink. "I'm good."

"So, it's gonna be like that?"

"It's not *like* anything. I'm doing the dishes. It's a one-person job."

Ashlie sighs, knocks her hip into my side again, and rolls up her sleeves. "Move over. Let me help." She grabs a stack of dirty dishes and dips them into the water. I know she's trying to connect, make sure our friendship is still intact. But I'm so lost, I just can't pretend right now.

"No."

"Hunter..." she grunts, trying to push me out of the way with her ass. "Move...over."

"No." Acting out the first impulse that comes to mind, I flick a wet hand toward her. My eyes widen when I realize how much water made it to her dress, and I try to stifle the laugh in my throat by biting my lips together.

She turns toward me slowly, mouth gaping, working hard to hide her surprised smile. Cupping a handful of water, she flings it sideways at me, hitting me square in the chest. Her brows raise in a feisty taunt.

I tuck my chin and challenge her with a stare. "You really wanna start this war?"

She slaps her hand into the water, laughing as the large, wet splatter plasters my button-down to my skin. "Yep."

"You're trouble. You know that?" I wrap my arm around her, pinning her wrist to her back while I repeatedly flick water toward her face.

"You cheater!" She laughs, twisting out of my grip and lunging for the sink sprayer. Pointing it right at me, she looks down the center like it's topped with a scope. "I'll do it."

"Naw, you won't. You're too nice."

"I will." She reaches for the faucet, and I fold my arms over my chest in a silent dare.

"Ooh, what's going on here?" Ashlie's mom, Jackie, asks, looking between the two of us with a smile. Jackie's dark curly afro is held back by a wide orange headband that matches her pantsuit.

"Just tryna clean up, and this troublemaker over here started a water fight," I say, tipping up the corner of my mouth as I turn toward Jackie.

"*Me*? You splashed me first!"

"Where's your proof, Little Miss Faucet Sprayer?" I tease. Ashlie drops it, placing her hands on her hips.

"You do look pretty guilty, Ashlie. I'm with him," Jackie teases. "While I have you here, did you get your application in? It's due in a couple of weeks."

Ashlie takes a deep breath, and I clock the anxiety in her eyes before I turn back to the sink. She already knows what I think about the situation. This is her business, and she can handle a conversation with her mom on her own, even if she doesn't think so. "Uh, yeah," she says. "The deadline *is* coming up. But I don't think I'm going to grad school this year."

"Ha. Ha. Very funny. Of course you're going. That was the deal we made. A year off, and then graduate school. Two weeks is plenty of time to get your application together."

"Um, no. I don't want to go anymore, so I'm not applying."

"Oh yes, you are." That prompts me to look over my shoulder, just in time to see Jackie put a hand on her hip, making it clear where Ashlie learned the motion. My body tenses, teeth grinding as I listen to this woman tell Ashlie how to live her life. "It's been your dream since you were little," Jackie urges.

"No, it's been *your* dream since I was little. Things change, Mama..."

"If it's a money thing—"

"It's not the money. I just don't want to go. And I'm not going, so you can stop pressuring me."

"I'm not pressuring you. I'm trying to keep your feet on the ground and your head out of the clouds. If this is a money thing—"

"It's *not* a money thing, Mama. *God*! You're not listening to me!" Ashlie's voice shakes as her volume increases. She's saying exactly what she wants, and Jackie is stomping all over it like it's nothing. I bite the inside of my lip to keep my mouth closed, but it's getting harder to act like I don't hear what's going on.

"You better watch who you're talking to like that." The authority in Jackie's voice makes me whip my head back to the sink. "You can't work at a fitness store forever. What can you possibly gain working there?"

"Happiness, Mama. I'm happy there, and I'm good at it, and I don't leave in tears every day. I won't work there forever, but I'm staying for now."

"You should be in the *classroom*. You were a good teacher. Don't selfishly hide your gifts. Hunter, you tell her. She listens to you."

My back goes rigid. I wasn't prepared for a direct call in. Grabbing a hand towel, I take my time drying the water dripping down my forearms before turning to Jackie.

"I think Ashlie has made it *unmistakably* clear that she doesn't want to go, and you can't accept her no for what it is. You're putting so much pressure on her to do this thing she has no interest in, she's having panic attacks about disappointing you. She doesn't want to, and for that reason alone, I don't think she should."

Jackie's mouth gapes at my boldness, and I turn back toward the sink, glancing at Ashlie as I do. The pure look of shock on her face leaves me feeling satisfied. *Someone needed to say it.*

"Ashlie, is that true? You're having panic attacks again?" Jackie asks.

"It's true, Mom," Willa says from somewhere behind me. "You and Dad put so much pressure on her. On us both. She hated teaching. If she wants to work in retail forever, that's something she gets to choose for herself. You need to deal with it."

"I just want what's best for you," Jackie says tearfully. "For both of you."

"And that's for us to decide. Not you, and not Dad," Willa replies.

I hear footsteps retreating, but I don't know who they belong to until I finish the dishes and turn around.

Ashlie's leaning against the island, in the exact spot as our first night here, as beautiful as ever. The mood is different, but she looks just the same, biting her thumbnail with a timid stare through her lashes. "Thank you," she whispers.

"Hey." I shrug, taking the few steps to stand in front of her. "I got you. Always." Raising my fist, I knock it lightly into the hand she's holding up to her mouth. I smile until she smiles back, and I feel like we're closer to the friends-who-don't-talk-about-that-night than we have been in days. *This is for the best.*

CHAPTER TWENTY-FOUR

ASHLIE

ME

🎄Merry Christmas, Hunt!

Surviving the fam?

"This is so bizarre," Willa whispers, unwrapping another gift. I glance at her as she juts her chin toward our parents. With their feet propped up on their worn brown recliners, they squint at the instructions for their new fitness trackers. My eyes wander to the old family picture hanging over the brick mantle. I think that might have been the last time we were all together like this. It's nice having the four of us under one roof again. Weird, since it hasn't happened for ten years, but still nice. "They haven't asked us any questions about life in LA."

"Huh," I say distractedly, turning back to my laptop. "You're right." I'll lose my nerve if I don't focus on the swim director application on the screen. Ever since we got here, I've been working up the courage to fill it out. I think when I stood my ground with grad school, and Hunter and Willa backed me up, it gave me the little bit of confidence I needed to open the email again. Granted, I've stared at the blank form for two days now, nervous as hell.

Here we go...

I type my name into the first box and get a rush. *My name is in there. I actually did it.* I stifle the excited yip in my throat, keeping this milestone to myself for now. Feeling unstoppable, I cruise through the personal information section like I've never been anxious a day in my life. And then it asks about my prior swimming experience.

A thick coil forms in my throat, my stuttered breath racing along with my pounding heart. My eyes flick to the bookshelf where my old medals hang around a few small trophies, and I cringe. *You're not that person anymore.* I quietly close my laptop and move it to the end table as a dark realization settles over me. *Who was I kidding?* I can't even look at a pool, let alone teach someone else to swim. *You're such a disappointment.*

"You don't think this is weird?" she whispers, snapping me out of my quick spiral. "It's been five days, and everything is still light and fluffy..."

I crisscross my legs on the brown floral sofa and squint across the room, hoping to hide the melancholy growing inside. *Failure.*

"No lectures, no arguing. I haven't left yet. *You're* not crying."

"Hey!" I whip around to glare at her. "I don't cry *every* time..."

"Yeah, but you want to." She bumps my shoulder and grins as she unwraps her last gift. I like the sisterly teasing we have now. All we did was fight growing up. I was sure she hated me, and was so hurt when she left, I didn't reach out for years. It was only when we both ended up in LA that we reconnected, and I finally found out I wasn't the reason she left Fort Bender.

"Okay, parentals," Willa calls across the room. "What's going on? We haven't had a single lecture, and we leave for LA tomorrow."

"I'm sure I could figure out a lecture if you really want one, *Wilhelmina.*" Mom peers over her glasses.

Willa throws a hand to her chest, gasping dramatically. "Not my government name! That was uncalled for."

Mom tries to hide her amusement with a roll of her eyes, but it's clear as day she's enjoying this back and forth by the smile twitching at the corners of her mouth.

"We figured it would be better to have a nice holiday than to pick at you," Dad says, dousing Mom's attitude as it hangs in the air. The lamp beside him gives a lustrous shine to his bald head, spotlighting his dark brown skin.

"You two are grown and can make your own decisions." Mom's carefully measured words don't match the pinched restraint on her face.

"If you want to share parts of your life with us, great. But we don't want you to feel pressured, and we don't want you to stay away for another ten years," Dad adds.

"Who are you, and what have you done with Robert and Jackeline Willis?" Willa teasingly cocks her head to the side. "Ash, I think there's something in the water. Do you feel okay?" She smacks my forehead with the back of her hand, pretending to check my temperature.

"Ha. Ha." Mom crosses her arms. "We're serious. We're turning a new leaf. As long as you're happy and healthy, then we're happy. You know you can always come to us for advice."

I look between my parents, then turn wide-eyed to Willa. "I think it's body snatchers. Willa, I'm scared!" Covering my mouth in mock horror, I curl into her. Mom rolls her eyes, and Willa's shoulder shakes against mine while we laugh.

"You two are so silly," Mom says, failing to keep her giggles from escaping.

Dad smiles at the three of us for a while. "I'm glad you two made it home. I've missed this."

"We'll see how long it lasts," Willa murmurs, giving me a look that conveys her skepticism.

My phone buzzes near my feet, and I dig through the shredded wrapping paper, tossing aside shiny ribbon fragments until I find it. Hunter still hasn't answered my texts from this morning. His phone hardly ever leaves his hands, so with each new message I receive that isn't from him, I get more and more anxious. He always answers me. Always.

I can't even attribute this to what happened at the lodge, considering we've been fine since getting back to LA. The plane ride after Thanksgiving was quiet and awkward, with Hunter and me trying not to brush against one another. But by the time our Wednesday lunch rolled around, everything was back to normal. He may have kept a wider distance between us when walking to the restaurant, but our easy, joking banter was back with a vengeance. This delayed response from him is freaking me out.

My phone buzzes again, and my fingers finally grip the rubberized case. I expect some snarky sentence fragment from Hunter, but it's not him. The disappointment that washes over me comes as a surprise.

TREVOR

Merry Christmas!

Can't wait to see you next week, pretty lady 😍

ME

🐼Merry Christmas. How's the corn?

TREVOR

It's too EAR-ly to tell 😉

ME

LMAO! That was so bad, Trev.

TREVOR

Bet it made you smile though! Get anything good?

I did, actually. A package from Hunter showed up on my parents' doorstep yesterday. Since I'm trying out old hobbies, he got me a few thriller novels, along with a gift card to Board'n'-Books. It was a really sweet surprise.

"You okay?" Willa asks, watching me from her side of the couch. "Your face is all frowned up like you just smelled Mom's mac and cheese."

"Hey! I heard that." Mom glares at us.

Fixing my face, I flash a grin. "Yeah, I'm fine." I don't know why I made that expression when I read the message. I like Trev; he's the nice guy I should be looking for. But a message from him isn't what I wanted to see right now. I shoot off another round of texts to Hunter.

ME

Did you lose your phone?

Should I be worried?

HUNTER...

"You sure you're good?" Willa asks.

"Yeah. It was Trevor, actually."

"Uh-oh. I thought you liked him..."

"No, I do. I just...was expecting it to be Hunter. He hasn't answered any of my messages, and it's almost lunchtime."

"I'm sure he's just busy with family stuff..."

"That's what makes me nervous. I've seen the dynamic between him and his mom. I'm worried he's spiraling."

My phone rings in my hand, which is surprising since the only people who call me are sitting in this room. *Kayla? She definitely doesn't call me.*

"Hello?" I say slowly, convinced I'm the victim of a pocket dial.

"Ash, hey, um, Merry Christmas..." There's a nervous edge to her voice.

"Kay, what's up? Why'd you call? Is everything okay?"

"Um..." She takes a beat before sharing the news. "Hunter's in the hospital."

"*What?*" Jumping from the couch, I knock wrapping paper

and bows to the floor. I'm across the room and on the carpeted staircase before I realize I'm climbing it. "What happened?"

"Well, we don't really know yet. Artie called me sobbing, and Chase and I are headed there now. I just didn't want you to find out some other way. We're pulling into the parking garage, so I'll call you when I have more info."

I hear the line go dead, but the phone is still up to my ear while I throw clothes into my suitcase one-handed. I have to get back to LA. Make sure Hunter's all right. Tell him...*shit*. Tears run down my face, splashing onto the clothes spilling out of my bag as I realize what I want to tell him.

"Hey, what's wrong?" Willa asks from the door. My back is to her, so she doesn't see the steady stream leaking from my eyes. When I turn to face her, I'm a sobbing wreck, trying to get the words out through snot and tears.

"Hunter...hospital...love..." I choke out, covering my face with my hands. Her arms wrap around me, and I cling to her as I try to regain control of myself. I can't see through the blurriness, can't think through my racing thoughts. My body just needs to move. Pulling away, I turn back to my bag and throw things inside. I don't even know what I'm putting in there, but it was full when I came and needs to be full when I leave.

"Whoa. Hey. Slow down. What happened?"

I wipe my face, shaking my head as I scurry around my bedroom to add more items to the suitcase. "I have to get to the airport," I say, maneuvering around her confusion.

Willa grabs my arms and holds me in place until I look at her. "Ashlie. What. Happened?"

I open my mouth to answer, but collapse in her arms with another sob. She shoves my luggage to the floor, contents toppling out as she sets me on the bed next to her.

Rubbing circles on my back, she offers soothing instructions. "In through the nose, out through the mouth. Good. Now, what happened?"

"Hunter's-in-the-hospital-and-I-have-to-fly-back-to-LA-to-make-sure-he's-okay-because-I-love-him." The words tumble out so fast, my tongue has a hard time keeping up.

"You—okay… Let's back up. What happened to Hunter?"

"I don't know. That's why I have to go. I have to fly back to LA and find out what happened and make sure he's okay and—"

"And taking your old penguin alarm clock is going to help with that?" She points to the mess on my fuzzy pink rug. Sure enough, there's Pengie, next to my hair bonnet and a pair of high tops. She bumps my shoulder playfully, and I laugh, wiping a stray tear from my cheek.

"I don't know. I was just throwing shit in there."

"Girl, I can tell. You have half your bedroom in that bag. How about we wait to hear back from Kayla before hopping on a plane, hmm?"

"But what if—"

"Exactly. What if he's fine, and you rush out there for no reason? We leave first thing in the morning. There's nothing you can do for him better than a hospital can, anyway." She stares at me like she's trying to send the logic through brainwaves with her eye contact. "If it turns out to be something bigger, I'll leave with you tonight. But for now, let's just wait."

I nod, glancing at the phone still in my hands. No new messages.

"Now for the other thing…" She squints at me.

"What other thing?"

"The 'I love Hunter' thing."

I shake my head emphatically, refusing to believe those words came out of my mouth. "I didn't say that."

"Ash, you literally said you had to make sure he's okay because you love him."

"No"—my voice trills nervously—"I don't think so." I thought it before, but I didn't say it out loud. *Right*?

"You're so distraught at the thought of him being hurt, you're panic packing your entire childhood bedroom to get back to him. That's not love?" She tilts her head to the side. "You love him."

"I..." I breathe out a shaky breath, coming to terms with the jumbled mess in my head. "...I think so. Shit. *No*... I can't."

Willa chuckles. "What do you mean 'you can't'? It doesn't sound like you have much of a choice."

"I...he...we... *No!*" The last word is guttural as I turn my wide-eyed panic to Willa. And she's laughing. *Laughing*. As if this isn't the most infuriating situation I've found myself in. Like it's not the stupidest conclusion for me to come to.

"Ash, you love him. It's okay."

"No, it's *not*." I slap an outraged hand on the bed. "You can love someone and know they're no good for you. That's Hunter. He's a one-way ticket to Hurtsville, and I don't want to take any more trips out there. *I can't*."

"Hurtsville? Are you a country singer now?" Her brow raises over the teasing look in her eyes.

"*Ugh*, this is serious, Wills. Hunter's just like Marcus."

"And Trevor is just like Bryan."

"Wha—no he's not." I glare at her.

"Don't give me that look. You know I'm right. He may not be controlling like Bryan, but Trevor's safe, predictable, and checks off all the boxes you think you're supposed to check off." I roll my eyes, and she bumps me with her shoulder. "And Hunter's not like Marcus. Maybe he is with every other woman, but not with you. He's some third, unknown anomaly with you, and only you, and *that's* what has you scared right now."

"*Oh, okay,*" I scoff. "So what do I do, Willa the Wise?" I scowl at her know-it-all ass calling me scared. Even though I am—terrified, really, about something I can't put my finger on—I don't need her telling me.

"You, my sweet sister, are the only one who can decide if you're going to keep playing it safe, or if you're ready to go for what you really want." With a sigh, she pats my knee and walks to the door. When she stops in the doorway, she turns and points right at me. "And don't get used to the hugging." She shivers.

I start to laugh, but my phone buzzes in my hand, and it's pressed against my ear impossibly fast. "Kayla," I say, staring at Willa as I listen to the update about my best friend who, apparently, I'm in love with.

CHAPTER TWENTY-FIVE

HUNTER

Christmas Morning

"Good morning, Hunter. Merry Christmas," Mom says from the front room as I trudge down the stairs. I need coffee and possibly a good whack to the head to get me through all of this family togetherness. I'm only twenty-four hours into a two-day sentence in this house, all because my stupid ass promised Theron I'd be here on Christmas morning. That was before I went and promised Dad I'd stay until after dinner. At least Chase and Kayla will be here by then, and I'll have a little bit of a buffer.

"Morning," I mumble, shuffling across the tiled floor to the kitchen.

She walks over from the couch, leaving the island between us. "There's coffee in the pot."

I set my phone on the counter and pour myself a cup, hoping the caffeine will do something for my sour mood. One big swig, and I promptly spit it out in the sink. The coffee coats my mouth with a bitter film. "What the hell is this?" I ask.

"Hunter, language, please. It's coffee..."

"Naw, something's wrong with it then." I scrape my teeth against my tongue and spit into the sink, repeatedly rinsing my mouth out under the faucet. Something's not right. The more I scrape, the itchier it feels.

"You always were so dramatic. It's mushroom coffee. It's good for you—"

"*Mushrooms?*" I screech, staring with the intense hope that she's joking. "*Shit!*"

"Hunter, *language*. And yes. It helps with focus and boosts your immune—"

"It boosts my death date, is what it does. I'm allergic to mushrooms!" I yell, marching back toward the entryway. "Dad!" I call up the stairs.

"Oh, please, you're not allergic. You've had mushrooms before."

I whip around, keeping my hand on the banister so I don't stomp back over and get in her face. "That's how allergies work, *Charlotte*. One day you're fine, and the next, you're gasping for air on the kitchen floor..." My words garble as my tongue swells in my mouth. "*Dad!*"

"Hunter, why are you yell—" Dad's eyes widen when I turn to him, and he beelines it back up the stairs. "*Stay!*" he booms over his shoulder, somehow knowing I was about to follow him.

I sit on the bottom step, staring at my hands to avoid looking at the Black Widow in the form of my mother. My lips feel puffy, and I want to claw at the itchiness in my eyes as they swell. A high-pitched stridor wheezes from my throat with each breath I take. Kneeling over the stairs, I try to heave in air. Dad rushes back down with an allergy pen in hand, and the diamond pattern tile swirls in a dizzying haze as I collapse on the entryway floor. I watch Dad jab the epinephrine through my plaid pajama pants, so worried about the lack of air I can barely feel the pinch.

"What happened?" he asks Mom.

"She...tried to...kill...me..." I rasp, each word harder to squeak out than the last. My heart pounds while looking at Mom's wide-eyed expression, my T-shirt clinging to my sweat-soaked torso.

Overwhelming panic surges over my rage as the edges of my vision fade.

"Hunter, just focus on breathing," Dad says, laying me flat on the cool tiles. He slides my body around, using the stairs to elevate my legs, and sits next to me while checking my pulse. "Charlotte, call 9–1–1, and stay in the kitchen. We need him to be as calm as possible. That won't happen as long as he's looking at you. Now! *Go now!*"

AFTER AN EIGHT-HOUR OBSERVATION PERIOD, ANOTHER anaphylactic attack, more epinephrine, and another eight hours of observation, I'm almost cleared to be discharged. I called it when I said Charlotte would ruin Christmas. *What fucking audacity flows through her that she can confidently stand in front of my hospital bed right now?*

"How are you feeling?" Mom asks softly, putting a hand on my blanketed foot.

"Half dead." My throat is rough and scratchy, my voice gruff.

She winces, shaking her head as she moves around the bed to stand at my side. "That's not funny."

"I'm not joking..."

"Hunter, if I would have known, I would have never—"

"You shoulda known."

"*How?* I haven't seen you in years, Hunter, and you won't speak to me otherwise."

"And whose fault is that, Mom? Huh? If you wouldn't have left me here to clean up your fucking mess, you would have known." The monitor's beeps increase with each word, a harsh, steady beat, only adding to the rage coursing through me. I set it free, my scowl deepening as I stare her down.

A tear slips from the corner of her eye. "Hunter, I didn't want to leave you."

"Bullshit."

"You were sixteen, almost grown, and I thought you needed your dad more than you needed me. You were so *angry*. The way you looked at me was awful. I thought I was doing what was best for you, but I didn't want to leave you. You're my firstborn, and I love you in a way that can't compare to your sister and brother."

"Naw." I shake my head. "You blamed me for telling Dad, took Artie away for revenge, and left a damn note on the fridge instead of saying goodbye."

"No," she gasps, reaching for my arm. I flinch out of her reach, and she moves in again, grasping my wrist firmly. "Hunter, none of this was your fault. I made these choices, I'm the one responsible for this. I was then, and I still am now. It was never your burden to carry; I shouldn't have asked you to." She takes a deep breath, eyes red with emotion. "Leaving the way I did was wrong, and I'll spend however long it takes making up for it. This isn't something I can fix in one trip, I know that, but I need you to hear how very sorry I am for leaving you. For ruining everything."

Silent tears roll down her face as she says the words. They sound genuine and full of accountability, which would have worked when I was younger. Now, they do nothing to dissolve the hate filled crevice reserved for her in my heart. She's saying the right things, but nothing in her behavior has suggested otherwise. My mother—the great deceiver—wants me to take her word for it. *That* is something I just can't do. Not with her.

"You can leave now." Turning my back on her, I face the window. I've said more words to her in the last twenty minutes than I have in the last ten years. There's nothing left to say. "I'm tired."

"Of course. You need your rest. I just came to give you this and say goodbye. Properly." I look over my shoulder as she reaches into her oversized purse and places a large square-shaped present on the bedside table. "Theron is in the waiting room, wanting to say goodbye too, and then we're headed back to Sweden a few days early."

"Of course you are," I huff, turning back to the window.

"Only until the divorce is final. Then we're coming back to live in the states. New York or LA, I haven't decided. But we *are* coming back, Hunter. I'll do whatever I need to fix this. No more running." She squeezes my shoulder, lingering for a moment before her heels click across the vinyl floor.

After discharge, I'm more than ready to go to my apartment and sleep. It's almost two in the morning. I want my bed, my space, and some uninterrupted quiet. But Dad is a hard sell when I ask him to take me home.

"Not happening. And I already hid your keys. The doctor wants you observed for another twenty-four hours. I can't do that if you're holed up in your apartment alone."

With the alternating light and dark shadows from the street-lights streaming into the car, I see the deep worry lines across his forehead. We've been through so much together. Apart from his depression after the divorce, he's been a solid constant in my life —one of the best people I know.

"...Thanks, Dad," I whisper, unsure of any other way to show my appreciation after all of the holiday chaos.

"Hey." He puts his hand on my arm, juggling his gaze between the road and me. "I'm just glad you're alright." His smile doesn't reach the exhaustion in his eyes. I don't think he's slept a wink since I've been in the hospital.

We're met with bright lights and a detective rerun on the TV when we walk into the house. Kayla pops her head over the couch and waves as we come into view. Chase is standing in the kitchen, hooking up a brand-new coffee machine. I spot my phone on the counter, right where I left it.

"What are you two doing here?" I ask.

"We volunteered for the first round of 'Hunter Duty.'" Kayla hops off the couch and wraps her arms around me with a squeeze. "Hey, big bro."

"Hunter Duty?" My brows furrow as I hug her back. *What kind of duty requires them being here at two in the morning?*

"Yeah. You two need sleep. We napped earlier, so we'll stay up and check on you every hour. Make sure you don't croak while you're knocked out." Chase chuckles, walking around the island and clapping me on the shoulder. "Glad you're okay, man."

The annoying burn behind my eyes from the concern in theirs sends me scurrying to hide. "*Aww...*" I slap my hand to my heart sarcastically. "I'm gonna go shower."

"There's the Hunter we know and love," Kayla mumbles, shaking her head. We drive each other nuts and bicker like we grew up together, but avoidance is something we have in common. Despite my discomfort, I give her another squeeze. An understanding smile lands on her face. She gets it, and I couldn't ask for a better sister.

After almost falling asleep in the shower, the queen-sized mattress in my childhood bedroom feels like paradise. I barely had the strength to slip on pajama pants, foregoing a shirt. My head hits the pillow, and I'm shaken awake in what feels like seconds. Groggy like I slept for a decade, I squint against the brightness streaming through my window. My heart skips a beat.

"Ash? What are you doing here?" Her golden-brown curls glow in the sunlight, the ends brushing her pink velour zip-up. The spark of her fingers caressing my arm is the only clue I'm not dreaming.

"Your dad made breakfast and asked me to bring it up to you." She smiles, but worry fills her eyes. "I didn't realize your allergy was that severe... How are you feeling?"

"It's not airborne for me, just can't touch or eat them." Slowly, I anchor my back against the slatted headboard, draping an arm across my bare chest. "Drinking them is generally frowned upon too," I joke to lighten the mood. But her face falls, and I feel like an ass. "I'm alright, Ash. Tired."

Hunger pangs scatter through my stomach when she hands me a plate of bacon and eggs. She settles on the edge of the bed, next to my feet. *Too far away.*

"Oh!" My phone buzzes as she slides it from her jacket. "I almost forgot... Chase charged it while you were sleeping."

"Are they still here?"

"Nope, they left about an hour ago. It's just me." She flashes a timid grin.

"Which leads me back to my original question. What are you doing here?"

"My flight got in at seven-thirty, and I came right over." Shrugging, she drops her eyes to the navy bedspread. "I'm on Hunter Duty."

"Yeah?" A smirk tugs at my lips. "For how long?"

Her cheeks flush, each shallow breath drawing my attention to her chest. She bites her thumbnail and slides her eyes to mine. "For as long as you want me."

What is that look?

Our dynamic feels different somehow. I try not to fidget as the charge shifts in the air, but my dick misses the memo. *I'm just a fucking horndog. Shit.* Nothing's changed, and now I'm a creep. Breaking our stare, I tap my phone, halted by several missed messages from Ashlie. "You, uh...texted me *a lot* yesterday..."

"Yeah, well, that was before I found out you were terrorizing the nurses in the hospital. You were stuck with your mom all week. I wanted to check on you."

"*Aww*, you were worried about me?" I tease, smirking.

"*Whew*, yeah, don't know what came over me..." She rolls her eyes, but I don't miss the smile on her face. We sit in silence while I eat my breakfast, until a yawn slips out of my mouth. "I should go back downstairs and let you get more sleep."

Don't leave.

She pushes off the bed, and I lunge for her wrist. "Wait!" The sun illuminating her freckles makes me flounder for an excuse for her to stay. "We, um...could watch funny videos?" I say slowly, finally gesturing to the flat screen mounted on the wall. It's the best I can come up with, but the smile spreading across her face is akin to striking gold.

"Yeah, okay. But if you get tired, you better tell me..."

"Just come over here." I scoot as she sheds her jacket and climbs in. Electric currents buzz through me when she settles against my arm, the undeniable urge to intertwine our fingers almost too hard to resist. But we're finally past everything that happened at the lodge. Making this friendly moment into something more will send her running for the hills faster than she ran from my room that morning. More than ever, I want her to stay.

CHAPTER TWENTY-SIX

ASHLIE

HUNTER

You're gonna be late for your date…

ME

And you're annoying.

HUNTER

The club shuts down in 4 hours. You gonna be ready before then?

ME

🖕 Give me 10 minutes!

I'm nervous. A New Year's Eve date with Trevor seemed like the best idea when he asked, but now the pressure of a potential kiss at midnight fills me with anxiety. It's not that I don't like Trevor. I do. We've been talking since our hiking date, and his flirting is top tier. He's sweet, thoughtful—I have no complaints so far. Kissing him would probably be great, but the last person I kissed was Hunter. And I haven't been able to move past it.

Hunter definitely has. When I brought breakfast to his room last week, his phone buzzed in my hand and I glanced at it. Ava and all her business were barely covered by the black lingerie. The reality check helped me box up the newly confessed feelings I shared with Willa. They're currently bundled tight in the crypt of memories we don't talk about. Hunter's already on to his next thing. I'm the one who needs to get control of my feelings. But he really should turn his text previews off.

"You're shiny." Hunter looks me up and down, his face unreadable as I slide into the passenger seat. He's in his standard black button down and jeans.

"Uh, duh..." I smooth a hand down the silver bodice of my mirror dress. "It's New Year's Eve."

"Oh, *that* explains it." He scowls as he pulls out of my parking lot, squinting as soon as we hit the first stoplight.

"You know, I can drive us if it's too hard for you to see at night...*or* you could just wear your—"

"I don't need my damn glasses. I'm fine."

I chuff. "Are you going to be this much fun all night? What's your problem?"

"Nothing," he murmurs, staring straight ahead. The muscle in his jaw flutters as he clenches his teeth.

"Is this because I was late? I'm always late."

"I said it's nothing. Can you drop it?" he snaps back at me.

"Miss me with that attitude, Hunter. I just got in here." Pressing my lips together, I settle back into the seat. Whatever his fucking problem is, I'm not entertaining any of it. Sending him the clear sign that I'm done talking to him, I open my phone and scroll. We're silent the entire drive to the club, and I keep my body turned toward the window, seething until I reach for the door handle to get out.

"Hey," he says, putting a hand on my arm. "I'm sorry. You look great."

"Oh, I know I do. When was *that* even a question?" I shoot him a playful look, waiting until he cracks a smile before getting out of the car.

Willa and Trevor meet us by the doors, and she already looks like she's ready to bounce. Her shimmery gold dress clings to her hips. Long, sleek twists flow down her back, almost reaching the hemline at her thighs. Trevor's in a simple gunmetal V-neck and jeans. The smile on his face grows when he sees me.

"Hey, pretty lady." He pulls me into a hug and whispers, "You look amazing." My cheeks burn, and I bite my lip while Trevor holds out his fist to Hunter. "What's good?"

Hunter taps Trevor's knuckles with his and quickly sticks his hand back in his pocket without a word.

"Don't mind him. He forgot to remove the stick from his ass today." I shoot Hunter a glare, and his eyes drop to the ground. "Should fit right in with my sister tonight."

Willa's middle finger is backed by a sarcastic smile, and all I can do is roll my eyes. *So much for a fun night.*

"You ready?" Trevor asks.

"More than ready," I say. He guides me to the door with his hand on my back.

"Come on, Hunter. You're with me tonight," Willa says behind me. We file into the building, losing them in the strobe lights.

Trevor pulls me onto the dance floor, moving in close as we sway and bounce to the beat. We make it several songs into the night before I lead him over to the bar for a drink. "Whew!" I say, flopping on a stool, mojito in hand. "I didn't know the Midwest had moves like that."

"The way you were dancing circles around me, I was just trying to keep up!" He runs his hand over his short hair and takes a swig from his water.

"Come on, you're a good dancer, Trev."

"I take all my inspiration from the cornfields." He shimmies in his seat, making me choke on my drink.

"Explains where all your corny jokes come from too…"

"*Ooh*, okay. I see how it is." Laughing, he knocks his knee against mine. I smile back, but it's short-lived when my gaze drifts over his shoulder.

"*Ugh*." I roll my eyes. Trevor looks behind him and back at me with his eyebrows raised. Marcus sits a few tables away, chatting up a blond. "It's my ex."

"It didn't end well, I take it."

"If you count a short-form email on official hospital letter-head as not ending well, then yep."

"Ouch. That's messed up."

"Little bit." I pinch my fingers together and take a drink.

"You didn't deserve that."

"Oh, I *know*," I say bitterly before taking another. It's clear as day now that Marcus treated me like shit. I deserved better.

Trevor pops out of his seat, reaching a hand toward me. "Come here."

"Wh-where are we going?" I ask as he pulls me off the stool.

"You'll see." He winks and walks me right up to Marcus's table, digging his phone out of his pocket once we get there. "Hey, bud. You think you could take a picture of me and my girl?"

Marcus shoots a surprised look at Trevor, then does a double take on me. My immense joy at seeing his face fall is off the charts. His mouth hangs open, and he blinks a few times before the blond across from him chimes in. "Oh, sure! You two are such a cute couple! Aren't they cute, Marcus?"

Shifting uncomfortably in his seat, Marcus slides a look to his date, before nodding curtly. He looks away as she takes a few pictures on Trevor's phone.

"Hey, thanks!" Trevor sends a wide grin over the table before pocketing his phone. His arm curls around my waist as he walks me out onto the dance floor. "Don't turn back, but that's a man who just realized what he lost."

"You are *messy*!" I laugh.

"Maybe, but it worked. Did you see his face?"

"I'll never forget it... Thanks."

"Hey, he clearly didn't deserve you. It was worth it just to see that pretty smile light up your face again."

I'm almost certain my cheeks are red, hidden only by the purple neon streaking across the dance floor. "Come on," I say, biting my lip. "We can get a few more dances in before the ball drops."

"Ten...nine...eight," Trevor and I count down to midnight, watching the ball drop on the big screen in the main dance hall. He's standing behind me, one hand settled loosely on my hip. My nerves from earlier return as I anticipate what may happen when we get to the number one. "Seven...six–"

But when we get to five, he whispers in my ear, "Do you want to get out of here?"

I nod, and just as the crowd explodes in a sea of the New Year's kisses I was worried about, he leads me by the hand to the exit. Outside, I pause on the sidewalk and pull out my phone. "I just need to tell Willa and Hunter we're leaving..." Opening a group message, I type out a quick goodbye as we walk to Trevor's rental car. The drive to his hotel takes about twenty minutes, and halfway there, my phone dies. "Do you happen to have an extra charger?" I ask.

"Yep." He reaches into the center console and pulls out a long charging cord, which is great, except it's not compatible with my phone.

I tsk, shaking my head. "Don't tell me you're a Pro-Phone guy..."

"Always. And by the tone in your voice, I'm guessing you have a StarCell."

"Yep. I just ran into your first red flag,"

His laughter booms over the soft music playing on the radio. It must be contagious since I giggle along with him. "Welp, if that's the only red flag so far, I'd say I'm doing pretty well for myself."

"Guess we'll see." I grin at him.

We pull into a parking spot, but he keeps the engine idling, turning in his seat to look at me. "I want to be perfectly clear about my intentions tonight... I plan to throw on a movie and cuddle the hell out of you, and then I'll drive you home after."

"Cuddling *and* a movie?" I click my tongue. "I don't know... You didn't say anything about snacks. Sounds iffy."

He sucks in air through his teeth like we're in serious negotiation mode. "You drive a hard bargain, but I think I can make that happen. I'll even throw in some overpriced water bottles." I laugh as those dimples accent his smile, and he shuts off the car and escorts me inside.

After clicking on the dim light in his hotel room, we dump our movie snacks onto the bed and agree on a comedy from a few years ago. Once we're comfortable against the headboard, he reaches for the fruity candy, then slides an arm around my shoulder. The tingling warmth coursing through me is a stark change from the heart palpitations I usually get with guys. It's nice, just... different. I follow the impulse to snuggle into him, and he drops his arm to my waist. My breath hitches when his thumb grazes my thigh.

"Oh, you want to *cuddle*-cuddle," I tease.

"Shh," he says playfully. "The movie's starting." With his hand on my hip, he tugs me closer. Biting my lip, I glance at him, and he's already watching me with a sly smile on his face. I reach forward for some chocolate, and when I settle back against him, his hand searches for mine until he hooks his thumb around my pinkie. It's so adorably sweet, I can barely stand it. Just like those high school movies where I'd be kicking my feet at the cuteness of it all.

But after the first few scenes of the movie, I can't take the quiet. "Sooo...you learned about my ex. Can I hear about yours?"

"I guess that's fair." He shifts so we can see each other better. "It's been..."—he blows out a puff of air—"a couple years since I had anything serious. She was a coworker, and it turned into a long-distance thing when she got promoted. We ended up wanting different things."

"What kinds of things?"

The smallest shadow falls over his face as he scrunches his lips. "Well, for starters, she wanted her boss, and I wanted someone who wasn't a cheater..."

"Ooh, yeah, those are very different things."

He shrugs, and just like that, the shadow is gone, replaced with a glint in his eye. "It was for the best. I learned a lot about myself."

"Like...?"

Chuckling, he nudges my shoulder. "Like, now I know I need to take things slow, keep things light and fun while getting to know someone. Only jumping into exclusivity when we're both sure it's what we want. Most women get fed up and call it quits because of my pacing, but I'm not rushing something like that again."

"I don't think slow is a bad thing, as long as you're upfront about it."

"Welp, that makes you different than most."

"You did *not* just hit me with 'You're different than most girls,' did you Trev? *What a line...*" I tease, bumping him with my elbow. He laughs, and I reach for more chocolate. When I sit up, a stray curl rests on my forehead.

"It's not a line if it's true," he says, tucking the curl behind my ear. His thumb trails to my chin, and my breath stutters as desire simmers in his eyes. I'm sure he's about to kiss me. *I think I want him to.*

He tips my head up with his finger under my chin, leans in, and whispers, "I really want to kiss you, but New Year's feels a little cliché." His thumb brushes my bottom lip, eyes flicking to my mouth. He breathes out a shuddered breath while shaking his head. "So I'm going to be a gentleman and wait. And then I'll kick myself in the morning when I replay tonight in my head."

I snort and immediately cover my mouth. His joking smile

gives me permission to let my giggles take over. *My friends were right about him.* Trevor's warmth and openness have sucked me right in, and he seems to be into me too. He isn't rushing this; I like that. His penchant for going slow could be good for me. I've tried jumping in quickly, which is probably why I've missed all the red flags in the past. Slow and steady might be exactly what I need right now. *Thank you, Kayla.*

CHAPTER TWENTY-SEVEN

HUNTER

If I clench my jaw any tighter, I'll crack a few molars. As I sit here against Ashlie's front door like the lovesick dummy from the lodge, wearing the same clothes I had on at the club, it's undeniable that I'm jealous. This is torture, waiting for her to come home from an overnight date with some guy. No. Not *some* guy. *Trevor*, the goddamn gentleman. My imagination runs wild as I battle the images in my head of what an overnight date likely entails.

I've never been the type to worry over what some other guy has. It always seemed like a waste of energy when I could blink and find someone new. I wasn't ever jealous of the other guys Ashlie's been with. They were idiots, and watching them touch her was aggravating, but game recognizes game. I could spot the end of her relationships before they even began. This Trevor thing is different. He's persistent and focused. Doesn't play games. I can acknowledge that threat for what it is: a real one.

And Ashlie's still not answering her phone. I've been sitting out here since 5:30 a.m., after waiting in my car since two, trying to get ahold of her. She took off without a second thought about me. I know I'm acting irrationally right now, but I'm going insane about all of this and don't know what else to do.

The sun crests over the horizon, and I check my phone for what feels like the thousandth time. It's seven in the fucking morning, and the only thing keeping me from shivering in the coolness of the dawn is this obnoxious, nagging envy coursing through me. It should be me having overnight dates with Ash, not some Boy Scout fuckstick.

I squeeze my fists tightly over my eyes, trying to scrub out the images of them pressed tightly together on the dance floor last night. No matter where I was in the club, I was hyperaware of their proximity to me and their closeness to each other. I sulked all night, knowing I wasn't who she dressed up for.

"Hunter?" Ashlie's voice snaps me to attention, the soft breeze tousling her curls. *Holy shit. She's a goddamn vision, just as amazing as last night.* My entire purpose for sitting out here all morning becomes as clear as the sky above. "What are you doing here?"

"You weren't answering your phone."

"It died. I left my extra charger in your car... Have you been out here all night?"

"You weren't answering your door either," I say stupidly. It's got to be the sleep deprivation, or the jealousy, because I'm not even making sense to myself.

"Because I wasn't home... Hunter, it's freezing." She nudges me out of the way to unlock the door, then ushers me inside her apartment. "What are you doing here?" Her back is turned to me as she plugs in her phone.

"Did you sleep with him?" I ask, steeling myself for an answer I'm going to hate. *Why beat around the bush?* Direct will get me the information I need before I confess everything to her.

"*Excuse me?*" Ashlie whips around, eyes narrowed as she slams a hand on her hip. "How is that any of your business? Is that why you're here?"

"You disappeared last night. I was worried about you. What happened to 'leave the way you came'?"

"That applies to leaving with strangers. You knew I was with Trevor. I texted you before I left."

"Naw, not me." I jam my hands in my pockets.

"Yes, *you*. I sent a group text to you and Willa."

I shake my head, and she smugly checks her phone, eyes widening as she scrolls. "I thought I sent... Hunter, I'm so sorry. I wouldn't leave without telling you."

"Okay." I slide my eyes to the floor and kick the shaggy white rug, watching the corner curl and fall with each tap.

"Hey," she says quietly. "I wouldn't just leave. I know that's a thing for you."

"Okay."

Ashlie walks toward me and wraps soft fingers over my forearm. "To answer your question, no. Trevor was a perfect gentleman. We watched a movie and fell asleep. Didn't even kiss."

"Okay." I nod quickly, unable to meet her gaze. Being a "perfect gentleman" makes this infinitely worse. Those are the guys who land a woman like Ashlie with no effort. Perfect gentlemen are on the opposite end of the spectrum from me.

"Hunt..." She searches my face, her voice full of regret. "Look at me."

I do, and if she isn't the most beautiful woman in the entire world, I don't know who is. I could drown in her. All of her. Suddenly, my hand cups her cheek and I'm drawing her in, brushing my lips against hers. I want this—want *her*—more than anything I've ever wanted before. She's a necessity. I'm aching to be the one she leaves the club with and the one she wakes up next to. Hiking dates through the forest and weekly lunch dates in the middle of the workday. The football game with flirty eyes and the water fights while doing dishes. I want it all—with her.

"Hunter..." Her breath stutters as she tries to pull away from our embrace. "W-what are you doing?"

"Ash, I want you."

Her body goes rigid in my arms, and her gaze drops, leaving my precarious words hanging in the air. "You already *had* me. At the lodge." She shakes her head, and I lift her chin until her eyes meet mine.

"I don't...mean like that. Ashlie, I want to be *with* you." Crashing into her lips again, I lose myself in their soft warmth. Her hands snake around my shoulders, nails scratching the back of my head. A quiver dances up my spine as I memorize her touch. She kisses me back, gently at first, then with a desperation that threatens to crack my heart in half from the euphoria. *This is really happening.*

But then she pulls away, pushing me with a palm on my chest.

"For how long?" she whispers with a fierce indignation that punches me in the gut.

"W-what?"

"How long until you toss me in the pile with the rest of them, Hunter? Huh? And how's Ava?"

"I...no. I want—"

"Why now?" The steel in her eyes hits me like a bollard to the chest. "Because Trevor's in the picture? Is that it?"

"I...don't know. I just do."

"You don't *know*?" Her humorless chuckle waves over me as the realization hits that I'm horrible at communicating my feelings. What a shitty time to find out. "We fucked in a cabin *one time* and, now, *magically,* you want—"

"That was more than just *fucking*, and you know it." The spark of frustration that hits when she reduces our night together to one meaningless word makes my head pound. There's no way in hell she feels that way.

"You're telling me you want a relationship? When was the last time you had one? Because in the five years I've known you, I've never seen it."

"...It's been a while."

"When?" She takes a couple of steps back, far enough away that I can't comfortably keep her in my arms. The full range of her anger glows in her eyes before realization crosses her face. "Don't tell me it was high school..."

It *was*. Right after my mom left, and I realized I was the only one who could protect that dependent part of myself. "Why does it matter?"

"Because you don't *do* this, Hunter!"

"But I could...maybe...with you." My mind races to understand everything I'm feeling right now. Hope? Fear? Desperation? *Fuck!*

"*Maybe*?" She balks and pokes a finger into my chest. "You think everything's going to be sunshine and rainbows if I say yes to your '*maybe*'? That's not enough when I see how you treat every other woman, Hunter!"

Trying to avoid shutting down, I shake my head. I'm losing this battle. "I know it won't be rainbows all the time. It'll be scary and frustrating, and we'll drive each other crazy while we figure it out. But you and I could be great together. Every single ounce of confidence I have knows that life would be amazing with you."

She takes a deep breath, closes her eyes, and hangs her head. I give her one, five, ten seconds, and right when I'm about to say something, she whispers, "I can't do 'maybes' anymore, Hunter. Not when there's someone willing to give me an 'absolutely.'" She walks to the door, using it as a barrier between us when she opens it. "I want you to leave."

I nod quietly, my feet shuffling across the room while my brain screams at me to beg her to reconsider. *Convince her. Show her you can be whatever she needs.* But I don't. *I can't.* She clearly told me what she wants. I would be just like everyone else if I walked all over it. As much as I don't want to, I go.

I TRIED SITTING AT THE BEACH, HOPING THE SOUNDS OF the waves would help rid me of this pit in my stomach. Sleeping it off at my apartment did nothing but make the black hole exponentially larger. So now I'm here, at the house of my childhood best friend, hoping he can help me categorize the dusty, unused emotions tenderizing my heart. The white Mediterranean-style mansion was my second home growing up, just a few blocks away from Dad's. Dark barrel tiles line the roof, with four stately columns framing the porch.

Slipping through the side gate, I walk past the covered fountain in the courtyard, going underneath the grand staircase to avoid the pool. When I get to the guest house where Chase and Kayla are staying, I knock with a sigh. Kayla answers, takes one disgusted look at me, and slams the door in my face. *Great.* She's already talked to Ashlie, I'm sure. Blowing a breath to the sky, I groan. *Fuck this entire day.*

The door opens again, with Chase standing to the side, inviting me in. "Hey, man," he says, closing the door behind me.

"I messed up."

"Yeah, no shit. Kayla just got back from Ashlie's place..."

Kayla rounds the corner, folding her arms in a huff. "Leave, Hunter."

"No," I say simply, knowing it will only add fuel to the fire blazing from my sister.

"*No?* Ashlie's inconsolable. What the *hell* is wrong with you?"

"Look, I don't know, but yelling at me isn't gonna help me figure it out. And that's the only reason I'm here."

"Like you didn't know what you were doing. First the lodge, and now whatever shit you pulled this morning? Get out of here with that, Hunt!"

"You told her about the lodge?" I turn to Chase, and the daggers he shoots from his eyes as he shakes his head make me take a step back.

"Oh, you *knew*?" Kayla sets her blazing glower on her fiancé. "You knew, and you didn't tell me?"

"...Yep..." he says tersely, nodding and shooting another glare at me in the process. He scrubs a hand over his face, stopping to stroke the hair on his jaw.

"Here." Kayla walks to the coat rack and tosses Chase his jacket and keys. "You can go with him. Both of you, go somewhere else." She opens the door, staring us down until Chase walks through and I follow. When I pass her, she stops me with a hand on my shoulder. "Fix this." Her indignation softens as sympathy flickers crosses her face. Somehow, that's even worse.

The air from the slamming door fans over our heads like a tidal wave, and I turn to Chase with a nervous grimace.

"Come on, Casanova. I'll drive." He clicks the remote with a sigh, and we climb into his silver crossover. The engine roars, but he makes no moves to drive. "What happened to leaving her alone?" His exasperated tone has me dropping my head in my hands.

"I can't." I groan, dropping my head back against the seat. "I tried, and I can't make the feelings go away. She's everywhere, even if she's nowhere near me. The only highlight to my week is seeing her. Hell, even texting her is a high point. I don't notice anyone else when I'm with her. It's just her."

"And you told her this?"

"...No?"

"Bro, *what*?" He laughs, shaking his head like I'm the biggest dummy on the planet. *I might be.* "You feel all of that for her and didn't tell her? What *did* you say?"

"I said I could maybe try with—"

"*Maybe*?" His eyes widen at my daftness. "Man, you really are bad at this."

"Bruh, you think I don't know that? I fumbled my way through this morning. I can't blame her for kicking me out."

"Listen, man... With women like Ashlie, you can't dangle a 'maybe' in front of their faces and expect them to follow you into the unknown. You have to be focused and intentional. Make plans and follow through. She spooks easily, so you need to go slow. You can't expect her to believe a word you say when you haven't shown her you're willing to put in the effort."

"So what the fuck do I do? I'm not good at this shit like you are."

"You date her."

"Huh?"

"I really have to spell this out for you?"

I blink at him, completely at a loss.

Chase taps his fist on his forehead in frustration before taking a breath. "You take all the complicated things out of the equation, and you date her. Woo her. Show her you're serious. And most importantly, *tell her how you feel*."

"How do you know any of that shit will work?"

"Have you met your sister? Do you remember how many hoops I jumped through just so she'd give me the time of day? I knew she was worth it, and I did everything I could think of to let her see that."

"And what if I put in all of this effort, and she still walks away?"

"That's the risk you take, man. But at least you stop wondering. At least you tried." He lets his advice soak in for a couple minutes, then, without warning, throws the car in reverse.

"Where are we going?"

"I'm not walking back into that house without Kayla's favorite ice cream. Since you dragged me with you straight into the doghouse, you're coming with me."

CHAPTER TWENTY-EIGHT

ASHLIE

HUNTER

Still on for lunch today?

ME

Can't. Short staffed.

HUNTER

You're not taking a lunch break?

ME

No, Hunter.

The "Day after New Year's" sale left the Fit4U building a disaster. I had the day off, but the employees who worked didn't bother to reset the store before closing last night. When I walked in this morning, it looked like someone had robbed the place. Disheveled clothing racks. Hangers scattered across the orange vinyl floor. Supplements peppered around the store. *I'm really starting to hate it here.*

Olivia called in "sick," so Hannah and I have been rushing around all morning trying to do two days' worth of store prep in a few hours. Exhausted is an understatement. Everything is in shambles today, mimicking exactly how I feel inside.

And now, Hunter wants to have our standing lunch appointment like this past weekend wasn't a completely shitty way to blow up our friendship. Like everything can go back to normal. The things he confessed, the conviction in his voice, it all sent me into a panic. There's no rug in existence big enough to sweep all of that under.

Thank God Kayla was still in town. If it weren't for her rushing to my apartment when I called, I'd still be curled up on my couch, devastated that Hunter thinks of me as just another woman on his roster. I bawled to her for hours at the thought of losing one of my best friends. Confessing to her about my feelings for Hunter was a messy, snotty display. But today is a new day, and I'm too tired to deal with any of it.

My stomach alerts me when lunchtime rolls around, growling with a fickle reminder of where I would usually be now. The clock on the wall confirms it, and I didn't have the forethought to pack a lunch from home. Leaning on the counter behind the register, I dig my phone out of my pocket and pull up a list of local delivery places. Right as I decide on a turkey wrap from Lunch-a-Bunch, a message flashes on my screen.

HUNTER

Hey…so, I brought you lunch.

ME

…

HUNTER

I realize you might not want to see me…

So, I'll count to 60 before coming in. If you want to hide out in the back, I can leave it by the register.

Frozen for several seconds, I reread his messages while lightning bugs dance around the muddled questions in my mind. I know he can see the bouncing dots as I type and erase potential responses, but I'm mind-blown. He's never gone out of his way to bring me lunch before. We've gone out to lunch, sure. But bringing lunch to a woman after everything he confessed doesn't feel like a friendly favor. It feels like a romantic gesture. I'm nervous to see him face-to-face, but my intrigue gets the best of me.

ME

K

HUNTER

Counting now...

It would take ten steps to get to the back room and avoid looking into those infuriating green eyes. Easy. Send the message loud and clear that I don't want to talk to him. Never mind my clenching thighs as I remember his lips on mine. Stepping into the breakroom would halt the flitter-flutter-flop in my belly long enough to remind myself. It would only take ten steps, and yet, I can't move one. Can't extinguish the glimmer of excitement inside. *I want to see him.*

The door chimes, and my thumbnail slips between my teeth. My eyes trail up the khaki-covered legs walking toward me as I will the triple *F* of my heart-stomach combo to slow down. *Flitter-flutter-flop. Flitter. Flutter. Fl—*

"You stayed." The relief behind Hunter's shy grin makes me bite my lip. He clutches a take-out bag from Lunch-a-Bunch in his hand.

"I..." No words. At this point, I don't know if staying was voluntary or a freeze response to my panic.

"Can you step out for five minutes? Hell, I'll even take three if you'll give me that."

I still have nothing, and the eager look in his eyes flickers to a timid stare.

"One minute?" His nervous chuckle is so cute, a smile slides across my face. "Yeah?"

"You're so annoying," I say, shaking my head as I come around the counter.

"Who, me?" He smirks. Damn those flutters waging war in my belly. "Naw. I've never heard *that* before."

"Hannah, I'll be back in ten minutes."

Hunter's car is front and center when we walk into the bright sunlight. He opens the passenger side—another new gesture. With the lightest touch, he places his hand on my back as I slide into the seat.

"You brought me lunch..." I say, when he gets in the car.

He settles behind the wheel, bag still in hand. "I did. Wanted to make sure you had something to eat...and apologize. I shouldn't have sprung everything on you like that."

"Thanks..." We sit quietly, awkwardly, as we try to navigate these new loose ends dangling between us. He's acting weird, and I don't know what to make of it. It's endearing, but *different*. "You're down to eight minutes, by the way," I say.

"I'd better get to it then. Ashlie, I want to date you."

My face falls in complete shock. "You—huh? What?"

"I. Want to. Date you." He punctuates his words with a smile on his face.

"No, I heard you. I just...what? Like go on a date?" *What would we even do? Argue with each other and call it a night?*

"Dates. Multiple. With you. *Just* you. I want to date you."

"But you don't do that..."

"That changes if you say yes..."

"But—"

"Bruh." He tips his head back, rubbing his eyes before looking at me again. "Okay, let's try it like this. How about a bet?"

"...A dating bet?" I blink at him. "Like a game? We're not twelve."

"I know, just...give me till after the wedding."

Sighing, I check the time on my phone. "I dunno, Hunt..."

"Look, hear me out... If I can convince you I'm not tryna entertain anyone else by then, you give us a real shot at being together. And if I fail—which I won't—I'll drop it, and we can add one more item to our list of things we never talk about."

I scowl at his logic. This sounds *all sorts* of complicated, especially after what happened a couple of days ago. "So if you win, you get me. And if I win, I get...secrets? How is that fair?"

"Okay, how about this: You keep dating what's-his-name too. And if I fail, which again, I won't, then you still have that."

"Oh, so now you're giving me *permission*?" I squint at him. My budding relationship with Trevor is decidedly slow, but I have fun with him. I'm not ready to give that up for whatever this is.

"It's not permission. It's acceptance that you might want to keep seeing what's-his-name."

"Boy, you know his name..." I laugh at how ridiculous this all sounds, but I'm amused. "And what am I getting out of this bet when you lose?"

"I'm not losing. But what do you want?"

That's the third time he's said he won't lose. His confidence makes me want to scoff in his face and curl my toes, all at the same time. The eager smile on his lips is convincing, but part of me is full of hesitation. Hunter's the epitome of the dating pattern I'm trying to break. I've seen him in action; knowingly signing up for that isn't a smart move.

But the part of me that made that confession at Christmas wants to see if he really can resist his playboy ways for more than a couple weeks, even if it's just a game. We've crossed friendship boundaries before and have always bounced back after. One more step over the line, even with an unserious bet, likely won't matter. *What's the worst that could happen?*

"If I win, you have to buy me tickets to the summer music festival of my choosing, with accommodations," I say.

"Easy. Done. But I'm not—"

"Losing? Yeah, I got that. And just so we're clear, I don't need your permission to date Trevor..." I purse my lips.

"I know that. My point is, do what makes you happy. As for me, I just want to date you...if that's okay?"

"So *now* you're asking if it's okay to date me?"

"Yes, Ashlie." He sighs. "I'm asking if it's okay for me to date you."

"Usually, you would ask someone out on a date, not ask *to* date them..."

"*Oh my God*, woman!" He groans, tipping his head against the seat. "Okay. If I ask you *on* a date, will you say yes?"

"Ask me and find out." Now I'm messing with him. A flustered Hunter is one of the cutest things I've ever seen. He holds everything so close to his chest all the time, watching him flounder a little is adorable.

"You're really making this so painfully frustrating."

"Three more minutes, Hunt."

"Ashlie, would you like to come to my place for dinner? Tonight? At seven? For a date?"

"*Oof!* Alone in your apartment on a first date? That's risky... What if you're some kind of creeper?"

"Ash..." He sighs again, scratching his forehead with his thumbnail. Watching him squirm feels like adequate payback for the chaos he laid at my doorstep over the weekend. But I think he's suffered enough.

"Okay, okay. Yes, but I should warn you..." I say, leaning in close to peer into his eyes. He leans in, too, as if my movement triggers an automatic response in him. Lifting his brow, he waits for me to finish, his breath catching as I hold his gaze. His eyes dip when I lick my lips, completely taking the bait as he follows the motion. Just to lay it on thick, I trap my lower lip between my teeth, and he leans in closer. With a smirk, I whisper, "I don't kiss on the first date."

"What about before the first date?" He wiggles his eyebrows, making my laugh come out as a snort.

"Nope. Times up." I reach for the door. "And I have one more condition. No one finds out about this. I don't want to look stupid when you lose the bet."

He shakes his head with a gleam in his eye. "I'm not losing this one."

"We'll see…" I say, pulling on the handle.

"Wait!" He stops me with a hand on my arm, his touch scattering goosebumps across my skin. Handing me the bag of food, he smiles. "Your lunch."

"Thanks," I mumble, taking the bag and stepping onto the sidewalk.

Right before I get inside, he rolls down the window and calls out, "See you tonight, *honey bear*."

My face heats from the surge of butterflies at the sound of *my* pet name. Once inside, I tear into the food bag. My cheeks ache from the grin on my face as I spot two of my favorite things: a small coastal sunflower and a turkey wrap from Lunch-a-Bunch. I tuck the flower into my hair, smiling like a fool. The lid on that box of feelings I buried a few weeks ago just cracked—wide open.

CHAPTER TWENTY-NINE

HUNTER

"So, how'd it go?" Aiden asks as soon as I step into our windowless office at EdTechU. I had the idea of taking lunch to Ashlie, but he suggested offering an out if she wasn't ready to see me. "Did you get to see her?"

"Yep. And she agreed to a dinner date tonight." Like I'm walking on fluffy little clouds instead of carpet-covered concrete, I bounce over to his workstation. I'm not sure what this feeling is, but it's light and vibrant. I wish I could fast-forward through the rest of my day just to see Ashlie again.

"Nice, nice! Where are you taking her?"

"She's coming to my place tonight. I'll cook something."

"Well, that's romantic. You can cook, right?" Aiden rubs his short black hair with a sheepish look on his face. "Giving her food poisoning will probably set you back a few steps..."

"Oh, I can cook." I laugh, sitting on the edge of his metal desk. "I've cooked for her a couple of times, just not in this capacity." Biting the inside of my lip, I try to stifle the ever-growing excitement in my chest.

"What is *this*?" A knowing smirk slides across his face as he leans back in his office chair. "Are you *giddy*?"

"Is that what it's called? My body is buzzing, and I'm springy. Bruh, this is all foreign to me..."

"It's fun in the beginning. Enjoy it, man."

When I slide my glasses on and stare into the black screen at my workstation, I notice a goofy-ass smile on my face, and I'm pretty sure it's been there since I left Fit4U.

Shit. Liquid flows across my glass top range. Boiling water roils over the pot and onto the espresso hardwood, hissing like an angry cobra. I rush for a towel, and pain shoots across my side when my hip catches on the countertop. It's like I'm like a bumbling idiot who's never stepped foot inside his own kitchen. I can't think as I race around the room, turning off heating elements and wiping up spills. The pressure to get this date perfect was motivating at first, but the more I mess up the cooking process, the more flustered I become.

At this point, the only thing working out is the vase full of sunflowers sitting on my dining table. Not the giant kind, but the small ones that line the sand at the beach. It's not quite blooming season, but with LA's warmth, I managed to find a few straggling heads. They're Ashlie's favorite, so it just seemed like a good way to start off on the right foot. So much rides on this date tonight; I'm freaking the fuck out. The doorbell rings, and I let out an audible groan, tossing the sopping towel in the sink on my way to the door.

Ashlie's hair is up, with a few curly tendrils framing her face. Her basic white tee and jeans hug all the places my hands are aching to touch. My fingers twitch on the knob while I painstakingly refrain from pulling her into a kiss. She doesn't kiss on the first date. Even though we've done so much more, I want to respect that. "Hey. You're early."

"Yeah... Is that okay?" Her fingers trail over my arm as she passes. Her perfume, the soft caress on my skin—it all sends a mind-glitching shudder through me. Every bit of my panic from before melts away, and I'm only aware of her and the way she tucks a stray curl behind her ear.

"Mm-hmm." I clear my throat.

"Why are you looking at me like that?" She scans her outfit with a frown, then flicks her eyes back to me with a tilt of her head. "Are you checking me out?"

"You just...look good. You look good." *Smooth, Hunter.* Let's just carry her straight to the bedroom. Way to make a good first impression.

"Uh, thanks...but you might want to go *check out* whatever's in the oven instead..."

"Shit!" I race to the kitchen. Black smoke billows up to the ceiling when I pull the charred breadsticks from the oven. I flip on the range hood and barely get the window open before a shrill beeping fills my apartment. When I turn around, Ashlie's standing on the countertop, in her socks, using the broom to push the button on the smoke alarm. Once the blaring stops, it feels like the entire world goes silent, somehow aware of my monumental fuck-up.

She climbs down and walks toward me, trying to hide her giggles behind her hand. I lean over the sink and cover my face, laughing at how bad everything is going so far. This and disaster are one and the same.

"*Ugh*, I'm crashing and burning here..." I mumble behind my fingers.

"Naw, the only thing burning is that bread over there." She puts a hand on my arm as she snickers at her joke, and when I look at her, we both fall out laughing again.

"*Whew!*" I whistle. "This is so bad..."

"No. It's cute."

"Cute? That doesn't sound any better... How is this fiasco cute?"

She lays a gentle kiss on my lips. Her fingers slide up my jawline, and she kisses me again, slow and deep. "It's cute because you're trying," she whispers, eyes locking to mine before dipping in for a third time.

I tug her closer, drawing on her lips a while longer. When she pauses for air, I nuzzle her nose with mine. "I thought you didn't kiss on the first date..."

She shrugs. "It seemed like you could use some encouragement."

"I think I need a little more." I steal a kiss of my own, her smile against my lips lighting my heart on fire. The risk, the stress —*everything*—was worth it.

Indian takeout and a movie cuddling session on my sofa save the night. Cradled in my arms, her back against my chest—I'm in complete bliss. Teasing, kissing, the ease of it makes my inner cynic question everything I know about relationships. She tickles my palm with her fingernails, and the small tingles rifling through me might be one of the best sensations I've ever felt. Being allowed to stare and flirt the way I've always wanted is like being set free from a high-security prison. I don't have to hide anymore.

"You smell so damn good," I murmur, planting kisses in the valley where her shoulder meets her neck. Her giggles are all the encouragement I need to continue.

Taking a deep breath, she turns to face me. "We can't tell Chase and Kayla about this right now. They don't need our... whatever this is...adding to their wedding stress."

I grit my teeth in a nervous grin. "Eh, Chase gave me the idea."

Skepticism pinches her face. "He told you to bet me for a date?"

"Naw, not that part." The opposite, really. This bet is nowhere near uncomplicated. I doubt he'd agree with it, but it got me here with her. "He's a pro at romantic shit. I needed some pointers. But I can be vague about it from now on if that helps you feel better... I'll just tell him it didn't work out."

That thumbnail slips between her teeth as she turns away and settles against me. "Can I ask you something?"

"Of course. Always."

"You said you're okay with me dating other people..."

"If you want to."

"But why?"

I take a minute to gather my thoughts so she doesn't mistake my words for anything other than what I mean. "You don't answer to anyone but yourself, and I think you forget sometimes. Do whatever feels right for you. If that means seeing multiple guys, then you should. Just...please, let me be one of them." *Fuck, I sound needy.* "I know I need to show how serious I am, so I'm putting all my focus on you. I want you to focus on you too, whatever that looks like."

"So, no other girls?"

"Just you, honey bear."

"What about Ava?" She whips around, cocking her head to the side with a scrunch to her lips.

"Ava? She's long gone..." I say. Ashlie's eyes narrow like she doesn't believe me, and I shrug, hoping she will. Ava's not anywhere close to being on my radar. I don't even know the last time I talked to her. A message might scroll across my screen occasionally, but I dismiss it as soon as it does. Responding would only encourage her. *Fuck that shit.*

"And if I keep going on dates with Trevor specifically, you're fine with that?"

"If that's what you want, that's what you should do."

"But what do *you* want?"

Her inner people-pleaser is trying to work overtime against our new situation. I stroke her cheek and grin as I stare into her eyes. "Ashlie, I want *you*, and I don't mean in a sexual way; that's off the table for now. I want to do exactly what we did tonight—dinners and movies, kissing and cuddling, laughing and whatever else we come up with. As long as you're there, I want to be next to you."

"And you won't get mad?"

"Mad? Naw. I'll be jealous as hell that he gets to spend time with you, but not mad. I can handle some competition, and after you get home from your little dates with Trevor, I'll enjoy making you forget all about him."

"Make me forget, huh?" Her eyebrows shoot to her hairline, and there's a playful glint in her eyes. "How so?"

"That's for me to know"—I leave a peck on her nose—"and for you to find out." Her face flushes, and I bite the smirk creeping across my lips.

Today has been an absolute whirlwind, but knowing I'm responsible for the redness spreading across her cheeks more than makes up for it. This silly-ass bet is my one chance to show how far I'm willing to go for a chance with her. Today feels like a good start.

Timidly, we walk hand in hand to her car. My stomach sloshes around as if this is the first date I've ever been on. Like I've never given a goodnight kiss before. It *is* the first to really mean something. Ashlie rolls her lips like she doesn't know what comes next either. We make it to her little red car and stand in an unusual, awkward silence.

I shouldn't be this nervous, but my heart is hammering like I'm sprinting on the track. "Can I call you tomorrow?"

She eyes me suspiciously. "Since when do we call each other?"

"Since now"—I tug her closer until she's pressed against me—"if you'll let me."

"What would we even talk about, Hunt?" she asks, tipping her head back to look at me.

I stroke her cheek with my knuckles. "Anything? Everything? I don't know. I just want to hear your voice."

"Oh..." Her cheeks flame again, her eyes dropping to the ground. "You're really giving this all you got, huh?"

I squint an eye and flash a nervous grin. "I'm trying... Is it working?"

She lifts a shoulder and smiles. "Guess we'll see."

CHAPTER THIRTY

ASHLIE

When Kayla leaves the dressing room with a grimace, I slide my phone in my purse. She's ethereal with the soft display lights glowing around her, but her frown deepens as she twists from side to side in her bridal gown. It's the one she found in LA months ago, but it just arrived at the San Francisco location this week. Maybe she hates it now? "Samson just confirmed the bulk order of peonies. We've got the ceremony location booked, the catering menu settled, and it's your final dress fitting. Everything's coming together, so what's with the face? You look like—"

"I'm going to throw up."

My widened eyes track her through the three-panel showroom mirror. She better not be dropping this news in a bridal shop.

"Again, *not* pregnant," she says quickly, holding up a finger to stop the question before I ask it.

"Honestly, no one would be surprised after how long you've been together..."

"One crisis at a time, please. I can barely think about becoming a wife; I can't imagine throwing a kid into the mix."

"Girl, *still*? It's February. You get married in three months..."

"*Ugh*, I know." She muffles a groan with her hands.

"Have you talked to Chase yet?"

Face still hidden, she shakes her head furiously.

"Kay, you promised!"

Kayla throws her arms at her sides, clapping her hands against her thighs. "I know, okay? But if you saw how excited he was when we got the confirmation email for Crystal Beach, you wouldn't be able to tell him either."

"He needs to know…"

"Why? I'm not doubting *him*. He's everything I could ever ask for. It's a *me* problem. I just have to get past it."

"Naw, if you don't tell him, I will."

"*Naw?*" she teases, effectively throwing me off her case. "You've been hanging out with Hunter a little too much."

"It's *almost* like we're friends or something…" I say with a bite of sarcasm. I haven't talked to her about the new Hunter arrangement. The last time she and I were together was on New Year's, when I soaked through three boxes of tissues telling her mostly everything that happened with Hunter to that point—including the *loving-him-but-he's-no-good-for-me* part.

"So he fixed it with you? I was so pissed and told him he better fix it."

"Yep, all fixed." I grin and drop my eyes to my shoes. She doesn't need to know *how* he fixed it, and I'll be damned if I'm going to stress her out even more with details of snuggling up to her brother multiple times a week.

"What aren't you telling me?"

"Nothing! It's all fixed. Everything is fine."

More than fine, really. There's a lot more romance up his sleeve than he lets on. I didn't think he'd make it a week, but most of my worries have been met with a lot of effort on his part. The make-out sessions are *very* steamy; however, I still refuse to tell anyone about us. He won't have me looking like a fool in front of everyone when he slips up. A month of consistency isn't nearly long enough for me to unsee years of the player excelling at his game. This can remain a low-key friends-with-benefits thing until it's done. I can do casual.

"YOU DO KNOW THEY HAVE NEW AND IMPROVED BOY bands, right?" I turn a teasing smile to Trevor, who's bopping his head along to the beat. A '90s boy band croons through the speakers of his SUV while we cruise down the street toward our dinner reservation. The moon peeks through the dark clouds in the sky, casting shadows over his brown thermal Henley.

"New, maybe. Improved? That's debatable. Nothing beats the stylings of the '90s." He chuckles at my scoff. "It's infinitely better. You're gonna tell me your little shoulder shimmy would be happening with a boy band from today?"

"You've seen me dance to modern music."

"But the shoulder shimmy? Today's music is all about twerking and beat drops. Those can be fun, don't get me wrong. But don't knock the simplistic grooves of old-school tunes. A good shimmy never hurt anyone. Plus, the lyrics are just"—he kisses his fingers—"*mwah*."

"Touché, Grandpa. You've got some good points." I shake my shoulders and wink at him, making him laugh again as we pull into the Poblano's parking lot.

"Grandpa? I'm thirty."

"Oh, is that all? You could have fooled me, Mr. *My-old-ass-music-is-better-than-yours*."

"Hold that thought." He comes around and opens my door, offering his hands for me to grab while I leap from the lift on his SUV.

"Whew! I feel like I just went cliff diving. Might need to bring a step stool next time."

"Short and cute, just how I like 'em." He winks, curling his fingers around mine as we walk across the parking lot.

The butterflies in my stomach collide with a pang of guilt when Hunter flashes through my mind. *Should I be doing this?*

But then Trevor smiles, and I brush it off. I'm not doing anything wrong by casually dating two people. It's just not something I'm used to yet.

Our conversation flows so easily over the next hour; I hardly notice when our empty plates are pushed to the side for an unobstructed view. Trevor doesn't take himself too seriously, which makes him easy to talk to. I don't know the last time I've laughed so much on a date.

"So tell me about your ink." I zero in on the tattoos peeking out at the wrist of his Henley. He's got to have a good story for that sleeve of his. "What was the inspiration?"

"Pure boredom." He chuckles, and I smile at the cute little dimples in his cheeks. "I got the first part at seventeen—right after boot camp—and I've slowly added to it. Every single addition was due to having nothing better to do at the time."

Oh… Guess not. "But you're right-handed. Why'd you choose your left arm?"

"You got a pen?" He nods to my purse.

I grab my pink felt-tipped pen and hand it over to him. "That's all I've got."

"Even better!" His smile grows as he rolls his sleeve up to his elbow, displaying more of the nautical tattoos on his arm. Mermaids, a ship, and various sea creatures cover his skin. I cock my head while he fills in the lines with pink. "It's my own personal coloring book for whenever I get bored."

"That might possibly be the cutest thing I've seen from a grown man. You listen to '90s pop *and* doodle on your arm when you get bored? You're adorable."

"Thanks." He comically raises a coy shoulder like a flirtatious Saturday morning cartoon.

I melt a little on the inside. With Trevor, it's like being wrapped in the middle of a warm, gooey cinnamon roll. He's comforting, and his sweet, open nature is an attractive safety feature I'm drawn to.

Vastly different than Hunter. He's snarky and sultry, with an intense air of protective—Why am I thinking about Hunter right now?

Guilt pinches my stomach again. I'm no expert in casual dating, but I doubt I'm supposed to be thinking of another man while *on* a date. At the very least, I need to tell Trevor I'm seeing someone else. It's only fair.

"So I should probably tell you something," I say slowly, scratching the furrowed lines on my forehead.

"Okay…" He caps the pen, rolling it in his fingers while he watches me. "What's up?"

"You and I… *We*…haven't really talked about what we're doing here…"

"Well, you see, we're sitting at a table, eating dinner, while you tell me how cute I am."

I cover my giggles with a hand. "No, I just mean…logistically, with how far apart we live, we haven't set any ground rules beyond taking things slow. You should know that I'm also dating someone else." I should tell him it's Hunter. It's the right thing to do—lay everything out on the table. But some little part of me wants to keep that blaring detail safe in LA. An even larger part is afraid of looking like the biggest dummy on the West Coast when this bet blows up in my face. So I keep it to myself.

"I mean, that's fair. We're having fun getting to know each other. You know I prefer to go slow, so I'm not worried about you seeing other people right now. Is it serious?"

Is starting a dating bet with your best friend, who you're secretly in love with but also terrified to admit it, serious? "It's… new."

He nods slowly, and I watch his face for flashes of wayward emotion—jealousy, rage, anything really. There's no change. "Alright. Good to know there's a little competition to keep me on my game." He winks, and I'm almost confused by his response. No clenching fists or grinding teeth. No intrusive questions or persuasive arguments. I'm used to guys needing that control, but he doesn't appear to be fazed one bit. I think I might like him more for it.

Trevor sits back and smiles. "Now, it's my turn... Will you be my date to the wedding?"

"The wedding?"

"Yeah, you know the thing happening in a few months, with the dresses and flowers. Rings...?"

"Boy, I know what a wedding is!" I laugh, shaking my head at his playful mansplaining. Biting my nail, I consider his proposition a little longer than I would have a month ago. Saying yes to him should be quick and easy. There's no doubt we'd have a blast together, and we'll both be at the wedding anyway...*with Hunter*.

If it wasn't for the effort Hunter's been showing, I'd have said yes immediately. But my people-pleasing ass is stuck trying to placate someone who's said he wants me to make these dating decisions for myself. It's time to stop doing that. I like Trevor, maybe even a little more than I did when we started the date tonight. There's no other reason to say no. *Except for Hunter.*

"Yeah, that sounds fun," I say, my conscience sounding off caution bells like we're headed into a nuclear war. *Should I be going through with this?*

"My thoughts exactly." He smiles and signals to the waitress for the check.

When we get back to Chase and Kayla's, Trevor insists on seeing me to the door. Our arms brush as the elevator settles on the fourth floor, sending warm waves through me that make me want to snuggle into him. He tangles our fingers together while leading me down the hallway, tucking my thumb under his as if for safekeeping. His hand completely encloses mine, and this gentle sign of protection has my heart thumping away.

"I had a lot of fun tonight," he says once we reach the door.

"Me too, old man," I tease, biting my lip as I look at him through my lashes. He laughs, but there's a simmering blaze in his eyes. Since he's so tall, he's bent to just about my eye level. *He's going to kiss me.* I'm pretty sure I want him to.

My lips part as they meet his, and broad fingers lightly graze my cheek. Fresh mint on his tongue, the soft pressure of his mouth on mine, his thumb drifting across my chin—it's all so sweet. Warm and comforting. I kiss him back, my belly fluttering as a sigh leaves my lips. It doesn't last long, but when he pulls away, his face looks as flushed as mine feels.

"Good night, Ashlie," he says, keeping hold of my hand until I enter the code on the door.

"Good night," I whisper, smiling and shooting him one last look before stepping inside.

Kayla and Chase are snuggled up on the couch with the TV on, laptops out, and books in their hands, trying to look nonchalant.

"You two were spying from the camera, weren't you?

"Nope—"

"It was his idea." Kayla's voice rushes at the same time as Chase's.

Chase turns to Kayla, mouth agape. "Oh, with *your* phone?"

"I was just making sure she was okay!" Kayla protests.

"Mm-hmm. Might wanna ask Artie how to improve your spying game..." I tease, backing up toward their guest bedroom.

"How was it?" Kayla asks, wiggling her eyebrows.

"I don't kiss and tell... Goodnight," I chime over my shoulder with a singsong voice.

The kiss was good. I had tingles in all the right places. Everything was what a first kiss should be. But I can't shake the guilt I felt when Trevor pulled away and my mind flashed to the green eyes waiting for me in LA.

CHAPTER THIRTY-ONE

ASHLIE

"You're being ridiculous," I say, feigning annoyance as my arms settle over my chest. "It's still on the secret menu. Just ask them..."

"Naw. It's almost spring. Pumpkin spice season is *definitely* over, and I'm not making a fool of myself by tryna order it."

The Saturday morning sun hits Hunter's tinted car windows, illuminating the space around him in a way that makes me want to skip our coffee date and straddle his lap. But I'm on a mission. Laying it on thick, I break out the puppy dog eyes, complete with a slight wobble to my lower lip. "*Please?*"

"*Not the lip...*" He drags a hand down his face, sighing loudly. "You know I can't fucking handle that thing."

I resist the urge to laugh as he climbs from the car, keeping up the act until he's pulled me from the passenger seat. He presses a kiss to my hand and weaves our fingers, and my smile breaks free with the eruption of butterflies in my belly. He's claimed to hate PDA in the past, but you'd never guess by the way he strokes my hand with his thumb. I reinforce his decision with a small squeeze. I love these cute couple things—especially with him. Silly little bet aside, intimacy is effortless with Hunter. As annoyed as I get when I'm horny and can't jump his bones, I see why he took sex off the table. It would only make this more complicated.

The fresh smell of coffee wafts over us when we walk into Cosmic Brews. A large chalkboard menu above the machines spans the entire brick wall. Small wooden bistro tables for two are lined on either side of the ordering line. We step up to the register, and because he was so insistent about this damn drink, I half expect him to order me something safe and sensible. I know I can make my own order, but I like having him take charge. It does things to me.

"Let me get a small Cuban espresso..." He hesitates, sliding his eyes to mine as I hang onto his arm. "And, um, a medium PSL."

I stifle my giggle in his shirt at his abbreviated rebellion. *Mission accomplished.* Staring up at him with a self-satisfied grin, I flutter my lashes. His eye roll doesn't hide the smirk twitching his lips.

"Anything for you, *Hunter.*" The long-haired brunette cashier smiles and winks before he has the chance to give his name, and the baristas at the coffee machines erupt into titters. I know he comes here multiple times a week, but this is a large coffee chain. Remembering him by name? That's suspect. They clearly see me hanging on his arm and just don't care. Judging by those heart-eyed responses at the machines, I'm sure he's had the time of his life with everyone behind the counter. My cheeks heat, and not in a good way. *Where the hell is this coming from?*

I can't get ahold of my jealousy, so I drop his hand and head for a table, murmuring obscenities the entire way. It's the pettiest kind of petty, but as I settle into a seat, I catch another woman ogling him dreamily. I just stepped into my own personal purgatory. *Everyone's staring at my boyf*—Shit. Nope.

He slides into the chair across from me, but I act supremely interested in my phone. The emotions rifling through me are messing with my head.

"Ash."

Raising my eyebrows, I continue staring at my screen. "Hmm?"

"Hey..." He puts his hand over my phone and lowers it to the table.

I glance up, and the knowing gleam in his eyes makes it clear he can spot my jealousy from a mile away. As if I'm the easiest book to read. I lift my phone back to my face and scroll, not willing to give him the satisfaction. With a sigh, he sits back in his chair, moving around for a few seconds before settling.

HUNTER

> Having a date through text is kind of weird,
> but if that's what you're into...

I snort, hiding my smile with a bite of my lip. Not even five minutes and he's making me laugh. How does he always find a way past my defenses? It's aggravating...*and sexy as hell*. Which is also annoying. But even being mad at the situation, I don't want to be anywhere else.

ME

> You're so irritating.

HUNTER

> Yeah. But I got your fancy drink. That must
> earn me some points.

ME

> How do you manage to flirt with three girls at
> the same time?

HUNTER

> I wasn't flirting...

"I just find it funny that they knew your name already, which means you've flirted with them at some point," I say out loud, glaring up at him.

He points at his phone. "Sorry, I'm on a date..."

HUNTER

I thought this was a texting date.

ME

You're ridiculous…

HUNTER

You started it. So, am I in trouble for anyone I may have flirted with in the past? I come here several times a week. Maybe that's how they know my name…

ME

No…

HUNTER

Then what's really bothering you?

I know I'm being irrational about this, but I can't help myself. With a sigh, I place my phone on the table and jut my chin across the room. "Even that lady over there is staring at you."

"Is it you?" he asks, following my lead and dropping his phone to the table. His eyes don't move from mine.

"Is what me?"

"Are you the woman staring at me?"

"What? No…"

"Then I don't care."

"You're telling me you suddenly don't care about all of the women falling at your feet?" I cross my arms and cock my head to the side, unwilling to let go of this stupid argument I started.

"Yep." He shrugs. "And it's not sudden. It's been this way for months. I care about one person in here—the woman sitting in front of me, tryna bait me into a fight."

"I am not!" I say in a huff. But my bravado fizzles as soon as he calls me out. When he hits me with that smirk, I let out a giggle. "Okay, fine. Maybe I *was*, but seriously, Hunt. It's like this everywhere we go. It's exhausting."

"Let's go home, then. Yours or mine, doesn't matter to me."

"We can't just stay home all the time."

"I agree. So what do you want? I can't control the staring, Ash. All I can do is reiterate that you're the only one I'm tryna see." He tugs my hand free from my grumpy stance and presses kisses on my thumb.

Although I roll my eyes, the heat filling my cheeks gives me away. I'm melting entirely, and he's the one responsible for it. I *like* it, clearly, since I'm still here letting him affect me.

"Hunter!" the barista calls from the counter. He doesn't move for several seconds, keeping our little moment alive. Another kiss on my hand is the pièce de résistance before he grabs our drinks. But the giggling behind the counter flies right to my ears, bringing back that annoyed heat in my chest. I try a few deep breaths before he gets back to the table, but when he slides my drink to me, I see red.

"*Are you fucking kidding me?*" Rolling my eyes, I turn my to-go cup around to him. Scribbled on the brown sleeve is a hand-written name and phone number.

"Give me your drink," he says, reaching forward.

I pull it back. "Why? What are you going to do?"

"Just give it to me..."

Hesitantly, I push the cup forward. He slides the sleeve off, folds it in half, and tosses the number in the garbage can behind him. "There. Problem solved. Now come here so I can kiss you and shut them all up."

"Wha—"

He pulls me from my chair and kisses me like we're the only people in the room, giving everyone in the coffeeshop a show that removes all the giggles from behind the counter. He pecks another small kiss on my lips and nods to my coffee on the table. "We good?" he asks with a smirk.

Trying to catch my breath, I nod quickly, my entire face burning while he leads me out to the car. I wasn't expecting him to stake his claim in public like that. Didn't expect to like it so much either.

CHAPTER THIRTY-TWO

ASHLIE

TREVOR

Last night in town. Quick dessert date after work?

ME

Yeah! What did you have in mind?

TREVOR

Ice cream on Layton's Pier? 6:00?

ME

😒Ice cream in March? Is this a snuggling ploy?

TREVOR

Maybe 😊

ME

That's right by my job. I'll meet you there.

TREVOR

Can't wait!

"Hey there, pretty lady." Trevor's smile lights up his face when he meets me in front of the permanent Melty King ice scream stand. The golden hour glow that illuminates the sky behind him adds to my growing affection.

"Hey!" I wave, turning away from the tiny blue and white structure. The familiar bear hug he wraps me in feels safe and warm as I breathe in the spicy citrus on his EdTechU polo. When we pull apart, his hand lingers on the small of my back. There's next to no one in line, so he guides me right to the register.

"Banana?" Trevor asks, skeptical eyes scrutinizing the pale-yellow dessert in my cup. "You gave me a hard time about bubblegum when you're over here eating banana ice cream?"

"Don't knock it 'til you try it!" I smile around another spoonful.

"Mmm"—he turns up his nose—"I think I'll just take your word for it." The breeze prompts us to gravitate for warmth as we walk down the pier. When our arms graze, I'm positive the goosebumps under my jacket aren't from the breeze.

"So how was work?" I ask.

He blows out a breath charged with the remnants of a long day. "Good. They're trying to get a new junior sales team off the ground here. Since they like what we're doing in San Francisco, I've stepped into a guest trainer role. Chase and I usually alternate, but I've been taking over so he can stay home and focus on wedding plans."

"That's really nice of you." I shouldn't be struck by the thoughtful actions of this guy. In my limited time spent with him, he's always shown kindness and initiative. It's refreshing, meeting someone who is exactly as they appear to be. Too many of the guys I've been with portray themselves as the knight in shining armor, only to reveal their tarnished tin a few months in. What you see is what you get with Trevor, and I'm liking what I see.

"Yeah. I mean, Chase is one of my besties, so it's no big deal."

"*Bestie*?" I laugh. "You're so hip, Trev..."

"Besties for the resties, or whatever the kids are saying."

"I'm confident no one is saying that except for you and

Chase." I bump him with my elbow, and laughter booms from his chest at my teasing.

He nods, digging his spoon into the blue ice cream for another bite. "Yeah, we've gotten pretty close..." At the end of the pier, he leans on the banister and takes a deep breath, staring out at the crashing waves below us. "Man, this makes me miss being on the water."

"Tell me about the Coast Guard. You said you entered at seventeen?"

"Yep. Graduated high school early, and the recruiter convinced me to give it a shot. I was active for four years, then went into reserves for another four. Always loved the water, so serving while helping people out of distressing situations was rewarding."

"Why'd you leave?"

He shrugs. "I just wanted a change, you know? Grew a lot over those eight years. Got my degrees. I realized I needed something different, started working for EdTechU shortly after leaving, and the rest is history."

"*Degrees?*" My eyes flash. "As in, multiple?"

"Yep." He nods with a sheepish grin. "They paid for it, so I took full advantage."

"Impressive. One was enough to last a lifetime for me."

"Kayla mentioned you used to teach..."

"Yeah. And burned out quickly. It wasn't the kids. I love working with kids. But everything else was just too much pressure for me. My job now is a much better fit. Leggings don't lecture you about test scores."

"You gotta do what makes you happy. I get that." He smiles with no judgment in his eyes, and my protective auto-response quickly dies in my throat. Defending my choice to leave the classroom is such a habit, I'm a little stunned I don't have to with him.

A shiver travels through me as the cool spring breeze blows off the Pacific. I set my ice cream cup on the ledge and reach for the zipper of my jacket. Trevor's warmth seeps into me as he wraps his arm around my waist, thawing the chill creeping up my back. Hugging into his side, I shoot him a smirk. "So, this *was* a snuggling ploy..."

Trevor laughs, but his smile falls slightly as he tucks a curl behind my ear. His hand settles into the crook of my neck, gently pulling me toward him. I lean in, and the coolness from his ice cream lingers on his lips as we kiss. Slow, gentle, and with just enough heat, it makes my head swirl with possibilities. He's breathless when we pull away, and I bite my lower lip, giving in to the warm-fuzzies blossoming inside me.

"I think I might have a new ice cream flavor," he whispers.

"Oh, really?" I giggle.

"Let me double-check." He leans back in, and just before his lips touch mine, the alarm on his phone rings out. "*Damn it.*" A wave of disappointment washes over me when he pulls away. He drops his head, digging in his pocket to silence the noise. "That's my flight reminder. I have to get to the airport."

"We have something to settle first." I guide his head back to me, moaning when our lips meet. His hands find my waist, and he gently tugs me against him, molding his body to mine. When his tongue darts past my lips for a taste, the warm-fuzzies burst into glittering sparks inside me. I clutch at the broad plane of his shoulders to get closer, my thoughts spinning into a blur. Where the first was just a simmer, this kiss sears into me. Passion intensifies with each caress and stifled sigh. *This is something I could get used to.* Pulling back breathlessly, I ask, "So, banana ice cream?"

He nods, eyes glued shut for a beat while he finds his words. With a smile, he whispers, "Banana ice cream tastes so damn good."

THE MCMAHON CENTER LIGHTS FLICKER OFF, BATHING my car in darkness as I wait for Willa to respond to my text. I've been driving here a few times a week for a month now, parking closer to the doors each time. I even threw swimming gear in my trunk last week, just in case my anxiety took a vacation. It's not much progress, but it's more than I've been able to do for years. *Now if I could just go inside.*

I channel my frustration into telling Willa off through text. She still hasn't answered about having another craft day. I'm running out of hobbies to try, and having her support would keep me from backing out at the first stray paint stroke. It's not my fault her hands were blue for a week after we tried knitting. How would I know indigo yarn bleeds all over the place? It was months ago; she should be over it by now.

I'm about to send my dramatic message when a banner floats across the screen.

> **HUNTER**
>
> Wanna go on another run?

Like hell. My legs still hurt from the last time. My foray into reading only lasted a couple of months, so I tagged along with Hunter on one of his runs. With the amount of time I've been spending with him, I haven't even thought about picking up a book. Running together felt like knocking out two birds with one stone. I used to do it all the time in college anyway, so I figured it could be the hobby I needed. But shin splints and side stitches reminded me how horrible it is, and I realized I only did it to keep in shape for swimming. Clearly, the more I try to avoid the pool, the more things point back to it. I glance at the darkened building, a dejected puff of air wheezing from my lips. *What the hell is wrong with me?*

> **ME**
>
> I'll pass.

HUNTER

LOL, ok. What are you up to tonight?

ME

Had a surprise date with Trev.

HUNTER

Ah... Where to?

ME

😳 Why are you in my business?

HUNTER

I'm just curious...

ME

We had ice cream on the pier, nosy.

CHAPTER THIRTY-THREE

HUNTER

That romantic asshole took her to the pier. It's chilly out, so I know he jumped at the opportunity to snuggle up to her. He'd be crazy not to. Competition is fine, but I really need to up my game. Candlelit dinners, movie nights, coffee dates—none of those top a stroll on the pier. I'm kicking myself for not thinking of it first.

ME

Beach tomorrow?

ASHLIE

It's March. It's freezing…

ME

LMAO, we're not going swimming.

ASHLIE

Then what are we doing?

ME

You'll see 😏

WE PULL UP TO THE BEACH A LITTLE BEFORE SUNSET. Ashlie still doesn't know what I've planned, and my body buzzes with anticipation. Having a surprise picnic while snuggled up on the sand should be enough to rival her date yesterday. Reaching for my hand, she starts toward the beach, eyebrows knitting from my abrupt halt at the trunk. She snorts behind me as soon as I pop open the back and pull out the picnic supplies.

Despite her shaking head, the smile on her face as she grabs the blankets conveys her amusement. She loops her arm around mine while we walk down the sandy path. "You're trying to top the pier," she says.

Small coastal sunflowers dot the trail around us, and I pause again, dropping the basket at my feet. I stoop to pick a flower and swipe my hand over her cheek, brushing back her curls to tuck it in her hair. Her sharp inhale makes me chuckle. "Is it working?" I smirk, already knowing it is. As much as she tries to hide it, she's eating this up.

"Jury's still out."

"Let me talk to that jury." I pull her into me and swipe a finger under her chin. But instead of the kiss she's expecting, I stare into her eyes. Those warm honey irises dance with mine, and I trail my thumb across her bottom lip, holding her there. Her face flushes, as if the heat in my gaze is tangible. She draws a shaky breath, the desire in her eyes morphing into longing. It's only then that I dive into those soft lips, and she melts like putty in my hands, exactly how I wanted.

I love that I know this about her. The ways to turn her on, weaken her knees. *Make her mine...hopefully...eventually.* She's still hesitant about us, but I get a little more reassurance during moments like this. I pull away, just to leave her craving for it. Her eyes remain shut as she swoons. "How about now?" I whisper, fully enjoying the view as I watch her regain her composure.

"G-guilty," she stammers breathlessly.

I chuckle at the flustered beauty in front of me, pick up the basket in one hand, and wrap my fingers around hers with the other. "Come on, your honor," I tease, leading her to the beach.

With one blanket spread underneath us and the other folded over Ashlie's lap, we casually graze the charcuterie style picnic. The flicker of flameless tea light candles dances rhythmically in front of us as the sun creeps across the sky. Gilded sunrays bathe the golden strands in her hair, illuminating her warm amber skin.

My jaw slackens, and I momentarily forget the sun, the waves, and the beach. I'm speechless, seeing her in this light. Enraptured. Captivated. Existence begins and ends with her, and my determination to win her over multiplies tenfold.

"I think that's one of my former students over there." Her voice breaks me out of my self-induced haze, my jaw snapping shut as I jump to attention. She nods at two elementary aged kids lobbing a football back and forth across the sand. Their parents lounge in the background. "Funny kid. He was missing his top front teeth and liked to tell the class he lost them in a bar fight."

"Do first graders even know what a bar is?"

"Oh, he made sure to tell them that too: a cafeteria where grown-ups go to get sad and throw up."

"Wise beyond his years." I chuckle. "When I have kids, I just know everything they say will be out of pocket." Ashlie's eyes bug out of her head like I admitted to kicking puppies for fun. "What?"

"You don't like kids," she says.

"That's not true."

"You complain about them all the time. I'm pretty sure you describe every child you see as bratty and annoying."

"That's other people's kids." I smirk, leaning back on my hands. "I'll like my own."

"That's not how that works. You don't suddenly like kids once you have them. You either like them or you don't."

"You wanna bet?"

She laughs, tapping her foot on my knee. "No more bets, Hunt. Your bets are outrageous."

"And yet, here we are...months deep in a bet *you* accepted."

She rolls her eyes and grabs a bottle of water. "You vex me."

"You like it." I grin back. "So how many kids should we have, then?" My brows dance as I wiggle them in her direction.

"*We?*" She crosses her arms over her chest, but the smile on her face gives her away. "Boy, who is we?"

"You. Me. Us. *We.*"

"God, could you imagine? *Us,* with kids together?"

"Just humor me. How many?"

Her face scrunches as if she's mulling over an algebra problem. "Four," she says, biting her thumbnail. "I want four kids."

My eyes widen before I can stop myself. Four kids are a lot of damn kids, even for someone who likes being around them. "Two," I counter back, shaking my head.

"Nope. Four. Or five. We could have our own mini swim team."

"*Five?*" A lump forms in my throat, my voice cracking as I lean forward, searching her eyes for the joke. Her face betrays nothing, and she shrugs at my incredulity. "Naw... That's economy van territory."

"Well, if it's an economy van, we can go up to seven or eight. Ten if we want to fill it up... And I wish you could see your face right now." Her head falls back as she lets out a loud cackle. "You look absolutely terrified! I don't want ten hypothetical children with you, Hunter."

I breathe out a sigh of relief. "Come here, you—" Wrapping my arms around her, I pull her to me. The cutest squeal erupts out of her, and with no effort, we're kissing like we were born to do it.

Ashlie lets the blanket fall between us as she kneels in front of me. Her fingertips graze my neck, and a shiver courses through me at a dizzying rate. A sexy giggle. Her smile pressed to my lips. I could live a thousand lives and never come close to this feeling. She kisses me like the falling sun kisses the horizon—slowly and full of anticipation. I kiss her back like the sun rises and sets on her. Like I'll never kiss another woman in this lifetime or the next. I kiss her like she's mine.

"Three," I whisper, pulling away just enough to nuzzle her nose.

Biting her lip, she shakes her head. "Two. Only two."

"You took me through that rollercoaster of emotion just to end back at two?"

"Hey, now," she says with a sassy tilt to her head. "You showed more emotion in that fake scenario than I've ever seen from you. I wanted to see how many I could introduce you to."

"What do you mean? I have feelings, Ash…"

"Yeah, maybe. Locked up in the abyss that is Hunter Jackson. You show two emotions—annoyance and anger—*sometimes*. But talking about them? Not you." She waves her hand in the air, batting away the notion as if it were a mosquito. Sitting back on her heels, she swipes a grape from the box beside her.

I don't have a response. What could I even say? Talking about feelings has always seemed like a waste of time. Hearing others talk about theirs makes me want to crawl out of my skin. Her assessment is spot on, and yet, it bothers me how she says it with such surety. As if emotional detachment is encoded into my DNA. Like she doesn't believe I can change.

"I feel happy when I'm with you…" I say quietly, my voice cracking as I slide my eyes to hers. It sounds supremely juvenile. I'm no good at this, but it's important to me she hears it. Her hand hangs in the air with a cube of cheese halfway to her gaping mouth. "And I'm excited whenever I hear your voice."

A cool breeze blows over us, but I doubt the shiver that travels through her body is from the wind. Still, I reach for the blanket and position it around her shoulders. "I feel a lot of things, and you've helped me see that it's okay to show it sometimes."

"I—oh..."

"Ash, this bet isn't for me. I already know what I want at the end of this, but I know you need time. So come over here, watch this sunset with me, and take all the time you need."

Ashlie continues to stare, cheese in hand and lips slightly parted. I think she's going to say something, but she shakes her head instead and tosses the cheese back in the box. She pulls the blanket off her shoulders and wraps it around mine, then settles in between my legs, gazing toward the horizon.

"You're full of surprises, Hunt," she whispers, leaning against my chest. Her hair tickles my cheek as I rest my chin in the crook of her neck, encircling her in my blanket-wrapped arms. "Thank you for giving me time."

I would stay in this jasmine infused love cocoon forever if she'd let me. I'll give her all the time in the world.

WHEN THE BREEZE BLOWS SO COLD OUR TEETH chatter, we drive back to her place. I walk Ashlie to her front door and lean in for one last goodnight kiss.

"Do you want to come in?" she asks, biting her lip.

"*Hell yeah*, I want to." I chuckle, tipping my forehead against hers. "But I shouldn't."

She trails a seductive finger down my chest, giving me a look that goes straight to my dick. "What if I want you to?" Her hand traipses lower, and she giggles when I press into her with an undeniable bulge. One firm graze of her hand, and I fucking moan like I've never been touched before. *God, this woman.*

I grip her waist and tug her closer. "You're trouble."

"So, punish me..."

Pinning her against the door, my kiss swallows her gasp. I pour out every ounce of lust and longing coursing through me, my mind and body screaming at me to take her up on her offer. She sighs and clutches my hips, conveying her desire for me to stay with each caress of her tongue. Thoroughly satisfied with the effect I've had, I pull away slowly. "The things I want to do to you are off the table until I don't have to share you," I whisper. "You'll be mine, sooner or later."

"There's that ego," she teases. "I was wondering when your cocky side would show back up."

"I think *confident* is the word you're looking for."

"Naw, I'd definitely say it's cocky..."

"I'd show you *cocky*"—I cant my hips, wiggling my eyebrows playfully—"but that's off the table right now too."

"Boy, quit!" She laughs, swatting my shoulder. "I'm going inside now." When she turns, I whip her back around, stealing another kiss. The soft moan she sighs makes me want to live in this moment forever.

"I'll see you Wednesday?" I ask, keeping my arms around her.

She nods, teeth sinking into her lower lip as redness flushes her rounded cheeks.

Fuck, I don't want this night to end. I'm tempted to march her straight to the bedroom and convince her to call off this painfully chaste bet. But she's still worried about my dedication to this, to her. Scared even. She won't admit it, but I can see it in her eyes when she thinks she's hiding it. And after dates like tonight, I feel so close to winning her over that I don't want to do anything to ruin it. The lengths I'm willing to go just for a chance with this woman are growing longer by the minute. So I say goodnight, wait for the lock to click in place, and take a deep breath as I walk away from her door.

CHAPTER THIRTY-FOUR

HUNTER

"Your place or mine?" I ask, pulling out of the drive-through. We're trying a new café for our Saturday coffee dates since Cosmic Brews is dead to me now. The best brown sugar espresso I've ever had isn't worth baristas upsetting the woman of my dreams.

"Yours." A mischievous glint in her eyes adds a charge behind the word, and my head spins.

Mine.

Hell fucking yes, please. I know she's into me. She wouldn't have agreed to any of this if she wasn't. The way she keeps coming back for more, it's easy to believe she'll actually give us a chance after the wedding. Trevor's still an issue, but since we don't talk about that aspect of her dating life, I have no idea how it's going. My choice. I don't want the details; I'd rather pretend he isn't a factor.

Ashlie's hand inches up my thigh as we drive back to my apartment. I barely have time to close the front door and set down our drinks before she drags me to my leather sofa. She falls to the cushion, pulling me on top of her and pinning me with a leg wrapped around my waist. Our lips feverishly work in tandem, the swirl of her tongue sending us both into hyperdrive as it darts around the tip of mine. She tastes like pumpkin spiced passion, and I can't get enough. The sound that slips out of me when she rolls her hips is salacious. I'm fucking drowning, and she's the torrent filling my lungs.

I desperately want to rip everything off her, manhandle her all the way to the bedroom, and burn this down in a blaze of glory. Putting myself on ice is a task, but any kind of sex would make our arrangement that much more complicated. Getting this right is important to me. She's worth the wait. I can power through for two more months.

She traps my lower lip between her teeth and giggles when I moan into the nonexistent space between us. I'm gonna nut in my pants if we don't stop.

"Ash." I pull away breathlessly. "We need... Let's take a breather."

"I don't want a breather." She teases my lips with hers, lying back with an irresistible gaze. "*I want you.*"

"*Fuck*," I whisper, dropping my head to kiss her neck. "This was *not* the deal, honey bear..."

"We made up the deal. We can change the conditions." Reaching a hand under my shirt, she trails her fingertips down my side.

My brain threatens to go offline. She's saying she wants this right now, and I damn sure want it too. But it was only a couple of weeks ago when she tried to pick a fight over some baristas. Giving in when things are trending upward won't work out in my favor. I went years controlling this instinct to run my hands all over her. I can go two more months...unless she keeps looking at me like that.

Pulling her hand from my shirt, I drop a kiss on her forehead and sit up. She props herself on her elbows and pins me with the sexiest stare.

"Stop looking at me like that." I chuckle, shaking my head. "I know what you're doing..."

"You *like* what I'm doing." She nods to my dick, which does nothing to deflate the need growing in my pants.

Tearing my eyes away, I head to the kitchen. "Yeah, and you're trouble. I need water."

"A cold shower?" Her giggle sends my eyes right back to the sinful way she's biting her lip.

"You're not seeing me naked today, Ash." I set my phone on the wireless charger on my island and open the fridge, sensing her gaze the entire time until I get back to the couch with two water bottles. But I look everywhere else. If she still has that seduction all over her face, I won't last a second before giving in. Just to mess with her, I place one of the frigid bottles on her exposed waist, laughing when she squeals and flinches away.

"*Ugh*, you're no fun." She drops her head onto the cushion. As much as we need to cool it, I pull her feet into my lap. The compulsion to feel her skin on mine, in any capacity, is constant.

"We both know that's not true." I tip the cold water to my mouth, and it strings a few threads of common sense back into my brain. After another sip, I'm around 85 percent sure I won't regret pumping the brakes.

She pops back up on her elbows, giving it one more try with her eyes.

"*Stop* looking at me like that. It's not gonna work."

"*Ugh*, fine!" She sits and pecks a kiss on my cheek. Hopping off the couch, she rummages through the fridge for a snack. I won this time, but I don't know how much longer I can touch her without being able to *touch* her.

My phone chimes with a text. Chase was supposed to send me color details for my wedding tux. "Can you check that for me, honey bear?"

Ashlie picks up my phone, the serenity on her face falling into fury. Her body stiffens. I don't even know that she's breathing.

"You good?" I ask. "Is it Chase?"

"*Hey there, handsome. It was nice seeing you yesterday.*" She reads from my phone slowly. "What the hell is this, Hunter? You're still talking to Ava?"

"What—no! We ran into each other at the gym yesterday." Ashlie's eyes flick to mine with the same expression from the fight over baristas. *Nope, worse.* She's pissed, and I'm confused as hell.

"Ran into each other, or *met up* with each other?" Her voice is eerily calm, but that ire in her eyes intensifies with each word.

"Are you being serious right now? I haven't talked to her in forever. Scroll up and check for yourself." Her thumb swipes several times, eyes steadily growing wider. *Shit.*

"She's *still* sexting you?" My phone dings in her hand, and instant rage heats her face. "With video, apparently..." Her irritated sigh fills the room as she tilts her head to the ceiling. "Look, I know this sounds hypocritical with the whole Trevor thing, but you told me you were done with her, Hunt!"

"I am! Ash, I swear to you, I haven't been talking to her. You just saw the messages. When was the last time I replied to her?"

"Oooh, so she's just sprinkling your inbox with nudes for fun, huh? With no response from you? Why would she do that?

"Fuck if I know." I throw my hands in the air and lace them over the top of my head.

"Why is she even saved in your phone?"

I shrug. "Everyone's saved in my phone. I don't bother deleting contacts."

Her nostrils flare. "So you have every woman's number saved that you've been with?"

"Probably. Go ahead and look."

She swipes around, snorting angrily with each glide of her thumb. I clearly shouldn't have suggested that. *Fuck.*

"I—" Dropping the phone, she steps back from the counter, holding out her hands like she's conjuring a force field between herself and my list of contacts. With her head steadily shaking, she huffs loudly. "God, I'm so stupid for agreeing to do this with you."

"You're acting like I use their numbers!" I yell, standing from the couch. But I stay across the room from her. This conversation is going nowhere fast. Being near her won't help a goddamn thing right now.

"Then why are they *still* in your fucking phone, Hunter? Why do you have your entire roster on speed dial?"

"Speed dial?" I chuckle at the absurdity, which is another wrong move that makes anger flare over her features. "You sound ridiculous, Ashlie. You're telling me you don't have any exes saved in your phone?"

"No. I don't feel the need to keep them around for a rainy day."

"What about emails?" I regret it as soon as I say it. The hurt that flashes across her face solidifies the punch to my gut. *I'm a fucking asshole.* That breakup email is still a sore spot for her, but frustration took over and I impulsively met her intensity with something to knock it out of the park. The lowest kind of blow.

"I can't even look at you right now..." she says bitterly, dropping her eyes to the countertop. A vice grip squeezes in my chest. My thoughts twist together as I try to even out my breath, but the pit growing in my stomach as she looks everywhere except at me makes me panic. *I need to get out of here. Fast.* Walking to the counter, I snatch up my phone and grab my keys by the door.

"Where are you going?" she snaps as I reach for the doorknob.

"I need air!" I yell, slamming the door closed. Everything inside screams to turn back around, but then I remember that look in her eyes. The one that shouted all her regrets about this. About *me.* My feet propel me out of the lobby and right into my car. It doesn't fully register that I left my own goddamn apartment until I'm on the road. *I just fucked everything up.*

I DRIVE AIMLESSLY, HOPING THE HEAVY BASS RATTLING my speakers will drown out the dark thoughts infiltrating my mind. It doesn't, and I'm surprised when I finally park in front of Dad's house. Trudging into the kitchen, I slump over the island. Despite everything that's happened here, it's still home. Still comforting. The lack of new messages when I slide my phone from my pocket makes me drop my head in despair. Why would she reach out to me when I'm the one who caused this mess? *Fucking idiot.* I roll my head around on the cool marble surface to unscramble the chaos twisting my insides.

"You alright there, son?" Dad says from the entryway.

"Fantastic," I mumble, not bothering to lift my head.

"No Ashlie?" His deep voice has a knowing inflection, and I pop my head up.

"Why are you asking me that?"

"Because you're here in my kitchen on a Saturday instead of with your girlfriend."

"She's not my girlfriend..."

He chuckles. "You two still playin' that game, huh? What happened?"

I sigh and get into it—the bet, Ava's messages, my contact list, the dig about Marcus's email. Dad stands opposite me, nodding and listening with a neutral expression. He doesn't interject, doesn't try to change my mind. He welcomes my messy word vomit, just like he did when I was younger. With burning eyes, my face hot from adrenaline, the dam breaks. My shoulders shake, and I'm tearing up so much, I can't see him anymore. "She's being unreasonable," I say, trying to convince myself I'm not wrong about this and failing miserably.

"You dealt with a lot after the divorce," Dad says. *The fuck?* What does that have to do with anything? "There were also some things you didn't see." He props his elbows on the counter and leans in. "Your mom may have left the house, but I abandoned her long before she ever left me, son. There were things she needed, things I neglected under the guise of being too busy with work.

Small requests that I thought were inconsequential. That I *ignored*. I convinced myself she was being unreasonable, but if I would have taken the time to listen, they wouldn't have turned into big things." He gestures to my phone with an arched brow. "You're a lot like me in that way, using distractions to hide from the tough stuff... But you're also like your mom."

"Like hell," I spit back as red seeps into my vision.

"I'm not saying you *are* her, but you leave like she does. I passed down my distractedness, and she passed down her avoidance. You run, Hunter. When things get uncomfortable, you get away as fast as you can. Hide behind your anger so no one can touch you. You leave first, so no one has the chance to leave you."

His words drench me in the kind of frigid reality that silences everything else. I have no rebuttal. How do you argue with the truth? Dad has a way of making things click, and right now, everything out of his mouth is making a hell of a lot of sense. I do run. Dipping before things get serious has been my entire MO since high school. I've never let anyone close enough to make me stay and fight. *Until now.*

"Son, you didn't ask for advice, so I'm not going to tell you what to do. You have to make your own choice with all of this. What I will say is, I see a change in you when Ashlie's around. If something is bothering her so much that she tells you about it, it's worth considering her side."

"And if I asked you for advice, what would you say?"

"Let go of all those trophies in your phone. Show Ashlie you care enough about her to move on from your past, like you told her you would when you presented your bet." He reaches over and claps my shoulder. "And go home. You're not fixing anything by sitting here in my kitchen." Chuckling to himself, he grabs a drink from the fridge and heads upstairs.

I leave. I avoid. All things I've known about myself for years, but sometimes, tough love is the only way to knock some sense into my hardheaded ass. Now that it has, my sole focus is making this right.

It's been hours since our fight, but since Ashlie drove to my place this morning, I doubt she stuck around after I stormed out. Fixing this on her territory might be for the best anyway, so that's where I go. But when I get to her apartment, her assigned parking spot is empty.

ME

Where are you?

ASHLIE

...

ME

Ash, please...

Nothing. And those damn bouncing dots are worse than her yelling at me. They're the clear sign that she's so furious she can't decide which words to tell me off with. I try again, calling her this time, but it goes straight to voicemail. *Damn it, she turned off her phone.* My head falls against my seat with a sigh. *Why would she come back to the first place you'd look? She's avoiding you, dummy.* But she has to come home eventually. I'll wait as long as it takes.

Settling into my seat, phone in hand, I do the only thing I can think of. It takes almost an hour, but by the time I'm finished, I feel a little lighter. With no answer from Ashlie, I decide to cut my losses and go back home. I'll come up with a game plan tonight, and hopefully, after a full night's sleep, she'll be ready to talk.

CHAPTER THIRTY-FIVE

ASHLIE

Three hours and twelve minutes since Hunter walked out, and I'm still lying on his couch, waiting for him to come back. Not my smartest move. My phone died in the middle of replying to his text an hour ago, but he's still not here. His chargers are all wireless, for his new StarCell model, so I'm just here with a dead phone and self-loathing.

The herringbone throw blanket cuddled around me smells like him, which only reinforces how stupid I am. I'm still seething over what happened today. Kicking myself for agreeing to this bet. Berating my decision to stay. Angry that I blew it all out of proportion. But my bleeding heart can't leave knowing he has abandonment issues, even though he's the one who walked out.

Just when I start to believe he's turned a new leaf, something reminds me he hasn't. He's always been avoidant, always been a player. I shouldn't be surprised, but it doesn't make it hurt any less that he didn't hesitate before walking out the door. No regard for the friendship we had before all of this. Not even a courtesy glance over his shoulder. *That* is what kills me.

I believe him about the Ava thing—the one-sided messages made that clear. In hindsight, I probably should have said that at the time. Hell, I'm dating someone else too, so my response was an overreaction. But in the moment, I couldn't get past seeing all those names in his phone. Why keep them if he had no plans to use them? Yeah, okay, this is all just a silly bet, but he's the one who set exclusivity for himself in the first place. Why string me along? *Have the rose-colored glasses I've been wearing for months obscured so much that I'm still only seeing what I want to see?* Guys like Hunter are my vice. I know how this plays out. *Why the hell am I still here?*

Just as I make up my mind to save my dignity and leave, the front door creeps open. I watch silently as Hunter hangs up his keys on the wall hook, unaware of my presence. The slump in his shoulders, the shadow over his face, his labored sigh—he looks as tired as I feel, and petty satisfaction simmers inside me.

His eyes sweep the room, and he freezes. "You're here... Y-you didn't leave."

"I wouldn't just leave." The bite in my voice is only enhanced by the tear-induced scratchiness in my throat.

"...That's fair." He drags a hand down his face, not daring to take a step away from the front door. "I didn't think... I mean, I assumed you'd—"

"Will you sit down so we can figure this shit out?" The blanket falls to my waist as I turn to face him. He nods, the leather squeaking as he quietly perches on the opposite end of the couch, keeping a cushion between us. Hugging my legs, I rest my chin on my knees, utterly exhausted. *Maybe we should end this now...* "What the hell are we doing here, Hunt? What's the point of—"

"I need to show you something." That fucking phone is still in his hand. He swipes the screen a few times and holds it out to me, but I've seen enough on that thing to last a lifetime.

I turn up my nose. "I'm good."

"Please?"

My reluctance fades when he pins me with a pleading gaze, and I drop my eyes to the screen as I accept his phone. *Aiden From Work, Artemis, Ashlie, Chase.* No Ava. My mouth drops. Hours ago, this was a personalized hook-up directory. I had to scroll several times just to get to the letter *F*. But now, I hit the bottom of the list in six swipes. Going back to the top, I read the names again. All the women from years past are gone. Silently, he taps to his blocked list where Ava is front and center. After one last swipe, her messages are permanently deleted.

"I don't even know why I kept them all, but they're gone now... I'm sorry." The tremble in his whisper grips me as unease shadows his face. He's beating himself up over this, and I can't stand it. I press a hand to his cheek, and his breath shudders as he leans in to my touch, red-rimmed eyes falling shut. "You didn't leave..."

"I wouldn't do that to you. I wouldn't just leave." Bracketing his head in my hands, I wait until his eyes find mine. The green is surrounded by fear, streaked with sadness, and tinged with fatigue. "I'm sorry I overreacted. I made it so much bigger than it needed to be...and I believe you about Ava." He nods, and I shift to my knees, kissing him lightly before sitting back. "You can't just walk out when we're fighting, though. This whole arrangement was your idea."

"I know..." He sighs, wringing his hands nervously. "Watching my mom walk out on my dad, seeing what it did to him, it convinced me I never wanted to go through that. I turned into someone who always leaves." His forehead drops to mine as his hands find my waist. "I don't want to be that person with you, Ashlie. For the first time in my life, leaving feels like a mistake, and I think that means something."

Oh shit. My heart fills my throat as all the air is pulled from my lungs. *This isn't a game to him?*

Dating two men was supposed to keep me from diving in too quickly, a safeguard for my heart. I'd convinced myself this was all just a fun arrangement. That he'd fail, and life would go back to normal after the wedding. But nothing about tonight has felt fun. It's been raw and emotional. *Real.*

"I can't guarantee I won't mess up, but if you give me another chance, I'll never walk out on you again. I'll fight that fear and do whatever it takes to be the man who deserves you."

My stomach drops as his sincerity barrels through me. His promise, the vulnerable timbre of his voice, that look in his eyes—it all scares the hell out of me. But uncovering the source of that anxiety feels tenuous right now. My head spins at the thought of processing any of this tonight, my pulse picking up speed.

Just when my breath stutters, his lips brush mine, and everything stills. There's a vague awareness that I should stop him—figure out where my head is—but calm washes over me as if the antidote to my panic lies in his kiss. I welcome the distraction and latch onto him, greeting his tongue in a languorous waltz. "Please tell me I didn't ruin this..." he whispers between panted breaths.

"You didn't," I mumble around his lips, tugging him closer. We fall against the couch, and nothing makes sense besides the warmth of his kiss lulling me into serenity. The musk in his cologne. His arms holding me. I'll work out my own mess some other time. Tonight, I just want him.

CHAPTER THIRTY-SIX

ASHLIE

"And he kissed my hand!" Hannah squeals, recapping her date with the musclehead. "I blushed so hard, I—"

The door chimes, and my head whips to the front of the store. I abandon the mess of hangers in the box at my feet as Hunter strolls into Fit4U, his smile spreading as soon as he sees me.

"Hey, *Hunter*." Olivia's voice is an octave higher than usual. The flirty tone makes me bristle.

She fits the mold of who Hunter would have gone for before our bet—tall, long hair, slender build. Opposite of me in every way. *What if he's back to old habits?*

I'm still conflicted about our fight last week. On one hand, I'm continually falling as I get to know the sensitive and vulnerable sides of Hunter. On the other, half of me still expects him to make a flirty pit stop at the folding table for old time's sake.

Oh.

He doesn't.

"Hey." Hunter nods hello but keeps his pace as he walks straight to me. "You ready?" he asks, tapping his fingers on the clothing rack between us.

"Yeah, just let me grab my bag." I walk toward the break room and glance back at him as I turn the corner, catching him staring at my ass. His eyes flick to mine, and he smirks before I disappear into the room.

It's not until we're at the end of the street that he grabs me by the hand and tugs me to him. This dating trial has been going on for a few months now, and just like with our friends, I've set a hard line with my coworkers finding out. *Don't want to look stupid if he slips up again.*

"Hey, honey bear," he murmurs as he pulls me into a lingering hug.

"Boy, don't 'hey' me. You were checking me out."

"Is that a problem?"

"Hell yeah, when I'm at work."

"Alright, noted." He gestures for me to walk ahead. "After you…"

I make it a few steps before I realize I'm walking alone. When I turn back, he's got that same look on his face as he stares at my retreating form. "Hunter!"

"What?" He chuckles as he strides toward me. "You're not at work anymore. I gotta get it in while I can…"

"*Ugh*, annoying." I roll my eyes, trying to stifle my smile.

"Yeah." He kisses my forehead and weaves our fingers. "I know."

We catch up on our workdays while walking the last few blocks to lunch. When we get to the doors of Lunch-a-Bunch, I glance at him, and his eyes are already on me. As much as I try to hide it, I'm obsessed with the way he looks at me. His gaze screams *desire*. Paired with his committed restraint, it makes for one sexy combo. He *wants* me, but he also wants *me*. Considering his past, that's a powerful feeling to hold.

Willa's at a booth inside, sipping on ice water. She stares at the cloudy April sky through the picture window. To keep from blowing our cover, I dropped Hunter's hand outside the restaurant before he opened the door. I slide in next to her, and Hunter sits across from us. His heated glances while we eat feel obvious as hell, but Willa says nothing. I'm so on edge when it's time to coordinate our schedules, I swear I've lived a hundred lives in the last hour.

"Okay. Our flight leaves for San Francisco on Friday night. We'll do the bachelorette party at a bar called Chickies on Saturday, and then home Sunday morning." I list our weekend itinerary while Willa plugs it into her phone.

"You said Chickies?" Hunter's eyebrows tick up. He pulls out his phone and scrolls quickly. "We're at Chickies..."

"They can't have their parties at the same place. That defeats the whole purpose." I huff. We should have had this all figured out by now, but it's safe to say I've been a little preoccupied lately.

"Does it? Isn't the purpose to unwind one last time before they lock each other down?" Hunter's skeptical look fuels my irritation.

"Yeah, but not together. It's a last hurrah to being single," Willa explains.

"They haven't been single in five years. They'll be riding home together afterward. We can just keep them across the bar from each other..."

"Uh, *no*..." My head falls into a frustrated tilt. "Have you met Chase? If they're in the same room, he's going to be next to her. Do you really want to watch their PDA all night?"

"Good point," he says.

"Besides, we already reserved a party room. You guys gotta move somewhere else."

"Can't you ladies stay in there while we stay on the bar floor? Problem solved."

Crossing my arms, I stare at him, an annoyed heat creeping into my chest. We've already made our plan. Kayla will flip if we change it now. "Oh, just lock us in a room, huh? How will that be fun?"

His jaw clenches as he stares back, and I think he's going to volley with his usual snark. *Typical Hunter.*

He doesn't.

Biting the inside of his lip, he looks at his phone with a sigh.

"I'll be back." He leaves the booth and walks outside. The cloudy springtime sky sets a moody backdrop for the scowl on his face as he paces the sidewalk, phone to his ear.

"Lover's quarrel?" Willa bumps me with her elbow, and I whip my head to her. I haven't told her anything about the last few months with Hunter. I haven't told anyone.

"What are you talking about, Wills?"

"Oh please. I saw you two holding hands as you walked up to the restaurant, and I'm pretty sure you've been rubbing ankles under the table this entire time. Not to mention the way he keeps looking at you. So are you two a thing now?"

Damn it. We've walked to lunch hand in hand so often lately; I didn't even think about Willa being able to see us.

"Look, you can't tell anyone. And no, we're not a *thing*. We're dating."

"How is that different?"

"I'm dating him *and* Trevor...casually."

"How the fuck is any of this casual, when you're in love with Hunt—"

"Can you *not* say that out loud! Damn." I glance around, making sure these perfect strangers didn't hear anything. "Look, I'm just seeing how it goes, okay? Plain and simple." She gives me a dubious look. We both know there's nothing simple about this, but I'm sticking to what I said.

"That shit sounds messy, Ash. I don't like it."

"*You* don't have to."

Maybe it is messy. It could all blow up in our faces at any minute. But it's also the most at ease I've felt in years. With Trevor, I've found the gentle, assertive affection I've been looking for. Kayla was right about him; he's an amazing man. And at the same time, I feel like myself when I'm around Hunter. There's no need for me to put on an act with him. He accepts me as I am: annoying moods and all. I like being with them both. *Shit, that's chaotic as hell.*

"It was all Hunter's idea. He's trying to convince me he's

serious with a bet. I'm not convinced yet." I shrug despite his words from last week echoing in my mind.

"That's bullshit, girl, and you know it."

"How would you know?" I snap, the sudden need to defend myself sparking in my chest.

"Have you seen Hunter back down from an argument? About anything? Ever?" she asks. Pursing my lips, I wait for her to finish. "With the force that man used to bite his tongue just now, all so you could get your way, I'd be surprised if he didn't leave marks. I won't say anything about your bullshit bet, but that man is serious about you."

"I just...don't know if I believe it yet." How easily that lie slipped out of my mouth causes me to shake my head. He's absolutely serious. There was a shift in him after our fight, one I've been trying to write off ever since.

"At this point, you're choosing to ignore it. Someone's going to get hurt."

Doubts surrounding this bet weave in and out of my mind, all trying to build a case for the men hanging in the balance. There are so many conflicting truths. Hunter's clearly trying, but will he give up as soon as he wins? Despite everything he said last week, what happens the next time we fight? When the novelty wears off?

Even with the distance, Trevor's clearly the sensible choice here. He's kind, consistent and open—everything I've been looking for. But we're still at the impressions stage. Will he accept me when he gets a peek at my anxiety?

I sigh as Hunter walks back to the door. It's not the time or place to be hashing this out with her. "Anyway, we're taking it slow. And I'm still seeing Trevor."

"You're playing dumb is what you're doing. But okay, have your little messy love triangle." Willa shakes her head, and I can almost taste the disagreement oozing out of her.

"Okay"—Hunter sighs—"we'll be across the street at a sports bar called Ripley's. It's far enough away that they can 'act single,' but close enough that we can throw them in a car together at the end of the night. Happy?"

"Yep." I send over the cheesiest grin I can muster, and he shakes his head, biting that same spot on the inside of his lip. This time, the silence is earsplitting. We argue all the time about the dumbest stuff, and he usually meets all my sass with snark of his own. Lately though, our arguments are short-lived, stifled with a change in subject or an abrupt kiss from him. And yeah, I notice his disinterest in other women when we're together. His effort is promising, but trusting he'll continue to do so is a big leap for me. One that worries me more than I'd like to admit. I'm not ready to believe it. Not yet.

When Hunter walks me back to work, he stops me just short of the Fit4U building. "You ever thought about being a swim coach?" he asks.

"Uh, what?" *How does he know about that?*

"I was just thinking about our conversation on the beach a few weeks ago..."

"I'm lost, Hunt."

"You know. The kids and making a swim team... Anyway, you like working with kids, and you like swimming. Why not combine them?"

Because getting back in a pool freaks me the hell out.

Nobody knows about this dream of mine. I can't even find the courage to say it out loud to myself. How did he pick up on it? "Maybe I'll look into it."

"Just an idea, since you're running out of hobbies," he teases. Wrapping me in his arms, he leans in for a kiss. I'm shocked he remembered the tiniest detail from a joke I made weeks ago. Still stunned when he walks to his car, and just a bit dazed as he waves from his window. He listened. He remembered. He heard me. *What about that is freaking me out?*

CHAPTER THIRTY-SEVEN

ASHLIE

"Girl, we're only going for the weekend. Do you really need that big ass suitcase?" Willa cocks her head to the side as my struggle-grunts fill the room. The stuck zipper made it perfectly clear I packed too much, but I'm not giving her the satisfaction of being right.

"Look, you never know." I collapse on my bag as the last couple inches finally zips. Blowing a stray curl from my forehead, I stand with hands on my hips, breathing heavily. "I could spill wine on myself on the plane, or trip again and break my shoe."

An unamused snort leaves her nose as she leans against the door frame. "Why are you always creating problems in your head?"

"You call it *creating problems*; I call it *preparing for the worst*."

"Shit's exhausting, Ash. No wonder you're always so stressed..." she says. Exasperated, I shoot her a glare, and she throws her hands up in a truce. "Okay, okay..."

I slide past her and head for the bathroom. Hunter should be outside any minute so we can catch our flight to San Francisco. I'm running behind, as usual. "Did you need an extra toothbrush or anything?"

"Nope. Some of us don't wait until thirty minutes before the trip to pack."

"Sounds fake," I murmur, digging through my medicine cabinet for deodorant. My phone goes off in my back pocket. A smile tugs at my lips as I dig it out, preparing for a snarky message from Hunter about my always being late. But it's Trevor, telling me how excited he is to see me.

"So, how's Trevor?" Willa asks from the door, snapping my attention from the disappointment rifling through my chest.

"How did you know it was Trevor?"

"You do this thing with your face whenever you get messages from him. Kind of like an upside-down smile. What's the word for that again?" she teases.

I scoff as I grab toothpaste from the drawer. "No, I don't." I was only expecting it to be Hunter because he'll be here soon. The message from Trevor was fine. Sweet, even. My phone buzzes, and I feel Willa's eyes on me as I tap the screen.

"You did it again," she says with an annoying smirk. "Do you even like him?"

"Of course. What kind of question is that?" Trevor's great. Caring and attentive, the opposite of what I'm used to. *He's who I should want.* I try to focus on finding my toothbrush cover, but her know-it-all "mm-hmm" sends my eyes back to her. "Why don't you just say it, Wills?"

"You're using Trevor and this bet to avoid your feelings for Hunter..."

Using Trevor? No. Well...I don't *think* so. How I feel about him has nothing to do with Hunter. And the bet wasn't even my idea, so I can't possibly be using that as a crutch. Just because I'm still a little worried Hunter will revert to his old ways doesn't mean I'm evading my feelings for him. I'm just being cautious. Protecting my heart.

"Oh, so dating Hunter is the same as avoiding feelings for him? Got it," I quip sarcastically, breezing past her to get to my bedroom.

She follows me and flops onto my bed. "You *know* that's not what I'm saying."

I toss my toiletries into my carry-on tote before facing her. "Look, I like both of them and—"

"Mmm, nope, let's fix that. You like one of them. You *love* the other."

With a sigh, I prop my tote on my suitcase and sit next to her. "Why are you making this such a big deal?"

"Because it *is* a big deal, girl. For you, especially. When was the last time you were in love?"

"Marc—"

"Not that shallow, codependent shit you hide behind. *Actual* love."

My skin prickles from her blunt veracity. She's the relentless lens magnifying my shadows, and I'm just the puny ant running for cover. She cocks her head, and I know she already knows the answer. *Bryan.* "I don't talk about him."

"I don't blame you." She gives a playful grimace, and we both giggle. "Now, when was the last time someone was so crazy about you, they'd do anything just to see you smile?"

"Trevor..."

She rolls her eyes. "Okay, fine, I'll give you that one. Let me rephrase... When was the last time you were loved?"

"Wills, we don't have time for this..."

"Humor me."

"I just told you I don't talk about—"

Willa holds up a finger. "Bryan and his weird obsession with you don't count. That wasn't love. I'm talking about the last time you were with someone who really knew you. Someone who accepted you as you are, despite"—she waves a hand over me with a teasing smirk—"all of this."

"Hey!" I push her shoulder, stifling my smile as she laughs. "You know, for a sister, you're really mean to me."

"You call it *mean*; I call it *honesty*. Now answer the question."

I shrug. None of my boyfriends cared enough. "Never, I guess."

"Until now." She leans back against the headboard, eyebrows raised like she just proved a point. "You have someone who meets the criteria *right now.*"

"Umm, yeah, I guess Trevor's—"

"*Ash!*" She smacks my arm with the back of her hand.

"*Ow!* What the *hell*?" I rub the sting away with a sneer.

"You know damn well I'm not talking about that man. What's with your Hunter-shaped blind spot? You're so dedicated to avoiding your feelings for him, you didn't even consider he's the one?"

The one?

Snorting a laugh, I reach for my bonnet and stand from the bed. *How can I have a blind spot for someone I'm actively seeing?* I have doubts. That's it. "I'm not avoiding anything. I literally just said I like—"

"*Love.*"

"Stop that!" My hand slams to my hip as I whip around. She keeps bringing up that little fun fact, like it's some kind of "gotcha." It's annoying.

"Why?" She laughs. "You've already told me you love him."

"*Exactly*"—I angrily stuff my bonnet in my carry-on—"I've already admitted it. What's the point in saying it again?"

"*It?*"

"The thing..."

The smirk on her face only grows. "*Thiiing?*"

"*Ugh*, the *L* word thing!"

"You can't say the word, can you?" Her cackle bounces off the walls, and all I can do is glower. She's right. I can hardly say it to myself, let alone out loud. "Point proven."

"Stop looking at me like that."

"No." If smug had a spokesperson, it would be her close-lipped smile. "Every time I bring up how you feel about Hunter, you change the subject. Are you scared?"

"Of Hunter? No." Okay, *maybe*. But it's confusing, and I don't want to think about it. Denial is safer. "Why would I be scared of him? He's my best friend."

"Your semantics game is getting old, Ash. I know you're not scared *of* him." She raises her eyebrows condescendingly. "You know what I think?"

"I'm sure you're about to tell me..." I murmur as I reach for my phone charger.

"Hunter makes you feel the way you've always wanted. That carefully crafted front you show everyone else doesn't exist around him. He knows you in all the ways you won't allow anyone else to, and that scares you."

Her words stop me in my tracks, threatening the thing inside of me that feels too daunting to acknowledge. She doesn't quite get to the source of my fear, but it's close enough that panic flashes across my face before I can control it. Based on the sympathetic expression on hers, she saw it too.

Shaking my head, I bury the little seeds of doubt she's been sprinkling in front of me. I don't even know why she planted all of this in my head, knowing how much I overthink. She's already made it clear she doesn't agree with my dating life right now. This is probably her way of looking out for me. "Whatever, Wills," I say, pushing my suitcase toward the door. "Hunter should be outside soon."

"Yeah...whatever." She follows me to the living room, her disapproval chasing me as we go.

A knock on my door makes us turn toward each other, her face looking as confused as I feel. Hunter always meets me outside. I reach for my phone, double checking that I didn't miss a message as I turn the knob. "What are you doing up here? Did I miss a text or something?"

Hunter smiles and shakes his head. "Naw, I just figured you probably packed that big ass suitcase, and I wanted to carry it to the car for you."

"You—oh..." I stumble over my words, my heart fluttering

wildly as I get stuck on his crooked smile. Willa's lecture taunts me. *You already have someone who knows you.*

"*Oh?*" The amusement in Willa's voice isn't lost on me, and I flash a shut-the-hell-up look at her. "That's so thoughtful of you, Hunter. Isn't that *so thoughtful*, Ashlie? And he just *knew* you packed your suitcase. *Wow...*" She ribs me with her elbow.

He juggles a confused look between us. "So...your suitcase?"

"It has wheels. I can just—"

"Give it to me, Ashlie." Eyebrow arched, he assertively wraps his hand over mine, and my coochie flutters like his command was a personal invitation. I give it over dazedly, my brain lagging at the spontaneous shiver that runs through me. I may not like being told what to do, but something about that was sexy as hell. *And when did I bite my lip?* "...Ready?" His eyebrows dip as he watches me recalibrate. I nod quickly, glancing at Willa, who's barely containing her laughter.

Grabbing my keys, I usher everyone out, fumbling a little when I lock the deadbolt. I'm not avoiding anything...except his eye contact right now. But that's just because he caught me off guard with that "Yes, sir" boyfriend move he made with my bag.

Boyfriend? Shit.

As we walk to the car, Hunter's arm grazes mine, and I surprise myself by flinching away. "You good?" he asks.

Chuckling nervously, I pull out my phone and increase the distance between us. "Yeah. Just...tired, I guess. I'm gonna make sure our flight is on time."

You're avoiding your feelings.

He glances at me a few times, his gaze burning into my skin. I act like I'm unaffected, but focusing on our flight details does nothing to silence my sister's taunt echoing in my head.

When we get to the car, I slip into the backseat, and both of them look at me like I've lost my head. "Can we go? We're gonna be late!" I sneer, hoping they'll think I'm just in a bad mood. Willa covers a laugh, and I ignore her know-it-all ass as I scroll through my phone.

When Hunter gets behind the wheel, he looks at me through the mirror. "You sure you're okay?"

"Yep. Just ready to go." I buckle up and try to ignore the festering dread in my stomach that Willa might be right. I'm avoiding him...and myself. *What the hell is my problem?*

CHAPTER THIRTY-EIGHT

HUNTER

Ashlie claimed the window seat on the plane last night, and the innocent bliss on her face as she watched the clouds turn purple in the night sky did something to me. Made me feel things. This was deeper than shielding her from exes at the club or defending her to her parents. It unearthed some protective brute inside of me that has clearly been biding its time.

I want to keep her softness safe from anything with the potential to eclipse her light. Be her refuge, her safety. *Hers.* That's what this all boils down to. Being completely hers is the only thing I want, which makes watching her exchange intimate whispers with Trevor over brunch right now an absolute nightmare.

"You rethinking that bet after seeing her with her boyfriend over there?" Willa raises her brow as she looks at me over her water glass.

The fuck? How does she know about the bet? "I don't know what you're—"

"Save it. I already know, and I won't say anything to the lovebirds." She nods toward Chase and Kayla. "Or her boyfr—"

"Naw, stop calling him that. He's not her…" The words catch in my throat. I don't know that. I don't know anything about their relationship, really—haven't wanted to. The whole "out of sight, out of mind" aspect has been working for me. There hasn't been a need to feel jealous when he's a seven-hour drive away. But *this*—her smiling while he slides his hand over her arm—this might tip the scale.

"You two are ridiculous. Why did you agree to that?" She shoots her eyes across the table and back to me.

"I didn't want to be another person telling her what she should do." I reach for my cup and try to wash down the lump forming in my throat. It grows. The look in Willa's eyes falls from condescension to sympathy, and I drop my gaze to discourage the knot clustering in my stomach. "And you know how skittish she is. I didn't want to scare her off."

"Aw. That's actually really sweet, Hunter." She smiles and nudges me with her elbow. "I still don't think it's going to last with him, by the way. You have the advantage here; no one knows about your situationship. If you wipe that scowl off your face, it can stay that way. It's just for the weekend. You can hash it out with her when we fly home tomorrow."

I nod, knowing she's right about my advantage and my face. I'm no good at pretending I'm happy when I'm not, but I've got to pull it out from somewhere because this weekend isn't about me *or* us. The food comes, and I focus all my energy on hiding the agony rifling through me, just long enough to eat and get back in the car.

When we pull into the hotel parking garage, Willa hops out of the backseat quickly, leaving me alone with Ashlie. "She knows about the bet?" I ask, glancing at her.

That thumbnail goes to her mouth as she flashes a nervous smile. "Yeah... She saw us holding hands on the way to lunch on Wednesday."

I bob my head, silence filling the air as she gnaws away. After several seconds, I can't take it anymore. I pull her nervous hand from her mouth and move it across the armrest with mine.

"What's wrong?" I wiggle my fingers into her fist until she lets me fill the space in between hers.

"It's nothing."

"It's clearly something. You've been in a mood since yesterday, and if you take one more bite of that thumbnail, you'll need stitches. So tell me."

"You're mad about the Trevor thing..."

"I'm not."

"You've been shooting fire daggers from your eyes all morning."

I snort at the imagery. "What the hell are *fire daggers*, Ash?"

"Whatever. You know what I mean. You're mad, and I'm just worried about tonight." She slips the other thumbnail between her teeth.

"It sounds like you've got some fun things planned..." I try to deflect. She's not entirely wrong. I've been pissed all morning. I don't want her to know, but seeing them together has made me hate this stupid-ass bet.

"I'm not worried about the bachelorette party. I'm worried about you and Trevor being stuck together all night."

"You think I'm going to, what? Challenge him to a duel?" I smirk.

She gives me a side-eye and tilts her head. "A duel is just a bet with weapons. I don't put anything past you." Letting out a heavy sigh, she turns toward me. "Look, I don't know what to think. Just...don't start anything, okay?"

"Me? Start something? Never..." I joke.

"I'm serious, Hunt." There's tension in her voice as she meets my eyes without an ounce of humor. "I know you're mad. You won't say it, but you are."

"Hey." I kiss her temple. "Nothing's going to happen on my end. I swear."

"Bruh, one month. You ready?" I clap Chase on the shoulder and reach for my beer.

He nods and takes a swig from his bottle. "More than ready."

"Are you gonna cry?" Trevor asks.

"Of course he's gonna cry," I say. "He loses it over that penguin movie."

"Hey, that was *one time* when I'd had a rough day."

"Okay, but what about that *other* penguin movie?" I smirk.

"Another bad day..." Chase says, chuckling before taking another drink. Trevor's laugh roars across the table, joining my chuckle.

Ripley's sport's bar has three big screens, each showing a different game. Small alcoves house pool tables and dartboards. Brown-stained concrete floors and dim track lighting make this place feel a few steps above a cave, but it's still been a pretty fun time. After a few rounds of beer, billiards, and way too much shit-talking, we're slowing it down back at one of the high pedestal tables. My scowl has gone back into hibernation, despite having to deal with the unsuspecting enemy across the table. It turns out, Trevor isn't too bad to be around. He's goofy as hell, but chill—when I set aside the fact that he's also vying for Ashlie's affection.

"Alright, well, you two don't need me for this roast. I'll be back." Chase leaves the table, and I realize just how much he's driven the conversation tonight. I have nothing original to say to Trevor, so I grab my beer and drink, just to help the quiet make sense.

"So, you're around Ash a lot, yeah?" Trevor asks, cracking open his water bottle.

Ash. I don't like that. I don't want to think he knows her well enough to use a nickname. If he only knew how much time I spend with her, and what we do with that time, this would be a completely different conversation. I snort a sarcastic laugh. "You could say that."

"What can you tell me about this guy she's seeing? How serious is it?"

Pretty damn serious. Locking eyes with him, I consider being an asshole and laying it all on the table. I'd enjoy seeing his face fall after having to watch them together all morning. But I won't, because Ashlie specifically asked me not to, and I want what she wants.

"Naw." I shake my head, taking another swig from my bottle. "No idea. She hasn't brought him around yet."

"But she talks about him, yeah?"

"Not to me. You might try her sister, though."

"Huh..." His eyebrows cinch skeptically. "Damn. Thanks anyway, bro."

"What's up?" Chase slides back into his seat, turning toward Trevor.

"Ah, nothing. Just trying to get some dirt on my competition. Ash has been kinda distant the last few weeks..."

"I'm telling you, man, whoever she's seeing in LA won't last long. Not with you in the mix. She hasn't even talked to Kayla about him."

Well, damn. I know I can't really be upset about this. I haven't told Chase anything about mine and Ashlie's setup. The last time I talked to him about it was after that first dinner date. I lied and said it didn't go as planned, that I decided to let her go. It was the only way to get him off my case and demolish any possibility of him asking more questions.

"Guess we'll see at the wedding," Trevor says.

I whip my head back to Trevor. "What's happening at the wedding?"

"Ah, yeah. I asked Ashlie to be my date to the wedding a couple months ago, just to lock in my position."

My mouth drops, and I hide it by grabbing that faithful bottle, drinking the last dregs of my beer. Sweat prickles across my scalp as I painstakingly regain composure. *Fucking Idiot! Why didn't I think of it first?* Of course he asked her. He's been preplanning dates with her for months. Why would the wedding be any different? *Why didn't she tell me?*

Flexing the frustration through my fingers, I catch Trevor's puzzled gaze dipping to my hand and back to my face. I scan the room to avoid him, focusing on the big screen to calm myself. As if she was summoned, Ashlie stomps across the floor, high pony-tailed curls bouncing with each determined step. She's wearing a white crop top and jeans, her waist beads prominently on display. My back goes ramrod straight as I adjust from my slouch.

"You guys ever heard of phones?" Her feisty scowl circles around the table. With a hand on her hip, she settles her eyes on Chase. "I called all three of you."

"Eh, that was my bad," Chase says. "We turned them off at my request."

"You need to come with me. I've been trying to reach you for twenty minutes. It's Kay—"

Chase is out of his seat before she finishes saying the last syllable in my sister's name, and I'm up a split second later.

"Is she okay? What happened?" Chase asks.

"I haven't seen her this bad in a long time. She's had *a lot* to drink." Ashlie starts for the door, with Chase right beside her. I'm a few steps behind, trying to keep up with the details. Kayla doesn't get drunk. She'll have a drink here or there, but for her to get plastered is unheard of.

We make it outside, and I'm surprised Ashlie's keeping stride with how fast we're walking. "Did something happen?" Chase asks.

"She's freaking out about the wife thing."

Chase stops suddenly, brows furrowed. "What wife thing?"

Ashlie swipes her palm across her forehead with a sigh. "She didn't talk to you?"

"This is the first I'm hearing about a wife thing…"

"Shit. Okay." Ashlie tugs his arm, coaxing him to continue across the street. "She's been stressed about becoming a wife, and all the changes it will bring."

"Wha—nothing's changing. We're basically married already."

"That's what I said, and I told her to talk to you about it, which she *clearly* didn't do."

When we reach Chickies, the brighter atmosphere is blinding. Soft purple lighting glistens off the chandelier at the center of the bar. A karaoke stage sits in the corner, surrounded by ornate white floor tiles. Plush seating surrounds low round tables throughout. The two of them head to the back while I stop at the bar for some bottles of water. If she's as wasted as she sounds, she'll need it.

I pass Willa at a table full of ladies packing up their things, and she points me toward the closed party room door. Chase and Ashlie are standing on either side of the doorway.

"What's going on?" I ask, looking back and forth between them. Choked sobbing seeps from under the door as Chase tries to push it open.

"She's sitting against it." Ashlie pounds on the door with her fist. "Kayla, girl, *move* so we can open the door."

"No! Leave me alone!" Kayla's voice shakes as a loud wave of emotion erupts out of her.

Chase knocks lightly. "Kayla, baby, please. Let me in."

Kayla's muffled growl is accented with a bang against the door. "I told you not to get him, Ashlie!"

"Then you shouldn't have locked yourself in there!" Ashlie fires back.

"Baby, please..." Chase pleads.

"No. You'll just get upset."

"I promise, I won't. Just...open the door?"

"No!"

"*Fuck's sake,*" I mutter, handing the water to Ashlie. My sister's as stubborn as I am, but I won't hesitate to use brute force to get in this room. Nudging Chase out of the way, I plant my feet. "Kayla..." I ram the door with my shoulder and gain a few inches, wedging my foot in the gap. "You know I'll push you out of the fucking way. Open the goddamn door." I shove again, and there's a responding yelp as glass crashes on the other side. The few inches I gained disappear as soon as she recovers and pushes back against it. "Kayla! I *swear-to-Go—*"

"*Fine!*"

The door swings open, banging against the wall. Kayla stands in the middle of the room, shoulders slumped, her locs covering half of her face. Her cheeks are shiny from tears. *Shit.* I haven't seen this version of my sister in a while. Her Type A personality can hide a lot, but every few years, something tips her anxiety off the edge. Wedding planning broke the camel's back, apparently.

I lean against the doorframe as Chase rushes in, crunching over the shattered bottle of wine on the floor. He walks her to a nearby folding chair, squats in front of her, and wipes her cheeks with his thumb. Watching him display this easy, intimate act of care—so similar but wholly different from the PDA I'm used to seeing from them—makes something click in my head.

This is what I want, this unapologetic display of love and devotion. The protectiveness I felt on the plane last night, the jealousy at brunch this morning, it all amounts to this. I want to be everything for the woman standing across from me with worry etched across her face as she stares at our best friends. I have half a mind to step over and comfort her, secrecy be damned. But this moment isn't about me, or us, so I slide my attention back into the room.

"Baby..." Chase sweeps the hair out of Kayla's face and reaches for a cocktail napkin. "We don't have to do this."

"Yes, we do. It's a month away. We've already paid for everything."

"You think I care about any of that shit? Kay, I'll shut it all down tomorrow if it's not what you want to do."

"I *do* want to."

"Then what's...?" Chase looks to the ceiling and blows out a frustrated breath. "Please, talk to me."

Kayla doesn't answer right away, and I glance at Ashlie, who shrugs, hugging the bottles to her chest. Just as I'm about to step closer, Trevor sidles up next to her and peeks into the room. Heat flames in my chest when he rests his hand on Ashlie's back. *Stop. Fucking. Touching. Her.* Trying to ignore the fiery rage building inside, I clench my jaw, molars grinding hard enough they squeak in the process. Resisting the reflex to spring forward is getting harder by the second, but reacting would make me look like a controlling prick.

"Here, let me hold those for you." Captain Gentleman grabs the bottles from her, then turns to me. "I closed out the tab at Ripley's, and I'll drop those two off at home whenever they're ready."

I tip my chin up to acknowledge what he said before turning my attention back to the room. Trevor leaves, but my impulse to stake my claim doesn't.

"What if I'm not good at it?" Kayla whispers, eyes cast to the glazed concrete floor.

"Baby, you're already good at it. You're the best damn wife I've ever had," Chase teases. "If it's a technicality causing all of this turmoil, then I don't want it. Just say the word, and I'll cancel it all."

"But—"

"But nothing. I'll do anything for you, including taking marriage off the table. I love you. My only priority is you and your happiness. Screw everything else."

My eyes shift to Ashlie at Chase's profession of love and dedication, and a split second later, she looks at me too. Chase has always been a pro at expressing exactly how he feels. I try to siphon his words from the air, transmitting them into a coded message for the eyes I could stare into forever.

I love you. My only priority is you and your happiness.

CHAPTER THIRTY-NINE

ASHLIE

There's no denying the passionate devotion in the air as Chase dedicates his entire existence to my best friend. He speaks brazenly, as if he was born to protect her happiness at all costs. I wipe away a sappy tear and glance at Hunter, but the intensity in his eyes feels like he's silently shouting those same words at me.

Shit. *He is.*

My heart threatens to beat out of my chest as I'm pinned by his longing, a look I now realize I've been seeing for years. More so over the last few months, but in this moment, it's undeniable. *Love.*

Hunter's been the one encouraging me to get back in the pool, to find a job I enjoy. Grad school, the bet, dating Trevor—Hunter's been concerned with my happiness through it all. Maybe for much longer than I've been willing to admit. *I know I have issues, but how did I miss this?*

Suddenly, the unspoken stakes of our situationship skyrocket, and I'm reeling. There's not enough air in this doorway to clear the panic infused haze from my mind. It's one thing for my easily won heart to be in love; it latches on to guys quickly and often. But that four-letter word is consequential coming from him. He's never attached himself to anyone in that way. *Until now.* This silly little bet, a facade I've been clinging to for dear life, has the potential to shatter our friendship. Failing with a new man is bad enough. But failing with Hunter would be devastating. No. Worse than devastation; I'd be gutted. He's the most important person in my life. My rock. *I can't lose my best friend.*

Chase guides Kayla from the room, heading toward Willa. Dread washes over me when I glance at Trevor. *What do I do now?* I'm completely aware of Hunter's eyes on me, but I can't deal with this—with *him*—right now. *Love changes everything.*

My eyes sweep the speckled floor as I walk toward the table, and I shake my head to fend off my thoughts the entire time. *Willa was right. I'm scared.* I'm so absorbed in this newfound shame, I'm surprised when I'm stopped by the handsy mustache who's been trying to get my attention all night.

"Hey, sexy. You leaving already?" Mustache grabs my elbow and pulls me toward him.

Sneering, I rip my arm from his grip. "Don't touch me, asshole." I take a step and feel his hand around my hips, fondling the waist beads under my crop top.

He tugs them, pulling me back to him. "These are hot." The pungent smell of liquor and cigarettes wafts over me. "Come on, baby, just one drink."

"I said, *don't touch me!*" Driving my elbow into his gut, I knock him back a step before whipping around to face him.

"Ooh, you're a fiery one. Just how I like—"

"Touch my girl again, and I'll rip those fingers off your hand and choke you with them." Hunter puts himself between us, the acrid rasp in his voice rumbling down to my toes. This calculated energy isn't the Hunter I've seen get into fights before. He's usually quick to hit first and ask questions later. But *this* is controlled and calm. The only reason I hear what he says is because I'm right next to him.

"Hunter, don't..." I warn, pulling on the back of his shirt.

"You hear her? Mind your business, man." Handsy Mustache

pushes Hunter's shoulder, knocking him into me. I stumble, failing to catch myself as I land on the ground with a thud. Pain shoots across my ankle.

"Naw, she is my business."

"Maybe you should tell *your business* to cover herself up instead of giving a peep show to the entire bar."

"The fuck did you say?" Hunter has him by the collar faster than I can scramble back to my feet.

Hobbling forward, I wince against the pinching. "Hunter, *don't!*" I grit out right as he slams the hairy hipster against the table.

Chase reaches them just before Hunter's fist smashes into the man's lip, pulling back on Hunter's arm. "Let him go, Hunt. Come on." Hunter doesn't move, the muscle in his jaw fluttering wildly. The air is thick with his rage, his labored breaths coming out in spurts. "Hunter, she's safe. It's over. Let's get some air," Chase urges.

There's several tense seconds before Hunter drops the guy. He throws Chase's hand off his arm and walks out the door.

All eyes are on me, and I want to crawl in a hole. That secret I've been adamant on keeping between us just exploded in my face. *What the hell did you expect?*

Glancing at the table, I catch Willa's wide eyes as she holds on to Kayla's drunken body. The rest of the bachelorette party is gone. *At least I have that going for me.*

A hand on my shoulder makes me jump. "Hey, you alright?" Trevor asks.

"Maybe... I fell on my ankle."

"Can you walk on it?"

"Not well." I titter nervously. My hands shake from the drop in adrenaline as I try to steady my breathing.

Trevor squats, peering at me with concern in his eyes. "Can I help you into the chair to look at it?"

I nod, and he lifts me at my hips, setting me on the nearest barstool. *You're using Trevor as a distraction.*

"I don't think it's broken... I'm gonna grab some ice. Are you okay by yourself for a sec?"

"Yeah." I hope my smile is convincing. Handsy Mustache retreated to the corner with his friends as soon as Hunter dropped him, so I don't think he'll be a problem anymore. "I'm fine." I wave him off like my thoughts aren't pulverizing me from the inside. *Love changes everything.*

When Trevor returns, he drags over another barstool and props up my leg, positioning the ice around my steadily swelling ankle. He's caring for me in all the right ways, but I'm so numb right now, I can't dwell on it. "I'm gonna pull my truck around. Do you want to ride along while I drop off Chayla? I can take you back to your hotel after."

"Yeah, that's..." It's probably for the best, really. My mind is moving at warp speed, and I need to sort through everything from the last thirty minutes. *I need to calm down.* "That's a good idea," I say.

Trevor smiles. *And I don't feel anything?* "Stay here. I'll help you to the truck when I get it out front." He squeezes my shoulder and walks to the table, stopping to talk with Willa before heading out the door. Willa pulls out her phone, juggling it while holding a weeping Kayla.

WILLA

You okay?

ME

Landed on my ankle.

WILLA

Girl, you know I don't mean your ankle... That was intense.

ME

Trevor's going to drive me back to the hotel.
Will you make sure Hunter's okay?

WILLA

You need to talk to him.

ME

I can't right now.

"Ready?" Trevor holds out both of his hands to help me from the stool. I land and immediately groan as the familiar twinge pulses around my ankle. Clamping my lips around my teeth, I squeeze his fingers and groan out the pain. "Nope, you're not walking on that. I'm gonna carry you to the truck." He waits for my nod before picking me up in his arms, grabbing the bag of ice off the chair shortly after. He's such a good guy. *So why don't I feel anything?*

A cool breeze blows through my hair when we get outside, and I realize my shirt is clinging to the sweat on my back. Watching Hunter jump to defend me like that *was* intense. *Willa was right. About a lot of things.* Just like everything else that's happened tonight, I have no idea how to feel about it. I've seen him get in fights before, but never with that hard-set jaw and focused rage. Never over me...*for* me.

Chase and Hunter sit on the curb, and upon seeing us, Chase stands and opens the doors of Trevor's SUV. Hunter's eyes grow wide when he glances at us over his shoulder, before he turns back to stare at the ground. Trevor sets me down in the front seat and props my leg on the dashboard, laying the ice on my ankle. *He's perfect for me, but I feel nothing?* Squeezing my arm, he tosses a smile my way, which only makes it all worse. He and Willa head back inside the bar, and I focus on the melting ice. That shameful feeling grows in my chest, a clear acknowledgment that I've been using him clanging loudly inside my head.

"Is your ankle okay?" Hunter asks. I see him watching me out of the corner of my eye, hear the concern in his voice, but the thought of looking at his face right now churns the anxiety in my stomach. I can't make my head turn in his direction.

"Uh, not really..." I bite my lip, dropping my focus to my lap.

Why can't I look at him? The confusion waging war between my head and heart is so loud, I'm not even sure what my problem is right now.

"Shit, Ash, I'm sorry. I didn't realize you were still behind me."

"It's okay... Trevor took care of it." I lift a finger toward the ice and try to ignore the defeated sigh that slips out of him. Reacting like this to avoid talking to him is wrong. I know it is, especially when he defended me the way I'd expect my boyfriend to in public. *But he isn't.*

Annoyance surges in my chest, trampling over my anxiety as I remember the embarrassment of everyone's eyes on me. *We're not together, technically, and he couldn't give me the one thing I asked for with this dating bet: keeping it a secret.* That bothers me more than my throbbing ankle at the moment, and I'm latching onto it, as wrong as it may be. Channeling my anxiety into petty anger feels a lot safer than addressing the shame I felt earlier, so I let it fester. "He's taking me back to the hotel."

"Ash, I can take you."

"I don't want you to take me." With my vulnerability safely tucked into a shoddy little nook, I finally look at him. He holds my gaze for several seconds, then slowly drops his eyes to the ground, stroking his chin with a sullen nod. The unsettling dejection creeping into his shoulders threatens to extinguish the flames growing in my chest. *Fight back, damn it. Show me the old you.* I know how to fight with Hunter. We're good at it. Fighting would give me just a little hope that we can go back to how it was. Maybe, if we stop all of this now, we can salvage what's left of our friendship. But he doesn't take the bait. He lets me have my way. How am I supposed to handle that? *Love changes everything.*

Staring straight ahead, I cross my arms over my chest, hoping it will stop the crack in my heart from growing. I can't move, can't breathe, and can't find the courage to take it all back. When Willa and Trevor reappear, juggling the supplies from the party, I reach forward and slam my door shut. Through the mirror, I watch

Hunter flinch at the sound, then I keep my eyes forward until we pull away from the curb. When I look back, Willa's sitting next to Hunter, his head hanging low. *This shit just got messy.*

THE RADIO FILLS THE SILENCE AS WE DRIVE TO CHASE and Kayla's place. I think everyone in this truck has a lot to process about tonight. When we pull up to the high-rise, Chase waves us off and ushers Kayla inside.

"How's your ankle?" Trevor asks when we get to the hotel parking garage.

"I think I'll live... Might need help walking though." I grin. It's a fake one, but it's dark enough in the truck that I hope he doesn't notice. When I glance over, he's studying me, drumming his fingers across the top of the steering wheel.

"It's Hunter, right? The other guy you're seeing?"

I blow out a puff of air and nod. Not only is the cat out of the bag, but it shredded its way out and left me with a giant mess.

"It all makes sense now... Look, we have a lot of fun together, but I can't compete with that. He's *intense* about you, Ashlie." Trevor's voice is as warm and friendly as ever. There's no anger in his eyes as he smiles that sweet, comforting smile. "In my experience, when a man is that passionate about someone, it means something."

"Yeah. It means he needs anger management."

"*Or*"—he turns in his seat—"it means he cares about you. Maybe more. Righteous anger while defending you is worlds away from punching anyone who looks at you."

"I just don't like controlling men." It's such a weak defense, I think I'm trying to convince myself more than him.

"There's a thin line between control and protection, and it lies within the motivation. A controlling man wouldn't have stood by quietly while you drove off with another guy. His display at the bar was protection, Ashlie. Are you really upset about that?"

With a sigh, I shake my head. I don't think Trevor's wrong about any part of what he says. I did feel protected by Hunter…*do* feel protected by him. He's always had my back, but the protection tonight felt significant. Steadfast and committed. *It felt like love.* I was smacked in the face with a reality I've been skirting around for months, and it's clawing at my deepest insecurities, making me defensive in the worst way.

My eyes sweep over Trevor, and I realize he's a really good friend. *Only* a friend. A sweet, caring, good-natured guy who I don't have feelings for. "You're not supposed to be talking up the competition, Trev," I joke, trying to lighten the serious turn of our conversation.

He laughs, showing off those dimples that used to make me swoon. "Hey, I can tell when I'm outmatched. Is it safe to say we've become friends at least?"

"Yeah, definitely."

"*Yesss.*" He pumps a cheery fist in the air, eliciting another giggle from me. "Well, I hope you and Hunter figure it out."

I take a beat, coming to terms with letting Trevor go. I'm more surprised I don't feel a sense of loss about this breakup—if you can even call it that after a handful of dates. "This is probably the nicest I've ever been dumped." A quiet laugh lilts my voice. "It beats an email by a mile."

He throws his head back, chuckling. "Well, good. So what are you going to do?"

"I don't really know." I shrug, rubbing my forehead. "I'm so confused."

"Yeah, I get it…"

"You do?"

He nods and shifts in his seat, leaning against the door. "Jumping into a romantic relationship with someone you've only seen platonically can be a pretty daunting step. Reconciling the person you know as a friend with a partner who's now asking for your heart, wondering if it'll work out, or if everything will end up ruined—it's a leap into the unknown. All of the dynamics change. The stakes are higher. You have the ammunition to hurt each other, but need to trust that you won't let it happen. They already know you so well, you have to face your own shit. It's a scary transition. Maybe that's part of your confusion..."

Chewing my thumbnail, I drop my eyes to my lap. Without knowing it, Trevor took the mess in my brain and turned it into a palatable dose of introspection. Made it seem normal. He explained it all in a way that makes it less shameful to admit to myself. I'm terrified to take that leap with Hunter and ruin it because of *my* issues. *So many issues.* The chance of us not working out looms over me like a dark cloud, the anxious drizzle threatening to turn into a destructive downpour. *Losing him would be devastating.*

CHAPTER FORTY
ASHLIE

Trevor carries me inside the hotel on his back. As soon as he steps from the elevator, I groan into his shoulder. *Shit.* I'd hoped to sleep on all of this and get some clarity tomorrow, but Hunter's sitting on the wall by my door. Trevor gingerly places me on the emerald-green carpet and helps me hobble the rest of the way.

"Night, Trev," I say, giving a side hug.

He wraps his arms around me in one last warm, friendly embrace. "Let me know how it goes," he whispers in my ear, squeezing my shoulder before letting go. I lean against the doorframe for support. "Night, man." He nods at Hunter, who pushes himself off the ground to stand.

Once Trevor is gone, Hunter's words rush out as if they're fighting each other. "I want to call off the bet." He takes a deep breath and shoves his hands in his pockets. If it weren't for the night we've had, the pleading look in his eyes would shatter my resolve. But I'm exhausted. *I'm not ready for this.*

Rubbing my forehead, I try to ease the sudden pounding. My chest tightens like a boa constrictor strangling its meal, my breaths turning shallow the longer I look at him. *Please, not tonight.* Call it avoidance or whatever, but I really need to sleep on this. "Can we do this tomorrow?"

"Naw, it needs to be tonight."

Frustration hisses between my teeth, my words sounding more intense than I intend. "Why, Hunt? I'm tired and confu—"

"We're doing this! Right now!"

My face heats when he cuts me off. The sea of anxiety I've been treading all night is quickly replaced with a vat of indignation. Why he thinks forcing a heart-to-heart will work is beyond me. Folding my arms tightly against my chest, I lean on the door for balance. "*Oh*, so talking it out is only allowed on your terms, huh? Where was this energy when you were pissed off all morning?"

Hands balling into fists in his pockets, he sets his jaw and meets my glare. For several seconds, the silence bounces off the walls. The tension twists to an undeniable strain, neither of us willing to let go.

Then a flash of vulnerability softens his face, leaving just as quickly with a shake of his head. "I wasn't pissed."

"You can't admit it, can you?" I taunt. My fatigue gives way to low-hanging pettiness. Consequences be damned, I let it lead. "You're so guarded with your emotions that you can't even—"

"Hell yeah, I'm mad!" He scrubs his face with his hands before looking back at me. "I've had to watch you with him all weekend, Ashlie! Had to push away my own feelings because that's the way you wanted it."

"*You're* the one who told me to keep seeing him, Hunter!"

"Naw, don't put that on me. I told you to do what makes you happy. *You* chose to keep seeing him."

"Yeah, well, he's not—"

"Were you ever going to tell me about the wedding?" Heat radiates as he steps toward me. "Or just make me watch you hang all over him again?"

"Trevor and I—"

"Do you want to be with me?"

"FUCK! Stop talking over me!" I throw my hands in the air, but quickly grab the doorframe when I start to wobble. Hunter reaches out to help, and I stop him with a scowl. His nostrils flare as he watches me, fingers twitching like they're aching to touch me. I know I'm deflecting and *should* make it clear that it's over with Trevor, but now I don't want him to have the satisfaction. He's coming at me like we're in a boxing ring, where my only means of fighting back is to bob, weave, and avoid. Expecting his next words to match my intensity, I purse my lips, ready for everything to ignite.

But it fizzles when he cocks his head instead, eyes flicking around my face. The air seeps from my lungs when his pinched expression eases into realization. That undeniable intensity is back in his stare. *Love.* My eyes dart away, but it doesn't help; he's still reading me like a goddamn book.

"…You didn't answer the question."

You already have someone who knows you.

Willa's words assault my mind, and I don't even attempt to respond to Hunter. What could I say? I'm not fooling anyone at this point—not even myself. But admitting I want to be with him twists me up inside, threatens to blow open the hatch and release the shadows I'm clinging to. I bite my lip as my mind races to find a way to reverse all of this. Uncross the line I begged to erase in Fort Bender. Pretend I don't know how it feels to be his. I want him safely back in the friendship box, but his eyebrow arches like he expects me to lie, and I realize it's too late. We couldn't go back if we tried. Not in a million years. *You've already ruined it.*

His humorless snort pulls me from my spiral, and I brace myself for whatever comes next. "I might not be the best at communicating my feelings, but at least I'm not lying to myself about what I want."

Don't fucking cry. I swallow the thick coil of emotion, but my voice shakes anyway. "What the hell is *that* supposed to mean?"

"It means I'm right fucking here, Ashlie!" Gruff frustration rattles in his throat, and all I can do is stand here and take it.

"You'd rather dive heart first into these shallow relationships when, deep down, you know they'll never give the depth you need. Meanwhile, I've been here for months, giving you everything you say you want—everything I have—and you're pretending not to see it. *Choosing* not to. I'm fighting for what we could be, Ash. Everyone else sees it; why can't you?"

You're a disappointment.

There it is. The reason I'm so afraid this won't work. Those nagging insecurities spring to my head so loudly, I wince. Hunter's changed for the better, changed for *me,* and I'm still the anxiety-ridden mess who can't face her silly little fears. *You don't deserve him. He's done so much for you, and you ignored it all. Selfish.* I shift uncomfortably as the thought grows to a roar, and when I look in his eyes, my defensive response dies in my throat.

He takes a deep breath, eyebrows drooping with a pleading agony. "I know you're still in your head about my motives after our fight, and I get it. You're used to striking out with guys and jumping to conclusions so no one can control you, like Bryan. But I don't want to break you like he did, Ash. I want to be the one you run to when everything feels broken. I'm not him. Hell, I'm not even the old me anymore." *He hasn't been for a while.*

"...But I'm still the old me." My voice shakes as I blink away tears. *Selfish.*

"I didn't... That's *not* what I'm saying..."

Look at what you're doing to him.

The way he's staring at me, like he's both fed up and can't get enough, threatens to smother the confusing inferno burning me up inside. But I'm drenched with worry that I've fucked everything up beyond repair, consumed by doubts having nothing to do with him. All I'm left with is a fear so raw, it feels like a second skin. *Everything is your fault.*

"Hunt..." I puff out a shaky breath, teetering as I try to balance on my good ankle. Air whizzes from my lips in short spurts, the edges of my vision blurring. "I don't want—" My breath catches, and I shake my head, searching for the words I've never been able to admit out loud. "I *can't*—"

"You *can*." The conviction in his voice briefly cuts through my panic, curling around my heart as if he understands what I'm battling inside.

But how can he? I don't even understand it myself.

Taking a tentative step, he reaches for me, and I know he's about to do the one thing we can't take back. Use the words that change *everything*. "You're smart—"

Don't say it...

"—and strong. Resilient."

Please no...

"I know you, Ashlie. Like the back of my fucking hand." He takes another step, and I have to tilt my head back to see him. "I know you, and I lov—"

"Please, don't!" The strangled cry rips from my throat, my chest heaving breathlessly. "Don't say it..."

Dropping his head in his hands, Hunter lets out a groan that reverberates through me. I feel every bit of it clawing at my chest, begging me to put him out of his misery. With a shoulder-raising breath, his arms fall to his sides in a surrendering pose. The wounded look in his eyes pins me in place. "Why. Fucking. Not?" He punctuates each word with a brusque staccato, his stare unwavering.

"Because I'll ruin it!" My heart plummets as I realize I have no more excuses left. Nothing but the truth. I'm always the common denominator. *It's me.* I close my eyes briefly to expel the thought, but it echoes.

"Wha—Ash..."

"I will." Nodding quickly, I blink away the spill of tears. "I always do..." The doubts I've pushed away for a lifetime come rushing to the surface, crashing together until they shout at me, *you'll never be enough.* "I don't think I'm ready." It comes out as a whisper but is somehow just as loud as the yelling from before.

He places a hand on my waist as the other tucks a curl behind my ear. I groan at the tweak in my ankle when he pulls me against him and brace my arms against his chest. It would be the easiest thing to say yes to him right now. Jump in recklessly like I always do. My head is filled with a raging river of confliction, the battle between the easy choice and the right one volleying in my mind. But those cool green irises convey so much amid the silence. Warmth. Support. *Love*. It's like gravity itself is pulling me into his orbit until we're only a whisper away. With one glance that threatens to shoot me into oblivion, he crushes his mouth to mine. Heated desperation simmers from him, igniting at our tangled lips until I'm clutching his shirt in my fists.

His kiss has always hushed all the noise inside of me, and without a second thought, I kiss him back. The slow stroke of his tongue lulls me into a trance, claiming, declaring, *pleading*. As his thumb comes to rest on my cheek, I desperately want to hold on to this feeling with him. This place where doubts and fear disappear, and we're floating together against space and time. It means the world. Another sweet peck on my lips, and he rests his forehead against mine. "You hold all the cards here, Ashlie. You always have. What do you need to feel ready?"

When I open my mouth to speak, one last thought scourges my mind. *He deserves more.* And that's the clincher. Failing the one person who's always been on my side is too much to bear. Doing what I've always done, being the way I've always been—it will only end in devastation. I can't do it anymore. Not to him. That morsel of resolve nestles in my head until it's the only thing that makes sense. My heart races as my trembling fingers slide his hand from my cheek. "I need some space."

"*Fuck*," he murmurs through gritted teeth, flinching as if my words slapped him across the face.

"Hey..." I secure his head in my hands and guide it back to mine. "Look at me, Hunter." Despite the tear trailing down my cheek, I give him a small smile, hoping it will ease the confusion in his eyes. "This isn't about you. It's me."

"Ash..."

"Just...let me get this out. Please?"

His eyebrows cinch, but he nods and waits.

I flick the newest tear and take a deep breath. "I'm a floundering disaster, Hunt—"

"You're not..." He shakes his head emphatically.

"I *am*. Look at us right now. We've been yelling in a hotel hallway because picking fights with you is easier than dealing with myself." Swiping my face, I straighten my shoulders with the confidence I don't feel. "None of this is fair to you. Dragging you into my mess when you've worked so hard to change yours—it's not the right way to start a relationship together. I need a little space to figure it all out *without*"—I wave my hands around us—"all of this."

He pulls away and drags a palm down his face. "So what? A couple of days to breathe?"

I bite my lip. "I'm asking for a month."

"A month?" He scoffs. "That's more than 'a little *fucking* space,' Ashlie!"

"We still had a month before the bet was over anyway."

"Naw, fuck the stupid-ass bet."

"You asked what I need, Hunt. Just...give me four weeks to sort some things out. To work on myself. We can reassess after the wedding..." My voice trails as I hesitate to deliver the option to walk away from all of this. But it wouldn't be right if I didn't. "...And if you don't want to wait for me, if you want to move on, I... That's okay too."

He tips his head back and blows his frustration to the ceiling. Several emotions scroll across his face. "Those are my only choices? Space or move on?"

My heart thrums in my chest, and I bite my thumbnail, hoping he'll give me this last request. Love might change things, but it can't fix the way I feel inside. As selfish as this all feels right now, focusing on myself is long overdue.

The tension in his shoulders slackens as he lowers his head, and his arms hang limply at his sides. Enshrouded in a type of anguish that wrings the breath from my lungs, his eyes meet mine before dropping to the floor. "After the wedding?" he asks dejectedly. "No calls, no lunches—nothing for four weeks? That's what you want?"

No. But I think it's what I need. I ignore the wet streaks coursing down my face. "Four weeks." My voice shakes as the reality of what this all means settles into my stomach like a lead weight. The torment etched on his face hurts more than I could have imagined. This break feels like the worst kind of failure, and I'm not even sure I can hold up my end of the bargain when the timer runs out.

Eyes trained on the floor, he nods slowly, stuffs his hands in his pockets, and shuffles a step back. He's giving me exactly what I asked for, but my heart breaks anyway.

CHAPTER FORTY-ONE

HUNTER

I didn't even try to sleep after the shitshow in the hallway last night. I took my time walking down to my room, and then rescheduled my morning flight for one in the afternoon. With everything that happened, sitting next to Ashlie on a plane—even for a couple of hours—would feel like feeding myself into a wood-chipper one limb at a time.

My plan to call off the bet worked, alright. Worked everything right into the ground under the guise of a "break." *Fuck*! I knew she was scared. I should have given her more time to see how right we are together. Should've kept my stupid-ass mouth shut and toughed it out until after the bet. But I panicked, hearing Trevor brag about their wedding date, and thought giving her a nudge would get us over that hurdle. Instead, I pushed her over the edge; fucked everything up. *And she left.*

I grimace as the word *space* echoes in my head, a speedy corro-sion that spreads through my heart like a canker. The thought of being away from her for any amount of time eats at me, but I can't force this. I can't persuade her to be with me or convince her she's perfect as she is. She has to make those decisions herself. Despite how wrong all of this feels, I'm giving her what she asked for. No matter how fast I feel myself sinking into a pit of misery, I can't be that person who doesn't listen to what she wants. *I just hope she comes back.*

Waiting for Willa and Ashlie in the parking garage, I gear myself up for the awkward ride to the airport. *I just have to make it twenty minutes.* My fingers drum across the steering wheel as my thoughts drift to the bar last night. Everything happened so fast. One minute, Ashlie was looking at me across the doorway, and the next, I had some motherfucker smashed against a table. When he touched her, I saw red. Lost my mind. I didn't even know it was Chase pulling me off until I was halfway outside.

Grabbing my phone, I recheck the rental car return process. The back hatch of the SUV pops open, and I'm terrified to turn around. I can't take looking into Ashlie's eyes right now.

"Hey, Hunter," Willa says from the back. She hesitates, and I glance at the rearview mirror to see her. "Thanks for getting her the crutches."

I clear my throat. "Yeah, no problem." By four in the morning, I was still wired, so I hopped in the rental and found a twenty-four-hour pharmacy to grab crutches and an ankle brace for Ashlie. I left it all at their door, hoping she wouldn't see it as a breach of "space."

Willa slides into the passenger seat and places a hand on my arm. "You okay? I heard...everything."

"Yeah, naw, not really. I, uh... I changed my flight to give her some breathing room... Just don't want to deal with the awkwardness."

"Wow, okay... That's a little extreme, but I guess she asked for it." She breathes out a quiet laugh and shakes my arm. "Hey, she'll figure it out, Hunter."

I nod, but there's no confidence in it. Even after everything last night, I still don't know that she wants this with me. A month is enough time for her to change her mind about all of it.

Ashlie clicks out of the hotel on her crutches, swinging methodically toward the rental car. I watch her through the rearview mirror as she pulls herself up and slides her crutches across the seat. Watch her click her seatbelt across her torso. Adjust her ponytail. Swipe a finger under her glossed lip. I watch everything for the last time, fix my eyes on the road, and I don't look at her again.

Despite the ache in my chest, I managed to make it to the weekend without a single tear. Mostly. Wednesday was hard, when I realized it was lunch time and picked my phone up to text Hunter without thinking. Seeing his name on the screen was all it took for me to crumble into a tear-soaked mess.

I miss him. It's only been a week, and I miss everything—the teasing, the touches, the kissing. His snarky comebacks and smart-ass jokes. Arguing with him about everything...*anything*. His friendship. *Him*. But I stand by what I said in that hallway. I need to stop relying on others and work on myself... I'm just not sure how.

I've spent the week petrified by indecision, the roar of anxiety growing with every passing day. I'm running out of time, but that deep-seated fear of failure is pressing me into the couch cushion so forcefully right now, I can't do anything but sit here and flip through channels. It's already Sunday afternoon. Doing nothing about it feels worse by the day, but I just *can't*.

Loud banging at my door snaps me out of my pity party. I slowly stretch as I stand from the couch, adjusting my tank top and pulling up my sweatpants while trudging to open it. Luckily, the tweak in my ankle was a small one. After babying it for the week, I'm only feeling a slight twinge when I lift my heels to look in the peephole.

Willa storms into my apartment as soon as I open the door, and I shield my eyes from her cheery yellow T-shirt. It's too bright for my mood. Her long twists sway as she shakes her head at the misery cocoon I set up on the couch. "Alright, girl, get dressed and let's go."

"Oh, dear sister. Do come in..." I say dryly, moving back toward the sofa.

Whipping around, her eyes narrow. "*This...*"—she waves her hand in the air, gesturing to me and then the living room—"is not healthy. I'm getting you out of the house. Go. Get. Dressed."

"*Ugh*, no. I don't feel like going anywhere. Can we just stay in and watch a movie or something?" Resuming my position on the couch, I wrap the blanket around myself, curling in tight like a depressed little taquito.

"No, Ash. You need sun and fresh air." She grabs my blanket and yanks it clean off my body, scrunching her nose after a few seconds. "And a shower."

I slice a glare at her. "Remember how we didn't talk for years? We should make that happen again. Right now."

"*Oh*, so you're just pushing everyone away now? That's a low blow and you know it." Willa's stare is withering, and I crumble.

"I... I know. I'm sorry." Tears drip from my eyes, and I squeeze them tight. That *was* uncalled for. No matter how bad I feel on the inside, Willa doesn't deserve that. It was a shitty thing for me to say.

"I forgive you. Now lose the attitude, and get dressed." She marches back to my bedroom, giving me more grace than I've been able to give myself this week. Drawers open and close while she mutters obscenities from the back of my apartment. I roll off the couch and follow her. "Here!" She throws a T-shirt, leggings, and undies at me. "Get in the shower. I'll grab the rest of your stuff."

"What stuff, Wills? Where are we going?"

"You ask too many damn questions, Ash. *Just go.*"

"WHAT'S THE BIG DEAL?" WILLA'S BEEN TRYING TO convince me to get out of the car for ten minutes now. I admit, the warm sun streaming through the windows is rejuvenating against my skin. It's a beautiful day outside, but I can't do it. "You used to do this all the time."

I shake my head as a lump forms in my throat. People say taking a break from doing something you love can make it harder to come back to it, and that's the type of dread rifling through me as we sit in the McMahon Center parking lot. What if all the wonderful memories are sullied by walking in there feeling the way I do right now.

"I don't know," I say, biting my nail. "It's...been too long. What if I don't like it anymore. What if I'm not good at it anymore?"

"Ash, this isn't open heart surgery. It's a hobby. No one cares if you hate it or you're no good."

"I care." Shaking my head again, I sink into the leather. I used to love swimming, so what about it has me terrified enough to freeze me in this passenger seat? What's so petrifying about the one thing that gave me an escape? The pool was my sanctuary. I only had myself to impress. That's what I loved about it. I could jump in the water and all my worries would wash away.

"How about this?" Willa's voice edges on frustration as she tries to convince me. "Just come into the locker room, put on the suit, and decide about the water later. You can lounge in a chair if you don't want to get in." She leans forward and peers at me like she would an irrational teenager. I guess I'm not too far from acting like one lately, so it's fitting.

"Okay." I blow out a breath, slowly unfolding myself from the seat as I reach for the door handle.

Trepidation builds in the pit of my stomach with each step toward the front door. I feel so far removed from the person who used to love this. *What if my passion for it has fizzled out*? If I discover I no longer enjoy this outlet, it will gut me more than I already am. It will leave me floundering in the worst way. *It'll prove I'm a failure.*

Willa hands over a swim cap with a small bottle of conditioner inside and a faded blue one-piece suit. It's the first one I received after becoming team captain in college. The yellow lettering barely clings to the worn, stretchy fabric. Of all the suits she could have grabbed, she would have had to dig deep in my stash to find this. When I glance at her, she has a twinkle in her eye and a knowing smile on her face.

"I thought you could use a little reminder of who you are. You're the captain of your life, Ashlie. *You* decide the path forward. *You* steer your ship any way you want it to go, around anything or *anyone* trying to get in your way." Willa squeezes my arm as I trace over the letters on my bathing suit. "You've just gotten a little lost on the voyage and could use a compass recalibration. Don't let your worry keep you from your joy, sis." With another squeeze, she walks inside, leaving me to decide which direction I want to steer this catastrophic vessel.

Don't let your worry keep you from your joy. My dad's smile from that first jump in the pool flashes through my mind. I begged him to teach me how to swim for weeks, but as soon as I saw the rippling water, nothing could convince me I wouldn't inhale it all the second I dove in. He tried everything he could think of to get me into the pool. But just like now, I was stubborn as hell. After a while, the only thing he could do was set me on the edge and wait for me to decide for myself. I can still hear his words in my head:

"You know, there's nothing wrong with feeling nervous. But

don't let your worry keep you from your joy. You won't know what fun you're missing if you never jump in the pool."

Dad sat poolside with me for close to an hour. The excited bellows of other kids splashing in the water made me jealous enough to find some courage. I tipped forward until I lost my balance, falling into the water face first. A surprised yelp from Dad registered in my ears just as my face hit the water, his arms wrapping around me right after I submerged. The panic on his face switched to surprise once he realized I was laughing.

The memory of Dad's hearty chuckle as he dropped me back in the water brings a smile to my face. A tear slips down my cheek as I finally accept that I've been letting my anxiety stop me for too long. Somewhere along the way, I started believing the worry was the compass, letting it guide me in all the wrong directions. Allowing the wrong people to change my course. I've been holding *myself* back. *Enough is enough.*

I march into the locker room and put on the suit. As I prep my hair for the chlorine, it feels like I'm gearing up for battle. Sectioning my curls into chunky twists, soaking my strands in the shower, smoothing on conditioner. Each step adds another layer of courage until I'm confidently snapping the swim cap on my head. *You can do this.*

My feet dangle in the water, and I use my shimmering reflection as the recalibration I so desperately need. I dive in—headfirst. My movements are slow, the long-underused muscles warming up as I glide back and forth across the pool. Soon, I'm practicing strokes I haven't done in years, the cool water clearing away my doubts and worries until I come out with a giant smile on my face.

"There she is!" Willa grins from her lounge chair after I've exhausted myself in the pool. "I knew you'd figure it out, girl."

I smile back and pull myself out of the water to sit next to her. Removing my swim cap, I shake my soaking wet twists in her face, just like I used to do when we were kids.

She squeals and throws up her hands as a shield from the droplets. "Okay, I don't miss *that*! Seriously, Ashlie?"

"Hey, this was all *your* idea." I smile, still breathing hard from my laps.

"Yeah, there's something else..." She slips her hand into her tote bag and pulls out my old ID card for the LA County Recreational Centers. The picture is probably seven years old, but it's me, smiling without a care in the world. "I went ahead and renewed your annual membership. That way you have no excuses for not coming out here to swim again."

"Thanks...but I'm confused. How did you know I had a membership here? I haven't been in years, and we weren't exactly talking back then."

She shrugs, smiling. "Hunter mentioned it might help you feel better. Told me not to tell you though."

My heart kickstarts, like the mention of his name is my own personal defibrillator. "You're talking to Hunter?"

"He was worried about how you're doing and asked me. When I told him you've been wasting away on your couch, he told me to get you in the pool. Dropped me a location pin and everything. He even offered to pay for the membership, but I didn't take him up on that part."

You deserve someone who wants your happiness as much as their own. The rapid beating in my chest is nothing compared to the whirlpool in my head as Hunter's words echo. After everything, in spite of everyone else—including himself—he still just wants me to be happy? Tears well in my eyes as I gape at Willa. If it wasn't clear before, *this* solidifies it. *I really don't deserve him.*

"He's figuring it out as he goes, just like you. Take the time you need to decide what you want to do, but he's good for you, Ash. He's only giving you space for your sake. He doesn't want it."

Chewing on my thumbnail, I nod at the sobering reality that I don't just need time to do this on my own. I need some help.

As WILLA AND I LEAVE, A BRIGHT PINK FLYER CATCHES my eye: Youth Swimming Director Needed. The details are vague, but seeing the job listing sparks another moment of clarity in my head, and I rip it from the bulletin board. Something about holding this flyer in my hand makes my dream job more of a tangible possibility than the unopened reminder emails sitting in my inbox. Words on a computer screen are easy to ignore, but a neon piece of paper is a beacon. I could really do something I love for a living, and for the first time in a long time, my mind is clear enough to seriously consider it. Hunter, without even trying, has been helping me find my way to this exact moment. Everything points back to him. It has for a while.

As soon as I get home, I fire up my laptop and sit on the edge of the couch cushion, poised to get this shit done. I don't even bother showering first, worried that doing anything but filling out this application will make me lose my nerve. When I get to the section asking for swimming experience, I take a deep breath and pause, waiting. For fear. Panic. Anxiety. But there's nothing except a rush of excitement for finally getting this far. I bite my lip, and my fingers fly across the keys. My determination to follow through with this takes me right to the submit button, and I click without any hesitation.

"I did it..." I whisper, staring at the words *Application Submitted* for longer than is necessary, soaking in this unfamiliar feeling. *Pride?* That's a new one, but I let it fill me up until I'm smiling from ear to ear and ready to burst. An excited squeal echoes off the walls as I jump up on my couch, bouncing around like a five-year-old. "I fucking did it!" Bouncing turns into a victory dance across the cushions. I *do* feel proud of myself. This is the most empowered I've been in years, and I wish I could capture it in a bottle to carry around with me. *I need to document this!*

Excitement bobs in my knees as I slip my phone from my pocket. Six blurry selfies result from my inability to keep my feet still on the cushion, but the smile in that seventh one is crystal clear. Containing the victory dance to my hips, I tap out a message to send with my picture, still giggling with excitement. Then my face drops. The squeeze in my chest stops me mid-shimmy. Hunter's name glows in the contact field, but I don't remember selecting his name. *Another clear beacon I can't ignore.* He's such an instinct, even my subconscious craves his praise. *And you pushed him away. He deserves better.*

I cringe, awaiting that black hole to suck me in. Waiting for the panicked tears, the berating doubt. But the fear that comes is marred by a tiny glimmer, a remnant left behind by what I overcame today. And the longer I focus on the gleam, the more capable I feel. I scroll through my contacts and hit the number I've admittedly been avoiding for far too long. The anxiety that was nowhere to be found several minutes ago now rolls around in my stomach as ringing shrills in my ear. *This is the next step.*

"Aisha Thompson's office."

I bite my lip and close my eyes at the receptionist's greeting. This jump into the deep end feels harder than my last, but it's the one that matters the most. "Hi... I need to make an appointment."

CHAPTER FORTY-THREE

HUNTER

*F*uck. *It's Wednesday again.* I've been struggling to push the thought from my head since I woke up. I'd hoped it would be fine once I got into work, but the closer it gets to lunchtime, the louder I crank the music in my earbuds to drown it out. It's been a couple of weeks since everything happened in San Francisco, and I still find myself reaching for my phone to text Ashlie. I miss...*everything*. That's the thing about giving someone space. They get a break, and you get a mandatory, miserable, lonely break yourself.

I glance at the clock above Aiden's empty workstation, which doesn't help me forget where I'd usually be at this time. Where I *want* to be right now. A tap on the shoulder snaps me out of my head, and I pull the music from my ear, swinging my chair around to face Aiden.

"You're in the zone today." His smile falters when I don't respond. "No lunch break?"

"Naw." I push my glasses up to the bridge of my nose. "I'm tryna reach a deadline."

"...I don't think I've ever seen you work through lunch before... Is everything okay?"

I nod, shifting my eyes to my screen. "Just have work to do..."

"Alright, alright. I'll take the hint and leave you alone." He chuckles at my brevity, but he doesn't walk away. "You, uh, sure you're good?"

"How about you just ask what you want to ask me?"

"How's Ashlie?"

"I wouldn't know. Anything else?"

"Do you want to talk about it?"

"Naw. I'm good."

Aiden sucks air in through his teeth, shaking his head. "You're a steel trap, man."

"What can I say? It's a gift." I shrug, dropping my eyes to my keyboard. His words are like a punch to the gut. *Ashlie said the same thing.*

"I didn't say it was good. It'll eat you up inside if you keep holding it all in. Shit's not healthy, man." He raps his knuckles on my desk and heads for the door. "Don't forget to eat lunch, boss!"

I got word about my promotion to remote supervisor when I got back from San Francisco. But after everything that happened, it's hard to feel excited about the new position. There's a lot more paper pushing, which is what I'm working on now, but nothing too difficult. Apart from extra meetings and phone calls during the week, it doesn't feel much different from what I was doing before. I worked hard to get here and do my job well; I just don't care about anything right now.

Out of habit, I grab my phone from my desk drawer, thumbs freezing over the screen as soon as I realize what I'm doing. This isn't the first time it's happened, where muscle memory takes over and I'm staring at a conversation full of comfortable affection. If I could go back to that night and redo everything, I would.

ME

Goodnight, 🍵 🐻

ASHLIE

You really like calling me that...

ME

You don't?

ASHLIE

I didn't say that… It's cute.

ME

As are you…

ASHLIE

Oh yeah? Why don't you come say that to my face?

ME

Bet

STAYING LATE TO AVOID EVENINGS ALONE IS BECOMING a habit. All I plan to do is shower and fall into bed. Not bothering to turn on the light, I lock my apartment door, hang up my keys, and feel my way back to my bedroom. Pain shoots across my hip, something clattering to the floor when I bump into the bookshelf.

Grumbling, I flip on the light, and the Christmas present from Mom lies on the herringbone rug in front of me. I've had it hidden under papers and random junk for months. I'd forgotten it was even there. But now it's taunting me. Pleading to be noticed. Begging to be opened.

"*Fucking why not*?" I sigh, curiosity getting the best of me. I'm already feeling low, why not sprinkle a little aggravation on top?

Settling on the edge of my king-sized bed, I turn the package over in my hands. It's not heavy, covered in a shiny gold foil wrapping paper. Nothing rattles when I shake it. I peek inside like whatever's in there will jump out and bite me, but it's just a book.

Leather-bound, with gold lettering that spells out my full name: *Hunter James Jackson.*

Pictures of me as an infant are scattered across the first page, listing my birth stats and the hospital I was born in. I turn to the next page, and the next, and the next, each with a progression of photos throughout my childhood. Tucked in between the pictures are basic milestones—first haircut, school awards, and the dates I lost all my teeth.

As I move toward the back of the book, the pages dedicated to my teenage years have less pictures and more news clippings of my records from the high school track team. All standard things you'd expect from a scrapbook. Several of the memories behind these photos make me smile, briefly forgetting for a moment who this book came from. It's a sweet little keepsake, even if my callous mother created it.

The last spread is filled with newspaper clippings of every running record I broke in college, next to pictures of me after each race. These aren't reprinted from the internet. They're original, neatly cut from the Gradford University Gazette. *How'd she get all of these?* Graduation was years ago. She was already living abroad when I did all of this. I doubt the university keeps a backlog of physical papers for long. None of it makes any sense...until it clicks. Four years of my collegiate athletic career stare back at me, and the only way Mom could've done this is if she had the original papers when they were printed.

I run my fingers over the yellowing newsprint. As the full reality of what this book means dawns on me, a tear drips on the back of my hand. *I'm fucking crying?* Over a basic-ass scrapbook from the heartless Black Widow, no less. Another drop stains my hand, and despite the armored insults swirling in my head about her, I feel cracking in my chest.

She's been there. Not physically, but she's always been with me—keeping tabs on my accomplishments from the time I was born until I graduated from college. In her own way—in the only way I've allowed her to—she's kept up with my life over the years.

It doesn't forgive anything she's done. I'm not that soft. But something wedges into the split in my chest and stays there, allowing a little more softness in and a lot more resentment out.

Fresh tears prick my eyes, and once they start to run, I can't get them to stop. Whatever mechanism I've held on to so tightly inside breaks, the floodgates releasing an onslaught of pent-up emotions. Years of angst, a decade of hate, and what feels like a lifetime of hurt all come to the surface. Sadness over Ashlie. Fear about losing her for good. The force of it makes me hunch over the open scrapbook, shoulders shaking as I sob.

"*Shit.*" My tears are ruining the pages in my lap. Tossing the book to the side, I lean back on the bed, causing the stream to drip into my ears. I press my hands to my eyes, trying to slow the leaking, to no avail. *What. The. Fuck. Is happening to me right now?* Weeping like a sentimental sap, over a damn scrapbook, is some fuckery.

It's more than that. She may have missed some things, but she didn't miss everything. Despite giving me the space I demanded, maybe—just maybe—she was telling the truth; she regrets leaving me behind.

Taking deep breaths seems to help, so I pull air in through my nose, blowing it out of my mouth until I feel the storm pass. With my arm draped over my forehead, I pull out my phone and dial a number I never thought I'd willingly use again.

"Hunter?" Mom's voice hesitates. "What's wrong? It's... early."

Shit. I didn't even think of the time difference. I glance at the alarm clock on my nightstand. It's close to 4 a.m. in Sweden.

"Uh, yeah. Sorry. I didn't realize the time. I can call back later." I'm pretty sure we both know I'm not calling back if I hang up this phone.

"No! No, it's okay." I hear shuffling in the background. "Is everything alright? Did something happen?"

"Naw, I just... I finally opened your Christmas present. Uh..." *Why is this so fucking hard for me?* It's two simply words, but the longer I wait, the more my eyes sting. *Again?* This is bullshit, and I'm already sick of it. "Thanks, Mom," I whisper, my breath catching at the release of fresh tears drowning out more of my resentment.

"Oh, Hunter." She sniffles softly. "I'm glad you like it. I love you, my son."

I nod like she can see me through the speaker, and another sob slips out of my mouth. *Fuck this.* My throat's raw from the strain of the tears, but they won't fucking stop. "I, um... Can I call you back?" I croak, realizing I'm not fit for a phone call after all.

"Of course. You can call me anytime—day or night—and I'll answer. I'm happy you called, Hunter."

"Me too," I say weakly, feeling like it's the truth for the first time in a long time.

CHAPTER FORTY-FOUR
ASHLIE

"So you're good?" I ask Kayla. Fort Bender's calming breeze swirls around us as the tide whispers in the background. The rocky shore sets a calming background against the navy-colored deck at The Bluffs Estates. She's busy fluffing the pink lilies I *just* placed out on the patio table, her chevron blouse rippling in the breeze. Our friend Samson delivered the perfect bouquets from Forget Me Nots, but the party planner in her can't leave the details to anyone else. She's been following behind us all morning, refixing the decorations for her bridal shower today. "We're still having a wedding here next week?"

"Yep!" Her smile beams across the table, her hands still at work on those flowers. "We talked everything out, and Chase had his finger ready to cancel all the reservations until I dropped him off at the airport last night."

"What was the issue, girl?"

She smooths her hands over the blush tablecloth. "Our moms got in my head, and I spiraled."

"Okay, but that's an easy problem to solve. Why didn't you just say that when I asked you fifty times?"

"I thought becoming a wife meant I was supposed to handle

all the pressure on my own." Kayla shrugs. "But I'm fine now. The wedding is still on."

"*Thank God!* Are you excited?"

"Yeah. I really am."

"Nervous?" I ask, walking around to her.

"Nope. Just ready."

I wrap my arm around her shoulders and tip my temple to hers. "I'm so excited for you, girl. You deserve your 'Happily Ever After.'"

"So do you, Ash," she says quietly, pulling away to look into my eyes. "What's happening with the Hunter thing?"

Chase filled her in about the bachelorette party the morning after. When my plane landed in LA, I had several voicemails from her, demanding I call her back ASAP. She kept me on the phone for hours, scrutinizing every last detail about Hunter and me.

Puffing out a breath, I sit on the edge of the patio table. "Nothing..." I swallow the thick cluster of guilt crawling up my throat. I'm getting comfortable in my inaction. It's not that I'm doing *nothing*. Over the last couple of weeks, my therapist has been helping me work through some of my fears—speaking them aloud, writing them down and burning them, feeling scared and doing it anyway. It just turns out they're a lot more deep-seated than I realized. I don't feel like I've made enough progress to talk to him yet.

She raises an eyebrow. "Ash, I thought you called your—"

"I did. And I've had a few sessions. I just..." I smash my lips into a flat line, hoping she'll see the panic in my eyes and give me a break.

Instead, her arms settle across her chest as she leans against the wooden table. I didn't think she could raise that eyebrow any higher, but here we are.

Speak the fears out loud, Ashlie. "I'm the one that asked for space, even though I'm the one that fucked things up in the first place. I'm nervous that it's too late."

"It's not." She doesn't even blink when she says it.

"How do you know?"

"Because you two make sense. You complement each other. He's impulsive and guarded, and you're cautious and wear your heart on your sleeve. You can't stand disappointing people, and he couldn't care less what people think. It's a balance that works with you two. Plus, you're both annoying, so..." She giggles as she dodges my swat to her shoulder. "You told me on New Year's that you love him. Did you ever tell him?"

"Girl, no," I say, slipping my thumbnail in between my teeth. "I could barely say it to myself..."

"Do you *still* love him?"

"*Ugh*, yes..." I whine, relenting to the clear case she's building. She knocks my shoulder with hers a couple of times until I look at her.

"So tell him."

"But I'm scared!" The vulnerable burn in my chest makes me drop my head in my hands with a groan. *Is this ever going to get easier?*

Kayla chuckles, giving me a small smile. "Tell him that, too, girl. Communicate. You saw what happened to me. What's the holdup?"

Speak the fear. "I want to make sure I'm giving him my best before I ask for another chance, and I don't feel like I'm there yet. I'm still a mess, clearly." I point to the tears dripping down my face.

"That doesn't have to happen in a vacuum, Ash. I understand wanting to give it your all; there's nothing wrong with that. But holding yourself back from happiness in hopes that you *might* reach some arbitrary goal isn't making anything better for you or him. You can work on yourself and still be loved. You *deserve* to be loved, just as you are."

Debatable.

She's making a hell of a lot of sense, but knowing it and *feeling* it are worlds apart. Still, as much as I want to stay in my cozy corner of caution, it hasn't served me well. Air puffs from my lips as I trample that limiting belief with an affirmation from my coping toolbox.

Affirmation: I am lovable.

"Look, I'm going to tell you the same thing you told me when I was too scared to get with Chase. You're forgetting the third thing."

"The what? What's the third thing?" I reach for a napkin to wipe the mascara from my cheeks.

"It could all work out, and you two could end up happy. Together. You have to let the fears go, Ash. They'll eat you up inside." She squeezes my arm and walks back into the rental behind us, leaving me alone to absorb all of her wisdom.

Don't let your worry keep you from your joy. It echoes in all four chambers of my heart, a little beacon of hope in this hurricane I'm clawing my way out of.

Affirmation: I am capable.

CHAPTER FORTY-FIVE

HUNTER

"Hey," Chase claps me on the shoulder. "Don't look so sad. One more week, and I'll give the spotlight back to you." The bright lights in the alteration room at Tom's Tuxedo Parlor augment my sullen reflection in the wall of mirrors.

"Funny," I murmur, knocking him in the ribs with my elbow. He chuckles as he steps to the side, adjusting his tie. Kayla had this dumbass idea for them to spend the week before the wedding apart from each other. Something about distance and the heart growing fonder. So Chase is here in LA for the week, while she's in Fort Bender. *With Ashlie. Fuck distance. It can kiss my ass.*

I turn to the side and straighten my jacket, checking the fit before reaching around my neck to secure my tie. The beige silk shines as it glides through my fingers, and all my attention locks in on forming a Windsor knot. When I look back in the mirror, Chase is watching me, all the humor in his face replaced by worry. "You talk to Ash?"

"Naw." I finish up with the tie and head for the leather lounge chairs. As soon as I hit the seat, my head falls into my hands, and I breathe out a strained sigh. The closer we get to the wedding, the more stressed I am. *What if she's changed her mind?*

Chase takes the seat across from me. "Man, if I knew you were the other guy, I wouldn't have encouraged Trevor so much. What happened?"

"She asked for space." I shrug, straightening in the chair. Tom's is the last place I want to get into this.

"Come on, Hunt. It's *me*. You think I don't know when you're hiding shit? Stop shutting down and walk me back. What happened?"

I rub my fingers across my forehead, pressing hard like it'll help me condense five years' worth of pining into a minute long synopsis. Chase kicks my Oxford, somehow tapping the correct cobblestone to unlock the secret passageway. Everything spills out. All the missing details from the night five years ago, Halloween, the lodge, and New Year's. I ignore his bulging eyes when I describe the bet. And once I tell him about the hotel in San Francisco, his hand settles over his mouth as if he's trying to hold the words in.

Eyes stinging, I massage my temples, hoping to stop whatever this is threatening to spill down my cheeks. *Frustration? Sorrow? Who the hell knows anymore?* Tears falling in my apartment is one thing, but I draw the line at it happening in an overpriced tuxedo shop.

"Okay," he says slowly. "So you had the bet"—he grimaces, clearly disagreeing with that choice—"dated, and wooed. Did you ever tell her how you feel about her?

"I tried to tell her I love her in San Francisco, but she freaked."

"Yeah, well, you went from friends to a fun dating bet to 'I love you' in the span of a couple of months. You changed the dynamic too fast."

"I know I did." I groan. "I knew she was scared, but I pushed her anyway and fucked it all up. Now she wants nothing to do with me." Tipping my head back, my hands cover the wetness leaking from my eyes. Apparently, the line of propriety has moved, and the tuxedo shop *is* an acceptable place to cry.

"Asking for space doesn't mean she's done with you."

"Fucking feels like it..." I mumble through my fingers. "Bruh,

I can't breathe. Can't think. It's been weeks, and I still see her smile every time I close my eyes. Knowing Ash doesn't want me around feels like a hot blade being twisted in my chest. I'm fucking miserable."

"Hunt..." He jostles me as he moves into the chair next to mine. "Did you talk about this in your session last week?"

"Damn it." I drop my hands. "Was I supposed to?"

An exasperated sigh rumbles through his lips. "Yeah, man. That's the whole point, getting everything off your chest so you can address it."

"How was I supposed to know that? All this shit is new to me." After that call with my mom, I couldn't get myself together for days. I was so desperate, I called my dad's psychologist to make sure I wasn't losing it. Turns out, all the shit I've been pushing down for years couldn't be held off any longer, and the remedy is *feeling* it. Oh, and I have ADHD.

"Look, space just means she needs a minute. This isn't about you, Hunt. Hey..." He knocks me with his elbow until I look at him, then places a hand on my shoulder with a pointed stare. A silent conversation passes between us, one that only he and I could ever understand. He saw first-hand how bad it was for me after the divorce, the blame I assigned myself, how scared I was. How scared I *am*. "It's. Not. You."

Heaving a sputtering breath, I plant my elbows on my knees. "She said she wasn't ready. What if she never is?"

"You can't think like that, Hunt." He sighs. "You know her. Just give her a little time."

"But what if she doesn't come back to me, Chase?" The thought alone makes my voice shake. "What the hell would I do? She's it for me."

"You have to *tell* her exactly how serious this is for you. No more games. *No bets*. Help her bridge that gap so she has no space to question how you feel about her. And don't stop telling her once you finally do have her."

"She asked for space until after the wedding. I can't just say all of that after a month of nothing." I wipe my face and straighten up in the chair. The tears were short-lived, but damn it if I don't feel a little better. "And there's still the Trevor issue."

His eyebrows dip. "What Trevor issue? They're—"

"Sorry I'm late!" Trevor comes from behind the wall of mirrors, and my face drops. I knew he was coming, but seeing him when I know he still gets to be around Ashlie pushes a wave of indignation throughout my body. "This new cohort needed a ton of guidance today. I have to run back to the office after this."

"No worries, Trev." Chase stands, slapping his hand with some cheesy grade school handshake. "Your tux is in that room over there. I'll grab Tom."

He leaves me and Trevor—the loser and the winner, the unpredictable storm and the reliable ray of sunshine—to settle the score. I make no attempts to be cordial, hoping he'll get the hint and take his ass into the dressing room.

"Hey, bro, uh," he says, taking a step toward me. "Look, I didn't know you were the other guy. If I had, I would have bowed out long before I did."

Confusion scrunches my face. "What do you mean?" *He bowed out? Of what? When?*

"Yeah, I broke things off after the bar fight. I can't compete with what you two have going on."

"We're not—We don't have anything going on anymore."

Now he looks confused. "Oh... You're not seeing Ashlie?" he asks.

"Not at the moment. *You're* not seeing Ashlie?"

"Nope, we decided we're better as friends. I figured she would have told you..."

I shake my head slowly. *Is he fucking with me?* I never pegged Trevor as the mind game type, but this would be a good way to do it. Kick me when I'm already down.

"I just wanted to make sure there are no hard feelings." His hand gestures between us like he's physically clearing the air.

"So, you're not dating?" My heart beats a tick faster as I try to keep the hopeful tone from rising in my voice.

The confused look on his face eases into an amicable smile, giving me the last bit of confirmation I need. "Nope. Just friends."

I laugh, cover it quickly with my hand, and laugh again. He hasn't been getting closer to her in the last month. *I still have a chance.*

"Well, since no one's dating Ash, that only means one thing." Chase steps into the room with a conspiratorial look in his eyes. "My wedding has unofficially become Operation: Get Hunter and Ashlie together."

I shake my head. "That's a horrible name."

"Yeah..." Trevor trills. "That's not good at all, man."

"Oh, you guys have something better?"

"Operation: Hushlie?" Trevor offers.

"*The fuck*? Does it have to have a name?" I ask.

"We have tuxedos and a secret mission. I'm pretty sure we have to name it," Trevor says.

"Pretty sure it's in the handbook." Chase nods enthusiastically.

"What fucking handbook?"

"The 'Pretending to be Super Spies Because We'll be in Tuxedos' handbook. Operation: Hushlie is the inaugural mission." Trevor nods like this isn't the dumbest conversation we're having.

"How old are we? Nine? You two are idiots. Don't call it that."

"Then what should we call it, Hunt?" Chase raises his eyebrows, challenging me to play along.

"Hell, I don't know. Literally anything else."

"Like...?" Trevor jumps in on the challenge.

I think about it, and only one name comes to mind. It won't make sense to either of them, but the more I think about it, the more perfect of a name it is.

"Operation: Sunshine," I say finally. They pause and turn toward each other, matching smiles creeping across their faces.

"Operation: Sunshine it is!" Chase chuckles and turns back toward his dressing room, loosening his tie as he goes.

"Nice name. I feel good about that one." Trevor holds a fist toward me. I shake my head as I bump his knuckles with mine, letting out a little snort. Without the lens of jealousy clouding my judgment, I can see why everyone gets along with him.

CHAPTER FORTY-SIX

ASHLIE

I *shouldn't be up here.* I'm supposed to be grabbing napkins from the downstairs storage room, but I couldn't resist this little detour upstairs. The sheer curtains around the French window, the light blue seashell paintings, the bed covered with the same tufted ivory comforter—I take in all of it.

With the ceremony tomorrow, Chase and Kayla requested a wedding party breakfast at The Bluffs Estates. I haven't seen Hunter yet, but standing in this room full of memories—the place where everything started years ago—makes me realize how much I've missed him. It's been a special kind of misery, so I'm allowing myself to replay all the things about that night and everything else.

Among last-minute wedding touches this week, I've had a panic attack, an emergency virtual therapy appointment, and several pep-talks with Kayla about seeing Hunter for the first time. She offered to help me come up with a plan, but I wanted to see if I could do it on my own. Now, I'm not feeling so confident.

My therapy work has centered on being open about my worries: from the unease related to work and my future, to my fear of disappointment and feeling unworthy. Hunter deserves to know what he's signing up for before we jump into a relationship.

I've stressed over the best way to talk to him after the wedding, considered contacting him beforehand too. Typed and erased dozens of texts. Hovered my thumb over the phone icon until it cramped. Abandoned an email or three. But none of it felt good enough. Anything other than face-to-face is a copout.

I've made progress, but still don't feel like there's been enough to keep from ruining everything. Hell, asking for this break instead of leaning on him might have already messed it all up. I thought I needed to suffer through this on my own, that having an anxiety disorder was a moral failing—but I don't, and it's not. Working on myself and being with Hunter aren't mutually exclusive.

"You good?"

I jump out of my skin. "God, Hunter! You scared me."

"Sorry." His mouth curls on one side, and my heart aches as I realize I've missed that too. "Did you, uh, find what you were looking for in there?" He nods toward the room as he settles against the doorframe.

"I wasn't looking for anything. I was just...remembering." Guppies glide around the nerves swirling in my belly as I study my shoes. Seeing him again, being this close, it's more intimidating than I thought it would be.

"Yeah... I did that myself when I got in last night."

Flicking my eyes back to his, I expect that telltale smirk, assuming there's some sly innuendo in his response. Instead, he's looking down as he toes the threshold. He taps his phone against his thigh, the silence growing thick around us.

Now's your chance.

"Hunt—"

"—Ash"

We both laugh nervously. I'd be surprised if he can't hear my heart hammering in my chest. "You go," I say, rocking back on my heels.

"No...you." His eyes lock to mine, the weightlessness of being pulled back into his orbit wrapping around me. *I've missed you. I'm sorry. I love you.*

His phone buzzes, and he glances at it immediately, the way he used to before we made a mess of things.

"You're popular..." I grimace at my awkward teasing attempt.

"Naw, it's my mom..."

"Your *mom?*" *What happened in the last few weeks that has him talking to his mom?*

He shrugs, typing something out on his phone before slipping it in his pocket. "Yep. We're...working on it."

"That's a big development. Is it a good thing?"

"Eh." He chuckles, tipping his hand back and forth. "I don't really know yet, but it's something. My therapist told me to take it slow."

My head juts back in surprise. "Therapist?"

"Yeah. Turns out I'm not so great at talking about my feelings...." His face pinches, his gaze dropping to the ground.

Yeah, me neither. "That's really great, Hunt."

His eyes slowly find mine until they're boring straight through me. "Things change."

"Yeah..." I whisper. The uncomfortable tension between us is almost too much to bear. This isn't us. Small talk, nervous laughter—it feels unnatural. We're talking, sure, but the longer we do, the harder it is to address the fact that I messed everything up with him. Taking a deep breath, I clench my fists to ground myself, hoping the right words will come out when I open my mouth. *Do it scared, Ashlie.*

"Ashlie!" Willa calls from downstairs. "Did you find them? Everyone's waiting."

Whatever confidence that deep breath just gave me flies right out the window. "I should go..." I say without looking at Hunter. I feel his gaze, but the thought of looking back into those green eyes when I just chickened out feels too embarrassing right now. Slipping past him, I hurry down the stairs, chasing after the courage that fled as soon as I saw his face. I think I need to take Kayla up on her offer.

Affirmation: I have friends who support me when I ask for help.

THE WEATHERED WOOD AROUND PATTI'S PLACE GIVES A rustic feel to the cheery blush place settings. We've finished the rehearsal part of the evening, and now everyone's mingling while enjoying dinner at the diner.

Willa sidles up next to me at the punch bowl, camera slung around her neck. She eyes Hunter across the room. "Have you talked to him yet?"

This is the third time she's asked me today, and it's *not* making this any easier. Keeping my eyes on the sparkling drink in my hand, I play dumb. "Who?"

"You know who." She squints at me, then tosses another look over her shoulder. "The guy who *should* be your date tonight. The one we spent all morning coming up with a plan for."

"Oh, him. Nope." I shake my head and take a sip.

"Why not? And why is Trevor staring at you too? I thought that was done with," she whispers, looking back and forth between me and the guys at the table.

"Because I'm scared, okay? You happy?" Scared doesn't come close to describing how I feel right now, especially after losing my nerve this morning. I failed. But I'm learning failure isn't the problem. It's what you do afterward that defines who you are. Ready or not, I need to have this conversation tonight or I won't do it at all.

"This is messier than it was befo—"

"Trevor's just a friend. And he's not looking at me, he's looking at *you*," I say, enjoying the way her eyes bug out of her head. He asked me a week ago if I'd be okay with him pursuing her, and I wished him luck. "He's been trying to talk to you all weekend."

"*Me*? Why the hell is he looking at me?" Willa scrunches her face and takes another furtive glance at the table, snapping her head back so fast her hair whips my arm. "Is that why he keeps asking for a chess game rematch? I'm not his type *at all*."

One peek at Trevor's eyes on her has me giggling. "But is he yours?"

She shakes her head, but her mouth pops open and closed like a fish gasping for air. I leave that planted seed to fester and walk across the room. Willa finally broke up with her douchey boyfriend. She's long overdue for a good man in her life. One who moves slowly and doesn't get discouraged easily. After watching Trevor *try* to chat her up all day, I can see the two of them happening. With Willa's independence, I doubt she even noticed all of his effort. But I bet she'll notice now.

I slide into my chair next to Trevor right as Chase's dad, Russell, cracks a joke that has everyone laughing. His once blond hair is completely gray now, smile wrinkles deepening on his ivory face as he titters with everyone else. Across the table from me, Hunter leans back in his seat. His eyes flick to mine with a smirk before looking back at Russell. Just that fast, my insides are flitter-flopping like a month hasn't passed.

"Hunter, I'm surprised you don't have a date this weekend," Russell says. "That's unlike you."

"Yeah, well, the one I wanted wasn't ready." Hunter looks right at me, and so does everyone else when they realize it. Clearing my throat, I reach for my drink to cool the heat rising up my neck. The quiet chuckle under his breath is loud as hell to my ears, though I doubt anyone else heard it. "I'm gonna grab another drink. Anyone need anything?" Hunter asks, standing from the table. I finally release my breath as he strolls across the room.

There's movement beside me, but I'm too flustered to realize Trevor's stood up and Kayla's taken his place until she says, "Hey, girl, you ready?" She puts her hand on mine, pulling me back into the moment. "Here's the key. Do you know what you're going to say?"

I bite my thumbnail and shake my head. "No. But I have to try."

"Just be honest. With him and with yourself." She squeezes my hand and smiles. "And if you come out of there single, I'm disowning both of your ridiculous asses. Now go. I'll handle the rest."

I smooth my dress nervously as I walk behind the counter. When I unlock the supply room, and the noises from the party disappear, I breathe a sigh of relief. This reprieve is exactly what the doctor ordered. The napkins and straws transition into a sandy beach when I close my eyes. *In through the nose, out through the mouth.* My breathing mantra loops until I feel calm and clear-headed. It's now or never, and I have a few more minutes to decide what I want to say.

Affirmation: I believe in myself.

CHAPTER FORTY-SEVEN

HUNTER

"Alright..." Trevor rubs his hands together. "Now we gotta figure out how to get you two alone."

"I still vote for the grand gesture route. Grab that mic and spill your heart out," Chase says.

I shudder at the thought of having all these extra people in my business. I'm nervous enough as it is. "Bruh, hard pass."

"Go pull her aside right now." Trevor nudges me toward the table. "Tell her you want to take her outside."

Scowling, I shake my head. "Naw, that sounds like I want to fight her in the parking lot."

"Yeah, that's not romantic at all, Trev," Chase says. "He's supposed to leave an impression, not freak her out even more."

Ashlie running from me this morning flashes in my mind. As frustrating as it was, I let her go anyway. Technically, I broke the agreement; she asked until *after* the wedding. But a full day of keeping my hands and eyes to myself has been agonizing. All I want to do is cling to her. I can't wait until tomorrow.

"You could show up at her parent's house tonight." Trevor tries again. "Borrow that boombox over there and blast it outside her bedroom window."

"See, *that's* what I'm talking about!" Chase gives Trevor a high-five.

"You guys are horrible at this." Kayla laughs beside me. I've been so tuned into the back and forth between these two dummies, I didn't even see her come over.

"Oh, and you have something better?" Chase cocks his head.

With crossed arms and an arched brow, she cocks her head right back. "I do, and I've already put it in motion. Operation: Sunshine will be a success. The three of you can thank me later."

"How do you know about that?" Trevor asks, wide-eyed.

"For three guys moonlighting as secret spies, you really need to check your surroundings. I heard you scheming through the open kitchen window while I was out on the deck last night."

"So, you gonna fill us in on your plan, or...?" I ask, impatiently scanning the room for my girl.

"I just sent her to the supply room to find blush-colored forks."

Blinking at her does nothing to reveal the hidden meaning in her message, and the other two look just as lost as I am. "How the hell is that helpful?" I ask.

"There *are* no blush-colored forks. All the plasticware tonight is champagne-colored."

I glower at my sister. *What the fuck do forks have to do with anything?*

Kayla sighs her frustration, twirling her hands around to emphasize her point. "She's going to be looking for a while. For something that doesn't exist. Alone. *Where no one will bother her...*" I still have nothing. "Oh. My. God. Hunter, go to the damn supply room, close the door, and tell her whatever you need to tell her."

"Genius." Trevor claps slowly. "That's it. That's the move."

"Baby, that's *so* good! Marry me?" Chase teases, pulling Kayla into a hug. She rolls her eyes, but smiles and hugs him back.

"Hunt, you're my brother, I love you, and I'm only going to say this once..." Kayla warns.

"What? If I hurt her, you'll kill me?"

"Nope." She gives me a gentle smile. "Don't hold back. She needs to hear all of it."

Without another word, I spring toward the hallway. I know what I want to say to her. Hopefully, this time, she's willing to consider it. Consider *me*. I open the door, prepared to sweep the love of my life off her feet, but I stop at the sight of her biting her thumbnail as she watches me enter. We're suspended in time for a few seconds, just staring, and I'm pretty sure my sister was working as a double agent.

"Kayla mentioned something about forks…" I take slow steps toward her. "This isn't about forks, is it?"

She shakes her head, dropping her trembling hands at her sides, and takes a deep breath. "I need to fix all of this. The last few months, I've blamed you for my hesitation and refused to acknowledge all the ways you've been changing. Made you jump through hoops. Avoided my feelings for you so I could keep hiding in a corner, scared." She reaches for my hand, her gaze studying our laced fingers. "I know I'm the problem here, Hunter."

I swallow thickly. This wasn't what I was expecting *at all*.

"I've been hypocritical, calling you out for keeping your feelings inside when I'm the one who wasn't communicating. And when I asked for space…" Tears fill her eyes as they slide to mine. "I realized I didn't deserve your effort when I hadn't put any in myself. You should be with someone who's working just as hard to be the best for you. I didn't want to be the disappointment that caused everything to crumble. I've been inconsiderate and stubborn during all of this, and I'm sorry." Her voice cracks on the last word as she hurriedly swipes her cheeks.

Words escape me. When I came in here, I was prepared to give my best pitch for why we should be together. Make her see how right we are. The notion that the woman of my dreams isn't good enough for me is nonsensical. She's apologizing, while my focus is solely on how much I've missed being this close to her.

She purses her lips and shifts her eyes to the floor, dropping my hand. "If you're done with me, I get it. I'm still a damn mess, and I won't blame you if you don't want to put up with it." Her voice shakes as she nervously smooths out her dress. Those beautiful brown eyes look so distressed, it breaks me.

I reach out and tug her back to me. "I'm not done with you, honey bear." My thumb travels across her freckled cheekbone, and I savor the feeling of her skin against mine. It's all I've ever wanted. "As long as I'm breathing, I'll never be done with you. With *us*. Life without you, even for a month, has been absolute hell." Her jasmine essence wraps around me as I rest my forehead against hers and breathe her in. *I've fucking missed this.* "I adore you, Ashlie. Everything about you lights me up inside. Your kindness, the sassy way you challenge me, and God, your smile. You wreck me with that thing."

She bites her timid grin, giggling when I tug her lip free with a gentle thumb. "That's the one," I say, smiling back. "Ash, when I tried to tell you I love you, what I should have said was you're the first thought I think in the morning. You're the one I want to tell everything to throughout the day, and the last face I see in my mind when I close my eyes at night. My dreams start and end with you because you're my wildest dream come true. You're the vibrancy to the bleak, the beauty to the mundane, and the light to all my shadows. You're everything to me."

Tears drip from her eyes as I cup her face in my hands. She opens her mouth, squeaking softly when no words come out.

"If you don't feel the same way, just say the word. I'll walk out of here and pretend like nothing from the past few months happened. It'll hurt like hell, but I'll do that for you if it's what you really want. I'll always be here for you. *Always.*" I graze her nose with mine, air stuttering from my lungs as the adrenaline settles. "But if there's any part of you that wants this—wants *me*—please tell me."

I close my eyes then, unable to bear the look in hers if she says no. My thoughts spiral the longer we stay like this, but I can't let go of her. Not yet. Not ever. *Not unless she asks me to.*

Her tears trail slowly over my thumbs, and I open my eyes as she squeezes hers shut. "I want to fail with you," she says, followed by a long, shaky exhale. My heart stalls as I search her face for clarity. "I want to fail over and over, until we get it right, because you scare me, Hunter. In a good way... In the 'I love you too' way..."

When I press my lips to hers, my world eases back into focus. A world where the driving force is, and always will be, her. I can't get enough, pulling her tightly against my body as I wrap my arms around her. The separation was torturous, but her warmth seeps into me, thawing the desolate remnants of every day we've spent apart until the only thing that matters is right here and now.

I rest my forehead on hers and drink in everything she is. "I want *all* of you, Ashlie. Your fear and everything else. For now, for always, forever. I don't ever want to know a life without you in it."

The soft pressure of her lips as she brushes them against mine once, twice, and lingering a third time has me sighing into her. "I want all of you too," she whispers. "Just you." Her hand cradles my face, and I lean in to her touch. "I've missed you." She smiles up at me, completely shattering all my worries as she nuzzles my nose.

"You have?" I'm pretty sure there are tears in my eyes, but I don't give a damn. I'm so fucking happy right now.

"So much. Your kindness, your confidence, your heart. You've always considered my happiness, even when I was too stubborn to consider yours. You're my safe place, Hunter, and I've missed everything about you."

Finally. I kiss her forehead, her left cheek, then her right, her nose. She giggles when my smile meets hers, and I dive into the one thing I'll never get enough of. With each tug of her lips, Ashlie's love seeps into me, a refiner's fire transforming my own into a river of pure devotion that flows only to her.

"No more leaving?" My voice cracks as I whisper through my vulnerability.

Pressing another peck to my lips, she gives a coy smile. "No more."

This shimmery lightness inside makes up for everything that led us here. Every ex, every bet, every misstep was worth it just to end up in this moment. I would redo it all if it meant getting back my everything—my sunshine.

I'VE ONLY BEEN TO A COUPLE OF WEDDINGS, BUT I'VE never been a fan. The tears, the cheesy vows, the lovey-dovey PDA. Everyone seems to embrace it just from being near a bride and groom, but it all makes me want to gag... *Made me want to gag*. Past tense. Since I'm standing here on Crystal Beach with a goofy-ass smile, staring across the aisle at the one who holds my heart. Her curls dance around her face with the breeze, the sun glistening off the sea glass, and only one thought crosses my mind. *She's finally mine*. I catch her eye, and she smiles back at me. Every single thing I've ever criticized about weddings makes sense now.

Chase's sniffling snaps me out of Ashlie's hypnotic pull, and Trevor bumps my arm from behind, handing me a tissue. The guests laugh when I make a show of dangling it in Chase's face. He dabs his misty eyes as I give his shoulder a reassuring clap.

The music switches from a light waltz to an intentional march. Everyone turns in their wooden chairs as Dad and Kayla appear at the end of the wooden plank aisle. The champagne fabric draped across the wedding arch flutters around us wildly. Chase loses it, blubbering like the love-sick fool he is. Desperately trying to wipe his face, he turns around, struggling to regain his composure.

"Naw," I say. "This is the part you want to remember. That smile on her face is just for you."

He nods, turns back around, and loses it all over again from the way his bride beams at him. Dad hands her off to Chase, and she reaches up to wipe the tears from his cheeks, which does nothing to stop the downpour.

I can't say I'll ever display this amount of unbridled emotion in front of a crowd, but when I slide my eyes back to Ashlie's giant smile, I get it. For the first time in my life, I get it.

CHAPTER FORTY-EIGHT

ASHLIE

"Presenting Mr. and Mrs. Chase Wilmington!" Hadley, Chase's sister, announces across the reception hall. The lights dim as a spotlight guides Chase and Kayla onto the dance floor. Everyone whoops and cheers when he twirls her to the C & K projected at the center of the room. The bridal party is scattered around the banquet table, and I'm right next to Hunter, where I should have been all along.

Every time I've looked at him today, his eyes were on me. I'm pretty sure I'll have a permanent mark on my lower lip from biting it so much. The anticipation of falling back into his orbit is off the charts. We haven't had a minute alone since our time in the storage closet. His hand stroking my thigh under the table right now does nothing to dampen the desire I've finally given myself permission to feel.

"Family and friends"—Hadley gestures with her hand—"please direct your attention to the dance floor, where the bride and groom will share their first dance as husband and wife." She pushes her glasses up her nose and sandwiches one headphone-covered ear against her shoulder, sweeping her blond hair behind her.

Lights flash around the room as people take pictures of the

happy couple. I recognize the slow, sultry blues song as one that holds a special place in their story. Watching them sway together as husband and wife is a nice reward after seeing their relationship blossom and grow over the years.

"You're so goddamn beautiful," Hunter whispers, squeezing my leg to get my attention. His warm breath on my ear sends goosebumps racing down my arms.

My cheeks burn as I turn to him. "You keep saying that…"

"Because I like the way you blush when I say it." He smiles, I bite my lip, and we repeat the timid tango we've been dancing all day.

I lean into him so he can hear me over the music. "I know you hate all this stuff, but don't they look so happy? It's adorable."

"It is." He places his hand on my back, his thumb leaving a tingling caress over my bare skin. "And maybe I hate it a little less than before."

"*Oh*?" My eyebrows shoot up in surprise. "Do tell…"

He shrugs, that smirk sliding on his face. "Things change."

"Like what?" The music fades out to an upbeat pop song, but I don't move.

"Like me. I've changed." His stare is unwavering, transmitting so many unspoken promises. He leans closer, and I'm sure he's about to kiss me in front of everyone at our best friends' wedding. I anticipate the shock to my system from his kiss as he slides his knuckles down my arm, but it doesn't come. "Dance with me," he says, pulling me out of my seat.

As he leads me onto the floor, I glance back at the table, and sweet Trevor sends over a smile and a thumbs-up. Hunter twirls me around while we dance and laugh like we would at the club, except his hand is tightly secured to my waist. When the music slides into a slow-moving ballad, he uses that same hand to bring me close. "One more dance," he says, then kisses my forehead. It's so romantic, I can't blame my burning cheeks on the energetic dancing from before. "You in this dress should be illegal, Ashlie," he whispers in my ear. "I haven't been able to keep my eyes off you all day long."

"Yeah, I've noticed," I tease, and he pulls me in tighter.

"I'm trying so damn hard not to kiss you right now."

"Why?"

"Because everyone can see us…"

"I don't care anymore." Sliding my hand around the back of his head, I pull him to my lips, a surprise that freezes him briefly. When he kisses me back, the jagged edges left by the mess I made snap into place, making sense of everything. The final piece in the middle of the most frustrating puzzle. He strokes my cheek, smoothing over the last of my doubts. This is perfect: me and Hunter, kissing while we sway to the music on the dance floor.

STRONG ARMS WRAP AROUND MY WAIST FROM BEHIND as I gather the last few cards from the gift table. I giggle at the soft kisses Hunter leaves on my shoulder. "You got Hadley all packed up?" I ask, turning to face the sexy-as-hell smirk on his face. The newlyweds have long since left for their honeymoon in Bora Bora, and most of the guests are gone too. If it weren't for our families still milling around the venue, I'd pull him into a storage closet to make some memories. The lights are still low, so I doubt anyone would notice we're missing. But getting caught with my metaphorical pants down at my best friend's wedding isn't how I want to be remembered in the history books.

"Yep. But I got roped into shuttling a few people to the airport." He presses a chaste kiss to my lips, but the look in his eyes is anything but innocent. "Come with me?"

"I promised Kayla I'd oversee cleanup." I gesture toward the catering crew clearing tables just as two of them collide, silverware clattering as it hits the hardwood floor. "She doesn't think her junior associates will do it right."

Hunter snorts and rolls his eyes as he pulls me closer. "That tracks. It should only take me an hour. Meet me in our room at The Bluffs?"

"*Our room*, huh?" Biting my lip at his implication, I shift on my feet, squeezing my thighs to relieve the pulsing between them.

His lips tease mine as he whispers, "*Our* room. Yeah." Then he kisses me, and I'm stumbling through a dizzying haze as I eagerly latch onto him. *Why the hell was I scared of this*? I clutch his broad shoulders as he presses me into the table. With one hand anchored on my hip, the other smooths up my side until his thumb caresses the fabric over my breast, steadily circling my nipple to a stiffened peak. A needy whimper slips from me when he nibbles my lower lip, and he snickers before diving back in. I trail my hands down his chest, over his stomach, until my fingers glide over his rock-hard bulge pressing into my stomach. A shiver scrolls through him, and *our room* can wait. It's time to find a damn closet.

"Hunter!"

"Shit," he murmurs, untangling from our embrace. Adjusting his tux, he turns from the doorway where Artie stands with a hand on her hip.

She takes one look at us, eyes wide with amusement, before bursting into a hooting laugh. "Really, guys?" Her shoulders shake as she tries to stifle it. I press fingers to my mouth to hide my own giggles, fixing my dress with my other hand. "A closet. A bathroom. A freaking car. All good choices. How do I know this and you don't?"

Hunter frantically pulls at his pants, glaring over his shoulder at the both of us. "Artemis, I swear to—"

"Hopefully you have some 'water balloons'..." She curls her fingers into air quotes.

"Did you *need* something?" Hunter sneers.

She titters, eyes glistening. "Yeah, I need to give you the talk, apparently..."

I snort, covering it with a cough when he glances my way. It really shouldn't be this funny. But something about us getting caught feeling each other up like we're a couple of horny teenagers who can't wait to be alone is hilarious to me. And from his nosy little sister? *We're never living this one down.*

Shaking his head, Hunter sucks his teeth. "You done?"

"Dad, uh, told me to come find you..." She flicks a tear from her eye, a shaky sigh hissing from her lips as she tries to get control. "But I can tell him you"—she snorts—"need to put something away..."

I cackle, and Artie loses it again. With an exasperated sigh, Hunter tips his head back and chuckles. "Fifty bucks, and you never mention this again." He turns to Artie with a defeated smile.

"One hundred, and you teach me how to drive your car."

"Naw. Not my car."

Shrugging, she turns back down the hallway.

Hunter groans, and a tight grimace pinches his face. "*Fuck.* Wait..." he calls after her. "Fine. But you saw none of this. You tell *no one...*"

Artie squeals, fists squeezed near her chin in excitement when she whips back around. "I can't believe that worked! Ashlie, you're a genius."

"Told you, girl!" I wink, and she bounds down the hallway, occasional squeaks echoing as she goes. When I turn to Hunter, his arched brow is only tempered by the smirk on his face. "What?"

"You're trouble." The sensual rasp in his voice as he trails fingers down my arm sends a shiver through me, but the fire in his eyes threatens to burn me all the way up.

"*Me?*" I scoff playfully, despite my breathlessness. "All I did was tell her how to negotiate with you the next time she had some dirt. I didn't know *this* would be the dirt."

Tangling our fingers, he leans in, his lips ghosting mine. "You're my favorite brand of trouble."

I giggle, and he pulls me against him for another slow kiss. That familiar haze consumes me as I clutch at his waist. A needy whine chases his lips when he pulls away too soon. He presses a peck to my temple, whispering, "If I don't leave now, I won't go... Meet me in our room?"

When I nod, he slips a key in my hand. Taking slow steps backward, he watches me with a smile until he reaches the hallway, then disappears around the corner. He's every single thing I've been looking for, and I'm already aching for more of him. An hour is an eternity.

CHAPTER FORTY-NINE

ASHLIE

The excitement buzzing through my body as I wait for Hunter to get back to The Bluffs is only partially soothed by my rapidly bouncing foot. I've had time to change out of my dress, shower, and get a snack, but he still hasn't made it back. For the last thirty minutes, I've been sitting cross-legged on the bed, balancing my giddy smile with the nerves I've had all day. The longer he takes to get here, the more my thoughts stray to how momentous this is. Tonight's the night I lay my heart on the line next to his.

The warm lamplight casts soft shadows over all the memories we've had in here—the bedroom where everything started. I smooth my hands over the tufted bedspread with a sigh, remembering that first night of connection we shared. The stark awkwardness in the room yesterday. How calm I feel now. We've come a long way. Reconnecting in this house—this room—is the perfect way to bring us full circle.

The door closes downstairs and my knees are loaded with springs, shooting me out of my seat. I can barely hear my sharp inhale over the pounding of my heart as I peek out the door, watching Hunter take the stairs by twos. And when our eyes meet, I'm simultaneously flung across the ocean and welcomed home. Embarking on my greatest adventure while settling into my safest haven.

He's lost his suit jacket and tie, the top buttons on his shirt popped open, partially exposing the tattoo on his chest. As he saunters toward me, I let my gaze wander to that mischievous smile quirking his lips. *God, I love him.*

"Hey, honey bear." The sensual hum in his voice threatens to melt me into goo right here. He pulls me to him with one arm, keeping the other behind his back as he kisses me.

"Hi," I whisper a smile against his mouth. "What are you hiding behind your back?"

"Kiss me again, and I'll give you a hint."

"And if I don't?"

He shrugs, raising his eyebrow expectantly.

"Boy, if you don't hand over those flowers..." I tease, nuzzling the tip of his nose with mine.

Hunter shakes his head, staring right into my eyes. "Naw, see, I'm not your boy anymore, Ashlie. I'm your man now..."

"Uh-huh... And what does that mean, exactly?" I tilt my head, baiting him playfully like I usually do. Only this time, his eyes spark with reckless abandon.

"For starters..." He tosses the sunflowers onto the desk and crushes his lips against mine. When my arms circle his neck, his hands tighten on my waist, lifting me. Our bodies melt together as I wrap my legs around him and peck kisses along his jawline. *My man.*

Carrying me to the bed, his safety curls around me like a weighted blanket. *How did I ever question his motives?* I bury my head in the crook of his neck, giggling as I breathe in the musky spiced ginger on his skin.

He sits, pinning my knees around his waist so I'm straddling him, his eyes fixed on mine. The gentle drag of his thumb against my hand paints desire across my skin while he waits for my next move. I want to dive straight into the intimacy we're both clearly craving, but I'm suddenly hyperaware of how significant this milestone is. Biting my free thumbnail, my gaze shifts to our laps.

Hunter chuckles quietly, maintaining eye contact while he places a kiss on my thumb. Then moves to the other thumb with another kiss. "So, are you gonna tell me what's on your mind, or do I need to keep tryna kiss it out of you? Don't think I won't—"

Cutting him off with my lips, my tongue slides past his to plunder, pillage, and claim, until my head spins at his matched intensity. His roughened fingers edge their way under my shirt, lancing me with a searing possession that I can't ignore.

A groan rumbles from his chest when he grazes my waist beads, and my nipples harden from the vibration. The sensual pull of his lips as he builds beneath me causes my hips to rock against him. He bites my lower lip, teeth grazing the edges of my sanity until his name cascades from my desperate sigh. "Hunt..." I whimper as he lances hot, open mouth kisses down my neck.

"Hmm?" He doesn't even pretend to pause, steadily brushing his lips against my collarbone.

"I...uh..." I pant, unable to stop grinding on him.

"I'm listening, honey bear," he murmurs.

"Uhmm," I whine, the internal battle between what I need to *say* and what I want to *do* waging on. I need to tell him he's my peace, my comfort, and everything I've been looking for. I need him to know I'm ready to be with him entirely, completely, wholeheartedly. But what I *want* is every part of him touching every part of me.

Each caress is the most welcome distraction, his kisses alone sending me through portals of delirium. He presses me into his stiff bulge as his hips buck, and a delectable jolt scrolls through me with a gasp. "Hunter, my love..." I say weakly, still fighting that pleasure battle. He stills, and when I register my own words, I freeze too. Even though I told him I love him in the storage room, this subconscious reflex feels like a big moment.

He pulls back, wearing the widest grin. "Say it again."

"*Hunter...*" I tease.

"Not *that*. The other thing. Say it again."

"Mm-mm"—I bite my lip—"it just slipped out..."

"So let it slip out again, then." His grin falls into that smart-ass smirk.

I squeal when he tickles my side, his laughter warming me from the inside out. How quickly we've fallen back into playfulness sets my heart at ease. He's changed, but he's still Hunter. *My Hunter.*

"Nope." I shake my head like the brat I am. "It's been, like, a day. It's too soon for all of that."

"Naw, it's been longer..." He sweeps the curls out of my face and trails a knuckle across my cheekbone, tenderly igniting my skin like a striking match. I feel every bit, wholly accepting the caress for what it is: his love. "Ash, it's been so much longer than a day." He kisses the tip of my nose, a devilish grin sliding across his lips as his eyebrows dance seductively. "Now will you please say it again? It made my insides feel all tingly."

I can't help but giggle. "*Ugh*, you're so annoying!"

"Who, me?"

I roll my eyes playfully. "Yes, you."

"And who am I?"

"My love..." I mumble.

"Your what, now?"

"You're my love, okay? And *you*, my love, are so very annoying."

"I know." Flipping me onto the bed, he peppers kisses all over my face. "Don't you forget it either," he says, hovering over me.

"Which part?" I bite my cheek to temper my smile. *Why was I ever worried this wouldn't work between us?* This playful intimacy has always been our brand of affection.

Dipping low, he snuggles his nose to mine. "Any of it." His eyes bounce around my face, taking in every line and curve. Stripping me bare, claiming my heart, and filling my soul, all before removing any clothes. When he presses his lips to mine, he molds his body around me, surrounding me with the safety he's provided all along. I shiver as he lifts my shirt over my head, goosebumps erupting across my skin in anticipation of finally being his.

CHAPTER FIFTY
ASHLIE

His lips brand me as they trail down my neck to his favorite spot. "Are you mine now?" he asks. *I am. I think I always have been.* With deft fingers, he unhooks my bra and tosses it on the ground. His torrid touch erases every invisible scar left by lovers' past, leaving me with only promises for the future. "I don't have to share you anymore?"

"Mm-hmm," I moan as his hands roam down my body. Warm breath fans over my breast, and I arch my back, seeking him, entreating for the connection I've been longing for.

"Say it." His fingers graze the base of my neck as he latches onto my nipple, stars bursting across my vision when he flicks my stiffened peak. "Tell me you're mine, Ashlie."

His spicy cologne fogs through my mind, unleashing the undeniable urge to bite. The insatiable craving to claim him, like he's claimed me. *Mine.* I nip the salty skin on his shoulder in ravenous desire, his ginger musk driving me wild.

Raking my hands over his back, I dig my nails into the taut muscles as they ripple under my fingers. A guttural rumble vibrates his chest as his mouth descends on my other nipple, the tingling pressure pulling a moan from me. His teeth graze my skin, every nibble paired with a soothing swirl. I'm consumed by each lick of his tongue, wet heat pooling between my legs. He can take all the time in the world touching me like this, and I'll gladly spend eternity a writhing mess underneath him.

Gone is my urge to bait him into playful intimacy. Tonight is different from the first time, and I let him guide me through his slow, assertive pace. I'll willingly follow him anywhere. "I'm yours, Hunter." My hands slide over his soft curls as he leads me down a path of blissful commotion. "All yours," I whisper.

"Damn *fucking* right," he murmurs. There's no smirk, no ego, or teasing when he lifts his head to mine. Just the scorching flame in his eyes. "And I'm yours. Always." His kiss demolishes the walls I've leaned on so heavily, replacing it with his devotion. We shed the rest of our clothes. Soft lips scatter promises across my skin as he works down my body, my whimpers offering sweet supplication in return. There's no more room to question whether we'll work out, and my heart surges at the realization.

He pauses when he reaches my thighs, eyes darkening with lust. "Open wider for me, honey bear. Let me taste what's mine." At the demand of his voice, my knees fall open, his carnal groan shaking me to my core with delectable madness. His desire for me leaves me a soaking mess, aching for his mouth, his fingers, *him*.

"All yours," I say, reveling in the truth of it all. I'm only his, and I always will be. The tip of his tongue twirls lightly over my clit before plunging into me. A shockwave scrolls through my body, the warmth from his mouth like white hot electricity zinging straight to my head after each taste. "Oh God," I gasp, clutching the cool sheets underneath me, clinging to gravity.

He props my legs on his shoulders and tugs me tightly against his mouth. His fingers grip my thighs with aching pressure as he devours my pussy, sucking and stroking my sensitive bud. He's feasting as if I'm his first meal after wandering through the desert. The sight of his head bobbing between my legs makes me moan, the tension in my core launching me into weightless hills and valleys. "Your tongue...feels so damn good," I rasp. He responds with a rhythmic glide of his tongue through my folds, around my clit, and back again. And again. Slow. Tortuous. *Exactly how I like.* Delicate sparks surge through me, my hips rocking with the sensation of stars colliding under his touch. "I'm—"

"Not yet," he tuts, punishing me with the loss of his mouth.

"*Whyyy?*" I whine, tossing my hands against the bed.

"So you remember"—he slowly slides a finger in my pussy, pulling indulgent whimpers from me with every inch—"who makes you come." I gasp when he curls it, dragging against that pleasure spot as he slides out. "Remember whose tongue your pussy craves." Two fingers slam back into me, the force lifting my shoulders off the bed with a moan. "Remember"—thrust—"you're"—thrust—"mine." Another thrust, and he leans over me, stealing a kiss. "Are we clear?"

I nod quickly, my breath matching the wet cadence as his fingers fill and retreat.

"Do you hear yourself, Ash?" He resettles between my legs, pumping faster to increase the sound. "You missed me this much?"

"Y-yes," the word stutters out of me while I dance through the glorious haze. "Missed you so mu—oh God!" A quick flick of his tongue dissolves all the words in my head.

"Show me." Hunter's husky demand twists the tension in my belly. "I want this pretty pussy dripping." Adding another finger, he pumps slowly, swirling his tongue over my clit before one forceful suck shoots me straight to the moon. I moan his name, rocking my hips forward. "You taste just like I remember," he murmurs.

"Faster, Hunter," I pant, moving against his motion, begging for more friction. His words are making my head spin, and I'm frantic, my body pleading to be ravaged by him. Raking my fingers through his hair, I press his mouth to me, ready to fall apart. "Please, I need...need to..."

"Fuck..." he mumbles. "You're so beautiful like this, begging for it. You gonna come for me?" With another curl of his fingers, I traverse through space and time, giving in to the sumptuous waves flowing through me.

"*Holy shit*. Don't stop, love," I moan. His name is a sacred whisper as fireflies dance before my eyes, my walls clamped around him while I tremble through the ecstasy. "I'm com—" His thumb glides over my soaking sensitivity, and my body levitates as he pulls a second orgasm from the remnants of the first. I'm floating and falling, screams of indulgence dying in my throat, and all I can do is hold on for dear life.

"Mmm, that's it. Just like that..." He slowly rubs out my pleasure until quivers zap through me. "There's my fucking good girl," he whispers. Soft kisses and the burning scrape of his stubble on my inner thighs brings me back down to this sphere, leaving me ravenous. I need all of him, *right now*.

"More," I demand, propping on my elbows. "I want you down my throat."

Hunter licks my release from his lips as he crawls up my body. "That filthy mouth is gonna get you in trouble." His lips crash into mine in a plunging kiss. My arousal on his tongue rekindles that primal urge, and all I can think about is licking, sucking, tasting him.

Reaching between us, I slide fingers around his dick, leisurely caressing his velvety shaft rippled with veins. He tilts his head to the ceiling with a sigh, eyes rolling to the back of his head. "Mine," I say, pumping slowly as he falls apart for me. He's irresistible like this, at my mercy, his face pinched in pleasure. *Mine*.

His breath catches when I rub my thumb over the precum leaking from his tip. I swirl methodically while I wait, enjoying the sounds coming from him. His throat bobs when he swallows, but he says nothing. I stop moving. "Say it, my love."

Nodding quickly, his hips rock to keep the momentum. "Shit, Ash. Yes, it's your—*shit*—I'm yours. Just...touch me. *Please*. Don't stop touching—*oh, fuck*."

Hooking a leg around his waist, I flip him down to the mattress and trail kisses down his body. When I wrap my lips around his tip, his brackish taste hits my tongue, and I have to remind myself to take it slow. I want every last bit of him, but I want to come together. Twirling my tongue, I slide off with a pop. The violent shudder that travels through him makes me smirk. "Looks like your needy dick loves my filthy mouth," I tease, and his voice rasps in agreement, pleading for more. I lick up his shaft, savoring every unbridled moan I pull from him.

Chanting my name, he fists my hair as if he'll lose all sanity if he lets go. "Your mouth...fucking amazing." When I suck his balls, he lets out a string of incoherent sounds, and I smile as I lick my way back to his crown. I love being in control like this. Seeing him give in to me, realizing it's my touch causing him to shatter. It's a powerful feeling, knowing he's mine.

I take him to the back of my throat and swallow. "*Shiiit*." His hips chase the sensation, my eyes watering as I adjust to the depth. Breathing through my nose, I take him deeper until I'm gagging. "You like choking on my dick, baby?" The words fall out of his mouth lazily, and I nod, humming around him while easing back. Hunter grips my head in both hands, taking ownership of my mouth, thrusting slowly. I'm tempted to make him spill down my throat, sucking him dry until he's completely wasted. But my need to be filled by him overpowers the thought, and I slowly drag my lips off with a smile.

He groans and glances at the door. "Condom... I didn't—"

"I'm on the pill. We don't need one." Having no barriers between us feels so right, I don't even have to think about it.

"*Raw*?" His voice cracks, eyes widening with giddy excitement. "...You sure?"

It's such an adorable transition from the dirty words he crooned earlier, I giggle as I settle onto the pillow next to him. "Unless something's changed since the last time..."

"Impossible." When he shifts over me, a soft smile graces his lips. "You've ruined me for anyone else." He lowers his body and kisses me slowly. We dance through light years, traipsing across the stars of our passion in a sensual meeting of lips and tongues, the taste of us mixing into a delectable tang. Slipping a hand between us, he slides his tip through my soaking slit until he's rubbing it against my clit. Down and back up, he repeats the motion, swallowing my moans with another kiss. My hips drift upward when I try to get him where I want him most, and his broad fingers tighten on my waist to pin me in place. "Just...give me a minute. It's my first time like this...without anything."

"So let me *feel* you," I tease breathlessly, rocking my hips again. "Fill me. Fuck me. *Please*."

"*Fuck...*" His head falls back, and he groans like he's not the one doing the edging. "So damn sexy when you beg." Pushing into me slowly, a low growl rumbles in his chest as his eyes roll back. "So damn tight," he grunts.

"Make a mess of me, love," I sigh as he ruts into me.

"Always." His lips move across my jaw, and he pulls out completely. Shudders course through me as he slides back in to the hilt. "Take it all, Ashlie." He pistons in and out at an achingly gentle pace, staring into my eyes with an intensity that sends my soul speeding through galaxies. That last part wasn't dirty talk. It's reassurance. His pledge to me. "Every single part of me is yours. This is perfect. *You're* goddamn perfect for me."

A tear slips from my eyes as I realize how right this all feels. Me and him, finally together. Everything feels complete. He's been right here the entire time. "I love you, Hunter," I say, wrapping my legs around him as he grinds into me.

He kisses the wetness from my cheek and presses his forehead against mine. "You're it for me, honey bear." His breathy voice as he picks up speed sends me into a frenzy. I meet his hips with enthusiasm, racing to the finish line together. "It's you, Ash. It's always been you." Rubbing firm circles over my swollen clit with his thumb, his words send one last shockwave through me. A swirl of lights flashes behind my eyes as a whirling black hole swallows me up. Every muscle tenses as he swells inside me, and I'm falling, spinning at a dizzying pace. "*Shit*." He latches onto me and blasts through the gateway shortly after, imploding with a stuttering buck of his hips. We collapse, left in a clinging, sated heap, unwilling to let each other go.

"NO MORE LEAVING?" HUNTER BRUSHES HIS FINGERTIPS over my spine as we lie tangled in the sheets.

"No more," I whisper. He outlines the shape of my lips with his thumb, smiling softly. "What?" I ask.

Shaking his head, he leans in for a kiss. "I'm just really fucking happy right now."

"I'm happy, too, my love."

"Never stop calling me that." His smile widens, but then his face takes on a layer of vulnerability as he bites his lip. "Did you like it?"

My eyebrows dip. "What? Sex?"

"Yeah... Feeling you—like *that*—was fucking amazing for me. I just want to make sure I'm doing things you like too..."

My heart cracks wide open at his honesty, bathing my soul in glimmering light. *He wants my happiness as much as his own.* "All three orgasms were perfect, love." I giggle, pressing a kiss to his lips. Laying my head on his chest, I trace the dark ink on his side, smoothing my hand over the burden of Atlas, the lightning on his ribs, the storm clouds. My fingertips curve around the moon and walk across the stars, dancing between the planets on his chest until he stops my hand, lacing our fingers right over his heart.

"Why don't you have a sun?" I ask.

"Because I use protection. Don't have a daughter either."

I flash him a confused look before his smirk clues me in on his joke. "Boy, I meant your tattoo!" I laugh.

"Again..." He leans down and gives me a forehead kiss. "I'm not your boy anymore. And I don't know. The tattoo artist didn't add one in his sketch. I've never really thought about it." He shrugs. "Things weren't exactly sunny back then anyway, so I guess it's fitting."

His eyes go distant as he strokes my finger with his thumb. I can only imagine what painful memory replays in his mind. The hurt on his face twists my stomach into knots. *I wish I could take all his pain away.* Propping on my elbow, I reach over him to the nightstand.

"What are you doing?" he asks, craning his neck to look.

"You'll see," I grunt, stretching my body across his to rifle through the drawer. I flick off the pen cap, getting a little black smudge on my thumb.

"What—are you *marking* me?" The amusement in his voice makes me giggle.

"It's only fair," I say, pointing the pen at the spot on my neck. "Now lay down and stay still." I drag the ink across his skin, the tip of my tongue darting between my lips while I make my addition to his tattoo. "There!" I grin, tossing it back on the nightstand.

Hunter reaches over the side of the bed and digs through his pants, grabbing his phone and handing it to me. "I don't want to get out of our little love nest to look in the mirror. Take a picture for me."

When I hand his phone back to him, he studies the picture longer than the simple geometric drawing warrants. His eyes lock on mine, full of warmth and love. "You gave me a sun..."

"Yeah, well, it's about time you had a little light in your life."

"I do, honey bear." He tucks a curl behind my ear, trailing his fingers down to my chin. "There's sunshine with you." The intimacy in his touch, the tenderness in his gaze, it all feels as familiar as the green in his eyes. And when I lean in to kiss him, it feels like home.

CHAPTER FIFTY-ONE

HUNTER

"Thanks for fitting me in on a Friday," I say, looking in the mirror at the line work on my chest.

Jimmy, my tattooist, pounds my fist and nods. "You were overdue for a touch up. It looks good. Let's get you wrapped."

After I pay and tip, I carefully slide the seatbelt over my sensitive skin. My next stop: the flower shop. Since my appointment went over, I don't have time to grab my weekly sunflower bunch from the beach today. Luckily, regular sunflowers are Ashlie's second favorite. It's cheesy as hell, but I'm surprising her for our one-month anniversary. I've become the guy who gets off on celebrating arbitrary milestones and buying flowers, all to see my girl smile. I barely recognize myself, but it feels so damn good to realize I don't hate it one bit. Everything with Ashlie is going great. Better than great. I'm completely gone for this woman.

I scroll through my phone as I wait for the florist to wrap up the small bouquet. The door chimes, and without looking up, I sidestep to give the next customer access to the counter.

"*Hunter*? Is that you?"

Everything inside me cringes. I look up, right into Ava's face. "Uh, yeah. Hey."

"How have you been? I thought you fell off the face of the planet the way you didn't respond to any of my messages..."

I drop my eyes back to my phone. "Just been busy with life. Work. You know..."

"Here's that bouquet!" the florist says cheerily from the cash register.

"Thanks." I reach around Ava to grab the flowers.

"Are those for your *best friend*?" Ava makes air quotes as she eyes the bouquet.

"My girlfriend, yeah... I gotta run. Bye, Ava."

"It's Awe-vuh."

Nodding, I purse my lips and hightail it out of the shop. I don't know how I ever entertained her and all the other women like her before. Looking back, it feels like watching a movie from an alternate timeline. I can't even fathom anyone else. All I see is Ashlie. Starting my car, I shake my head at the bullet I dodged. *Fucking drama.*

Dinner's out of the oven, the three-wick vanilla candle is lit, and sunflower heads are scattered around my small dining table. I've dimmed the lights in my loft to set the mood. All I'm waiting for is my sunshine to walk through the door. And when she does, I almost abandon everything I set up in the kitchen for another kind of cozy evening. Even in sweatpants and a crop tee, with her hair secured in a loose bun at the top of her head, she knocks the wind out of me. I slide the overnight bag off her shoulder and wrap her in my arms, leaning in to drown in her kiss.

"Are we celebrating something?" she asks, looking at the setup in the kitchen.

"Mm-hmm. It's our anniversary."

She looks at me like I've grown another head. "Our what, now?"

"Well, it's our month-i-versary. It's been a month since I swept you off your feet at Patti's and convinced you to give me a chance."

"You made this fancy dinner, and I'm dressed like—"

"You're beautiful, honey bear." I kiss her again. "Take a seat. I'll be back in a minute." I grab her bag and take it into my bedroom. Stepping out of my jeans, I reach for a pair of sweatpants to match hers.

When I get back to the table, Ashlie eyes me with suspicion. "...We're matching..."

"We *are*?" I tease. "What a coincidence..."

"You hate when couples do the matchy-matchy thing."

"Yeah, well, maybe things change." I grin and reach across the table to squeeze her hand. "And maybe it's easy when I've met *my match*..."

Ashlie tilts her head to the side, biting the smile creeping across her lips. "You keep talking like that, and we'll have matching love bites by the end of the night."

"So my plan is working then?"

"Yes, my love. I think all your plans have worked out so far..."

The way my heart still pounds when she calls me her love solidifies my motivation to do whatever it takes to keep her in my life. I'll do anything—everything—if it means she'll always call me hers.

After dinner and a sensual, kiss-filled dessert, we sit snuggled up on the couch in our matching sweats. "What's that?" Ashlie points to the leather-bound photo album on my coffee table.

"It's the scrapbook my mom gave me at Christmas. Which reminds me, I need to text her back." Despite things with my mom still being strained, the paper-thin lines of communication are open. I'm making more of an effort, but our issues run deeper than her abandonment. She still has a long way to go in addressing her own prejudices. Trust isn't easily built, so I'm giving all I can right now. My therapist says that's enough.

"Can I see?" Ashlie smiles with an excitement in her eyes so pure, it lights me up inside.

"Of course." I walk over to my phone on the counter. This is another new development. When we're together, which is every day lately, we make a point of putting our phones away. I can honestly say I don't even miss it when my focus is on our quality time.

I reply to Mom's text about me chaperoning Artemis on a trip to Sweden this summer, and slide my phone back onto the counter.

"Aww! You were so cute!"

"Naw, don't lie. I'm still cute." I slip a kiss on her cheek as I slide back on the couch and throw my arm around her shoulder, snuggling her against me.

"Yeah, and that humility...*whew*!" she teases back. "I think I have a picture with this same haircut when I was little. Hang on."

Ashlie jumps up to grab her phone, and the sent message tone chimes across the living room. She props her elbows up on the counter, doing a cute little dance while she waits. Just watching her be herself is enough to get me going. I can't imagine life without her.

My phone dings, and I stifle a laugh at her furtive glance. She knows she can see my phone at any time. I have nothing to hide. "Can you check that, honey bear?"

She clears her throat before flicking her eyes to mine with a smile. "Your mom says she can't wait."

CHAPTER FIFTY-TWO

ASHLIE

"So..." I turn to Hunter, flashing my teeth in a nervous grin. He pauses the movie I chose for his "month-i-versary" surprise tonight, then adjusts on his sofa. "I got called for an interview."

"Fuck yeah, baby! I knew you'd get it. When is it?"

"This week, at the Jensen Center. It's two parts. Monday, I'll be in the rec center offices, and if that goes well, I'll do a swimming interview at McMahon on Saturday."

Pulling me closer, he nuzzles into my neck. "I'm proud of you, honey bear."

I smile as he kisses my temple. "Yeah, thanks. Me too. How was your day?"

"*Oh*, I forgot. Guess who I bumped into at the flower shop?" Hunter rubs his hand up and down my thigh. "Awe-vuh," he says in a pretentious voice.

I snort. "Was she wearing green?"

"No idea. I got out of there as fast as I could." He laughs and presses a kiss to my shoulder, which I return with a kiss to his lips.

"Thank you for telling me." Ava's been such a hot button issue with us, I'm relieved I have no lingering suspicions. Hunter's changed for the better, and I'm working on changing too.

"Always... How was your session today?"

"Good! We talked about you, actually." I bite my lower lip nervously. He raises a brow, but waits for me to explain. "All good things. Promise. We discussed how supportive you've been with my healing journey. How much I appreciate your patience with me. And how I hope I can give that back to you."

"You already do," he whispers. "So much."

"Thank you for all the surprises tonight, love."

He tilts my head back with a finger under my chin, taking a deep, slow draw on my lips. "I need to show you something else." Reaching for the hem of his shirt, he scoots away from me and pulls it over his head. The soft smile on his face as he takes my hand and moves it to the freshly wrapped ink on his chest sets me at ease. My eyes sweep over the retouched Atlas and the expanse of the heavens, the stars, the planets, and the moon. And peeking out from behind the storm cloud is the not-so-temporary sun I drew on him weeks ago.

I've made a show of pulling out a pen and retracing the lines whenever my rudimentary drawing fades. Hunter huffs like he hates it, but he lays back and lets me do it every time. And here it is, my simple sun shining with a little twist. The skinny rays shine on one side, with the expertly drawn inflorescence of a sunflower on the other.

My eyes sting as they meet Hunter's, the explosion in my chest vastly different from the panic I'm used to. My heart is gone, burst open by this display of devotion. He added a sun to his tattoo. *No.* Not just any sun. He added *my* sun and my favorite flower. He added *me*, right over his heart. I can barely hear my voice when I ask, "When did you do this?"

"This morning," he says with a smile.

"*Why* did you do this?" My mouth hasn't closed yet, and I blink rapidly, my eyes moving from his face to his chest and back.

"Ashlie, you're a part of me, forever. You have my heart. You *are* my heart—my sunshine gleaming out of the darkness. And now, I have a little piece of you to take with me wherever I go. I love you."

"I love you more." My trembling voice stutters out of me as I struggle to keep the tears at bay.

"Wanna bet?" Hunter smirks and pulls me forward, kissing me slowly, encircling me in his arms. He clutches to me like a hard-won treasure he'll never let go of, kisses me like he'll never stop. On both accounts, I hope he never does.

TWO YEARS LATER
ASHLIE

Breathe, Ashlie.

My arms fall across my chest as I plant my feet in front of the door. "You're not driving without those glasses."

Hunter leans against the kitchen counter, his exasperated sigh aiding the scowl on my face. "I wore them all day at work. It's fine, Ash."

"No." *In. Out. Breathe.* "Glasses at night. So either grab them or give me the keys."

"Naw, you're not driving my car." Hunter eyes me for several seconds, running his tongue across his bottom lip. "I've seen the way you drive yours."

You control your reaction. "Then I'll get the glasses." I start back toward his office.

"The sun *just* started going down. It's not even dark yet," he gripes as he follows me. "We're gonna be late. Let's just go."

I shuffle through the mess of papers on his desk and scan over his workstation, finding nothing. He's watching me from the doorway. "Did you *hide* them? Where are they?"

"They're in the dresser. Top drawer, my side."

"Okay... Go get them so we can leave for dinner."

"Naw."

My nostrils flare as I watch his stubborn ass pull out his phone like he didn't hear me. No amount of breathing will help the annoyance simmering in my chest at his obstinance over these stupid glasses. Because of his astigmatism, the glare from taillights creates starbursts when he drives at night, making it hard for him to see. I finally dragged him into an eye doctor who gave him a new prescription for special lenses. But he doesn't like them because they *cramp his style*, which is his way of saying he feels nerdy in them. I think they make him look sophisticated, but he's not hearing any of it. It's been a month of having this argument with him, and I'm this close to leaving him here and driving myself to family dinner at his dad's house. If he thinks I won't call him out for being childish, he has another thing coming.

"Over some damn glasses," I mumble, breezing past him to get to our bedroom.

I deal with children all day at work. Despite the chaos, being an associate youth swim director for the LA County Recreation Centers is the best job I could have asked for. I get to oversee a few of the programs around LA, with one day a week where I'm teaching eight-year-olds how to swim at McMahon. I'm good at it, and still have a nice work-life balance. Even on the hard days—like today when we had to drain the pool after a stomach flu incident in the water—I still love it. But I'm not putting up with his stubborn ass today too.

The dresser shakes as I yank the drawer open, and I grumble obscenities while rifling through his boxer briefs. I don't make it far, finding the glasses tucked in their case in the corner of the drawer. When I grab them, I notice a small black velvet box underneath it. I stop breathing.

My whole body stills, heart pounding as my hand hovers. It's the right size and shape to be *that* kind of box, and we've been together long enough for it to be *that* kind of box. *Is this it? Has he finally picked up on all my hints?*

"Did you find them?" Hunter asks, but his voice is a lot closer than it would be if he were standing back at the doorway. I'm stuck staring so hard at this damn box that I can't turn around.

"I... What is that?"

He chuckles. "Why don't you open it and see...?"

Gulping down an entire fleet of butterflies, I lift it out of the dresser. I open it slowly, holding my breath as my heart skips several beats. Then I purse my lips and breathe out a growl. *It's empty.* Nailing him in the head with this stupid empty ring box is my first instinct. I don't do it, but I'm pissed enough to think about it. He knows how much I want to marry him. We talk about it all the time. This kind of prank is just cruel, especially when we're about to go to dinner with his family.

I spin on my heel, ready to lay into him. "You're so damn annoy—" The words fly out of my mouth before I realize he's down on a knee, holding up the white gold solitaire ring I've been hinting at since I moved in with him a year ago. I drop the box, the glasses, and my jaw.

"Yeah. I know." His sly grin pins me in place. "I couldn't make it *that* easy." He drops his head, takes a deep breath, and looks right into my eyes. "Ashlie Janiece Willis, you are the best thing to ever happen to me. You've made me see life as more than something to endure, given me a sense of purpose beyond my own selfishness. You came into my life and illuminated every ounce of darkness I kept hidden until the only thing left was you and your light. I want to spend the rest of my life making you the happiest woman in the world, because that's what you deserve. I am yours, always, and it would be the greatest honor to call you my wife. Will you marry me?"

I've thought about this moment since I was little. Had it all planned out. I would cry, jump for joy, and tremble as the ring slid on my finger. It would be wonderfully dramatic, and my water-works would be worthy of a cinematic award. So color me surprised when there isn't a tear in sight as I stare at the love of my life down on one knee. I walk toward him slowly, and an audible gulp travels down his throat as I get closer. I drop my head to his. "It took you long enough."

He breathes out a nervous chuckle. "Ash, I'm freaking out here. Is that a yes?"

"Put the ring on my finger first."

"Naw, not till you say yes..."

I grab for the ring, and Hunter sits back on his heels, holding it up in the air, just out of my reach. The nervousness etched on his face melts into exasperation—but I'm still miffed about his prank. He said it best: *can't make it that easy.* If I had to get my hopes dashed by opening an empty ring box, he can flounder for a bit while he waits for me to answer. He can work for this *yes.* I eye him suspiciously. "How long have you had this?"

"Ash—"

"How long?"

"A year. I got it right after you saw it in that magazine. Ashlie, are you going to answ—"

"*A year?* And you're sure now?" I mock sarcastically. "Do you need some more time to think about it?"

He drags a hand down the frustration on his face and tips his head back with a groan. "You're gonna be the death of me, woman."

"It took you an *entire* year to decide whether you wanted to marry me?"

"No. It took me a year to convince myself you'd actually want to marry *me*... And you haven't said yes yet. So do you?"

Of course I do. He *knows* I do. It's all I talk about. "Do I, what?" I tease.

Hunter's gaze is equally annoyed and amused as he waits for me to finish my outburst. He's come a long way in showing vulnerability since we've been together. Between a lot of patience, on both of our parts, and some couple's therapy, being open with each other about our fears comes easier to us. I almost feel bad for dragging this out. *Almost.*

"Okay." He stands and slips the ring in his back pocket. Plucking me off the ground, he throws me over his shoulder.

"Put. Me. Down," I squeal, unable to hold in my laughter. "What are you doing?"

"You've clearly lost your mind. I'm performing a factory reset on my girlfriend." He tosses me on the bed and hovers over me, smothering me with kisses across my face as I lose the giggle fight.

"Oh, I've been downgraded from fiancée to girlfriend that fast, huh?"

"Say yes, and we can work on installing the system upgrade." His eyebrows dance, and that smirk I've come to love slides across his lips.

This man, *my man,* has my whole heart. I could never in a million years see myself with anyone but him. I'll take all the sarcasm, teasing, and silly bets as long as I get to wake up with him by my side.

"Ask me again," I whisper, biting my lip as I let go of the last of my tenacity.

He cocks his head to the side, waiting to see what other games I have up my sleeve. "I'm not doing the whole knee thing aga—"

I interrupt the rest of his snarky commentary with a kiss, and he melts into me, pouring all his frustration into his lips while we battle it out on the kissing field. As much as we tease one another, this passionate pull we have together has never lessened. I think the playfulness brings us closer, and I wouldn't change it for the world.

After we've taken our fill of each other, I pull away, breathless. "Ask me..."

"Honey bear..." The huskiness in his voice sends tingles down to my toes. "Will you marry me?"

"Yes!" And that's when the tears come. It's not a downpour. The two or three that slip aren't award winning, but they'll be ingrained in my memory forever. "My love, there isn't any time-line in the universe where I wouldn't say yes."

Hunter kisses the wetness on my face, and in a sweeping

motion, brings my left hand between us. He slips the oval cut moissanite ring on my finger with a smile on his face. Holding my hand out, I admire the way it glints, gleaming brightly enough to shout to the world and everyone in it that it's finally my turn. *I've found my person.*

Hunter nibbles my ear, pulling me away from the gorgeous symbol on my finger. He slowly works his way down to his favorite spot at the base of my neck.

"We're already late, love." I gasp, jolting at the way he grips my hips.

"Sorry. System upgrade in progress," he says breathily, chuckling at the shiver that travels through me. Moaning softly, he weaves his fingers with my recently engaged hand, holding tight, like he'll never let go.

"Fiancée loading." I giggle. We're definitely going to be late. "We have to be quick."

"They'll wait for us," he mumbles around the shoulder he's freed from my top.

"They, who? I thought it was just dinner at your dad's."

He smiles with a mischievous slant to his eyebrow. "Everyone. Our parents, Chase, Kayla, Willa, Trev...everyone. They're at our engagement party, waiting for me to tell them we're on our way."

"But you hate that kind of thing..."

"Yeah, but you don't. And I want whatever makes you happy." He leans in and nuzzles my nose. "But first, I want you all to myself."

"I'm yours, Hunter James Jackson. Always." And that's all the assurance he needs before diving back in, taking me with him as our souls swim to the blissful depths of ecstasy together. Quick ecstasy, though. There's no way I'm missing my own engagement party.

COMING SOON

Willa and Trevor are in for the ride of their life. Catch up with them in the third book of the Fort Bender series, coming Fall 2025.

ALSO BY LAYNA JAMES

Some Kind of Forever (#1)

Sunshine with You (#2)

Always Will—Coming Soon! (#3)

ACKNOWLEDGMENTS

Ashlie and Hunter were never supposed to have a book, but I couldn't get their banter out of my head after finishing Some Kind of Forever. These two fought me the entire way while I worked out their love story, and I'm thankful for that. Now, it's become my favorite thing I've ever written. Thank you for reading. You've made my dreams come true!

Thank you to my family for all the sweets, hugs, and extra time to write interrupted. I couldn't have done it without you! To Olive, your encouragement through all fifty-leven versions of this story saved me from tearing my hair out. I appreciate you and your pep-talks so much. And Kenz, everyone needs one of you in their life. You're the greatest hype woman. Thank you for seeing me!

A huge thank you to my editors, Kourtney and Jessica. From beginning to end, you've helped make this story everything it is today, and I couldn't ask for a better editing team.

To my beta readers, Anna, Riya, Olive, Melissa, Samantha, JB, and Oona, thank you for all of your advice! Y'all saved the entire third act.

Last, but not least, I want to thank my writer's club for being the best resource and comedic relief when I got stuck in my head.

—LJ

ABOUT THE AUTHOR

Contemporary Romance author Layna James writes love stories with swoon-worthy banter, Happily Ever Afters, and just a little angst. Her stories feature diverse characters who navigate the complexities of life while falling in love.

She lives in Texas with her family and an anxiety-ridden Rottie named Ruby. Layna loves fuzzy socks, most types of dessert, and all genres of music.